I0652872

Contents

Cadillac Fin Suitcase

Michael Joseph Walsh was born on January 13, 1960 in Buffalo, New York of Irish, German, and Italian ancestry. Walsh's father, John Walsh, Sr., was a talented physician who specialized in internal medicine. He died of a heart attack in 1985 at the age of fifty-one. Walsh's mother, Joan Hoffmann (now Joan Hickey), graduated *summa cum laude* from the State University of New York at Buffalo in 1956 with a bachelor of science degree. She has resided in Minneapolis for many years where she's been a successful artist, primarily using oils to render landscapes.

The second oldest of five children, Walsh was a rebellious and adventurous youth, leaving Minneapolis for Florida at nineteen. He hitchhiked frequently, and journeyed to San Diego, California soon after he turned twenty, where he spent six years working as a construction laborer. Walsh resided in California for eighteen years; also living in Sacramento, and the San Francisco Bay Area.

In 1995, Walsh graduated *with distinction* from California College of Arts and Crafts (now called California College of the Arts) in Oakland. The following year, in 1996, Walsh created the book titled *Graffito*, a photo essay of the graffiti phenomenon in the San Francisco Bay Area. The book was well received in the United States and Europe.

Walsh ventured to Prague, Czech Republic in 1997 and began work on *Frontier Town*, a photo essay which explores the remnants of forty one years of Soviet communist rule and occupation in Prague (1948 – 1989). When Walsh arrived in Prague in November 1997, the monolithic statues of Stalin and Lenin and most other fear inspiring symbols of Soviet might and oppression had long been dismantled, but their ominous shadows continued to haunt the landscape. For the next year he traveled the city extensively by tram and subway with his camera.

In 1998 Walsh's work in Prague was cut short when he was awarded a Fulbright Scholarship in Photography to Taiwan. That fall Walsh arrived in Taipei, determined to create a capacious photo essay of Taiwanese culture later titled *Shangri-la Motel*. While based in Taipei, Walsh made frequent excursions to other regions of the island traveling by bus, motorbike, and train, stopping in major urban areas and many townships. In 1999, while taking photographs in the southern Taiwan city of Kaohsiung, Walsh met Julia (Mei-Hsiang) Wu. They married in 2000. Walsh's passion for street photography led him to shoot over 600 rolls of film in Taiwan between 1998 and 2000, and more between 2005 and 2007; when he abruptly stopped, declaring burnout. Between 2002 and 2005 he began recording some of his Taiwan experiences in writing. A third of the work in *Cadillac Fin Suitcase* has been taken from these writings; the remainder was written in 2009 and 2010.

for my wife, Julia

Also by Michael Walsh
Graffito

Cadillac Fin Suitcase is a Grind Show Editions book / In association with Frontier Drifter Productions

ISBN-13: 978-0615420134   ISBN-10: 0615420133

Published in the United States of America by Grind Show Editions, 2011

Cadillac Fin Suitcase

Legions of ravens drifted across a flame-colored horizon like a veil of coal dust, transforming the merciless sun god, Shen Yi, into a bloodless apparition. Alarms sounded . . . doors slammed . . . a young woman wailed. Without warning, a great wave of Red Chinese soldiers surged down the emerald hills that surround Taipei . . . propaganda babies no older than twenty . . . jackboots and sweat-soaked uniforms . . . mouths agape in a black chorus. They spread like a wind-whipped grass fire, descended upon the flats, thundered through fallow cabbage fields toward the lights of the city, swallowing every tree, every dog, every house, every Taiwan dollar, every living thing on the island so they could return to Beijing and vomit it all up at the Paramount Leader's feet. The chalky old man was sitting upon a crate of Russian fairy tales tearing the wings off white doves as casually as a child plucking the petals off a daisy—a dozen of the small bloodied creatures lay twitching on the floor in front of him. Carnival music groaned as a tiger tied to a stake ran furiously round and round. My ears began to pop—could faintly hear the high whine of landing gear. The sound of the wheels hitting the runway woke me . . . passengers rummaging through their belongings . . . pulling weeds out of their asses . . . someone begged for another varicose sandwich. . . . I was wrapped in butcher paper and twine from twenty hours in coach . . . Taipei City . . . Shangri-la wrapped in a plastic bag . . . rolled like a shiny ten dollar coin down Chichi Hill . . . rubbed my face and looked out across the moonlit pitch . . . baggage carts hissed by. . . . Ray Harryhausen's Medusa, followed by a Cyclops, heaved past my window and faded into the twilight. . . . I yanked my Cadillac fin suitcase from the overhead.

The captain's scratchy voice came over the intercom and announced, "I and the entire cabin crew would like to welcome you to Taipei. The weather's as pleasant and inviting as a burn ward—even fish sweat here. The relative humidity this evening is cotton candy, and the temperature is charred water buffalo. We hope you have a pleasurable stay in Taipei and thank you for flying Flash Gordon Airways."

I laughed, as I could still hear Mexicali Frank's raspy voice in my head cackle, "What the fuck did you expect?"

I would soon discover that Taipei's also supersonic, ultramodern, and hip as hell.

Before my arrival in Taiwan, I was slumming in a Prague ghetto palace that had dead Nazis' hides for wallpaper and live carp in the bathtub. I'd been there a year putting *buku* miles on my camera . . . at night, after a long day working the old quarter's mystical streets, I'd tack the day's photographs on the wall with all the others, and sit at the SS Exitus table in the middle of my room . . . a box of Cubans and a black beer next to the typewriter . . . I'd study the take as patriotic Bohemian folk songs on the phonograph marched gloriously over an assemblage of red men who'd fallen on their hammers and sickles. Late one evening, after a few dances with the Green Fairy, I found a pig's blood cake nailed to my door wrapped in a Fulbright Scholarship. It was a prize I'd hoped for, and also sadly, a notice of deportation. Sure I was grateful, but hated to leave my photography work in that magical city unfinished; knowing I probably wouldn't have the opportunity to return to it. My gut told me that I'd be exploring Taiwan and Asia for years. I was right. In Taiwan I would forget about Prague, traveling every inch of the dragon's scales for a full year and recording it all on 35 mm film. They'd pay me for that.

Some sweet and terribly thin Taiwanese immigration cop with a cracked porcelain face stamped my passport and slapped a Get Out of Jail Free card into my hand . . . stumbled out of the airport into a goddamned steam bath. . . . I stank like a fat man's hangover . . . quickly scanned the mad street for my ride. A brand new little taxi pulled up to the curb honking. I waved him on. My back ached from the long flight. A pint of Ten High rattled in my suitcase—what music! No rotgut clank! Yearned for the solitude of the hotel room—the bed . . . stripped down to boxers . . . a cigar and some of that Kentucky dye on the rocks. Something was biting my leg . . . felt in my pocket . . . too much fluid in the Zippo . . . it cried hot tears down my thigh . . . thought of the blonde on the plane . . . playing stick pony with a flirtatious Marine—the aisle over . . . her skin-tight black stretch pants . . . perfect nylon-encased feet . . . the way he dragged her to the john . . . the way she changed planes in Osaka.

The Fulbright Foundation slid up in a white van. Two blushing escorts wearing bell-bottom jeans and tank tops and platform moon-boots loaded my bags into the van. We sped down Highway 1 toward downtown Taipei in traffic thick as creosol. Taoist temples glittered on brooding hilltops. Watch out! The humidity turned the windshield into grilled cheese. Rice fields boiled and the Tamsui River spat in the hazy distance . . . scorched mullet flopped on the road, big as tomcats. The van slowed down as we entered the city—the Kuomintang (KMT) party's gold mine . . . an endless maze of bellowing cement canyons burning with neon lights, foaming hypermarkets, and zillions of mom-and-pop stores—a swarming thing that gyrates and sputters all twenty-four. Its enterprises are buttered with the sweat and genius of the Taiwanese, and billions in US cash showered on the KMT in the 1950s and early 1960s, Lady Liberty holding the island to her bosom, peering over her shoulder to mark the strategic military position in Southeast Asia.

I could feel the orbs of both girls running over my weary, wasted frame like Matchbox cars on a figure eight track. As the van crawled through traffic, people scurried past yakking on cell phones ... racks of lamb wearing gold neckties ... cascaded out of frill stores ... gangs of puffy-haired roosters laughed and joked as they window-gagged ... tread marks on my rib cage ... balls deep into jet-lagged stupor ... loaded from the sci-fi episode drifting past my window ... mothers swollen with virtue and credit card receipts ... 1970s pantsuits and dainty flower-print dresses ... dragged their children along as kids in designer labels and fresh Nikes sparkled on the curb—choking on the island's newfound wealth.

I sprawled out on the back seat ... hoping we'd stop at a blood bank for take-out ... the girls, who were in the seat facing me, continued to chat in Mandarin and shoot quick nervous glances my way.... A group of shirtless bronze laborers drank Taiwan Beer and smoked Japanese cigarettes under yellow street lamps along the roadside ... naive boys from Thailand, Indonesia, and Manila. They didn't know the paintings from the far west—only fish, tobacco, and the savage Taiwan sun. A big man around forty-five with bad skin, wearing a wifebeater, red shorts, and black biker boots, waved electric clippers around the bristled head of a young Filipino tough sitting on a stool with a powder-blue sheet draped over his stout shoulders—his girlfriend, a looker with a pixie cut and orange miniskirt scuffed her six-inch heels seductively as she slowly circled the stool inspecting the work. A jump away, a small group of bandy-legged boys in dark shades with pacifiers hanging around their skinny necks bopped mechanical heads to the drone of a boom box. 7-Elevens glowed on busy corners in the sticky mist. Betel nut girls sat in fish tanks with flashing neon signs—one every hundred meters. Locals call betel nut "Chinese chewing gum." The sweet-and-sour sisters twirled on high stools—wearing lingerie or clear plastic miniskirts and snazzy heels—selling boxes of the precious green nuts, mostly to taxi and truck drivers for the little boost like chewing tobacco . . . boxes the size of a deck of cards with bikini-clad models on the front and breezy palm tree-lined beaches on the back.

Swoosh! Motorbikes growling like a pack of dogs on the hunt . . . two hundred on a rosary . . . stormed by spewing blue smoke. The drivers wore bright head-to-toe rain slickers. One of the scooters looked like a mother possum, three kids and two adults clinging to its back. . . . Dozens of food vendors . . . the gods of Taiwan's streets . . . stretched to the singing fairies . . . shiny aluminum carts full of fish, pork, and noodles . . . fish oil, smoke and steam from the carts ascended high above the tiny island, making it glow like a red torch in the East China Sea.

One of the polite bell-bottom girls nudged her friend, who was staring out the van window . . . she turned and handed me an envelope stuffed with cash . . . thirty-six thousand NT dollars—twelve hundred US.

"It's your first month's stipend," she said.

The mention of cash spun the driver's head around. I thumbed the large blue thousand-dollar notes. The waxy face of the Generalissimo, Chiang-kai Shek, smiled up at me— arrogant prick!

"Uh, how was your flight?" asked the other girl.

"Like ten thousand miles in a dentist's chair," I replied.

"Oh, really?"

"Yeah. I'm bruised, kid."

"What?"

"My sunflowers are dried up, sister."

"Oh, I know. I just got my braces off, see?" the girl giggled and grinned to show her beautiful teeth.

Both of them eyed the blue Cadillac fin suitcase resting across my lap.

"Where'd you get that?" asked braces.

"It's a tailfin from a 1959 Cadillac Eldorado. Woolly Bear Lyle from Sonora, California, made it for me."

"It's from a real car?"

"The lights are real. He replaced the steel with aluminum."

"Do the lights work?" asked the other girl.

I hit a button on the side of the case, and the taillights lit up.

"Oh, my god!" said the girl.

I lurched into the lobby of the Taipei Teachers' Hostel with two flat tires and a rusty chain. The bell-bottom girls carried my bags. A staff of several women dressed like nurses fluttered around the reception desk.

"Is this really my hotel?" I asked the girls with a mouthful of jet fuel.

They giggled and covered their mouths in embarrassment. Bright fluorescent lights washed the white tile floor and walls in a greenish hue. The acidic smell of industrial cleaning products made my eyes water. I fished in the Cadillac fin for a box of Punch I bought in Madrid for the price of a shoeshine . . . grabbed one of the stubby cigars . . . bit the end off and lit it. The bell-bottom girls carried the suitcases to my door . . . octopus-eye peep hole . . . below it a smudged disclaimer and a list of warnings— including "you will be charged for massage oil on the sheets" . . . put my finger bone in Tom Turner, twisted the greasy knob and braced for the scene. The girls took a few steps back toward the elevators. Back down the winding stairs, people laughed in the lobby. I opened the door . . . the room was almost as big as a tin of baby squid . . . smelled about the same . . . all mattress with a cruddy little TV with a clothes-hanger antenna perched on a stand at the end of the bed. Cig burns pocked the TV's cheap plastic woodgrain. The carpet was 1980s lime-green shag with coffee stains like a map of Indonesia.

"Fuck."

The bell-bottom girls blushed.

"Sorry, we have to go now," one of them said. "Please call the Fulbright Foundation if you have any questions."

"Can someone help me find an apartment?" I called after them.

"After seven days you pay," one of the girls said over her shoulder with a nervous smile.

Moon-boots clomped toward the elevator. . . . Threw my bag on a chair, set the Cadillac fin suitcase on the bed, and opened it . . . the bourbon sleeping comfortably between my camera, the gars, and thirty rolls of film in Ziploc baggies . . .

grabbed one of the plastic cups in the bathroom and poured three fingers of the paint, drank half of it in one gulp, then walked across the street to a 7-Eleven. Two cans of Sapporo beer . . . a ham sandwich in a plastic box . . . a pack of Dunhill and a bag of ice for my back. Returned in a quarter hour . . . turned on the TV . . . flipped through the channels—a ridiculous commercial, magic cream for tiny tits . . . watch 'em grow! Four weeks later! Eight weeks! *The Kill Kill Fun Fun Hour*—a camera inside an ER busted in behind a curtained-off bed where a rape victim lay beaten and unconscious. The camera showed close-ups of the victim's battered face and body, and then turned on the sobbing mother who was trying to shoo the camera away—then a cut to shots of three gangsters in a Taipei police station handcuffed to wooden chairs, pulling their shirts over their heads to hide their faces. . . . Turned to some censored Japanese porn . . . a cute kid no older than sixteen in blue fishnets and lofty heels getting it from behind from some middle-aged Japanese with a gut . . . blurry crotches . . . black bars over the girl's eyes. She struggled and cried. He made love to her like he was mounting a tire. Every once in a while he gave her ass a good swat. I drained my drink—cracked a beer and relit the cigar . . . put Johnny Cash on the megaphone . . . lay down on the bed and set the bag of ice on my lower back . . . the pounding in the ceiling wasn't the people dancing upstairs—it was Buddha running away. . . . Checked my watch—eight thirty . . . after ten minutes, the ice deadened the pain . . . have had this toothache in my back for years . . . everybody's got to carry coals. . . . The Japanese guy rolled the girl roughly over on her side . . . got her top leg up over his shoulder and tightened down the rest of the lug nuts. The sound of rain on the window helped me relax. Then I grew somber remembering it poured the last time I saw my ex-wife's son Shane . . . trying to find his way in the cold Wisconsin woods.

Slept for an hour—until nine thirty . . . then grabbed the camera . . . hopped a cab in the rain toward the Wanhua district. Neon lights flashing from crowded storefronts fucked with my eyes as we cruised along Poi Ai Road, a long, stately promenade behind the Presidential building. Dr. Seuss had planted the dandelion palm trees that ran down both sides of the street. A ten-foot concrete wall covered with snakeskin and surveillance cameras surrounded the compound. Grim plainclothes guards stood on every corner under streetlamps chain-smoking and yelling into their cell phones. They wore black slacks, dark sunglasses, and white dress shirts drenched with sweat and rain . . . dozens of cig butts lay at their feet like dead night crawlers. Soldiers with M-16s stood frozen at attention at a gated entrance.

Ten minutes later we reached Wanhua, where all the streets are named after liver diseases. Yinglong, the winged dragon and god of rain, snickered and threw the lever down on the storm machine as I got out in front of legendary Longshan Temple. Clouds of incense smoke burped out of its tall doorways . . . like Johnny Fong, the "Human Volcano" with indigestion. In the rolling sea of pedestrians on the sidewalk and in the street, food vendors jockeyed their carts for position. Some of them wheeled quickly across the street to a night market . . . I followed, past blind people giving back rubs to folks sitting on folding chairs . . . old women in straw hats and rubber boots peddling fragrant hand-size bouquets of *lan wa* flowers to passing cabs and cars . . . people gawking—a kid pointed at me, yanking on his mother's pants. Food vendors and clothing stalls curled down both sides of the street for two hundred meters. People swarmed on foot and on motorbikes. A midget scurried past, whacking legs and carts with an umbrella, disappearing into the crowd. Hawkers screeched into megaphones. Japanese pop music blared. A sweaty crowd wearing steampunk goggles stared vacantly at a giant wall of televisions showing a chorus line of Japanese showgirls . . . their scissor kicks sent a jar of Uncle Choo's Go-Go All Night lotion splashing onto my dozing libido. A blind man wore a sandwich board painted with Chinese characters . . . felt along with a cane, holding out an empty aluminum bowl . . . another blind fellow followed as if they were tied together with a rope.

I dropped into a stall for stinky tofu and a beer . . . people continued to gape at me like I was the goddamn Elephant Man

... two Sapporos later I rolled up in the half-drunk crowd ... was sucked into the open jaws of a salt lick for tourists called Snake Alley—a flatline of vendors French-frying snakes and turtles ... a macabre show hall ... occupying a lofty spot on the Humane Society's shit list ... the torrential rain played a cemetery lullaby on the tin roof ... ta-da! Wire cages holding the unlucky dolled up the stall fronts ... a vendor barked into a bullhorn ... a transfixed throng looked on as his flamboyant pal held up a live yellow boa ... red lights flashed ... a drumroll ... he sent it over with one swoop of a butterfly sword ... a communal gasp! ... hung it on a hook ... drip drip ... poured shots of its blood for kids named Fang and Meow Meow. Nearby, boxes that held the organs of other recently slain were stacked neatly, like to-go orders after a Chinese prison execution ... the stench of bile and cig smoke singed my nose hair and sent my libido to the South Pole. There were tables piled with knock-off Rolex watches and Zippo lighters ... cheap switchblades, brass knuckles and nunchakus ... and enough dildos and butt plugs to stock every cathouse in Bangkok ... booths for tattoo artists and trinkets and fortune-tellers who sold ten-dollar dreams. Several plump American tourists plodded along in sneakers and Hawaiian shirts, wide-eyed as children at a petting zoo. Middle-aged local men with slicked-back hair and silk shirts wore their gold Rolexes low on the wrist so all could see, and I thought of the Taiwanese businessman who went to Macao for a weekend of gambling. A group of local thugs, disgusted by his arrogance, hacked off his Rolex arm with a machete, took the watch off the stump, and threw the arm in the river.

Narrow side alleys veered off the Snake into the darkness ... picked one at random and glided toward it ... shadows reached out and sneered like some dopey hired gun swinging open his lapels ... was a little worried about dopey, but guessed he was bluffing. ... The photos? ... They're sketches of a broader, deeper canvas that I'm more comfortable rendering with words ... the camera gives me a reason to be almost anywhere ... sometimes, as on this night, I'd use it as a prop with no film in it—and had been known to flash it like a dime-store cop badge. The sound of a woman screaming with laughter coming from one of the other alleys slashed the night open; her steamy guts poured out into the dank air like a butchered snake's. I turned, and headed into the abyss toward the scream. After fifty feet I came to a deadhead and saw light coming from the passageway to the right . . . switched on the camera for show and crept ahead slowly. Every twenty feet there was a door with a bright red or blue light bulb buzzing overhead, and against the old brick walls leaned a dozen Chinese imports with crazy hairdos and gaudy jewelry. Gals riding on their rims smoked and gabbed loudly in nylons and stuffed bras while dreams of a good life left rotting in the creaking hulls of Mainland junks. A dessert wearing a red silk robe jumped off the wall as if she were spring loaded—her pointy boobies bounced around as she skipped toward me in her fuzzy pink slippers.

"Everything all right?" she asked, letting the robe fall open, exposing sheer white panties and a peek-a-boo bra.

The old gals hooted and roared at their young companion's bravado. Behind me, down the alleyway, the wide, somber face of a man peered out of the blackness. A smoldering cig dangled from his purple lips. I followed my gut and picked up the pace . . . my camera, I thought—they might try to steal it . . . and I forgot to put my damn cash in my shoe . . . passed more doorways crammed with girls.

"Hallo, hallo, come back!" cackled one of the women.

I turned to look without slowing down. Suddenly, the man leaped from the shadows and landed in the middle of the alley twenty feet behind me. I immediately stopped and turned to face him. He snapped his fingers, and the whores rolled up behind him like a string of mottled pearls. He was a young thirty-five, handsome as Elvis, wearing a monogrammed black silk shirt, finely tailored beige slacks, and alligator shoes. Uh-oh, I thought, a real rail-splitter. He held out a pack of smokes—placed his hands together and bowed. This was a language I could understand. I walked to him. He handed me the pack and in an instant held a lighter under my nose. Then he clacked his teeth with a sound like a shotgun cocking . . . and rapidly fired off some Taiwanese. Immediately, a group of buff, shirtless men appeared out of the darkness, and with the hookers, circled in around us. Brilliant tattooed scenes covered the men's sweaty chests and backs. I held the camera up to my face and made a sweeping arc with my arm.

"Photographs of Taiwan," I said. "A book."

Elvis's dark eyes rolled over me, up and down, shoulder to shoulder—as coolly as an undertaker measuring a condemned man for a pair of crow's wings. And then his eyes locked with mine for a long moment. Then his face broke into a sudden, beaming smile ... wanted to exhale like I'd just escaped from Houdini's Chinese Water Torture Cell, but kept my composure as he bowed again and again ... pattered around humbly ... hands calmly folded across his barrel chest. He gestured for me to follow him and led me and the entourage out of the main alleyway ... into a crowded maze of lit passageways between the red brick buildings. Our collective smell of sweat and cheap perfume left a hundred-foot vapor trail. As we passed through the crowd, some sloe-gin Joe with plastic teeth and a wad of blue skins skidded over on rubber legs and threw a lasso around one of the girls. She smiled, took his trembling hand, and they disappeared into the crush. We stopped at the back of one of the red brick buildings, at the top of a wide flight of stairs with a metal railing leading to a plain double door under a soft light. Elvis nodded at two of the tattooed guys and two of the whores. The others peeled off and sulked down one of the alleys.

"Hungry?" he asked me in broken English, smiling.

"Yeah, sure," I said.

He led us down the stairs and pressed a small red buzzer on the wall. A tall slender Taiwanese man in a World War II Japanese soldier's uniform cracked the door slightly and popped his head and shoulders out as though wiggling out of a narrow pipe. He had a long nose and oily, pocked skin yellow as parchment.

He smiled at Elvis, threw open the door, pointed a Nambu pistol in our faces and said, "Welcome to Cellblock One. You are under arrest!"

Three or four other soldiers materialized, handcuffed us and led us inside to what looked like an old underground jail. A Japanese flag hung above the front office door. A sign on the wall read "No Picture Taking." Inside, crusty black and white pictures and many other official-looking documents cluttered the walls. Elvis and the others produced VIP cards to be scanned, and immediately their mug shots appeared on a large video screen. One of the guards led me to a small booking room, took my fingerprints and mug shot. (Wish I could tell you it was the first time I'd held the alphabet soup across my chest.) He tossed a black-and-white-striped prison uniform at me and motioned for me to hop to.

Back in the office, the others were waiting with their con clothes on. The guard who'd taken my picture handed me my own VIP card and opened the door on an immaculate cell-block. Ten cells on each side ... stone walls ... the taste of iron in the close, cool air ... the raucous voices of the prisoners. ... The guard stopped in front of the first cell on the right. It appeared dark and empty. All of a sudden zap! zap!—the cell lit up like a lightning strike, and inside a man was screaming and writhing, strapped in an electric chair. I jumped and shrieked like a junior high school kid getting a bar of soap shoved up his ass in the locker room shower, and everybody laughed.

The other cells were full of Taiwanese fat cats—politicians and gangsters and local celebrities, which in Taiwan often mean the same thing—dining on gourmet cuisine, champagne, and fine spirits. We were shuffled into cell number 6 ... the door slammed shut, *kachunk* ... the lock clanged into place ... my nervous laughter made me conspicuous again. Inside the cell, a table, a bunk bed, toilet, and sink, ink drawings and girly pictures pinned on the walls. A monotone voice in Chinese murmured over a loudspeaker. Tough-looking guards toting nightsticks and submachine guns paced slowly up and down the block, sometimes escorting individual prisoners—I mean guests. The only thing that seemed out of place was the lovely wait-staff, a half dozen of them in modified blue guard uniforms that consisted of miniskirts, thigh high hose, and the sexiest army boots I've ever seen.

We plopped at the table. A bottle of Kaoliang 58 sat in the middle hissing like a rocket ship on a launch pad ... 116 proof of nipple clamps and honey ... glanced around at my cackling companions ... they crammed bubble helmets on ... scoundrels! I radioed ground control to scrub the launch—the line was dead. Elvis grinned rascally ... slid the smoking bottle and a shot glass in front of me ... 58 kicks in the liver ... screwed on my Major Tom bonnet ... someone cut my oxygen ... everyone shouted *ganbei*! (bottoms up) ... poured a shot and took it—my Prague drinking legs broke into pieces ... shoved the booze back to Elvis ... smirking like a jack-o'-lantern, he poured himself and everyone else a slug, and so it went until we lost sight of earth.

A fawn wheeled a cart full of beer, cigarettes, and Cuban cigars up to the bars and handed whatever we ordered through the old serving slot. Soon thereafter, wave after wave of platters of bluefin sushi and sashimi, sautéed shrimp, lobster, *Kung Pao* chicken, pickled cucumbers, and more poured through the glory hole ... there were no rules to this savory gastronomical orgy ... food was served family style ... we all grabbed a set of chopsticks and dug in ... twenty minutes later we got off the kill drowsy as a pride of lions after feeding on a wildebeest ... one of the tattooed guys flopped on the bunk and lit a smoke ... Elvis shoved one of his girls at me—Fuzzy Slippers ... she pulled off my shirt as though it were on fire ... began to run her fingernails up and down my back ... the others oohed and awed, and it became obvious they were conversing about the whiteness of my skin. ... A sassy drag queen swinging his ass around was being escorted past our cell ... wearing a red skirt and a white silk top with a tarantula collar—his sugar daddy's cock and balls for a necktie ... he took a small camera out of his purse, ran toward us, and took my picture ... his guard looked on indifferently ... Fuzzy abruptly stopped the rake job ... I turned around—she gave me that blank, ashen stare ... the one I saw for the first time in my bathroom mirror when I was fifteen after half a bottle of Irish Mist. . . . Fuzzy's puke truck began to idle at the bottom of the hill . . . her anxious eyes darted to the toilet . . . it puckered its lips.

As we sat locked in our cell eating and drinking and smoking, I heard a commotion begin in the cell directly across from us. The cells were well lit, so we got a good look at the drunken man in the tux bashing around the woman he was with. She was crying and yelling for help, but all the guards seemed to have disappeared like East L.A. cops on a Saturday night. Other guests started yelling for help. They began throwing food and empty bottles out of their locked cells to get someone's attention. We stood shaking the bars helplessly as she was beaten. Her eyes rolled back in her head as he smashed her terrified face up against the bars. Blood ran from her mouth and nose. She frantically clutched the bars with both hands as the man tried to pry her away. The terrible sound of Fuzzy Slippers's puke truck dumping its load snapped my head around. As Fuzzy continued whispering into Mr. Porcelain's ear, I quickly turned back around and joined the others screaming for help even after realizing most of the people there couldn't understand a word I was saying. After five long minutes of pandemonium, it got real quiet. The woman being thumped across the cellblock began calling to me in English for help.

"Hey you, you American, please, your country is so strong. Why can't you help me? You, you fucking asshole! What the hell is wrong with you! Are you afraid? You are a real chickenshit! Why don't you just go away?"

The idiot in her cell began throwing bottles of wine and food through the bars. I watched in horror as he ripped her shirt off. Then she began to laugh.

And, as if on cue, everybody in the entire cellblock started laughing, and over the loudspeaker a man's voice said, "Mr. Walsh, Mr. Walsh, can you hear me? This is a little joke we play on our first-time customers. We hope you don't mind. The woman in cell number sixteen is perfectly all right. She works here. Please enjoy the rest of the evening."

"Bravo, fucking bravo," I said feeling a bucket of blood rush to my face.

The patrons stood up against the cell bars ... clapping like seals.... I took a phony bow. We floated out to the main drag a half hour later ... I was a cosmic boy burning up in reentry ... Fuzzy Slippers was a cherry bomb with a wet fuse—and Elvis glowed like Zeus's half brother. I thanked him and reached out to shake his hand ... Elvis hesitated, as it's not the custom in Taiwan, then he feebly held out his strong hand like an old man with arthritis. I shook it gently. He smiled, placed his hands across his chest and bowed repeatedly.

On the way back to my room, had the taxi driver drop me at a 7-Eleven on the corner of NanHai Road and Roosevelt for beer ... sat on somebody else's motorbike and drank ... the long line of parked bikes stretched and wound down the sidewalk for blocks like a colossal sleeping monster.... It was two o'clock and the streets were still humming ... that made me smile.

I came across Elvis again months later in the Wanhua district ... on a night for wolf men and bad cops ... in the dim, shabby lobby of a hotel with no guests ... no twinkling ones, anyway. The cold damp air created rivers of moisture that ran down the windows like tears at a saint's funeral ... one for every loser strewn around Purgatory's waiting room on dusty sofas ... I took a number and tried not to trip over the stacks of empty KFC boxes and bottles of Hard Luck whiskey ... didn't mind taking a wrong turn ... had found that Taipei's seedier streets and lower income neighborhoods, which first appeared to be dangerous, were as deadly as a Boy Scout jamboree encampment ... the past few months had also worked in the city's rundown Sanchung District.... In Taiwan, I had a free pass to a parallel world I would previously only enter with extreme caution—the midnight streets of urban California ... here, I was a halfback racing in the open with blockers downfield ... and no one was going to catch me. I stopped in the middle of the lobby and turned on my camera ... a shirtless Elvis was casually leaning against the reception desk—the Lord of Wanhua ... a tattoo of the yin yang symbol big as his hand encompassed his naval . . . it spun around like a Skilsaw blade . . . Elvis scanned the lobby and the urban plain beyond the windows with the aloofness of a cheetah . . . I smiled at him as he approached . . . a skinny kid wearing a Jimi Hendrix T-shirt stumbled toward me, fell face down, and didn't move . . . the lord giggled, stepped over the kid, took a look at my camera, and gave me a wink . . . a young prostitute in white fur fell out of the darkness . . . Elvis flashed his wily eyes at me and wrapped her around his arm like a slammer tying off . . . stumbled up the stairs like giddy kids on prom night . . . I followed . . . stared at the track marks on the backs of her knees . . . they spelled out "What the Fuck are You Doing Here?" . . . her legs white as the ceiling of an ambulance . . . caught a glimpse of myself in the mirror on the second floor landing—the biggest whore and addict in the whole palace. Room 17 . . . scenes Joel-Peter Witkin would've drooled over . . . the narcotized occupants wouldn't have known the difference if I lined them up in the sights of a howitzer . . . didn't really go into room 17 for the pictures . . . they're the cigarette after sex . . . it's the adventure, the adrenaline, seeing how long I can ride the bull . . . had become completely hooked by the non-stop action on Taiwan's streets since the first day of my arrival . . . roaming city landscapes lean and ornery as a springtime grizzly . . . couldn't see it all . . . could only capture a small fraction of it on film. . . that was the best part—knowing this whirl had no end . . . the hunt is satisfying enough . . . that rare image that doesn't make me want to throw up when I look at it a month after I take it is enough . . . the camera is a vehicle . . . it opens the doors of possibility. I believe Elvis and others here let me into their worlds because of the camera . . . they perceived a purpose. As for the Lord of Wanhua, he was more than just another image on a contact sheet. He was my trusted and gracious ambassador to Taiwan's underworld . . . he satisfied my desire to travel briefly in that realm . . . I sensed that he enjoyed hanging out with me, a *waiguo ren*—a foreigner. His kindness toward me, contrasted to the often brutal and unforgiving path that he has chosen continues to resonate. I never saw Elvis again.

Later, when I looked at the photographs of that night, I saw past them ... to the li'l gal curled up on a red sofa next to a banana cream pie with a stallion's neck and a coy smile that belonged on a can of Beef Chunks 'n' Gravy ... she reached into Tarzan's ear, pulled out a fried chicken leg and smiled, ate some and passed it around ... reached into his ear again and pulled out a stiletto heel ... his ex-wife attached to it.

Besides being my carte blanche in Taiwan, the camera led me to my future wife, Julia ... my Formosa rose ... met her while working in Kaohsiung eight months after dropping in. Taking street photographs, along with creating art and writing, have also helped me come to terms with my reckless and wayward youth, and somewhat appeased my restless nature— it's muscled up my self-respect and grinded the tips off my horns. However, as in Prague, as this work progressed, at times I began to feel insidious—pathetic ... swiping strangers' images ... what the hell for? ... I had no answer ... still have no answer ... chasing after people like they were trophies or bugs ... I was paparazzi's mongrel cousin—that was a cold river to swim in ... but, I couldn't stop ... the "noble scholar" in three-day-old boxer shorts ... with a hard-on for blacktop ... unshaven, a toothbrush and a fish head in shirt pocket ... merrily lost in Taipei's entrails ... jerking open "hey you" doors ... ablaze as a bug-eyed kid elbowing his way front stage of a rumble-tumble show ... had learned more about Taiwan's enthralling culture hanging out with locals in five-dollar noodle shops and karaoke clubs without the camera. But, the picture machine had me doped up—seduced ... careening down bright avenues ... hollow as a gun barrel ... my delirious face smeared with mortician's makeup ... and after a long day shooting on the pavement, I'd sit alone at the bar in an Edward Hopper painting—and like it.

We Ain't Ever Going Home

We dropped claw a Tom Thumb mile from Yellow Jack La-
goon on a night the Admiral of the Black took a bite out of the
moon, and promised me buckos free passage to Junan Town
Threw our boots and britches into the weeds
rode into town on a centipede
Passed around a bottle of Rangoon Red
That clap of thunder made Bela Lugosi fly out of our heads
Stopped in No Man's Land Theater where Bunny Boy
Wong got rich playing laugh tracks to porno flicks
It was a packed house just like every night of
middle-aged foreigners in turtlenecks and tights
Powdered girlies swung from the ceiling on silver trapeze
selling shrunken heads and baubles from the seven seas

Oh, hoist sail boys, we ain't ever going home
too much of this world we need to roam
Oh, hoist sail boys, we ain't ever going home
too much of this world we need to roam

For a year we've been dodging the bow chasers of two
Royal Navy hounds, crisscrossing the shallows from
Palau to Padang destined for Dead Man's Sound
Because we sent our Captain Mean Billy Banks waltzing
down the plank for murdering our beloved First Mate Kale
with a hundred lashes from a cat o'nine tails
Mean Billy and Kale were besotted with our cook
a real fair-haired Nel, but she loved Kale more,
this turned the Captain's eyes green as a sea turtle's shell
So he put Nel under the knife and stashed her corpse below
deck, and hung the killing around the First Mate's neck

Oh, hoist sail boys, we ain't ever going home
too much of this world we need to roam
Oh, hoist sail boys, we ain't ever going home
too much of this world we need to roam

The scurvy-ridden crew, the black and the blue
jumped every stockade from Bombay to the zoo
We live on rum and starfish fritters and coconut
marinade and cow heel soup from a hangman's parade
We're praying to sniff out an island that hasn't seen
an Englishman's boot print in a thousand years
of the likes which became refuge for the Bounty's mutineers
We'll run this sea rover ashore and set her decks ablaze
and carouse in the sun the rest of our days

Oh, hoist sail boys, we ain't ever going home
too much of this world we need to roam
Oh, hoist sail boys, we ain't ever going home
too much of this world we need to roam

After gorging on whisky and swine, we left No Man's Land
Theater and arrived in the bull's-eye of Junan Town. We
watched thunderstruck as a very hairy and brawny man rode
his bicycle up to Mangrove Fountain. He wore he-man Her-
cules garb—a one-shoulder-strap leopard-skin bear hugger that

stopped mid-thigh . . . a wide black belt wrapped around his gargantuan waist. With great pomp and swagger he waded out to the middle of the fountain, did a handstand, and sucked up all the water until his gut and his buttocks swelled up like a Zeppelin. . . . He staggered to his bike and rode off slowly, tee-tering, with a wild crowd following behind, including a band of moonshiners, who belted out a lively tune on banjos and squeezeboxes. . . . Christ, he rode for blocks and blocks, until the city stopped and the countryside jumped up everywhere with palm trees and bamboo and bald green hills. . . . In the dis-tance I could see a big top sitting alone in the middle of a great dried-up brown field. . . . Lots of hollering and shouting came from the tent; we could smell animal manure as we neared. . . . Fatso rode his bike to the center of the tent, and the crowd whooped and cackled like mad . . . like they expected him . . . and he rolled off the bike onto his back, and into the ring came the Zing twins, Chee and Mee—the precocious little gals wore fluffy red princess dresses—stood on his chest, and the ring-master counted to three, and wow the girls jumped up, and Fatso let that water go, and the gals rose in the air twenty feet on the fountain he was spurting, and when they got up near the top of the tent they did summersaults and cartwheels and other tricks, and the crowd went over the falls, and after three minutes the girls' Boston terrier, Bug Eye, got up there, too.

Oriental Sideshow

Stuck at Taipei Teachers' Hostel for a week—flickering like a gypsy moth inside a specimen jar ... the heat worked me over like a homemade tattoo needle ... my skin smelled like sulfur and bullet casings ... Muddy Waters was bending two-by-fours ... below my steamed up window, phantom '47 flatbeds crammed with wailing children standing on their parents' corpses circled Taipei's salty streets.... Ate out of 7-Elevens and show-me cafeterias ... people stared as I walked by ... six foot three of flour, inconspicuous as a T-bone in a Buddhist monastery cafeteria ... felt like some oddity in an Oriental sideshow ... cut out my tongue at the airport ... face like a rubber mask handed to me by a gravedigger at an Iggy Pop show ... time ran down ... belly flopped into the gray evanescent surf ... edgy after the first day ... train in my gut ... slashed through blue station mist ... chased farting angels around the room.... Wanted to roam every back street and alley in the country with my camera 'til there was nothing left of me except a bag of spent film and a shiny grease spot on the pavement of some bright sing-song boulevard. . . . By day two I was hopping buses, cruising the city on foot. . . . They gave me money . . . heavy as a dead horse . . . dragged it around by the tail . . . I owed a year of sweat . . . karma cops sat on my shoulders . . . trading smirks and dirty ammo . . . calling me beatific and obscene . . . I was resolute as a branding iron . . . gliding like a stingray. . . . Needed to find a place to live that was not here . . . the dumpy little ten-by-ten took on the clutter and must of a locker room . . . paced back and forth across the shag with a bit in my mouth skimming the want ads for a shack—waiting and drinking Myers's Rum . . . Hong Kong martial arts flicks gushed from the TV . . . a fountain of smutty dialogue and wired actors . . . the sun imprinted the delicate lotus flower patterns on the window shade into the wall . . . bumped into the TV stand . . . cigar butts in a glass of warm beer splashed around like drowning sailors . . . reminded me of Taiwan's peril and rabid dogs—China with a thousand thunder bolts pointed down our throats. . . . Women from the front desk called constantly—nervous because I didn't let them in every morning at seven-thirty with rubber gloves and vaccines to clean my room? . . . What was the damn use?—I've slept under cleaner bridge overpasses. . . . Pork Chop Chen the wrestler and former teenage runaway with sweet-potato biceps and boom-boom entourage roomed next to me . . . his men in T-shirts and red tights hung out in the hall all hours smoking and practicing gymnastics. . . . One night I saw one of the fluttering nurses taking a break by the cigarette machine on my floor . . . sipping a bubble milk tea with pearls (tapioca balls) . . . tried to ask her with tongue-in-cheek if she wanted to join me for a shark bite in my room, and she scampered away like a scared rabbit.

The steady old guy at the 7-Eleven across the street was entertained by my daily visits scavenging for food and drink . . . had a smile like Christmas morning in Cheyenne . . . thoroughly amused by my disorientation. We had a long discussion about ice the first night. He kept pointing to his head, saying *eyes, eyes,* and then led me to the sunglasses rack. He got a belly laugh when he finally figured out what I wanted . . .

began a longtime relationship with Cheyenne's snacks and drinks—the roasted lima beans and sweet red plums and li'l dried fish with li'l dead eyes . . . cold red tea and Sapporo beer.

After seven days at the teachers' hostel found a small apartment downtown . . . Chin-hua Street near the corner of Roosevelt and NanHai Road . . . fifth-floor walkup . . . a red railing and shiny aluminum doors with taped-up paintings of protective Taoist gods in cherry, mustard, and blueberry . . . the eggshell walls in the stairwell wound around, narrowed and then bulged in places like a giant intestine—if my room wasn't the asshole, it sure felt that way . . . a hundred square feet with a small bedroom in back with a yellow door . . . white tile floor . . . the plaster job on the walls done by an epileptic cake decorator . . . holes in the window screens . . . bought two fans . . . a two-inch futon mattress stuffed with Cap'n Crunch. . . . A blue pay phone sat on a lamp table on the third-floor landing . . . dropped plenty of coin in big blue those first weeks getting situated. . . . After working all day, used to lie on my thin mattress in the dark with a candle burning and listen to the rain, the cars honking, the voices on the street below, their loud, sharp tones . . . Tom Waits, Elmore James and other beauties on the bop player comforted me like biscuits and gravy in this Taiwan parade . . . their voices like a red wind roaring through a bullet-riddled Mojave mining shack—blowing roses off the hood of a '66 Pontiac "Goat" sleeping out back after torching the grandstand at Palmdale. . . . I thought about all those innocent kids living happy in dreary Chiang-kai Shek soldier buildings like this one—peeling and wounded with metal stairs that echo with the clomp of some four a.m. drunk. . . . Giant antennas on the roof flapped in the wind crashing out sad tunes . . . the whole damn building was stuffy as a rice cooker . . . newspapers crammed between the walls for insulation . . . cockroaches lived in the dreary little kitchen under a pile of old news—they visited often . . . mosquitoes tormented me nightly—waking me from a sound sleep . . . duct taping the gaps between the flimsy window screens failed . . . bought an electric zapper that looked like a tennis racket ... the metal strings cooked them until they popped—crack! ... The Fulbright money didn't make it past rent and food ... getting around by bus, motorcycle, and train was cheap—motel costs were the rub ... to do this project right I would have to stay at least another year or two ... welcomed that thought.

The Pigeon Racers

I was drunk as a Donggang fisherman when the horn blew. I'm always drunk when the horn blows. Picked up the receiver. It weighed more than a notice from the draft board. Looked at my watch. It had taken a boat to Peru. A gentle voice that sounded pleasing as a Bangka back rub was saying something about pigeons—stolen racing pigeons. I sat up on the sofa and belched out a fireball that parboiled the doorman's *ba-wan*.

"What was that?" asked the girlish voice.

"The grouper I swallowed for dinner mouthing off," I said as I wound my Timex.

"Oh?"

"I guess he didn't like the whiskey and the five-thousand-year-old egg I chased him down with."

"You mean the thousand-year-old egg."

"This one was five thousand and then some," I crowed. "What day is it?"

"Oh, it must be Saturday, June 12, 1965, I believe," said the delicate voice with a shot of sarcasm stiff enough to knock

Lenny Bruce on his ass.

"Thanks for including the year. I forget that sometimes, just like I forget the name of my favorite brand of hooch after the second bottle. I'm sure you also have the time?"

"Excuse me, I'm trying to reach Mr. Chang. Big Guava Chang."

"I'm Guava."

"Will you please come down and take a look? It's 9:45, by the way."

"Pigeons, huh. Where?" I asked, and set my sundial and switched the conch to my other ear.

"Lukang."

"Lukang? I've only passed through."

"Lukang is a captivating port township on Taiwan's west coast famous for its preservation of early twentieth-century Taiwanese culture with many historical temples, buildings, houses, and narrow alleys and—"

"Okay, okay. Spare me the five-dollar tour. I need two thousand NT per day plus expenses. And I'm not agreeing to the job until I get down there and speak to Mr. who?"

"Mr. Kung."

"Have Mr. Kung meet me at the Lukang depot at eleven a.m. sharp tomorrow morning. And for god's sake, tell him not to be waiting there holding up one of those pathetic little signs with my name on it. I don't want any hard-ons or scribblers getting wind of my arrival."

"How will he know it's you?"

"I'll be the biggest animal at the station, unless there's a rhinoceros convention convening in your charming district tomorrow," I said and hung up the phone while fumbling around for my pack of smokes.

That's how I got myself entwined with the beings that dwell in the seamy underworld of Taiwanese pigeon racing. I shouldn't have answered the phone. I should never answer the phone. Especially after skinny-dipping in a bottle of turpentine like I had the previous night. I needed the berries. I'm three dimes and some copper and have been a shamus since the beginning of Ike's second term. I've never been a cop. I've never been to Las Vegas. Well, that's not entirely true. I like almost anything eatable and thin ankles wrapped in sheer nylon. I loathe how Hollywood stereotypes Asian detectives in movies as with the likes of Charlie Chan—some white actor in a phony Fu Manchu trying to act like a chink. I've got three rooms over a wise house off Shin Yang Street in downtown Taipei. The dump looks like a flophouse for walruses and schizophrenic wallpaper hangers. I never did make it out of Mrs. Moo Moo's Etiquette and Finishing School. A sweet little sister comes in once a week and tidies up the box with a fire hose and wrecking ball.

On Sunday morning, two hours after the sun's yolk began to run; I dressed in a sweet potato suit, dark yellow shirt and hazel tie, and made my way to Taipei Railway Station with my favorite brown Fedora in hand. The taxi's shocks belonged on a Roman chariot. The bumpy ride caused the ray gun warming my ribs to jump around like a maniac in a straitjacket. I'm licensed to carry it. Or I was last year, I think. Anything larger than the snub-nosed .38 would be about as inconspicuous as a flasher in a maternity ward. Sometimes it still attracts brown birds and other things that slither on the pavement.

Bicycles, motor scooters, and rickshaws darted around in all directions as we neared the train depot. The station looked like a hornets' nest that had just been knocked silly by stone-throwing adolescent boys. That thought caused me to reminisce of tender youthful days before I discovered that my pecker had a dual purpose. I was surprised by the crowd, and then I remembered that this weekend was the annual Dragon Boat festival, during which groups from all over Taiwan race traditional hand-carved boats on the local rivers. There's an ancient story behind this holiday, but I forget what it is.

I hopped a Casey Jones and took a window seat. A fresh copy of the *Central Daily News* was lying on my seat. I shoved it to the floor under my seat where it belonged. Since 1950 it's been the only newspaper available in Taiwan—a mindless propaganda squawk box for the venomous Kuomintang Party.

Martial law and a ban on a free press and freedom of speech was instituted shortly after Kuomintang leader Chiang-kai Shek and a million troops fled to Taiwan in 1949 after being run out of China by Mao's peasant army. Actually, the KMT were given control of Taiwan in 1945 after Japan's defeat in World War II. Shek claimed that Taiwan would only be the temporary home for the KMT, and vowed to return to the mainland and defeat Mao. Unfortunately for us Taiwanese, they've never left our beautiful island and continue to oppress every facet of our lives with authoritarian rule. They serve intimidation, torture, and murder breakfast, lunch, and dinner.

The rattler arrived in Changhua three hours later. I jumped on a big car and arrived in Lukang in thirty minutes. I stepped onto the platform and looked at my ticker. It was 11:15. A sleek, wiry young man wearing a traditional bamboo paddy hat, workman's blue pants, and a matching button-down jacket made from locally grown hemp was sitting in his rickshaw staring at me. He waved me over.

I walked over and said, "Mr. Kung?"

The kid nodded and hopped out. He was around twenty with matinee idol looks and a smile that made Cupid work overtime. He took my brown leather suitcase and my smaller case and set them behind the driver's seat. He offered me his pack of Treasure Island cigarettes. I took one, and we proceeded down Lukang's busy little tar roll—Chungshan Road. It was four hundred meters of small traditional shops that included furniture factories, casket makers, and lantern and incense craftspeople.

"What's in the small case?" he asked, turning to flash his bright clear eyes at me.

"Two very lovely dancing girls from the Hwa Hwa Club in Taipei," I joked. "Want one?"

The kid laughed so hard he nearly choked on his cigarette.

"It's a portable bar."

"Really?"

"I never travel without it. It holds one bottle, two pony glasses, a corkscrew, and a little booklet titled *How to Pick Up*

Girls in Fifteen Minutes. I'm Guava. What's your name?"

"Jun-po. Call me Po," he said with an innocent smile.

Two Taoist temples guarded either end of the road—the Longshan and the Tien Hou. In between the shops I noticed the maze of old winding alleys that candy tonsils had told me about on the phone. Many of the alleys were only one to two meters wide. A stout woman sat in front of her house doing the wash by hand with a hose and a red bucket. A bald old man with a potbelly stood proudly in front of his little castle enjoying a smoke. A reptilian crowd gathered around several vendors cooking oyster omelets. I had the kid stop and bought three of the fish pies. I ate two as we drove along—gave the kid the other one. He looked like he'd been dining on chain oil and blown tires.

As we proceeded down Chungshan, through all the dust and commotion, we came upon a delicate teenage girl in a pink cotton dress at the side of the road. She stood pristinely on the shoulders of a white tiger. She was as delicious and out of place as a mooncake in May. In one hand she held a handmade wooden umbrella over her head to block the sun. In the other hand she held a peachy bouquet of white lilies. As we neared she held them up in our direction and smiled. Po slowed down and pulled over and parked next to the girl. She handed Po the flowers and pecked him on the cheek.

"Girl friend?" I asked.

"Wants to be," Po said with a smile as he turned left into one of the narrow streets about halfway down the main run and pulled over in front of a smirking three-story house with a Tokyo facelift. The imposing palace towered over the humble red brick houses that populated the neighborhood.

"No charge," Po said with a smile as I reached for my wallet. "I'll wait in the shade across the street."

As I floated across the moat toward the front entrance, the wide red wooden doors of the home swung open and an elderly servant woman in a dark gray dress and white apron gazed at me with an austere expression. The last time I saw a face like that it was marinating in a jar of formaldehyde. The place reeked of Beluga and exotic tobacco. I handed Irving my hat as I walked into a large, sparsely furnished room with a freshly waxed wooden floor that looked like it was stolen from the French embassy. Rare watercolor paintings and calligraphy scrolls hung on whale-rib walls.

A woman sat upon an immense emerald cracker up against the back wall of the alcazar. She was kissing the cobra from a silver Malabar hookah. The water pipe sat on an etched glass coffee table along with a vase of pink and white plum blossoms. The tangy scent of the flowers made me feel woozy as a box of newborn kittens. From a hundred bucks away she looked like a shapely and benign thirty-year-old princess in a very attractive light blue silk *chee-pow*. From striking distance she looked as sober as an obituary column with elegant eyes that pierced me like a hollow point. A bob cut ran along a sharp jawline framing an aloof face that along with her curves wouldn't quite make the final twelve on a pinup calendar. My gut told me she'd spent her entire life eating pie and splashing around in warm shallow water at the bottom of a golden rice bowl the size of Borneo.

"Please sit," she said dryly, blew on the cobra, and shifted slightly in her intricately carved mahogany throne. "What I've heard is true. You're very robust."

"You should've seen me before I molted last spring. And Mr. Kung?"

"Mrs. Kung. Would you have come if you knew I was a woman?"

"I don't know," I said, and sat down in a Judas chair. "I never know what I'm going to do, and I like it that way. Would you have contacted me if you knew I was a woman?"

"Oh, and you're funny, too," she laughed and shrugged at the same time.

"That's pro bono."

Angel face brought in a traditional tea set, placed it in front of Mrs. Kung and poured tea into two small porcelain cups. She set three new packs of cigs on the table in front of me in a neat little row—Revival, New Paradise, and Shuang Shi. I opened the pack of New Paradise, flipped one of the butts into my squawker and lit it.

"Would you rather have giggle juice?" asked Mrs. Kung.

"Whiskey, neat," I said.

Teddy hurried out of the room and returned shortly with a bottle of good bourbon and a bottle of sake. She set them in front of me along with a pony glass.

"There've been a few Mr. Kungs."

"Uh-huh. The last one's in a million-dollar urn in the other room. Would you like to speak with him?"

"Maybe, after a few more of these," I chuckled. "So what's this about birds?"

"I've heard you're as unforgiving as a riptide."

"I usually prefer my flattery in a warm spring roll served by something pubescent," I said as I poured myself a double bourbon and took a swallow long enough to make most mortals feel like the object of a taffy pull. "But, I'll take it chilled from you."

"I like you already, Mr. Big Guava."

"Just Guava is okay. Don't like me too much. I don't come cheap. Word is your family's flush with dirt taking up half of Changhua County and you've been through more daddies than the queen of Sheba."

"I'm so embarrassed! Who told you, Guava?" she said sarcastically and lifted her dress up a rung, exposing shapely alabaster gams.

"A little pigeon."

She smiled and said, "Speaking of royalty, I've heard you have a joo joo that Nefertiti could hang her hat on."

"She did."

"Oh, really!"

"But you'll never find out. I never sleep with clients."

"Aren't we presumptuous? But you have."

"Slept with clients? Twice, and both of them mistakes."

"Your frank manner doesn't bother me at all. My late husband ate communists for breakfast and could curse in seven languages."

"So you know how to say *fuck you* in Swahili?"

Her eyes blushed. "Naturally," she said.

"My business hardens a man faster than a three minute egg."

"Exactly what is your business?"

"You know. That's why you summoned me down here to lovely Lukang. Usually something with a toe tag attached. Or, as in this case, a leg band."

"I've also heard you were unpredictable."

"Another asset that's kept me out of the morgue. Don't confuse unpredictability with unreliability. I'm your man and will see this through to the end if I agree to take the job."

"Uh-huh," she said with an air of uncertainty.

"Ask around."

"I have."

"Then you know my track record stacks up against the best bangtails at Happy Valley or Sha tin in Hong Kong."

"I wanted to meet you in the flesh before deciding."

"Okay, you've said hello to my flesh. Now, tell me about the birds."

"Last Wednesday two extremely rare and expensive racing pigeons were stolen from me. I, we had just purchased them. They were imported from Belgium."

"Stolen from here?"

"Oh, god no. From a meeting place here in Lukang that was arranged and agreed upon by me and the seller. Nice boys and girls don't meet at this kind of place."

"Uh-huh."

"And they sent a ransom note the day before I had my assistant contact you."

"May I see the note?"

She handed me the scrawled note. It read: *half a million NT or curtains for the chickens. We'll contact you.* Two serial numbers from the pigeons' leg bands were written on the bottom of the note.

"The birds really worth it?"

"It's one of the only things that excite me. To enter a group of birds into a high stakes 700 kilometer race and wait for them to come in to the finish is really something."

"What other things excite you?"

"Big, reckless men," she purred. Her eyes measured my inseam. "Know any?"

"Yeah, we just passed a bunch taking a nap in the cemetery."

"Do you know anything about pigeons?"

"In my racket they usually can be found blubbering and sucking their thumbs in some secret police detention."

She took a sip of tea and said, "The Japanese introduced pigeon racing to Taiwan at the beginning of the century. Sometime early in the occupation. Without exaggerating, it can be said that the Taiwanese are the most fanatical pigeon racers in the world."

"Because of the loot?"

"Exactly! The money. Gambling. The amounts bet on each race are worth a fortune. And racers like me can also cash in big if our birds win."

"Uh-huh."

"Will you deliver the ransom and get my birds back? I'll pay you handsomely—twenty-five thousand NT."

"If we're talking that kind of money, could you have Sweet Face bring me a '61 T-Bird with whipped cream and strawberries?"

"Ha!" she laughed.

"Tell me as much as you can about exactly how the birds were lifted. Were you there?"

"No, it was my assistant Mr. Lee."

"Where is he?"

"Resting," she said. "He got hit on the head after the lights went out."

"The lights went out where?"

"At an underground gambling den in town. In the back room. In a private room where he was to meet the seller and pay for the birds. I can arrange to have you taken there."

"Can he describe the birdnappers?"

"No, he said he didn't see anyone. He's met with this same seller many times before. We've always been able to trust him."

"Who and where is the seller?"

"He's local. I don't know who he is. I instruct Lee not to tell me these things so I can keep my distance from these types."

"I'm going to need to see Mr. Lee and the seller pronto. What about the money?"

"Mr. Lee gave the seller the $300,000 NT we agreed upon.

The seller left with the money, and Lee was knocked out and the birds taken a short while later."

"Expensive ducks."

"Awfully."

"And you trust Mr. Lee?"

"Completely."

"Anything else?"

"I have my suspicions. Most likely creatures that inhabit the Taiwan underworld."

"Unfortunately, we play in the same sandbox."

"That's one of the reasons I asked for you."

"And the other?"

"As you said, you're hard-boiled."

"Did you notify the khakis?"

"Who?"

"The brown birds. The local cops."

"No."

"They're not the ones to worry about. The Taiwan police have as much clout as the local Girl Scouts. The KMT has them directing traffic and looking for lost goldfish."

"Who should we be worrying about?"

"The KMT's secret police."

"Oh, them!" She shuddered.

"So, you've had a run-in with them before."

"Hasn't everybody?"

"With this much dough involved, those jackals will get wind of it soon enough, anyway."

"They always seem to, don't they?"

"So we wait until whoever wrote the ransom note contacts you for the exchange."

"I've reserved a room for you at the Gold Dragon," she said as she picked up the telephone and dialed it. "I hope you don't think I was being presumptuous. Lee," she said into the elephant ear. "Mr. Chang is here, and he will need to interview you soon concerning the incident. Uh-huh. Well, he's handsome, and he's in his early thirties with a broad, boyish face, and he's a slightly rotundus man. Actually, he's very stalwart and well-built with heavy shoulders and a lot of pluck. He has well-kept hair that's combed straight back with pomade or something or other that smells nice, and he's wearing a rather sporty ochre sharkskin suit with a yellow shirt and hazel tie. Goodbye, Lee."

"I'll let you know as soon as I get something," I said and walked outside and hailed my rickshaw driver parked across the street.

The Gold Dragon Hotel was midway down Chungshan Road. There were several other hotels nearby, but this was definitely the pick of the litter. I paddled into the lobby. A good looking woman in her late twenties sat on a high stool behind the front desk with her sexy bare feet propped up on the counter. She smiled and gently rubbed her feet together.

"You must be for Mrs. Kung," she said with a smile that was almost certain to end up on my bathroom floor tonight.

"Hey, you're the voice on the phone who gave me the five-dollar tour."

She gave me a girlish smile and the key to room 23. I followed her up a posh mauve-carpeted staircase with a gold railing that doubled as an amusement park slide, and as I watched her ass sway under her tight yellow silk skirt, I could feel the needle in my moral compass begin to swell up and jump around. She walked down a long hall to the last room on the left—opened the door and turned on the lights and the black-and-white. I followed her in. The room was so clean you could have eaten off the floor—if you were a Siamese cat. It was a big room with a large double bed. A small refrigerator sat next to the TV. The frail walked into the bathroom and flipped on the light. She pointed toward the door, smiled and walked out. I hurried after her and stuck my head out into the hall. She was standing there waiting for me.

"Yes, Mrs. Kung owns the hotel, and no I usually don't work at the front desk," she purred. "Mrs. Kung thought you might like someone to talk to since you're from out of town. They call me Panda."

"Let's talk later Panda girl," I said. "I'm beat."

She smiled and glided down the hall toward the stairs. I lit a butt and flipped through the TV channels, stopping at Star Showcase, one of my favorites. I was sitting on the end of the bed enjoying a sweet looking canary's performance when there was a knock on my door.

"She's back!" I thought. With a certain amount of enthusiasm, I opened the door—and a Taiwan Garrison Command thug pushed me aside and blew into the room like a ruptured sewer main. His dark suit and polite manners were a dead giveaway. He had a thin steamrolled face with a mole on his cheek the size of a sunspot and goose barnacles for ears. These goons are the most feared of all of the Kuomintang's secret police. They trimmed roses and learned how to bake cookies at the same summer camp as Stalin's KGB boys. They cut throats. They make people disappear. They're in bed with the devil's sister. They had starring roles in the 2-28 Incident and many other atrocities inflicted upon the Taiwanese since 1947.

"Where have you been?" I asked. "I've been in town for an hour and no welcome from the TGC?"

"Where is she, peeper?" he growled and flashed his buzzer in my face. It read *Officer Whoops*.

"Who?"

"The round heel in the yellow skirt."

"You wouldn't know a nice dame if she chopped off your tail."

He muttered something in pig Latin.

"I bet you look for women the same way the khakis drag a river."

"Watch it," he snarled.

"I'm just down here for the dragon boat races."

"So am I," he hissed as he snooped around the room, jerking closets and drawers open.

"A visit from one of you characters is always like eating a plate of bad clams—and takes just as long to get out of my system."

"Cute, shamus. Where the hell is she?"

"Get wise, needle dick."

"Got a license for the flamethrower?" he snapped as he eyed the .38 in my shoulder holster.

"Want to see it?"

"No."

"Want a Molotov cocktail? I'm buying."

"I grazed your file," he said with a menacing smirk, straightened up and faced me. "Mr. Shao-lin Chang, private detective, AKA Big Guava Chang. Taiwan Naval Officer five years. Stationed in Long Beach, California, four years. Graduated from Cheng Kung Provincial University near the top of his class, 1952. Single, with a passion for anything with a cork in it. We know why you're here. Go back to Taipei tomorrow morning."

"You can read! That's something for a mug with a head that's been plucked out of a cabbage field. Okay, why am I here?"

"Tweet, tweet."

"I know a good speech therapist."

He shook his head in frustration and burst out of the room with the same grace he'd entered with. Ten minutes after he left I phoned Mrs. Kung from a payphone on the street a few doors down from the hotel, as I was sure my horn was bugged. I informed her of the TGC's visit and that they were on Panda girl's trail. I advised her to tell Panda girl to lie low for a few days. Then I went back to my room, collapsed onto the bed, and fell into a sweet pile of fairy dust.

I woke up two hours later, ate two roasted ducks and a wedding cake in the hotel restaurant and went to visit Mrs. Kung's assistant Mr. Lee. He lived in a simple, well-kept two-story place a few blocks away from Mrs. Kung. Mr. Lee answered the door with enough gauze around his melon to wrap a mummy. He was a very proper and polite bespectacled middle-aged gentleman dressed in a white shirt, dark slacks, and a tie he'd pulled out of a bag of licorice. A faint scar on his left cheek looked like something he could get taken care of at a dry cleaner. He'd bunked with Confucius at college and admired *Moby Dick* and Sun Yat-sen. He led me into a small dining area, and we sat down at an oval rattan table.

As he poured oolong tea over our heads I said, "That lump looks the size of Kilimanjaro."

"Oh, yes," he said and gently patted the back of his head.

"I suppose your ego is just as black-and-blue?"

"We've never had a problem with this kind of matter before."

"Mrs. Kung spilled the milk about what happened at the exchange," I said looking him in the eye. "I'd like to hear it from you, if you don't mind."

"Oh, most certainly," he said with a smile. "As instructed by Mrs. Kung, I took $300,000 NT and met the seller."

"What's his name?"

"Mr. Woo," he said. "Everyone refers to him as Red Moon Woo."

"Where did you meet Mr. Woo?"

"At the same location where we've made many exchanges in the past," he said. "It's a gambling establishment that locals call the Shut Out."

"Underground?"

"Aren't they all?"

"Yeah, sure," I said. "Then what happened?"

"We met in a private back room," he said. "We've met there many times, like I said previously. I inspected the birds and made sure their leg bands matched the numbers provided by Mrs. Kung. They did. So I gave Mr. Woo the money, and he walked out into the playing area. I stayed behind for a few minutes covering the birds, and then the lights went out, and I was hit very hard. I must have been unconscious for at least five minutes, and when I awoke the birds were gone."

"Did you see anyone or hear anyone say anything before you were sapped and the dodos were nabbed?"

"Nothing."

"Does Mrs. Kung know where the Shut Out is?"

"I believe she does."

"Anything else?"

"Red Moon Woo owns the Shut Out."

"Uh-huh."

"And there's a mysterious name I've heard several times over the years that may have something to do with the incident."

"The name?"

"Horse Brother," he said. "I've never met the man, but I believe he's connected with the local underworld; possibly someone that oversees Mr. Woo's establishment."

"Any idea what cave he's hanging in?"

"No, sorry."

I thanked Mr. Lee and asked him to buzz me if he remembered anything or anyone else that may be connected to the string.

Mrs. Kung owned a palace, a hotel, enough mud to start her own country, and half the politicians in Chunghua County; and Red Moon Woo owned a nice little gambling dive smothered in gravy and onions. I owned a worn pair of wingtips, a glowing bouquet of hemorrhoids, and a swell little corner plot in the Odd Fellows Cemetery. What the hell did I care? I'm as materialistic as a Tibetan monk. I used Lee's telephone to call Mrs. Kung and instructed her to have Po pick me up and take me to Red Moon's pig farm. Turns out she did know where it was. I hoped Po could be trusted.

Po arrived in his flying carpet soon after my call and dropped me in front of the Shut Out at around 9:30 p.m.

"Careful in there," he said with a nervous smile.

"Wong's Fish Meal Factory" was painted in large red Chinese characters across the nondescript, shabby facade of the Shut Out. The boy pointed to a narrow alley to the right of the building and drove off, disappearing into the shadows. I lit a smoke and walked down the alley and stopped at the only door on that side. I knocked a few times. The door creaked open halfway. A slender, cute little pro skirt in a short blue dress stood there with her hands on her hips. She looked like she'd been hopped on by more men than the diving board at the YMCA.

"Want a massage?" she asked and primped her poofy bouffant hairdo that had been set with rollers the size of gin bottles.

"Not today, little sister. I'm looking for Red Moon Woo."

"Come on, soup's getting cold," she whined. "When was the last time you dropped trow?"

"When was the last time you stuck something in your mouth that didn't have a hole at the end of it?"

"Bouncy bouncy," she said seductively, tilting her head to

one side and pushing up her small pointy breasts.

"Sorry kid," I said. "Get him for me, would you?"

"Come on then," she sniveled, and grabbed me with a hand soft as a lobster claw and pulled me into a dark hallway that reeked of fish meal and tobacco smoke.

She led me twenty feet down the hall and stopped at another closed door and said dejectedly, "In there. I'm Echo if you change your mind."

I opened the door to a scene that I was well accustomed to. I felt welcome as a pinched nerve. A boisterous and raucous crowd of men sat around twenty green-felt-topped tables in a thick sea of cigarette smoke. They were playing the usual; roulette, fan-tan, pai gow, and mahjong. A chandelier made out of plastic spoons and wet dreams shimmied above the tables. Baby dolls in bikini tops and hot pants carried trays of drinks and food around. A bar long enough to bowl on ran the length of the entire right wall. The ceiling was painted with dozens of mythical Chinese gods floating around on puffy white clouds against a blue sky. A clam bucket of other rentals sailed around in the mist and perched on the bar. On a cruddy little stage opposite the bar, a lithe yellow torch wearing a mermaid gown was chirping in front of four cat men in slick white suits and bow ties who were blowing horns. A juiced gambler in a pinstripe zooty was stepping on the fins of one of the red ladies on the dance floor. She was twice his size and as young and shiny as a new bicycle. Later, in one of the peeling and curdled rooms upstairs she was going to shoot a fire bolt inside the mattress and teach him a new set of vowels.

I walked up to the end of the crowded bar and sat on a stool. A big tacky clock hung on the wall behind the bar above an impressive line of booze bottles. The ticker was one of those last-minute things you can find at tourist shops all over the South Pacific from Saipan to Tahiti—something to get for your brother before you board the plane. The face of the clock was a map of the region, and on either side stood two topless porcelain hula dancers. In subterranean dice joints like this, foreign booze and tobacco were always available for a premium, as they were strictly on the black. All the legit joints on the island only sold beer and tobacco produced by the KMT-owned and humbly named Taiwan Tobacco and Wine Monopoly.

A slim fellow with snowman eyes and a mug that looked like an order of *pai-goo fan* that someone had left in the middle of the street brought me a glass of water, a pack of Hwa Kwang cigarettes, and the man I was looking for. Mr. Red Moon Woo had a violet crescent-shaped birthmark next to his right eye, a ruddy sun-baked complexion, and an enormous mouth with thick lips I'd seen attached to a fishhook off a Luodong pier. I guessed he was around forty. He had long sideburns and wore his hair pompadour style like many of the local hoodlums and Yakuza in Japan. A sharp yellow-and-blue Hawaiian shirt draped over his medium build, but it couldn't hide the feeling that he was stained as the floor of a slaughterhouse bye-bye room.

Woo didn't give me anything that could move me over to second base. His story corroborated with Mr. Lee's: He gave Lee the birds, took the money, and left. He got his, though. He was $300,000 NT richer, and Mrs. Kung was left holding an empty bag of birdseed. Red Moon Woo was still in the lineup. Everybody was. I didn't mention the name Mr. Lee gave me— Horse Brother.

I telephoned Mrs. Kung from a phone at the bar and told her of my conversation with Woo. I knew something had happened, as her voice sounded jittery. She said someone had called ten minutes earlier and demanded that $450,000 NT be delivered in one hour in exchange for the birds. I hustled outside to the rickshaw and arrived at Mrs. Kung's in five minutes flat. She met me at her front door dressed in a gaudy white nightgown that looked like the upholstery inside a coffin.

She handed me a satchel and said, "Do you still have the ransom note with the leg band numbers?"

I nodded. "Anything else?"

"Tell the driver to take you to the sugar factory. He knows where it is. You'll be okay, won't you? I suppose you're a black belt in something or other, aren't you?"

"I wouldn't know the difference between a karate chop and a lamb chop," I said. I opened my jacket and let her say hello to my .38. "Better get Mr. Lee over here and wait by the phone. Don't answer it unless it's me. I'll let it ring twice and then hang up. Then I'll immediately call you back."

"Okay," she said, and squeezed my arm.

I slung the satchel over my shoulder and got in the rickshaw. Po was proving to be reliable as a field of spring rice. We drove off into the maze of lonely dimly lit alleys off Chungshan Road. After fifteen minutes of winding and weaving the kid turned around and gave me the high sign that we were getting close.

"Drop me fifty yards from the meeting place," I said, as I didn't want him anywhere near what was up ahead. "And sit tight and wait for my return."

Seconds later a rickshaw pulled out of an alley behind us. We were drenched with a bright spotlight. Another magic carpet pulled out in front of us and began to slow down.

"Get the hell out of here, fast!" I yelled at the kid.

Po swung left into the nearest alley and took a quick right and another left and parked in the darkness underneath a tin overhang on the side of a building. We looked at one another with wide eyes and didn't make a sound. He grabbed my arm and led me on foot down a long alley that was only four feet wide. We scampered fifty yards down the narrow vein and ducked into a small open space that was ten feet wide.

"Who do you think they were?" he asked.

"Could have been our drop or maybe the secret police or who knows. I'm glad you know these alleyways."

We waited there for nearly an hour before making our way back to the Po's rickshaw. To be extra safe we didn't double back. The kid took us through Seoul and Singapore and who knows where else. I had no idea if we were anywhere near our destination. Then I received a blow to the back of my head that must have been thrown by Godzilla. I woke up and looked at my watch. It must have been drunk again. It read 2:30 a.m., which would mean I'd been out for nearly two hours. The satchel was gone. I looked around for the kid—my only friend in town. He was gone, too.

Somehow I managed to find my way back to the rickshaw. I found Po lying in the back seat. I knew he was dead by the way he looked like he'd been through the spin cycle in a cement truck. My guts were on the bargain shelf of a butcher shop—right next to the monkey scrotum and horse mane. I checked for a pulse in his neck to make sure. I couldn't determine the cause of death in the darkness, but there was plenty of tomato sauce on his torso. I guessed it was a carve job. I slid the body onto the floorboards behind the front seat and covered it the best I could with the newspaper Po had been reading earlier. The poor kid probably put up a fight and saw the face or faces of whoever jumped us. In my line of work murder is part of the deal, like visits from a mother-in-law. But this was different. Po was a real sweet kid.

I limped along through the alleys and finally found my way back to Chungshan Road and hailed a cab to Mrs. Kung's. I arrived there at three thirty and found her sitting in the spacious front room. She was always sitting in the front room. A cage containing two cooing pigeons sat in front of her on the coffee table. She looked worse than I did. I told her about Po and said I'd phone the local khakis in the morning and report it anonymously.

"I couldn't sleep, as I was worried sick about the both of you," she said somberly. "I heard a knock and they were left outside the front door. That was about an hour ago."

"You mean worried about your money," I said.

"No, that's not true! I checked the leg bands. It's them."

She handed me a large white envelope and said, "Thank you Guava. I hope you're not hurt too badly. Count it. I don't mind."

I shook the envelope a few times and said, "It feels like twenty-five grand."

"So, you'll be going back to Taipei in the morning?"

"Maybe."

"Maybe?"

"Someone's just killed the only friend I had in town over a couple of birds. I need to find out who it is."

"I'll have another driver take you to the bus depot tomorrow at your request."

"Don't bother," I said and walked out.

I hobbled back to the hotel feeling all wet and tingly—like I'd just crawled out of a bottle of Novocain. I spent some time getting reacquainted with my portable bar and mulling over the day's events. Drinking to help ease depression is like trying to put out a fire with napalm—tonight I didn't care. It was too easy. The birds being dropped off on her doorstep. Maybe the kidnappers were just being cautious and thought I might bring heavies to the drop. The whole business began to smell like a fat lady's leotard. It always does. Was there really a birdnapping, or was I being played? I fell asleep with my clothes on.

I was awakened at 5:00 a.m. by someone tapping on my door. It was Panda girl, standing there in a sheer wrapping that she got from a florist. Before she could say anything, I yanked her into the room and tore at her packaging. She didn't resist. I was exhausted. I stripped and lay on the trampoline on my back. She did all the work.

I woke up alone at nine, showered, dressed, and ate half the breakfast buffet at the hotel. I made the anonymous phone call to the brown birds and told them where to find Po's body, put my twenty-five grand in the hotel safe and hopped a rickshaw to the Family Records Bureau. I bribed the clerk for the price of a movie ticket and got the information I was looking for. Panda girl was the only daughter of the latest late Mr. Kung.

I took a cab back to the hotel and tried to decide if I should tell Mrs. Kung I had some new paint for her walls or keep it to myself. There was an anxious knock on my door. The door flew open before I could get there. It was the same TGC goon, and this time he brought a friend. They weren't polite like before as they waved their heaters in my face, cuffed me, and dragged me down the back stairs to an unmarked crow. Neither of them uttered a single word as they pulled a black bag over my head, shoved me in the back seat, and drove off like we were heading to the Hindenburg crash. The sweat dripping off my face and down my back told me exactly where we were going—to the worst possible place imaginable; a secret Taiwan Garrison Command detention center.

It only took about twenty-seven years for us to reach our destination. I was hustled into a building and seated in a tin chair that was clammy as Hitler's smile. Someone jerked the hood off and stuck a cigarette into my mouth. I rested my elbows on a greasy, lumpy metal table that smelled like mackerel filleted last week. It was bolted to the floor. The entire wall in front of me was a one-way mirror. I wondered if an ashen and buggy Mrs. Kung was on the other side with her asshole puckered up like a pregnant jelly doughnut. My friend Officer Whoops, who had now twice visited my hotel room, was lurking around like a hollow tiger near a far wall. He shot me a scowl that bruised my ribs. A new man sat across from me. A man that looked like he'd never heard of Mickey Mouse or children. He was bolted to the floor, too. His wide sallow face had pockmarks that belonged on the far side of the moon. A wrinkled monkey suit that was two sizes too small squeezed him until his cheeks turned red. His scornful bloodshot eyes danced over my face like a drunken ballerina.

He reached over and lit my cigarette and said plainly, "I'm Mr. Sun."

Officer Whoops noticed that the mention of his name raised my eyebrows.

"That's right, friend!" cackled Whoops. "AKA Deadbolt Sun."

I was an Eskimo Pie in a waffle iron.

"I heard you learned how to fold napkins and curtsy at a Russian charm school," I said as coolly as possible.

Sun gave me a derisive little smile from one side of his mouth that exposed a yellow fang.

"Don't look so flattered," I said. "I also heard that guys like you go home to bullwhip twirling wives in black-leather bodysuits and stilettos. Does she tie you up before or after she shoves the yellow plastic ball into your blow hole?"

Officer Whoops hit me from behind with something that made my head feel like a Mickey Mantle home run ball.

"You're reckless," Mr. Sun said plainly.

"I try to be, and I like your smooth delivery," I said. "Officer Whoops's voice sounds like a pussy fart in an echo chamber."

"We found your driver."

"The three wood?" I said.

"Answer our questions and you'll be back at your hotel for a pleasant lunch."

"Why would I bump off the only friend I had in town?

"Where's the money?"

"You clowns would love to get your mitts on all that cake. And just how big a sliver would you give back to my client?"

"Get wise, Chang."

"Business with my client is confidential. Even if I did know, I wouldn't be spilling to you Kuomintang stooges."

"We're not so bad, really."

"Oh, really?"

"When we arrived in '47, Taiwan had been stripped and fucked by the Japanese like the class slut. Twenty-eight sugar factories are now under operation, and all profits are going directly into rebuilding Taiwan's infrastructure."

"Congratulations!" I blurted out. "But, what about all the dead bodies you boys keep piling up?"

"General Shek has implemented agricultural programs to give land parcels to individual farmers."

"You can take some of the credit. But, as you know the US has been pumping billions of dollars into Kuomintang coffers since the late 1950s—and for purely selfish reasons. Their only concern in the region is fear of the spread of communism. Look at the troops they're pouring into Viet Nam. Hell, if Taiwan wasn't such a strategic geographical location we'd all still be walking around barefoot."

"We've been gracious enough to allow them to let their enlisted men R & R in Taipei."

"Have you heard the one about the diplomat from the US State Department?"

"Uh, no."

"He had his nose jammed so far up the general's ass the US feds had to file a missing person report."

"And?"

"You and the general and the Kuomintang are extremely lucky to be running your little show here at this particular time in history."

"Mr. Chang, tell us what we want to know."

"What?"

"Who killed Mrs. Kung's rickshaw driver and who took the ransom money?"

"I don't know."

For the next three days we were a ducky little three-man band with Mr. Sun on vocals, Officer Whoops on various percussions, and me on the Uilleann bagpipes. I didn't spill. In between our recording sessions they strapped me to a love seat in a dark room with a giant movie screen, taped my eyes open and played loops of *Monster A Go-Go* and *Glen or Glenda* for hours on end. I still see Dolores Fuller in my dreams. They dumped me on the side of the road near a chicken farm about a mile from the hotel. I ate for two hours in the hotel restaurant. I ate the carpet. I ate the furniture. I ate the waiter's brother. I went up to my room and fell asleep.

I woke up early the next morning, put on my olive suit and a fresh shirt, and went directly to Mrs. Kung's without breakfast. I was getting close. Sweet Face met me at the front door and led me up a stairway to the top floor. She opened the door leading out onto the roof and pointed across it to a well-built and well-kept pigeon coop. I walked to the coop and looked through the narrow open door. Mrs. Kung was holding a chirper in her cupped hands. She was looking more appealing this time in an airy brown rayon dress with white polka dots and brown heels.

"Isn't she precious," she said with a big smile. "Please come inside. I want you to see my birds."

I ducked through the door and walked inside the coop. Fifty birds cooed in their cages.

"These gorgeous racers compete when they're only five or six months old."

"Is that a fact?" I said, trying to seem interested.

"And I baby and spoil them and feed them secret mixtures of food. I rub their bellies and genitals and sing to them."

"I heard Chairman Mao lives like that."

"Many of them don't make it back from a race. They either get lost or decide they want a new life. But Singing Boy over there, he's my champion and the coop stud. He's won us a lot of money. He's retired now and takes care of my lady birds."

"I know Panda's your stepdaughter."

"Oh?"

"What does somebody have on you?"

"What do you mean?"

"How did your late husband die?"

"That's none of your damn business."

"Are you being blackmailed?"

"No!"

"This birdnapping was a cover, wasn't it? You just needed an honest delivery boy to do the drop."

"Ha!"

"Ho!"

"You were paid well."

"I expect the truth from my clients, especially if I'm being chased around dark alleys with a bag of loot and an innocent boy's corpse turns up next to me."

"Are you married?"

"What does that have to do with the price of fish balls?"

"Well, are you?"

"No."

"Girlfriend?"

"The last one couldn't stomach the hazards of my trade."

"What was she like?"

"She had hips that could have made Gandhi join the French Foreign Legion."

"It must be tough being a greasy gumshoe dick," she sneered.

"It must be tough being as endowed as a female Beluga—swimming around all alone in this li'l backwater always having to fret about some slippery character coming along wanting to filet you to get at all those expensive blackberries."

"My, that was quite an oration. You staying around?"

"Someone just tenderized my friend with a Taitung toothpick."

"Must you always sound so, so indelicate?" she asked pretending to be coy.

"Still playing a bluff hand, huh? I owe Po's mother," I said, and with an agitated shrug, I left.

I passed Tienhou Temple as I walked back toward the hotel. It was crowded. The dragon boat festivities were rolling down hurly-burly hill. Several open-air tents were set up out front with a row of tables that stretched sixty feet. A dozen puffing wooden steamers sat on top of the tables. Many people anxiously pushed and shoved their way in around the steamers. A smiling man with a white beard opened one of the steamers and held up a stringer of baseball-size rice dumplings wrapped in bamboo leaves. People clutched at the *tzong-zu*—shouting and begging, holding out their hands. He passed the tzong-zu out freely, then he handed me one. Inside the temple a throng of people were praying and making food and ghost-money offerings.

I worked my way through the crowd toward the front door. Old men telling stories sat on benches next to the doors. A woman in a wheelchair sold yellow bundles of ghost money. On a makeshift stage next to the temple, a chorus line of twenty darling young women walked onstage wearing matching black skirts, nylons, and heels designed by Vertigo. Floral scenes were painted on their backs and shoulders. The inside walls of the stage were decorated with painted landscape scenes of animals and nymphs. A small group of old men played traditional instruments next to the stage—long horns that made a high pitched sound and a *gueh khim*—a banjo-like instrument that makes a beautiful plucking sound. Someone lit a bundle of firecrackers nearby. A small hand grabbed my arm from behind as I was enjoying the dancers' routine. I spun around. It was Echo, the cute little pro from the gambling den.

"I'll meet you at your hotel room in fifteen minutes," she said anxiously.

"Sorry, sister."

"I have information about Po's murder. I can't be seen with you. Now, where are you staying?"

"Gold Dragon, room 23."

Echo disappeared into the mob. I grabbed a few more of the tzong-zu and headed back to the hotel, stopping every few blocks to see if I was being followed. I went up the back stairs, opened my door and walked into the room. The sexy little jade was sitting on the sofa smoking a cigarette. She was looking as expensive as a ghost-month pig in a black miniskirt and zebra-print top.

"You move fast on those swizzle sticks."

"I know who killed Po," whimpered Echo.

"That so?"

"My boss, Red Moon."

"Proof?"

"I heard him blabbing about the ransom money."

"We need more than that."

"Well, fuzzy, how about this," she said and pulled a blood-stained watermelon knife with an eight-inch curved blade out of a paper bag.

"Where'd you find the toothpick?" I asked, making no move to take it from her.

"Please have it checked for fingerprints and blood type, okay."

"Why are you doing this?"

"Po was my cousin!" cried Echo. "Please help me find the ruthless killer!"

"Does Red Moon know you were related to Po?"

"I don't think so. Nobody does."

"You better hide out for a while. If he's our man and he finds out who you are, I don't know if I can protect you."

"I know," she purred and leisurely crossed her legs, making sure I got an eyeful of her hayfield. "So, how about some cash?"

"Well, aren't we sentimental."

"I just cracked your case."

"You couldn't crack your own knuckles."

"Why don't you give it a try," she said and pulled her top down.

"Better cover up those gumdrops before I get out the clothespins."

"Ooh!" cooed Echo.

"I mean it. Scram!"

She pulled her top up, set the knife down on the table and walked out with her nose up in the clouds. After she left I ordered room service—one of everything on the menu. I gorged and took a short nap.

I had the name of a local cop that I was told could be trusted. My source said he hated the Kuomintang's secret police as much as I did. I phoned the crow house and asked him to meet me somewhere discreet. I met him at a noodle joint an hour later. He wore the usual khaki uniform with a khaki hat that almost all Taiwanese police wore. I gabbed with him for thirty minutes before I sprayed about the case. My gut told me he was okay. I took a chance and spilled most of it and gave him the bloody watermelon knife. I made him promise to keep this on the hush-hush and not to tell even his beat partner or his wife or any of his girlfriends. He agreed and said he'd get back with me in two or three days. That seemed like an eternity. Mrs. Kung, Mr. Lee, Panda, Red Moon Woo, swizzle-stick legs, the Secret police goons—they were all still in the lineup.

For the next day and a half I caught up on my sleep and played yo-yo with some local canaries. I discreetly fished around for info about the shadowy character Mr. Lee said was called Horse Brother. One source said he took a powder to Hong Kong shortly after Po turned up with silver dollars resting on his eyes. The local cop I hoped I could trust finally phoned and informed me that the prints on the knife matched Red Moon's and the blood type matched Po's. I threw him some stardust and pork skins as a professional favor. In return he promised to sit tight and not squawk until I put bracelets on Red Moon Woo.

I waited until 2:00 a.m. to put the drop on my man. A rickshaw driver I whistled off the pavement left me off a hundred yards from the Shut Out. I told him to get lost. I didn't want to find another kid with a Hong Kong street map carved into his belly. I hid in the shadows of a clump of orange trees across the street from the front entrance and waited. I shuffled around chain smoking until it felt like I'd swallowed a comet.

At three I watched the last vehicle leave the front of the building. Thirty minutes later I sneaked in the back door. The place was black as a fortune-teller's account book except for a light coming from underneath the closed office door. I put my ear to the door. There was no sound. I pulled out my ray gun and eased the door open. Red Moon was lying face-down on the floor. He was cooked as a Peking duck. I searched his wallet and his person for a lead as to where he may have hidden the stolen ransom cabbage. Nothing. I didn't think he'd be stupid enough to hide the loot in his office. I went through his desk and file cabinets anyway. I was halfway back to the hotel when it hit me. I remembered the kitschy wall clock behind the bar. I walked back to Red Moon's and ran my fingers along the top of the clock. Nothing. I groped around one of the hula dancers and was able to pull it forward. In a small compartment underneath rested a key to what appeared to be a public locker, like the kind they had at the bus depot. It had a number on it—7B. I was careful to wipe my prints off everything before I left. The locker at the bus depot could wait until morning.

At 4:30 I opened my hotel room door, made myself a drink stiff as a sailor's hard-on and plopped onto the sofa. I took off the shoulder holster, set the rig on the end table next to the sofa and lit a smoke. Ten minutes later the door swung lazily open. Echo drifted into the room like vapor from belladonna.

"The grieving cousin," I said and quickly glanced over at my rig trying to judge if I could reach it from where I was sitting. It was on the other side of the world. "I figured you'd show up."

"Any word yet on the knife?" she asked with feigned innocence as she took a few steps toward me.

"Oh, please help me find whoever killed my poor cousin Po," I said mockingly.

"Well?"

"I did a little checking around. He wasn't your cousin, sister. He was probably the only kid in town who hasn't humped you."

"That doesn't mean Red Moon didn't kill him."

"True, but that doesn't mean it wasn't a frame job. You and Red Moon were in on the bird napping scam from the get go."

"No way, hammerhead!"

"You knew you couldn't trust your partner Red Moon. You knew he wasn't the sharing type. So you gave me the murder knife to set him up for the fall and hoped I'd lead you to the hidden ransom loot. But, you two must have had somebody else. Somebody with brains. Somebody running on the inside rail to set this whole thing up."

"You've been reading too many pulp magazines."

"But I have it, swizzle sticks. I have the key you were looking for. I beat you to it."

Echo pulled out a .32, pointed it in my direction, and walked within six feet of me.

"You can come out now, Panda girl," I said. "That is you hiding in the bathroom, isn't it? I recognize the perfume— Auschwitz No. 5."

Panda slunk out of the bathroom cherry-faced.

"What's the matter?" I chided. "Mrs. Kung take away your lunch money?"

"All of it," she muttered underneath her breath.

"Ain't that a shame, sister."

"The key, buster!" Echo said, and held out her idle hand.

I flipped her the key.

"You dumb twit!" Panda shrieked at Echo. "I told you to wait and I'd get the key! Then we'd make the split."

"The same way you split with Red Moon?" said Echo.

"Which one of you two ladies fitted Po for the wooden kimono?" I demanded. "Who, damn it?!"

"She did!" they both yelled out.

"If you two she-cats are going to tussle and roll around on the floor, could you strip down to your bras and panties first?" I said as I inched my caboose over on the sofa to try to get closer to my rig.

Panda lunged at Echo and the two crashed onto the floor. I grabbed the .38 out of its holster and held it ready. Two shots were fired. Echo popped up off the floor with gun in hand faster than a jack-in-the-box. Panda girl wasn't moving. I squeezed two. Both of them hit Echo in the windbag. She wasn't dancing now. I took the key out of her clenched hand and went over to check on Panda. Her breath was faint. The dark puddle of oil spreading underneath her told me it was a liver sandwich.

I shook her and said, "Who else was in on it?"

She wheezed something unintelligible.

"Come on! Who else, damn it?"

"You were nice the other night," she slurred with a dumb little smile, and then she pulled the zippers.

Two dead birds on my hotel room floor—and pouting angels sitting on my shoulders. I needed a drink. I needed a drink and a gasoline chaser. That's the only time I ever sent a woman to the sawmill.

I took a long pull from my bottle, lit a butt, called the khaki who'd helped me with the murder knife, and told him the score. I leaked everything except that I had a key to a bus depot locker. The Taiwan Garrison Command boys had some fun grilling me until eight the next morning. I made it easy for them and laid it out like a connect-the-dots drawing for five-year-olds. They swallowed it like a horse pill, convinced that I had the ransom loot hidden somewhere. But they couldn't prove it.

Late the next night I crept down to the bus depot and opened locker 7B with the key I'd found at Red Moon's joint. It was all there; the $450,000 NT ransom that was taken from Po and me, and the original $300,000 that Mrs. Kung's assistant Mr. Lee gave Red Moon to pay for the birds. I went to sleep with all that loot underneath my ear.

The next morning I put the $450,000 NT ransom into a large manila envelope and left it in the hotel safe to keep my salary company. I put the $300,000 NT into a potato sack and hopped a cab to Mrs. Kung's. When I got there I said hello and dumped the cash onto the table in front of her. All that loot spread over the coffee table went well with the décor.

"That's all of it, pigeon lady," I said. "I don't have any leads as to where the ransom may be."

"The police were here earlier," she said. "They told me what happened at your hotel room last night. I can't believe that my stepdaughter was, uh—"

"Can't believe your late stepdaughter was in on it?" I said, and pictured Panda girl standing naked before me the other night.

I imagined Mrs. Kung would be chewing on that for quite a long while.

"Never cared much for the girl anyway," she said, and lit a butt.

"Po was the sole supporter of his widowed mother and younger sister," I said. "But you knew that."

"Yes, I know."

"I'll be leaving for Taipei in an hour. I guess this is goodbye."

As I neared the door she called out across the spacious wooden floor, "Mr. Chang! Mr. Chang! Please wait a moment."

When I turned around she was standing there cradling the sack of cash in her arms like a newborn baby.

"Please take this to Po's mother," she said and handed me the loot. "And tell her I'm so sorry."

I looked at the cash, then into Mrs. Kung's eyes, and said slowly, "Not bad for a woman who's used to eating her dinner with an ice cream scoop."

"Ha!" she laughed.

"Why don't you tell her yourself?" I said. "It'll do you some good to get out of this palace for a while and rub up against the salt of the earth."

"I might do that," she said as I walked out. "And thank you, Big Guava, for everything!"

"Thank you, and get a little sun," I said and popped a butt into my craw.

I went directly back to my hotel, got my $25,000 NT salary out of the safe and checked out. I put my salary into my portable bar and stuck the box into the potato sack with the other three hundred grand. I had the taxi driver stop at a flower shop, where I bought a bouquet of yellow chrysanthemums. Then I had him drop me at a plain Jane red brick house on Da Ming

Road. It was Po's mother's family home. I asked the driver to wait and stuck my head in the open front door. She was sitting alone in a modest front room. I was a wet fart on a trans-Pacific flight. I was surprised by how young she was. She must have had Po when she was only a teenager. I handed her the flowers and told her how terribly sorry I was that Po was killed and how I was partly to blame. I assured her that Po's killer was found and that justice was done. What I didn't tell her was that I didn't know exactly who killed Po; I was nearly certain it was Red Moon Woo, Panda girl, Echo, or even the Taiwan Garrison Command. That was good enough for me. As for who killed Red Moon Woo, I didn't really care. He got his supper. The man called Horse Brother, who may or may not be connected to the case—well, I won't be running off to Hong Kong looking for that surreptitious character. Besides, there's always a Horse Brother or a Mr. X behind the players on the street. Maybe we'll cross paths down the line.

Before I left I gave Po's mother Mrs. Kung's three hundred grand. After that, she had every right to kick me in the face and throw me out. I wished she had. It may have made me feel better. I was fortunate that she was a wonderfully humble and gentle soul and accepted the money without any questions. I asked her if I could use her telephone. She showed me into a private hallway off the main room and left me there. I phoned Mrs. Kung and informed her that the other $450,000 had been located and she could find it in the safe of her hotel lobby with her name on it. I wondered if she was still feeling generous. I wondered if she had the heart to at least give Po's mother a courtesy visit. I didn't feel guilty about holding out on Mrs. Kung about the cash. I like to think she'd have given the sorrow-ridden mother all of it, but in the end I wasn't sure she would have. I had to make sure Po's mother didn't end up empty-handed.

I walked out into the bright Lukang sun, hopped a flying carpet, lit a butt, and on the way to the bus depot couldn't stop thinking about how that innocent boy and three others had been killed over two lousy birds. Sometimes, I think I must be nuts to be doing this kind of work. But I can't imagine doing anything else.

Ting Ting Pageant

Kaohsiung's habanera streets gave me a gasoline rubdown and the fatigue of fifty men I was having a smoke taking a rest in front of a red onion near the train station crammed with salary men a voice in my head chanted "beans on Sunday" work songs reminding me of the tough Twenty-Seventh and I Street years I knocked down in Sacramento that reel of night school and shit low-wage jobs playing so I can appreciate how good things are now I'll keep punching the breeze and doing my art 'til the reaper pulls the lion out of my throat I was looking up and down Jiangwo Road for more action so damn tired but happy after another day of working the great Hail! Hail! ting ting pageant but didn't want to go home to sleep even after twelve hours of pavement slapping and trumpets because I would lie awake exhausted thinking about all those scenes I was missing from the never-ending Moviola playing on the riotous blinking-sea-of-flashbulbs street the twisted up staring faces at the Taoist temple and the men cutting themselves the blood and smoke and banging clang music with high scream-

ing horns piercing me like a Vacaville nail gun and the hey hey
chaos and the devout looking on that misty throng of gently
swaying souls rolling on their heels to the trance music clutch-
ing worried breasts with burning incense prayer sticks held in
both hands up to chin three shakes forward *bai-bai* and the ec-
stasy men the zombie sci-fi shamans gushing like great marble
fountains with masks and black lungs lunging around like
rogue hippos loose in camp ready to fuck a tree or an over-
turned canoe in a Conrad lagoon with someone's clothes scattered on the bank my weary legs had had enough so I went to
the curb to wave down a cab Taiwan cab drivers are cool men-
thol tom cats not rattled by anything they see on the electric
prairie I've seen them do a disco turn on a worm a roscoe a U-
boscoe a Spider Man crawl up the President Department Store
wall I've seen them flat out disappear and then come back to
life on the other side of an impossible stockyard intersection
and yes I've seen a cab fly at 120 MPH sweet as Key lime pie
they go underground when the cops ain't around and travel
the ammunition tunnels that the Japanese built in WWII
they'll pick up your clothes at the all-night fat iron dry clean-
ers with steam irons big as a blacksmith's anvil tethered to long
veins of electrical cords hanging from nineteenth-century tim-
ber ceiling the hazy hissing and pictures of dead ancestors on
stained flowered rice wallpaper Kaohsiung taxi drivers millions
of them in a great kid game rush little yellow cars some
crunched up and sloppy others new and brilliant buffed with
short roofs so I can't sit up straight in back seat with rolled
bead mat to massage my back the driver had pictures of his
kids and good luck mementos on the dash the conservative
chain-smoking drivers play the sweetest old Taiwanese native
music from the forties and fifties on their stereos with some silver girl cooing under a big yellow moon with a watercolor wa-
terfall dancing beside her the driver is quiet and cordial we try
to speak a little but my Chinese smells up the cab like stinky
tofu they buzz around the city slurving in and out of alleyways
always honking their horns and hey you and let me in that space
as big as a cigar box they whoosh in the rain the lots-of luck streets

and yes brother they are known to chew betel nut and spit long flashes of that red juice out the window onto frothing Kaohsiung streets with aluminum gals and elegant-suited guys trying to get to work was lying on my side in shrunken cab backseat the calm driver's hard turns shook me like liar's dice as we passed the bright lights and pomp of Liouhe Street night market the cabs all ten million of 'em prowl slip gazoom ba-boom dash ride waves all around the race track known as Kaohsiung City just stride up to the curb with chest thrown out like some grumpy wolf don't get out there in the flow or you'll get slammed and there will be two or three cabs playing stock car race drivers trying to cut each other off and damn near kill a vendor or a flock of schoolgirl swans for your fare compared to the States is a rock bottom deal cheap as hell!

Meeting Chairman Mao

A month of Sundays before I first met my *amor aeternus*, Julia, I was on a lilac wonder out of Chiayi rolling north, back toward Taichung and then Taipei. The train was a slowpoke. I liked it that way. For the past two weeks I'd been southbound, hopping on and off that plush run, working the small towns between Taichung and Kaohsiung. I wanted to track down the warped, resin-caked doors of an opium den this ramble. It was something I'd never tried, and I wanted to let the black gas knock me around until I was a double-amputee tumbling toward Mirage City—wrinkled as a prune, sprawled on a bamboo mat laughing at the firing squad, the Red mechanics, my empty bank account, and visions of running naked on a deserted Mexican beach with skinny stray longhorns pulling out each others intestines in the fizzing turquoise surf. Lizard-headed Taiwanese men in luxurious silk robes would be planted next to me spitting up joy-joy bills and shark fins as the devil's smoke poured out the tops of their heads. But Pingtung bartenders and Siamese twins Earl and Pow Babang—the

"Spider Boys of Jakarta," told me there weren't any opium dens in Taiwan. They suggested I go to a sauna to relax. I remembered what the boys said as the train screeched into Taichung Railway Station. It was a hazy afternoon sticky as flypaper. I got a cheap room above an aquarium shop that also sold used prosthetics and betel nut. With a wink, Gil, the suave proprietor with a curling mustache and delicate hands the color of a cuttlefish, pointed me toward a rubdown shop some half mile away. The place inhabited the lower levels of a tall, modern-looking office building. An elevator let me off in a spacious, empty lobby. My ears stood up as several attractive young women in green and gold uniforms smiled at me from behind a marble counter long as a landing strip. The fee was sporting—fifteen US dollars for twelve hours.

One of the women led me to a locker room. I stripped naked, which is the custom in Taiwan at these kinds of places, and walked through double doors into a brightly lit cavernous space big as a ballroom. Fifty men were sitting on the sides or walking around in a two-hundred-foot-long rectangular cold-water wading pool in the center of the room. Many of them turned to look at me as I entered—the only pale foreigner within light years. A small gathering of beefy, mean-looking buzz saws sat jabbering on the edge of the coldwater pool. Some of them had gorgeous tattoos on their backs and chests like the gangsters I'd met my first night in Taipei. Four smaller pools of varying degrees of hot water were situated around the room. A glass-walled steam room puffed like an oyster cooker against the far wall. A mess of sweaty arms and legs and other body parts—like a tangle of angry octopi—appeared and suddenly disappeared through the swirling, wafting hot white cloud inside. The biggest Swedish-style sauna I've ever seen took up the entire left end of the space. Inside, over one hundred motionless men roasted at 450 degrees Fahrenheit.

One of the towel attendants slithered toward me from across the room through the maze of naked bodies. He was a squat Filipino with greasy hair and a smile that belonged on a dingo. The word "laser" was tattooed across his forehead in blue ink.

He walked up to me and said, "Hey, you from the US, huh?"

"Yeah," I replied.

"Know what's in there?" he said, all-knowing, pointing to a large metallic door next to the Swedish sauna.

"Little guys who write funny things on people's foreheads?" I said with a smirk.

He smiled and tilted his head back.

"Oh, good one—you're funny. It's a lounge. There's girls working over there, know what I mean? You like hand jobs? They do it for you but will cost a lot. Hey, you like number sixty-nine? Hee! hee! Maybe Chairman Mao is in there, hee! hee! hee! Hey, maybe you want to buy some pot? Hee! hee! hee!"

"Not today, friend," I said and walked into the Swedish sauna.

For the next forty-five I went back and forth between the Swedish sauna, the steam room, and the coldwater pool. It was heaven. I was relaxed as a bloodhound's face. I found Towel Boy and told him I wanted to check out the lounge. He handed me a flimsy cotton robe.

"Put this on before you go in," he said. "You going to get some, huh? Hee! hee! hee!"

I put on the robe. It didn't do much to conceal my you-know. That was the idea. I opened the door to the lounge and was surprised at what I saw: a gigantic dimly lit room with at least a hundred La-Z-Boy recliners lined up in rows pointing toward two king-sized video screens showing porno flicks from the same Japanese sex channels I'd seen in the hotels. Half the recliners were full of curled up men. Some smoked. Some slept. Some drank tea or beer or whiskey. Some had giggling prostitutes bouncing around on their laps.

I found a chair somewhere in the middle of the room and collapsed into it, tilted it back as far as it would go and closed my eyes. I quickly fell asleep and began to dream. I was in the circus scene from the noir classic *Gun Crazy* with my old Sacramento pal Onions McElroy—we were tied up to huge straw targets on a crummy wooden stage ... Harpo Marx dashed on-stage with a pair of scissors and cut off our neckties ... in front of us, behind a chicken-wire barricade, a throng of wild-eyed kids bobbed up and down in an enormous vat of dirty motor oil . . . they cussed and whooped and made catcalls . . . a dozen clowns sat on the edges of the vat throwing cream pies at the oily kids . . . empty booze bottles flew through the air . . . a shaved donkey with painted zebra stripes was led around by Babe Ruth . . . there was a loud explosion, and out of a cloud of white smoke, sultry actress Peggy Cummins appeared twirling magnificent ivory-handled six guns . . . the crowd went nuts . . . Peggy gave the audience a big wink and strutted over to inspect us . . . she smelled like a donut shop.

"I always aim better when I'm a little drunk," she smirked.

Her assistant placed a short lit candle on the top of each of our heads . . . Peggy stepped back about twenty paces . . . the crowd got quiet . . . the rat-a-tat-tat of a drum. . . . Suddenly, I was at my silverback friend Roy Kendal's house in Oakland on Howe Street drinking single malt and smoking Royal Jamaicans. Some of Roy's work covered the walls—Goyaesque paintings of Spaniards with tormented faces. Roy took a beautiful and enormous clear glass shotgun out of its trombone case and gently laid it on the dining room table on top of his oil paints and brushes. He opened a box of glistening diamond bullets big as beer bottles and stuck it in my face.

He shook the box with both hands and said, deadpan, "These bastards can go through the walls of ten houses." Then Roy sneered and said in a slow drawl, "Hey Mike, I'm going to shut myself in the house all weekend and get really weird. I'm going to wear my sunglasses in the house all day, even to bed."

We walked up to Joey's Liquor and bought Hershey bars, a bottle of Old Grand-Dad, and a box of Pall Mall red. A tough-looking black Great Dane in a Hawaiian shirt rang up the order standing on its hind legs.

"He's a real mean sonbitch. Killed two kids last week trying to rob the place," whispered Roy. "He's got one hell of a poker, too. Gals always hanging around here."

Roy handed me a note as we walked back to the house with the booze and the treats.

"I wrote that today during one of my fucking boring intro

painting studio classes," he said matter-of-fact. It read:
To do list—this weekend
blender fish heads extra chorizo
rip ears off asshole upstairs neighbor
practice bullwhip on side of garage
hunt wild possum sleeping in basement
phone Robert Mitchum
I handed the list back to Roy and thought, he's going to really lean into the rails this weekend.

"Hey Mike," he said slowly and a sly grin appeared on his whiskered face. "Why don't we go out back when we get back to the casa and I'll show you how that goddamned glass shotgun goes. Man, Oscar and Pete were here last week and well, Jeezus Christ we blasted the hell out of those—"

I felt a tapping on my shoulder and woke up. One of the young whores Towel Boy told me about stood over me smiling. She was sexy as hell—all suntan lotion and martinis—wearing a robe like mine that stopped just below her crotch. The outfit looked a lot better on her. Her puffy nipples poked through the thin material. One pirouette with her was guaranteed to put lightning flowers across your back. A thin bead of sweat began forming on my brow. She held up a copy of some skin magazine called *Bargirls of the Orient*.

"Page thirty-six," she said proudly and dropped the mag into my lap. "That's me!"

I thumbed to the double-page spread of her lying alone on a bed in nothing but her whisker biscuits; glanced at it briefly and looked back at her.

"It looks like the Doberman had a good time," I said, and handed the magazine back to her. "How about you?"

"You're cute, but not very funny," she said disappointedly.

She was probably only twenty, but the bags under her eyes and a few skid marks made her look thirty. Calf-high white leather platform boots—taut thighs. She gave me a devilish smile, lifted up her robe, turned around, and bent over. Her entire ass was covered with a huge tattoo of Chairman Mao Zedong's smiling face. I was dumbstruck—the blue-and-red-inked portrait was amazingly lifelike. Oh my fucking god I thought! What a photograph that would be! She spun around twice, wearing a cool victorious smile, knowing she had shocked the hell out of me.

"Sphincter, mister?" she asked casually, like she was offering me a cigarette. "Oh, you like that? I'll take you to Venus if you want, okay?"

"Can you make him smile?" I stuttered, still astonished.

"For you, 2,500 Taiwan Dollars," she said toying with one of her hefty gold earrings.

"Come back in fifteen minutes, okay?" I said.

"Okay," she said with a smile.

She squeezed my shoulder like she was checking a muskmelon for ripeness and walked across the room toward a door marked PRIVATE ROOMS in bold black letters. I watched her tempting ass harrumph under the short rob.

"If you go with her, everyone will seeeeee you," said a singsong voice in an English accent.

I looked over at the guy in the La-Z-Boy next to mine. I couldn't see his face. He had a large towel draped over his head.

"What'd you say?" I asked. "See me what?"

"You'll become part of the live entertainment, my boy!" he laughed.

"What do you mean, man? Who are you?"

"I'm someone who's been burned at the altar."

He turned his head and leaned toward me so I could get a look at his face. He looked around thirty-five, and he had a long, sad sunburned face and sweet, boyish eyes the color of mud.

"They'll video you having a naughty with her from behind a two-way mirror, and it will be up there," he said pointing to the two massive video screens up front. He chuckled, "But then again, how many times will you ever get the chance to fuck Mao in the mouth?"

I could feel myself frown as I gazed at the gigantic naked bodies swimming on the screens.

"You can't trust her, man. She's all full of piss and wind, that one is. Oh yes, they love it when a big dumb American like you comes in. It's good for business. They'll make a video and sell it all over Taiwan and Asia. She'll take her time with you, too, so they get plenty of footage. She'll put a dollop of Tiger Balm on your asshole, and you'll send smoke signals clear to Ho Chi Minh City. They'll fillet you with a straight razor and hang your skin on a nail on that door over there and sprinkle salt on your muscles and watch you twitch. You'll be famous, you will."

He smiled, opened his eyes wide, stared at me mockingly and said, "Your warm entrails will be on school kids' lunch pails."

"How you know all this?"

"They'll blackmail you. For some cash, maybe you can keep the video off the street. How do I know all this? Because, my American friend, it happened to me."

"Where?"

"In Bangkok a few years back. Oh, bullocks! What a fucking mess that was! I had to leave town and ditch everything in the river. I'm still quite upset about it."

"Tell it," I said.

"I had been teaching English in Bangkok for a few years. I had my fun, don't get me wrong, but I kept a low profile and was very careful until, until I met Wanda."

"Wanda?" I said.

"You know how it is, mate, some of these Asian birds always giving themselves funny English names. Wanda was seventeen and ravishing. A genuine beauty. Ever been to Bangkok?"

"No. But I'd like to." He looked disappointed with my answer.

He hesitated a moment, smiled again, and then continued, "Oh yes, I met her in the red-light district. She was up onstage in a thong bikini and cowboy boots dancing around with a lot of other birds. She had the number 23 or 27 or something pinned on her bikini. They gives all the girls in places like that numbers, and if you see what you like, you tell the boss the number and you order her up for the hour, week, or month, just like at the baker's shop. The first night she washed me entire body with her pussy. I made the mistake of falling in love with her cause she promised me the moon, you know, if I would take her back to England. The sex was out of this world, and after a few months of seeing her regular, I let my guard down. And it was all done very nice and slick, you know, the way they got me. They told me at the club she worked at that since I was such a regular we could use a room like the one that little bird that was here a minute ago wants to drag you into. What a fucking setup: bright floor lamps, a long massage table, a bar with about fifteen bottles in an exquisite line—Johnnie Walker, Bombay Sapphire, Courvoisier, Absolut. A few tinklers and treats. Grass, too. A comfortable black leather couch. A Siamese torch singer cooed softly from speakers I couldn't see. The wall-to-wall mirrors. The bloody fucking mirrors! Get the picture?"

In my mind I could see the Filipino towel boy and about thirty brutes sitting behind mirrored walls on high stools with video cameras filming my cock sliding in and out of Mao's mouth from half a dozen angles. They'd be drinking Kaoliang 58, and I'd be up on the big screens in front of me. A live feed, Jesus Christ!

"Then what happened?" I asked.

"The blokes I was with that night, some of me pals from London, they saw me shagging Wanda on the video screens up at the bar. But it was too late by then. They couldn't find me. They didn't know where the hell I was in that damn bloody maze of rooms. That's why I'm here in Taiwan. I was the butt of a lot of jokes and was always worrying about my school finding out. They threatened to blackmail me. It was a bad scene."

"Thanks man," I said and stood up.

"Right oh, man," he said. "Hey wait, you know that pro with Mao on her ass is owned by some local gang. Maybe you could get her number and meet up with her somewhere away—"

"A look was enough."

"But, don't you *at least* want another look?"

"Nope, the first trip through the fun house is always the one you remember," I said, and walked into the sauna room a little dejected without looking back.

Yes, I did want another look—to get Mao on film, but knew I

didn't have a chance. Thunder pussy was most likely an illegal from China and, like the Englishman had said, literally owned by the local mafia. There was no way they were going to do anything to jeopardize all the money that that sweet little hussy brought in. And I wasn't about to go looking for the mob and asking them for any favors. In case you're wondering, I had no interest in taking the trip to Venus that Mao girl had promised—sure, I've seen a few hustlers in my day, but that was when I was a young buck full of rock salt and mescal drifting around the San Diego beach scene in the early 1980s. I found out that the Englishman's yarn about foreigners getting secretly filmed with massage girls was not true. It has happened to a few high profile locals, but those were isolated cases at small "love motels."

Mango Road

A U-shaped house called a *san-ho yuan* sat serenely behind a five-hectare mango orchard in the Ciatou countryside. Its red brick walls and elegant sloping orange tile roof were reminiscent of nineteenth-century southern Chinese architectural style. The tiles shone like imperial topaz in the onset of dusk. The shade of six bountiful papaya trees caressed the west side of the house. A single strand of incense smoke curled out between the two red wooden front doors, which were swung open completely and gave the appearance of the wings of an exotic butterfly flattened in a dusty, wearied album. On the facade of the building around the entrance, Chinese characters in relief revealed highlights of family history, mostly hidden by the red wings. The man who had meticulously handcrafted the characters one hundred and twenty five years ago lay buried with other ancestors in a well-kept mound in the field behind the house. Above the door hung five hand-painted yellow lanterns to protect the home from spirits of the underworld. Out here, northwest of the perpetual rumble and clamor of Kaohsiung City, maternal flatlands teeming with rice, cabbage, cauliflower, and sugar cane flowed out for miles to the sanctuary of the goddess of the sea as the sun rolled over the landscape as faithfully and as true as a great golden dharma wheel.

A dark-skinned old man wearing baggy brown shorts and a snug white T-shirt was sitting in an archaic rocking chair beside the front door. His handsome, weather-lined face had the appearance of a freshly tilled red clay field. With content, boyish eyes, he gazed at the triumphant mango orchard as it began to dissolve into the tide of evening. People said Mr. Lee was indomitable and valorous and scarred as a battle-worn bull elephant. People also said he was an angel, a bigot, a boy-hero, a son of a bitch, and the grower of the best mangos in Kaohsiung County. A traditional wide-brimmed bamboo hat hung on the wall next to the door. A single light bulb in a shaded fixture on the other side of the door threw its shallow arc into the dusk several feet beyond the sinewy old man. His mind strayed to his late wife, and he thought of the black and white photograph of them that sat in a gilded frame upon his dresser. His eyes hardened a bit and his mouth became dry and tight. He reached into a small plastic bag in his shirt pocket, pulled out a betel nut, and popped it into his mouth.

A late-model Toyota sedan with a wake of brown dust stormed up the narrow dirt road that ran along the right side of the mango orchard from the main road, passing a humble, hand-painted sign nailed to a fence post that tittered in the wind. Its orange Chinese characters read: Mango Road. The car stopped abruptly in front of the house. A rangy teenage boy got out of the passenger side and stood uneasily in the dirt road. He wore a new pair of white Adidas, Levi's blue jeans, and a dark blue T-shirt. A brown suitcase trembled slightly in the boy's hand. He squinted and held up the other hand to shield his eyes from the setting sun.

The old man stood up as tall as he could, straightened his wiry shoulders and muttered to himself, "She hates me. But you need me now, don't you, you old sucker fish?"

The car quickly pulled away. The old man stared silently at

the boy.

"Uh, hello, Grandpa!" the boy called out. He walked gingerly into the red tiled courtyard, as if it were a minefield.

"Damn strawberry," grumbled the frowning old man, and he looked the boy up and down and spit a stream of betel-nut juice that landed, a red splotch, between him and the boy. "You look pretty, like a goddamned girly boy."

A look of shock appeared on the boy's face. "That's what you have to say, Grandpa, after not seeing me since I was six? Everybody calls me Curtis now."

"You call me 'Grandfather' or 'sir,' or I'll plant you with the mangos," the old man grunted and grabbed a bright yellow pack of Long Life cigarettes from his shirt pocket, flicked one of the butts into his mouth and lit it with a cheap butane lighter. "What the hell's wrong with your real name? Why some damn fag foreigner name?"

"A lot of people have English names now."

"Well, you're Strawberry to me, pussy lips."

The boy frowned.

"Set that damn monkey box down and hold out your hands."

"What for?" the boy asked meekly.

"Palms up, Straw Boy." The boy set the suitcase down at his side and held his hands out in front of the old man.

The old man didn't look at the boy's hands. He gave the boy a hard stare, turned his head, spit a splotch of betel-nut juice that nicked the boy's shoe, and muttered with disgust, "Soft and pretty as lotus blossoms."

"So," the boy whispered under his breath, and he looked down dejectedly at the red stain on his pristine shoe.

The old man sat down in his chair and said, "You'll get your badges starting tomorrow morning."

"Badges?"

The cell phone in the boy's hip pocket began to ring.

"Take a seat," commanded the old man, ignoring the boy's question.

The boy opened his cell phone and said, "Hello?"

The old men sprang out of his chair, grabbed the cell phone

out of the boy's hand, turned it off, and shoved it into his own pocket.

"Take a seat!" growled the old man. "This ain't aunty's."

The boy hurriedly sat in the cane chair across from his grandfather. The old man eyed the boy with suspicion for a long while.

"How old are you now?"

"Fourteen."

"You looked a helluva lot more promising at your parents' funeral."

"So did you." The boy looked scared, even as he said it.

"Your aunt told me you've been a real asshole," scolded the old man, not letting on that he liked the boy's retort. "Extorting money from a young girl at school with a group of thugs. Terrorizing a girl? Is that true?"

The boy bowed his head in shame, looked at the timeworn red tile beneath his feet, and shifted uneasily in the chair. It felt hot. Visions flashed in his mind from an underground video he'd seen of an inmate getting fried in Old Sparky, the infamous Texas electric chair.

"They forced me to or they said they'd, uh—"

"Damn it all, Straw Boy! You've disgraced our family name! What kind of punks are you going around with?"

The boy continued to look down.

"Well, I spoke with the doctor, and he said that you're fit to work. And that's what you're going to do here for the next two and a half months until school starts. Your precious aunt sent me enough insulin and needles for you to poke holes in about every goddamned thing that walks or crawls within a fifty-kilometer radius."

The boy peeked up at the old man momentarily with the big sorrowful eyes of a runaway hound expecting another blow on the snout from its master.

The old man said, "I suppose you're feeling sorry for yourself because of your medical problem and because of what happened to your parents. You better learn to take it boy, because life ain't a bowl of cherries."

"How much will I get paid?"

The old man laughed mockingly. "Prisoners don't get paid," he said, shaking his head. "You've got five hundred hours with me for what you did to that girl. And I hear you're getting shitty grades, too. Are you stupid, is that it?" He didn't give the boy a chance to answer. "You're going to work, boy! You're going to work until all that silly shit is leached out of your damn bones!"

"Says who?"

"Says your warden, your jailer, and the meanest old bastard in the county," said the old man, and he stood up and walked into the house. "I'll never bleed the damn strawberries out of this kid, wife," the old man muttered, and he opened a drawer in the kitchen and pulled out a pair of electric clippers.

He returned with the clippers and a white towel, which he threw around the unsuspecting boy's shoulders.

"What are you doing, you crazy old man?!" the boy yelled with fright. When he tried to rise, the old man held him lightly, easily in place. "You go to work tomorrow. You look like a damned girl with this Japanese devil's hairdo. You don't want some neighbor's dog or some convict on the lam to come along and fuck you in the ass, do you?"

The boy squirmed when the old man turned on the clippers. The old man grabbed one of the boy's ears and twisted it hard as he began shearing the back of his head. Five minutes later, the job was complete. The boy ran his hands over his shaved head defeatedly.

"Why did you want a Japanese dog haircut, anyway?" asked the old man as he quickly ran the clippers over his own shorn scalp.

"It's the style," said the boy plainly trying to conceal his humiliation.

"Don't they teach you your own history?" said the old man in disgust. "Those Japanese devils enslaved us for fifty years. Made me learn their damn language. Beat me in school if I spoke my native tongue. Forced our young women into becoming comfort women."

"That was a long time ago."

The old man turned off the clippers. "Clean up this mess, Strawberry, and come in for supper," said the old man and he walked into the house.

The old man woke at five thirty the following morning, put on black cotton work pants, a white T-shirt, and calf-high rubber boots. At 5:40 the boy was sitting on the end of his bed preparing a syringe for his morning insulin injection. He had been performing this routine for over a year. The old man appeared at the boy's door ready to roust him out of bed. Instead, he took a step back and looked on silently, pitifully, and the boy cursed and plunged the needle into his arm.

The old man waited until the boy was finished and said, "Breakfast," then he turned and headed toward the kitchen.

After a quick breakfast of rice soup and egg sandwiches, the old man threw the boy a pair of old work pants, rubber boots, a wide-brimmed bamboo hat, and a white T-shirt with the word "hoodlum" scrawled across the front with felt-tip marker.

"I'm not wearing this," exclaimed the boy as he examined the T-shirt.

"That's what you are, ain't you?"

"I told you I didn't really—"

"You'll wear it every day in the fields until I tell you it doesn't fit you any more, if that ever happens. You should feel lucky. In my day they might have tattooed it across your damn chest."

The boy stripped off his blue T-shirt, exposing a medical ID necklace hanging around his neck that read "DIABETES" in bold Chinese characters.

"I've already got my mark," he said, and put on the "hoodlum" shirt.

The old man barked, "Well, now you've got another one!" He looked at the black and white wedding portrait of him and his wife on the wall and said slowly, "We've all got marks, kid."

The boy hastily donned the rest of clothes and followed the old man to a traditional Taoist family ancestral shrine that occupied the small room inside the front door. The walls and wood-beam ceiling were smoked a deep reddish brown from decades of burning incense, the Taoists' way to communicate with the spirits of gods and ancestors. A twelve-foot-wide mahogany altar spanned the back wall. A small wooden statuette of the goddess Kuanyin—her head and face blackened by years of smoke, sat in the center of the altar. To Taoists, Kuanyin is the goddess of mercy. They believe that faithful prayer to her will assist in facing any problem. Offerings of snacks—pineapple, mango, and banana—lay in front of her. These offerings were gifts for her and for departed ancestors. A vase of lilies and a vase of orchids sat at either end of the long table. The old man was a devout Taoist, praying at the altar each day. He took great pride in attending the shrine, changing the offerings often and making sure at least one stick of incense was always burning. The old man lit six sticks of incense and handed three to the boy. They knelt down in front of the altar and prayed in silence. The boy waited for the old man to raise the incense in front of his face and wave it forward three times. The boy did the same. The old man stood up and placed the incense in a small urn that sat in front of Kuanyin. Again, the boy followed his grandfather's movements exactly.

Without uttering a word, the old man walked outside, grabbed the wide-brimmed bamboo hat that hung on the wall beside the front door, put it on, and marched through the courtyard and around the side of the house toward a small shed fifty meters away. The boy followed. The betel nut chewing old man came out of the shed leading a white bull by a long thin rope. He used his other hand to balance a wooden plow on his shoulder.

"You didn't jack off last night, did you, and shoot strawberry juice all over the walls?" barked the old man and spat a splotch of betel nut juice.

"No!"

"You jack off in the bathroom or outside somewhere. I don't want you messing up the bedding with your young restless birdie."

"Yes, sir."

"I suppose you've never worked an honest day in your

whole damned soft strawberry life have you?"

"I'm in school."

"School's school. It ain't work. Oh hell, school's all right. But you kids get too much of it. Problem with you strawberries is that the whole damn society coddles and wet nurses you kids 'til you're not worth a shit. Parents should be imprisoned for the way they pamper you and wipe your asses. The cops are useless. We got a whole stinking nation of computer game addicts with the attention span of a flea that at twenty-two years of age after college haven't worked one day in their lives, not one damn day, and have never earned a dollar. Bunch of damned sissies."

"What about when you were a kid?" the boy asked, following the old man toward the fields and looking sideways nervously at the bull.

The old man ignored the boy's question. "Mr. Shih in town owns a motorcycle repair shop—he's a smart one—has two boys about your age, and he's taught them how to work. One of them goes to high school in the day and works at the shop at night, and the other works at the shop during the day and goes to school at night. They run the place by themselves half the time. Real fine young men—polite, courteous, hell they're years beyond you, kid."

"What about you?"

"Hell, I was working in the fields right alongside my mother and father when I was seven. And it was work, boy, eight hours a day, or we didn't eat. We were bent over all day long working a shovel or a hoe—no one ever saw our faces, we were all assholes and elbows. When I was eighteen I did my mandatory three year hitch in the Army. Nowadays, you pansies are only required to do thirteen puny months."

"Did you have to fight?"

"It was peacetime in the mid 1950s. You don't pay attention at school, do you dumbfuck?"

"What about your school?" the boy winced as if stung by the remark.

"Some," said the old man, and he stopped next to a barren

patch of ground and dropped the plow. "I made it to the sixth grade. That's why I've got balls made from steel and you've got numb nuts, you little pecker."

The boy laughed, and the old man pretended not to be pleased. He dug the plow into the rich black earth, bent down, grabbed a handful of the moist soil, and said, "Hold out your lotus blossoms."

"What?"

"Hold out your damn hands!"

The boy held out his hands. The old man placed the soil into the boy's cupped hands, and the boy held it without appreciation.

"What's that for?"

"Smell it."

"Why?"

"Go on."

The boy lifted his hands to his face and smelled the soil. "I don't get it," he said.

The old man gazed at the boy in silence for a long moment, bent down and hooked up the plow to the bull and stood behind it. "Now pay attention, boy," he said, "so when it's your turn that old bull won't kick your nuts into your tonsils."

The old man set the tongue of the plow into the earth with his foot, gently flicked the long rope, and he and the bull began to walk slowly and gracefully along the empty field. Every few meters the old man flicked the rope so that it barely brushed up against the bull's side. The old man and the bull plowed fifty meters, turned around, and plowed back a parallel row one meter over from the first run.

"Your turn," said the old man, and he handed the rope to the boy and reached in his shirt pocket for his cigarettes.

The boy fumbled and stuttered along during his first run. The old man walked behind him barking out directions. It was slow work. By eight the bright sun was breathing on the back of their necks like an angry dragon. By ten the boy and the bull had plowed six crooked rows while the old man watched from the shade of a tree.

"Lunch time, Strawberry!" called out the old man.

The boy's sweat-covered shoulders dropped.

"Okay," he said.

"After lunch you're going to plant some corn."

"Corn?"

"What the hell do you think we've been doing here all morning, dingleberry? Playing with ourselves? This is your cornfield, boy. You plowed it. You're going plant it. You're going tend to it. And you're going pick it. And you're going to cook it. I suppose you don't know how to cook, either?"

"Not really."

"Add that one to your list."

"Are we going to eat the corn, too?" the boy asked meekly.

"Damn right. Now you take that animal into the barn and make sure he's got plenty of water. When you're done, come on up to the house."

"Okay," said the boy, and he led the bull toward the barn.

After lunch the old man taught the boy how to plant corn by hand in the eight rows they'd plowed in the morning. The boy worked hard next to his grandfather in the hot sun. At three the planting was done.

"Come on hoodlum," said the old man, and he walked toward the mango orchard without looking at the boy. "Time to bust your cherry."

Curtis followed his grandfather into the orchard. The old man walked slowly in the short grass in between a row inspecting the trees. He reached out his hand and brushed it against many of the impressive Chin-huang mangos that hung down on long vines. The boy mimicked his grandfather's every move as he walked behind at a safe distance. The old man stopped and climbed a step-ladder that was under one of the trees.

"Get the other ladder and get your ass up here," barked the old man.

"I don't see it."

"It's next to a mango tree."

"Smart ass," said the boy under his breath. He scanned the

orchard, then he ran and retrieved the other ladder, set it down next to his grandfather's, and climbed up so that his eyes were level with the old man's. The boy looked around at the multitude of hefty greenish-yellow mangos.

The old man gently cupped one of the large fruit in his hand, leaned over, smelled it, and said, "Abroad they call these beauties 'Golden Queens.' I know what you need honey," he said softly, smiled, and let go of the mango. "Try it."

The boy reached out, roughly grabbed one of the mangos, and yanked it hard toward his face causing the branch to creak.

"Son of a bitch," said the old man. "These ain't five dollar whores, boy. These are the bosoms of goddesses—our goddesses."

"Sorry."

"Try it again. And no squeezing and pinching like it's the titty of some betel nut beauty."

The boy reached out, took a different mango in his hand, leaned over and smelled it.

"Give you a hard-on?" asked the old man.

"No."

"It will, if you ever wise up. You've got too much city running through your veins. Guess we'll have to leech that shit out of you, too."

"When will they be ready to pick?"

"Know why these are so special?" asked the old man ignoring the boy's question.

"Why?"

"They're virgins, like you—one hundred percent organic. There's never been a drop of chemical in this orchard. Harvest is from early July through August, usually. It depends on the spring weather, the rain, and how many typhoons wallop us," said the old man, and he climbed down the ladder and walked toward the shed. "Wait here," he shouted over his shoulder.

The old man returned ten minutes later with a long pruning saw, and a plastic two-gallon spray bottle with a long hose and nozzle. He set the spray bottle down at the base of his stepladder and climbed back up with the saw.

"Watch close," he said, and he reached out with the saw and

made an inch cut on the underside of a branch that had grown too long and was tangled in the adjacent tree. He finished the job by cutting down through the top of the branch.

"We don't want the trees to shed one another. It inhibits growth. I missed this little son of a bitch during the pre-flowering pruning back in the spring. We won't prune much at all until after the fall harvest." He handed the saw to the boy and said, "Prune six inches behind on the same branch. Remember, make your first cut from the underside, about one to two inches; the length of your dick. It ensures a clean cut."

The boy followed the old man's instructions perfectly, and looked at him hoping for a compliment. The old man said nothing. He hopped down the ladder, picked up the spray bottle, and strapped it onto his back. The boy followed the old man as he headed twenty meters down a row and stopped, set up a nearby ladder, climbed to the top, and began spraying a clear liquid onto the mangos.

"What's that for?" asked the boy.

"It's a family secret. A special herbal concoction with fish amino acid that your great-great grandfather conjured up with the help of Kuanyin. It makes these darlings grow bigger and taste sweeter. You've got to promise me to guard our secret with your life if I'm ever dumb enough to give it to you."

"I promise."

"A few of the other growers use chemical pesticides."

"Why?"

"They're lazy assholes. Hell, that's like rubbing down an infant with turpentine every night after its bath. Did you notice the curry shrubs planted around the perimeter, and how clean and weed-free the orchard is?"

"Yeah, I guess," the boy said indifferently and shrugged his shoulders.

The old man scowled at the boy's disinterest. "The curry ain't for show," he growled. "They attract insects that will kill off most insect pests. And weeds attract all kinds of destructive bugs."

For the rest of the afternoon, under the old man's direction, the boy lopped off several more stray branches, cultivated around the perimeters of trees with a hoe, and pulled weeds that had recently sprung up in the otherwise clean, dark soil. At four the boy rested his hoe against his shoulder, wiped his sweaty brow, and inspected several large blisters on his palms and fingers. The old man took notice and walked up to the boy, who quickly got back to work with the hoe.

The old man grabbed the hoe away from the boy with one hand, and one of the boy's hands with the other and said sarcastically, "Congratulations Straw Boy. You've been officially deflowered. Better learn to like those badges, because besides chow and a bunk, they're the only thing you're going to get around here unless you get wise and learn how to *see*."

The boy gave him a quizzical look and asked, "See what?"

"Between the winds," said the old man, and he walked away.

At around five the boy was humming a happy tune as he worked the hoe. Then he began to sing in a beautiful voice. This got the old man's attention while he was working from a ladder thirty meters away. He hurried down the ladder hoping the boy would continue to sing. The old man quietly approached the boy from behind, walked past him a few meters, stopped without turning around, and let out a long resounding fart. The boy immediately stopped singing.

"I never liked a cappella," said the old man loudly, and then he continued walking without looking back.

The boy shook his head and laughed. He resumed singing when the old man was several meters past him. The old man immediately stopped walking, but he didn't fart this time. Again, the singing abruptly stopped.

The old man turned his head and yelled, "Pussy! You shouldn't give up that easy!"

"I was waiting for an F-sharp. What, are you tone deaf?"

The old man smiled and chuckled at the boy's remark as he kept walking, but he didn't let the boy see his face. He was pleased with the boy's progress and work ethic, but he didn't let that on to the boy, either. They continued to work for another hour and knocked off at six.

"Follow me, Straw Boy," said the old man as he walked toward a five-foot mound of graves in the rear right-hand corner of the property.

The boy ran to catch up to his grandfather. The old man stopped and faced the graves. In the fading sunlight, four ornately decorated stone tombs glowed like sculptures of ice on top of the well-manicured mound.

The old man said softly without looking at the boy, "My great grandfather, your great-great-great grandfather is buried on the far left with his wife. He built our house by hand, by himself in 1875. Brick by brick. If that doesn't make you feel proud, we should dig a hole for you shortly. Next to him are my grandfather and grandmother, your great-great grandfather and grandmother, and next to them are my father and my mother. And next to them is my wife, your grandmother," he said and his voice trailed off. "You probably don't remember her very well."

"Only a little."

"You should. My queen doted on you something awful."

The old man knelt down in front of a weathered foot and a half tall shrine that sat in front of the graves. A yellow robed statue of Tu Di Gong, the earth god, sat inside. His smiling, bearded face and chest were blackened by generations of burning incense. The boy knelt down next to his grandfather.

The old man reached inside the shrine, grabbed six sticks of incense from a box and said, "He's been watching over our family and this land for more than one hundred years," and he lit the incense and handed three sticks to the boy.

The old man held the incense in front of his face and prayed in silence. The boy watched his grandfather closely, and followed his every move. Several minutes later, the old man shook the incense forward three times, set it in a small urn in front of the deity, and stood up.

"What's that grave over there?" asked the boy, and he stood up and pointed to an unmarked grave in a small mound of its own twenty feet to the right of the larger mound.

"Let's go on up to the house and get some supper," said the

old man, and he turned and walked toward the house, pretending not to hear the boy.

The tired boy went to lie in his bed soon after supper. As he was nodding off, he heard footsteps outside. He sat up on the bed and looked out the window. He watched the old man turn off the front porch light, peel off his T-shirt, kick off his sandals, and stride twenty feet past the courtyard and out into the broad moonlit clearing in front of the dirt road. The old man looked up at the full moon and began the slow graceful movements of tai chi chuan. The grove of mango trees swayed gently in the cool evening breeze as if directed by the old man's movements.

"He looks like a swan," the boy thought in disbelief as he gazed at his grandfather. "He's changed."

The boy watched the old man for a long time. He picked up his wallet off the dresser and pulled out a small color photo of his parents. He held the photo up in the moonlight and studied it while running his fingers along its edges. He soon fell asleep.

The next morning the old man woke the boy up at five thirty and said, "Harvest today, dum-dum."

The boy rolled over, sat up in bed, and wheezed, "You said next month."

"You haven't seen the mothers of all the goddesses."

"What's that?"

The old man leaned against the door frame, smiled, and rejoiced theatrically, "My Irwin mangos. Now, do your doctoring, and make it quick. Breakfast is waiting." The old man left.

After breakfast the boy followed the old man into the home's small family shrine, where he again mimicked the old man's every move and gesture. When the old man finished his prayers, he sprung up off his knees, walked onto the porch, grabbed his bamboo hat off the wall, and barreled out into the courtyard. The boy followed behind. An old blue coaster bicycle that looked like it had been pulled out of a World War II bomb crater was propped up against the house.

The old man jumped on the bicycle and yelled, "Train's

leaving!" and he rode like the wind out of the courtyard, across the dirt drive, and into the mango orchard.

The boy ran after him as fast as he could and yelled as he entered the orchard, "Where's my bike?!"

The old man turned his head and yelled with the glee of a child, "Come on, Strawberry!"

The boy chased after the old man, who was fifty meters ahead and pulling further away each second, then he abruptly turned right on the rickety old bike, and disappeared into the mangos. The boy laughed, and continued to run after the wily old rascal until his lungs blew their gaskets. He turned right where he saw his grandfather disappear, and heard the sound of women's voices. He ran down a row following the cooing sounds, and after several minutes he came upon the old man, who was standing in the shade near two lean women, watching them as they separated red mangos into two flat plastic bins that were sitting on top of a meter high stack of their empty brothers. The panting, sweaty boy stopped in front of his grandfather.

"Pussy britches!" yelled the old man. "I thought we'd have to unchain the hounds. You got a load in your drawers?" The boy's face blushed with embarrassment.

The two women, who were clad in knee-high rubber boots, cotton pants, and bamboo hats with scarves wrapped around their faces, giggled while they kept working.

One of the women looked up at the boy and noticed his "hoodlum" shirt. "So, *this* is your grandson, Boy Hero?" she asked.

The old man winced when he heard the words "Boy Hero," as if he'd been struck with a bamboo stick. "Uh-huh," he said.

Curtis saw the old man's face change, and he thought that he looked almost afraid.

The woman's companion, the taller of the two, cupped her hand over her mouth and shouted into the trees, "We've got a convict here!" and squealed with laughter.

From somewhere up in the bounteous trees a female voice yelled, "Is he cute?!"

"He's a real pretty boy!" she yelled back and everyone laughed, even Curtis.

The old man picked one of the hand-sized mangos out of a bin, held it up to his face and smelled it; then he reached out and held it under the boy's nose, and said tenderly, "The sweetest smell in the world." He outstretched his arms and looked at the surrounding ten-meter tall trees, and exclaimed boastfully, "These boy, are my Irwin—my gold mine. I've got thirty producing trees that run to the property line next to that rice field over yonder."

The boy looked through the rows of Irwin and into the sun-drenched rice field, the meter-high stalks swaying in a gentle breeze like hair of a goddess.

The old man looked at the bin on his left and said, "These pick of the litter go to Japan, where they can sell for as much as thirty US dollars a piece." He held the pristine mango out in front of the boy, slowly turned it, and said, "This is the only way the Japs will take them—without as much as a mark the size of a mosquito's ass on it. Those Jap devils have to be the most anal beings on the planet."

"Thirty US a piece?" said the boy, and raised his eyebrows with a look of surprise. "Why are they called 'Irwin'?"

The old man smiled broadly, pleased with the boy's interest, and orated with the pomp of a proud statesman, "F.D. Irwin was a mango grower from Miami, Florida. In 1939 he cross-pollinated a Haden mango variety with a Lippens, and the Irwin was born, first bearing fruit in 1945. In the early 1960s, the first Irwin seedlings arrived in Taiwan, planted in Tainan's Yuching Township. A grower from Tainan County, a friend of your great grandfather, gave the seedlings to him over forty years ago. And now look at them."

The boy was impressed by the old man's knowledge. "You know the whole history," he said.

"Damn right, I do," quipped the old man. Then he stood silently for a long while, the proud look on his face turned to melancholy, his shoulders slumped, and he looked off into the mangos. He turned his head quickly, stared hard at the boy, and asked, "Why do you think the Irwin was brought to Taiwan, school boy?"

The boy fidgeted, shuffled his feet, and squint his eyes waiting for the storm to hit. "I don't know," he said softly without looking at his grandfather.

"Because we Taiwanese were too damn poor—poor as poor can be. Hell, a man that ate rice and sweet potatoes every night was considered a rich man. Most of us only ate sweet potatoes and sweet potato leaves, what they fed pigs with."

"I didn't—"

The old man cut him off and said, "You should know your history boy, and be proud of it, and what we've become."

The old man put the mango back into the bin, reached into the other bin, plucked out a slightly blemished mango, deftly cut four sections away from the large center seed with a pocket knife, and handed one of them to the boy.

The boy cupped the piece in both hands, put it against his lips, quickly ate the fruit away from the skin, smiled, and exclaimed, "Wow!"

The old man grinned and said, "Now you're learning dumbfuck," and he discarded the mango seed into a nearby bucket and handed each woman a section. "The blemished ones taste just as delicious as their fair-haired sisters. I sell them domestically for less than a song." The old man devoured the remaining mango section, looked at the boy sternly and said, "I'm counting on you today. Remember, handle these beauties as gently as you would a newborn. Follow the ladies. They'll hold your hand and walk you through it."

"Okay," said the boy.

The old man looked the boy in the eye and said, "I'm going to tend to the Chin-huang mangos. No fucking off, or I'll lash you to a mango tree with your ass sticking up in the air, and let the neighbor's dog hump you until he goes blind," and he hopped on his bicycle and disappeared down a row.

Curtis worked all morning with the women, who watched him keenly, and instructed him how to separate the choicest mangos for export to Japan. The old man returned throughout the morning to check on the boy's progress, sitting under the shade of a mango tree admiring the stacked bins full of Irwin proud as a new father of quintuplets.

After lunch the old man walked up to the boy and said, "Get your straw butt up in the tree with Miss Lily over there. And don't go falling down and break your ass. I hate going to the damn hospital."

The old man followed behind the boy as he walked over to the mango tree, climbed a step ladder leaning against its trunk, and slowly and carefully climbed into the tree.

"Holy smokers!" bawled the old man. "You'd think you're walking a tightrope strung across Taroko Gorge by the way you pussyfooted that one." Everyone laughed.

The old man walked directly under the tree and called out, "You stay right on Miss Lily's hip, boy! Don't get any foolish ideas that you know what the hell you're doing. You only pick a mango after Miss Lily tells you which ones are ready."

"Okay!" the boy shouted.

"You mind this old bull, or I'll come up there after you, and don't think I can't. Hell, I can still jump around in the mangos like a damn monkey if I'm in the mood." All of the women cackled.

By sundown, the boy and the four women had picked and packed ripe mangos from ten of the thirty trees. A local exporter who the old man had been working with for years showed up at six with a truck and a bundle of crisp, thousand-dollar NT notes. He handed the cash to the smiling old man, loaded up quickly, and drove off.

The old man and the boy stood in the wide, grass covered path at the edge of the property that separated the Irwin mango trees from the adjacent rice field. The sun waned—the sky a brilliant red-orange. As the women began to ride away on their bicycles the old man called out after them. They stopped in unison, turned around, and saw the old man holding up a big sack of Irwin mangos.

"Please take some home!" he called out.

The women rode up, and one by one, the old man deposited a sack of a dozen choice mangos into the baskets hanging in front of their handlebars.

"Thank you! Thank you!" they cooed softly, giggled, and rode away.

The old man looked at the women affectionately as they disappeared down the dusky orchard row.

"Fine, fine people," the old man said, and placed his hands on his hips. "Every one of them on the far side of fifty. Hell, any one of them is worth three men in the field." Then he gazed at the boy and said, "I hope you know that you just had the privilege of working with children of the soil."

"I know that," said the boy.

The old man strode to the narrow, two-foot tall concrete irrigation channel that ran along the property line in front of the rice field. He propped one foot up on top of the channel, folded his arms across his chest, and looked in admiration across the rice field toward the sunset. The boy followed, stood near his grandfather, and clumsily propped his foot on top of the irrigation channel. The old man reached into his shirt pocket, grabbed a cigarette, popped into his mouth, lit it, and in his mind revisited the scene from that morning watching the boy inject himself with insulin.

The old man fixed his eyes on the rice field, and said without looking at the boy, "If you meditate on a rice field like this one long enough, it'll teach you something you can't express in words. It's a feeling that'll creep into your bones, make you a little better."

"And the mango trees?" asked the boy.

The old man took a long drag off his cigarette, exhaled and said, "Them, too. Nature is perfect. Man, at his absolute best, is a bumbling fool."

The old man turned his gaze back toward the sunset, and with a contented look upon his face, smiled and said, "That's where dreams are born, boy. I hope you'll have the courage to dream, because this life isn't worth a damn without them." He turned, looked the boy up and down, and said, "Every butterfly starts out as a caterpillar."

The boy smiled, relaxed his aching shoulders, and took a long slow breath, as if he were trying to inhale his grandfather's words. He took a few steps closer to the old man, and surveyed the rice field and darkening, red horizon. Since after lunch, Curtis had been nervously contemplating the possible consequences he might suffer if he asked the old man a question that had been burning in his mind all day. The boy stood silently next to the old man until the sun was nearly asleep. He remembered the pained look on his grandfather's face from that morning, and he asked weakly, "What did she mean when she called you, 'Boy Hero'?"

The old man ignored the question, threw his cigarette on the ground, popped a betel nut into his mouth and said, "You ride that foul contraption up to the house and get cleaned up for supper. I want to walk."

That night before bed, and the following five nights, the boy sat watching quietly out the bedroom window as the old man practiced tai chi. On the seventh night he stood and tried to follow the old man's movements.

"Why don't you come out here?" said the old man, and he turned his head toward the window.

"How did you know?" asked the boy.

"Come on!"

The boy walked outside and stood next to the old man as he continued with his slow graceful movements.

"Breathe," said the old man.

The boy began to awkwardly follow his grandfather's movements. The old man looked on in silence.

During the second week of Curtis's incarceration on Mango Road, the old man woke up at five fifteen on Wednesday morning, walked to the boy's room to wake him, and stood in the doorway. Curtis was sitting on the bed in his boxer shorts unzipping the diabetes travel kit that his aunt bought for him. He didn't notice his grandfather. The old man stood and watched in silence as the boy took out the palm-sized glucometer, a lancet, a test strip, and set them on his lap. He switched on the glucometer, inserted the end of the test strip into it, picked up the lancet, pricked his finger, and carefully dabbed a tiny drop of blood onto the test strip. In a few seconds his blood sugar level appeared on the meter. The boy took one of the five new syringes out of the kit, popped the orange cap off, and eyed the fresh needle.

The old man walked into the room, sat down on the bed next to his grandson and asked, "Do you think I could give it a try?"

The boy looked up. "What, this? Why?"

"In case I ever find you flopping around on the ground foaming at the mouth." The old man knew he made an error in judgment.

The boy frowned, shook his head in disapproval, and said, "What made you so damn mean?"

The remark caught the old man off guard. He felt like an ass. "Since your dear grandmother passed away nearly ten years ago I've become even more ornery than before," he said softly. "She'd find that impossible to believe."

A little smile appeared on the boy's face.

A faraway look appeared in the old man's eyes. "And other things too, made me the son of a bitch you see here," he muttered, his voice trailing off. "Won't you let me give it a try?" he asked quickly before the boy could crack that nut and see what popped out. "It's plain common sense for me to know how to doctor you up."

"Okay," the boy said reluctantly. "You're right," and he put the cap on the needle, put the syringe back into the case, zipped it up, and handed it to the old man. "I have Type 1 diabetes."

"What's Type 1?"

"My body can't produce insulin like normal people. Oh, and I forgot to tell you I carry special glucose tablets with me at all times in case you find me *flopping around on the ground.*" The boy picked up a small insulated bag. "See, I keep this in my pants pocket."

The old man nodded, quickly unzipped the case, picked out a syringe, popped the cap off the needle, plunged it into the small rubber top of the insulin bottle, turned the bottle upside down, drew out the medicine until the syringe was full, held it up to his face, and pressed the plunger slightly until a small jet of insulin shot out.

The boy was amazed at the dexterity of the old man's gnarled, calloused hands and fingers.

"You've done this before?"

"Oh, I've jabbed that old bull and his predecessors with enough concoctions that'd be worth a small fortune." Then his face hardened a bit, a small, fragile smile appeared, and he said, "And toward the end I uh, you know to your grandma."

"Insulin injections might be a little different," the boy said politely, and he slid closer to the old man and turned his arm so that the back of it faced away from him. "Hold the syringe like a pencil, pinch up some skin on the back of my upper arm with your other hand, stick the needle in, release the pinch, and then push down on the plunger. Got it?"

"Just like pork and rice," said the old man, and he wiped the back of the boy's arm with an alcohol swab, and gently followed his instructions to the letter.

The boy's eyes were glued to his grandfather's face during the whole process. He felt protected and safe in the old man's hands.

The boy let out a deep breath when the old man pulled out the needle, smiled and said, "If it's an emergency, it doesn't matter where you inject, as long as the needle reaches the fat layer under the skin."

The old man threw the syringe into a waste basket next to the bed, put the insulin back into the case, zipped it up and said, "Let's go have some breakfast, and then I'm going to work you to death Type 1," and he stood up and walked out.

Curtis shook his head at the old man's audacity, smiled, and followed him into the kitchen.

Curtis worked alongside his grandfather from sun up to sun

down six days a week for the next month and a half. Several nights a week, when he wasn't too exhausted from the day's work, the boy walked out into the warm night air and practiced tai chi with his grandfather. He worked very hard trying to match the old man's movements exactly. This pleased his grandfather. Curtis also worked with the four women when they returned two weeks after the initial Irwin harvest to complete picking and packing the rest of the fruit. The harvest was bountiful due to mild spring weather and steady, warm temperatures. This delighted the old man to no end, giving him bragging rights among his fellow growers. In mid-July, several weeks after the Irwin harvest, Curtis again worked with the women and harvested the Chin-huang mangos. The old man continued to teach the boy every aspect of tending to the mango trees. The corn he planted started to grow and flourish, and the boy could barely contain his excitement about it. On his day off, the boy usually slept most of the day. Monday mornings before work the old man repeated the ritual of placing soil in the boy's cupped hands. When the boy asked him why, the old man always gave him the same blank stare.

After supper one evening the old man and the boy were sitting on the front porch watching the sunset. The old man went into the house and returned with a large flat rectangular box. He handed it to the boy and sat back down in the rocking chair. The boy opened it. He pulled out a new white T-shirt and held it up. The word "asshole" was written across the front in Chinese characters with felt-tip marker. The boy sighed heavily and looked at the old man with disappointment. The old man stared at the boy with a straight face, and then he looked down at the box. The boy removed a thin layer of soft white paper that the T-shirt had rested upon and gasped, "Oh my god!"

The boy held up an authentic New York Yankees warm-up jacket with "Curtis" sewn in small script on the right breast.

"Oh, shit! It's awesome!" cried the boy.

"That T-shirt I gave you when you first got here doesn't fit you anymore, Curtis," said the old man. "I think this will."

The boy stood up and put on the jacket.

"It fits great," said the boy, and he ran his hands along the shiny black material.

"Now, there's my grandson," said the old man with a smile.

The boy rushed over, got down on his knees and wrapped his arms around his grandfather. The old man held his grandson tightly.

"Thank you," said the boy, and he began to cry. The old man held the boy even closer as tears ran down his own cheeks.

Several minutes later, the boy stood up and began to walk nervously around the porch in small circles as he rubbed the slick material of his new jacket.

"The girl got so sick from our persecution that she had to change schools and go to a psychiatrist," he said without looking at his grandfather.

"Uh-huh," grunted the old man with a surprised look, and his face went sour.

"I didn't have many friends. A group of older boys at school scooped me up. Began to threaten me with beatings if I didn't join them in their cruelty. Extorting money from this poor girl. I was the one. I was the one who threatened her the most. Got the money from her. At first I planned that I'd later give it all back and tell her that these guys made me do it. But I was too weak. Then it was too late. She'd already left school. It was my fault for being such a 'pussy' as you say. I don't know if I'll ever be able to forgive myself."

"We all stumble sometimes, Straw Boy," whispered the old man. Then he stood up and walked into the house.

Curtis was sleeping in on a sunny Sunday morning when the old man whispered into his ear, "Wake up. We're going to town."

The boy jumped out of bed. He hadn't left his grandfather's since his arrival more than six weeks earlier. They had their usual simple breakfast of rice and eggs and rode toward Ciatou Township on the old man's cruddy, sputtering Kymco 125cc motorcycle. They rounded a bend a few miles outside of town and came upon a spectacular field of sunflowers that stretched for a quarter of a mile. Next to it another immense field with rows of purple, white, and yellow lilies glowed in the bright sunlight.

"Slow down!" yelled Curtis.

The old man slowed down, and when they got to the end of the lily field he turned around and slowly drove the entire length of the fields and back again.

As they neared town, a teenage boy roared past on a shiny new scooter.

The old man turned his head back toward Curtis and yelled, "Another asshole strawberry with a custom muffler to make his little pecker of a scooter sound like a big bad street bike!"

"I know!" screamed the boy. "A lot of kids are doing that now!"

"I hate those damn kids! They don't give a shit in hell that that racket irritates the shit out of people! He's the kind of kid who stuffs a pair of socks in his underwear to make it look like he's got something other than a minnow of a pee-pee!"

The boy laughed and asked, "Where are we going?"

"Whorehouse!" yelled the old man.

"Really?"

"If a whore got a hold of you she'd grease your head and shoulders and use you for a dildo!"

"Oh, shit! You're sick."

The old man whooped with loud laughter and slowed down as they entered the buzzing streets of Ciatou Township. People were streaming in and out of the big open-air fruit and vegetable market that lined the narrow main street. They drove down another street, where an elderly woman was standing in front of her san-ho yuan placing sardines to dry in the sun on a long black net strung between four corner poles. When she saw the old man, she yelled and waved him over.

As the old man slowed down and pulled over and stopped in front of the woman Curtis asked, "Who's that?"

"An old friend," said the old man, and he got off the motorcycle and walked up to the woman.

The woman smiled and said, "Who's the handsome boy?"

"My grandson, Curtis."

"What are you up to?"

"Been bleeding the strawberries out of this kid. He's still about half strawberry, maybe more."

"Uh-huh!" laughed the woman.

"We need supplies. And the boy needs to blow off some steam."

"Well, my granddaughter's here. You know Mei-chi. She's about his age. Please come inside for some tea."

"Well, okay," said the old man, and he and Curtis followed the woman into her home.

The woman called for her granddaughter as she walked into the kitchen. The pretty long-haired girl came bouncing down the hall. When she saw the old man, she walked up to him, bowed solemnly, and placed her hands in his.

"This is Curtis, my grandson," said the old man, and he turned toward the boy.

"Well, come on," the outgoing girl said lightheartedly as she passed Curtis. "I want to show you something."

The old man looked at the girl with pleading eyes and shook his head slightly. Curtis followed her to a small room at the end of the hall, although his grandfather, who watched them the whole way, seemed not to want him to. The room contained a small shrine set up against the rear wall. A framed black-and-white photograph of a boy a few years younger than Curtis rested on the table in the center of the shrine. Orchids and offerings of fruit sat next to the photograph. A single thick stick of incense burned in an elaborately engraved dragon urn.

"Do you know who your grandfather is?" asked the girl.

"What?"

"That's him," she said, indicating the photograph with a glance.

"Huh?"

"He hasn't told you the story? Many people in Ciatou know it. They call him the boy hero of Ciatou."

"He hasn't told me anything."

"Oh my god! I would love to tell you, but I think he wants to tell you himself. Maybe you should ask him."

"Uh-huh," Curtis said, confused but intrigued.

"My granny has told me the tale many times. She was there."

"Where?"

"Come on!" giggled the girl and she ran out of the room.

Curtis followed the girl into the kitchen, where the old man and the woman were sitting at the kitchen table drinking tea. The youngsters joined them, and munched on crackers and sliced pineapple while the older pair continued with their light conversation. The old man and Curtis said good-bye to the old woman and Mei-chi an hour later. The old man dropped Curtis off at a video arcade before he went to buy supplies and food. Curtis met some local kids and shot nine-ball with them. He had fun but was surprised to realize how much he didn't miss his friends in Tainan. His grandfather hadn't given back his phone since that first day, and Curtis had barely thought about it or his friends back home for weeks.

On the ride back to the house Curtis didn't say anything to his grandfather about the shrine or what Mei-chi had told him. The old man and Curtis carried the supplies inside. The old man took a bouquet of white lilies from the market and marched slowly and solemnly toward the graves at the rear of the property. The boy followed. The old man approached the lone unmarked grave, bowed, bent down, and arranged the flowers tenderly on the headstone.

"Today's the day," he said quietly. He did not look at the boy.

"What day?"

"The anniversary of August 19, 1944. I was twelve years old."

"We didn't stop at that lady's house by chance, did we?"

"I always stop at that house on this day."

"Why?"

"And I always come back here. I stop there because she wants me to or maybe because I . . ."

"Was that your picture on the shrine?"

"People around here have been retelling the story of what happened on that day for more than sixty years. I've never told it to anybody, not to one soul except your grandmother—what really happened during that damned war. Each year on this day I walk out here and my legs get heavier and heavier. I'm . . .

I'm turning to stone."

"What, grandfather?" Curtis didn't like seeing the old man this way. Although he stood as straight and strong as usual, something about him seemed bent and weak.

"I need to lift this thing off me."

"What happened?"

The old man hesitated, and then he glanced at the boy quickly with a small apprehensive smile. "It was a beautiful clear day—like today," he said. "The Japanese had been here for what seemed like forever—long before I was born. The colonization began in 1895. My father, your great grandfather took me into town for supplies. On a blue bicycle with a big shiny basket in front of the handlebars."

"The same old bike you ride in the orchard?"

"Yup. I felt ten feet tall riding with my dad. We got the supplies, and as we headed out of town the air-raid sirens sounded. It was a terrible noise. People were running like hell and screaming. I remember the screams of children and women. We heard the planes coming in low. American fighters had been targeting Japanese airfields here for some time. The one not far away, near Gangshan, was a popular target because of all the planes and fuel. The fighters had recently begun strafing houses and Japanese command centers in Ciatou."

The old man became silent, got down on one knee and said, "We were taught that during an air raid you were to go into the nearest home possible for cover. We were passing the house we stopped at today. We heard a woman screaming inside. It was a different scream from those running for cover. It sounded to me like she was being attacked. My father jumped off the bike and ran into the house. I followed. We were met at the front door by the woman you met today. She was just a young girl then, about my age. She was frightened and pointed to a back room. The room little Mei-chi showed you today. We ran toward the room and looked inside. A menacing Japanese officer, a captain, we later found out—he was in his underwear standing over a woman lying in bed—the girl's mother. He was agitated and waving an empty bottle of sake or wine over his head like he was going to thrash her with it—the woman was half-naked and crying terribly. I reacted without hesitation. I saw the officer's saber laying on the dresser between us and him—in those days all Japanese officers carried razor sharp sabers. I grabbed it, pulled it out of the scabbard and ran toward the officer. As he turned I lunged and thrust it into his stomach. I'll never forget the look of horror and shock on his face. I don't know how I did it. I had never been in any kind of fight before that day. He was bleeding like the devil and the woman was squawking and crying over him. He died thirty minutes later. It seemed like forever watching that handsome young man die. My father took the saber and was ready to finish him off if the wound I inflicted didn't kill him. If he would have lived, all of us in that house would have been strung up by the Japanese."

"Oh, my god! Then what happened?"

"I'm so grateful that my father didn't have to kill that man," whispered the old man. "That's the only time I ever saw my father afraid. His face changed. It became small and weak."

"And?"

"We were lucky the air raid occurred when it did. In all the chaos and confusion we were able to sneak the body out of town. We placed it under some hay in the back of a friend's wagon. We cremated the body that night at a temple's fire chimney used to burn ghost money. Then we placed the ashes in an urn and hid it for years in our house. We only put it here some years after the Japanese left."

"The Japanese looked for the officer, didn't they?"

"For weeks. It was said that he was quite a dashing ladies man and had several mistresses in town. But the town kept the secret. The Japanese also couldn't rule out that the officer was obliterated by a bomb that day."

"You're a hero, grandfather!"

"I'm no hero, boy."

"Why not?"

"The Japanese officer, Tanaka, was having an affair with the woman. Her husband had died, and she was alone with her children. He took care of them. He got drunk sometimes and roughed her up, but he didn't rape her or try to kill her."

"But, you didn't know that."

"Maybe the bastard deserved to die? Maybe. But not by me. That single moment, that single error in judgment has stalked me every day since like a hound from hell. That's my sentence for taking a life."

"You were only a little kid."

"To save the woman and her family's face, we never said anything. The woman created a story to make it look like I had saved her skin. It went something like, just as he was about to run her through with his sword, I pounced on him, wrestled the saber away, and filleted him like a mackerel. People have been telling similar versions of that lie for decades. Don't ever kill anyone son, for any reason. It's the worst possible thing for a person to carry around the rest of their life. That moment, that instant changed me forever. It sent me to a desolate place where the landscape is like the surface of the moon. It hardened me—turned my skin into wax. This beautiful countryside, these mango trees, that's what's saved me ... that and your grandmother. Do you know what it's like to live with a lie for sixty-five years?"

"No," the boy whispered compassionately.

"It's a curse—a hell of a curse to brand a young boy with."

"Maybe it's not too late to do something about it." Curtis was thinking of the shame he had carried here to his grandfather's farm and how the old man had helped lift it from his shoulders.

The old man looked at the boy affectionately. He bowed and prayed in silence for several minutes in front of Captain Tanaka's grave.

Then he spoke to Curtis again. "That's not all," he said quietly. "What?"

The old man knelt there silently for a time.

"Come on! You have to tell me the rest!"

He rubbed his gnarled, weathered hands over his shaved scalp, leaned over and fussed with the lilies, looked down at the grave, and spoke to it, as if he were trying to explain to Officer Tanaka. "On my tenth birthday my father told me that my mother was raped by a Japanese officer before I was born. He said that he felt that it was his duty to tell me who I was. To tell me what I was, before I heard it from someone outside the family and rain more shame down upon us."

"You mean you're . . ."

"I'm half Japanese."

"Officer Tanaka was your father?"

"It was different back then. The Japanese were our lords and masters. My mother and father dared not try to get any retribution. They could have gotten killed for less. So they lived with this shame, and my poor father had to take it. And he did. My dear father, my mother's husband, he took care of me like I was his real son. Abortion was out of the question, being both extremely dangerous and illegal. I was an ornery kid, ahead of my years, and hard as the bark on a white pine from all the work I'd been doing in the fields since I was small. I was determined to find out which officer raped my mother and fathered me. I wanted revenge, damn it, for my mother and her husband's honor. There weren't that many of these Japanese officer devils around. So for the next two years I kept my ears eyes and ears open. I got wind of Officer Tanaka. He had a reputation for being a real brute and a bastard with local women. After talking with people and learning more about him, I was absolutely certain he was the cruel son of a bitch who raped my mother. He had to be."

"So you got your revenge."

"I killed the wrong man."

"What?!"

"I was so certain the gods threw all their luck on me when my father and I came across Tanaka the day of the air raid. It was so perfect. The way we were there at the opportune moment for me to exact my revenge."

"You mean you, you . . ."

"I killed him in cold blood. The real bastard got away."

"How do you know that?"

"It turned out the real scoundrel bragged about it at a card game in town one night when he was drunk. He knew all the details only the real culprit could have known. One of the cooks at a gambling hall told us some months after I killed Tanaka. We trusted this man's word completely."

"What happened to the officer who raped your mother?"

"We learned he shipped out a year or so after Tanaka's death. I had the opportunity to try to do him in, and probably could have gotten some help. He was still fucking around in town. Abusing more local women. By that time, Tanaka's death continued to devastate me. I couldn't think about taking another life."

Curtis shook his head, his eyes filled with the sorrow he felt for his grandfather.

"You needed to know who you are, what you are, too," whispered the old man.

"Yeah."

The old man grew quiet, stood up, and looked off into the dusky sunset for a long moment before walking back to the house. The boy followed far behind.

The old man was subdued in the days after telling the boy his story, with few of his usual wisecracks. One evening toward the end of the summer the two of them were sitting on the front porch after supper.

"That might be the best damn corn on the cob I've ever had," said the old man, "besides your Grandma's, of course."

"Thanks Grandpa," said the boy with a triumphant grin.

This was the first night that they had tried any of the boy's corn, and he was anxious to hear the old man's verdict. The old man's face was serious as he lifted a box that was sitting next to his chair and handed it to Curtis. The boy opened it and found a beautiful old trumpet inside.

"Is this yours?" asked the boy.

"It's yours now," the old man said. "I was a bugler in the army when I was not much older than you."

"Really?"

"I'd like you to learn how to play, Curtis," said the old man.

"Why?"

"So your soul can speak."

The boy gently picked up the trumpet and looked at it with great admiration. It had obviously been well cared for; the brass gleamed softly in the dim light.

"A friend of mine will teach you. He'll come twice a week on Tuesdays and Thursdays after supper. And when you go back to your aunt's for school, I'll pay for your lessons there, too."

"I don't know if I can do it."

"You've been singing in the mangos all summer like 'an oriole from the valley.' You have a very expressive singing voice. I know you can do it. Just try."

"Okay."

"You've done a fine job here, Curtis. You've learned to take pride in your work, and you've learned self-respect. You can take that with you anywhere."

"Thank you, Grandfather," said the boy. He went to the old man, wrapped both his arms around his shoulders, and hugged him for a long while.

The old man stood, walked out of the courtyard, and stopped and gazed at the mango orchard. The boy came out and stood next to his grandfather. The old man bent down, scooped up a handful of the moist black soil, and placed it into Curtis's hands. "What's that?" he asked.

The boy rubbed the soil between his hands and said, "There're no words for it. It's a feeling like—like home."

The old man smiled, put his arm around the boy's shoulder, and he said, "Not bad for an ex-strawberry."

They both laughed. Then the old man faced the swaying orchard, stripped off his shirt, and turned his head quickly to one side to signal the boy. The boy pulled off his shirt, stepped a few meters away from the old man, and then he began following his graceful tai chi movements.

"That's it Little Dragon—breathe," said the old man.

That same fall, on a warm October morning, the old man dug up the grave of Officer Tanaka and carefully carried the urn containing his ashes into the house. He removed the ashes and placed them into a beautiful light blue urn that he had recently purchased. The old man also retrieved a small black and white photograph of Officer Tanaka, his wife, and his infant son that he had taken from the man after his death, along with several medals from the officer's uniform. He had kept these items hidden in a metal box. Several days later he put on a new suit, placed the urn, the photograph, and the medals into a handsome white gift box, and took the subway to Kaohsiung International Airport, where he boarded a flight to Tokyo. He was met at the airport by Officer Tanaka's son, a man not much younger than himself. He told him the truth about the death of his father and asked for forgiveness. Moved by the old man's tale, Tanaka's son accepted the apology, the urn, and the other items on behalf of his family. He consoled the sobbing old man as best he could, and once he had composed himself, the two men shared dinner in a small restaurant near the airport.

The food was served, and after a long, uncomfortable silence, Tanaka's son said, "I think about my father every day, and wonder, what if?"

"So do I," said the old man. "So do I," he whispered, and his voice trailed off.

Tanaka's son leaned forward, looked searchingly into the old man's eyes, and asked, "Was my father an honorable man?"

The old man thought about Officer Tanaka's reputation as a brute and a womanizer with the local Taiwanese women, and decided to spare the son from any of this information.

"War kills everyone in some way," whispered the old man, and he looked down. He sat silently for a long moment. Then he looked into the son's face and said, "Yes, I believe your father was an honorable man."

Tanaka's son smiled, and tears welled up in his eyes. A small, forced smile appeared on the old man's face. As they continued to dine, Tanaka's son sat and ate in silence for over an hour while the old man confessed more details concerning the officer's death. The old man stopped talking momentarily a few times, and each time the son's mournful eyes pulled more of the black report out of him like a doctor extracting poison from a snakebite. The old man returned to Taiwan late that night and reached home even later. He went to sleep in the early hours of the morning feeling a sense of peace he didn't remember ever feeling before.

Top Boy Society

I'm sitting at the drafting table in red boxers in my Tainan apartment in a sublime haze of acrylic fumes hoping to conjure up the spirits of famous artists like Yoshito Usui and Jack Kirby and others the gods have wounded with thunder bolts dipped in India ink. Call me Yellow Boy. By day I work as an eye surgeon, but I moonlight as a comic book artist, my true vocation. If you could look around, you'd see that I'm also superstitious as a Taiwanese grandmother—my red boxers and enough lucky charms are hanging around the room to impress a soothsayer, just a few signs of my obsession.

It's 34 degrees Celsius in here, and I'm melting faster than a strawberry sundae in a hothouse. I've been camped here for two days—ever since the power went out when the latest typhoon blew across the island. The storms frequently roll up from the Philippines from June through October. It's quite unsettling waiting for one of these monstrosities to reach shore, watching the weather reports and pretending everything is business as usual for several days as the gluttonous thing slowly gains strength, churning across the South Pacific like a Death Star.

I've been living off sustenance from a local 7-Eleven. 7-Elevens are as much a part of Taiwanese culture as betel nut or Kymco motor scooters. They're everywhere. There are around five thousand of the twenty-four-hour stores on the island; more per capita than in any other country. They're different from your average US 7-Eleven. Besides an enormous assortment of snacks and junk food from the US, Japan, and Taiwan, at a Taiwan 7-Eleven one can buy a bottle of Macallan eighteen-year-old single malt scotch, fine French wine, cigs from a half a dozen different countries, or a pint of Guinness. In Taiwan 7-Elevens, the clerks sit out in the open rather than shuddering behind three inches of bulletproof glass as they do in the States. People can't purchase or own a gun in Taiwan unless they're cops or wearing military fatigues. At any 7-Eleven in Taiwan, one can pay all their monthly telephone and utility bills with either cash or credit card, and also order books from many online Taiwanese bookstores. It's funny. I hardly ever went to a 7-Eleven during the summers I spent working for my uncle in Seattle while I was in med school at the University of Washington. The prices are jingled too high. In Taiwan the 7-Eleven prices are jacked, but not thirty or forty percent like in the States.

Besides drawing, to pass the time I've also been killing mosquitoes and contemplating if I should ever tell my parents that I'm gay. I've nervously run through the recital in my mind more times than I've fantasized about having intercourse with NBA stars. Pop's sitting there (in a schoolboy tie and a white short-sleeved shirt stiff as canvas sailcloth) unruffled and stoic as Zeno in his dad chair reigning supremely and judiciously over fifty pings of the universe. Mom in her flowery cotton housedress is cooking madly and miraculously taking care of everyone's problems besides her own or trying to.

I sit calmly in front of them like a good son and set them on fire with a single sentence: "Mom and Pop, I'm a hopeless queer who likes to slobber on as many cocks as I can get my hands on. By the way, thanks for medical school."

What's it like to be gay in Taiwan? The closet here's big enough for a fleet of jumbo jets—and it's standing room only, with queers packed into the rafters in K-Y Jelly and cocktail umbrellas. The closet door isn't constantly banging open and shut like in San Francisco or in Paris or Miami, either. Occasionally, the door will open just long enough to toss out a dead body. It wasn't easy for me to accept what I am. I shudder, remembering typing long guilt and angst ridden manifestos in high school—with a gun to my head. I've never showed those to anyone. The scary part was I became comfortable typing with one hand. The suicide watch lasted until I went to university, where I met some other aliens and ran with the wolves. Jerry the Wonder Boy, a broad shouldered lumberjack from Tacoma, popped my cherry in the back of his old Dodge camper during my sophomore year—his slobbering Pointer Buster watched. Being gay in Taiwan isn't really that bad—they're not arresting cocksuckers and holding public hangings. In fact, in hip Taipei the number of gay bars has steadily increased in recent years. Gay awareness in hetero land has improved. Three hundred fags marched in the National Women's Coalition parade in 1996 for the first time. Even though I've been told it resembled scenes from a funeral march, I give those courageous queer pioneers a lot of credit. The first Taiwan Pride parade was held in Taipei in 2003—chickenshit me watched from a safe distance. I was actually sitting in a tree masturbating. The Taipei government kicked in 70,000 NT dollars, as they helped sponsor the Taiwan Lesbian and Gay Civil Rights Movement. The 2009 parade had the most participants of any gay pride parade in Asia—twenty five thousand. But most of us, including myself, continue to chew our nails and hide in silence.

I've been an eye surgeon at a large local hospital for the past three years. You may have heard about individuals taking advantage of Taiwan's national health insurance system. Or you may be wondering what the fuck is he babbling about now?

The health insurance system isn't as bad as the news media wants you to think. However, I have had some strange and rather odd experiences. Two elderly couples have been regular and frequent visitors to our department for the past several years. The four of them always come in together. It's something of a social hour for them, a place to meet and brag about their children. And sometimes they actually need medical treatment or advice. But most of the time, they only pretend to need treatment, and we pretend along and give them placebos, pat them on the shoulders, and send them home. About a month ago only three of them came in.

When one of our nurses asked them about the missing spouse, his wife responded," Oh, he's home sick."

I've also been thinking a lot about my little sister, Meko. She's a nurse in the ophthalmology department at my hospital, which is so cool because I get to see her nearly every day, and we sometimes get the opportunity to work together. And yes, I may have breeched office protocol with my pithy and arrogant superiors and used what scrawny influence I have to assist her in landing the position. I may have even done things that I'm certain would make a merchant seaman blush if I did do such things. Okay, okay, to sum it up in a word; sodomy, which by the way, is one of my favorite words because it covers so much territory in three juicy syllables. Meko knows I'm gay. We share everything. She inspires the hell out of me. I wish I had her courage. She's had to deal with kidney disease since her early teens.

A gust of wind just shook the baby rattle hanging in the window. Oh, I must tell you about it! It's a cherished memento from a weekend I'll never forget. Last summer I performed a routine cataract operation on a Taiwanese CEO. This guy's so flush that a colleague of mine had to use a crude oil drip to hydrate him after removing his gall bladder a few years back.

The gentleman's wife brought him to my office the day after his surgery for a post-op follow up. Mr. Lin is in his early sixties, tall and slender, with a gorgeous head of wavy silver hair. He'd look aces in a G-string.

I sat him on the exam table, slowly began to remove his bandages, and said, "Please keep your eyes closed until I ask you to open them." I completed removing the bandages and said, "Your eyes are a little crusted with dried residue from your eyes watering last night," and I soaked a cotton ball with saline and gently washed away the crust. "Please open you eyes."

Mr. Lin opened his eyes.

"Can you see this?" I asked as I wiggled my fingers in front of his face.

He squinted several times and burst out, "Yes! Yes!" and then he looked at his wife and began to weep, but quickly regained his composure. I love this job because of moments like these.

"Is your vision clear?" I asked.

He raised his arms in jubilation and said, "It's a little blurry. Oh, I was so worried that I wouldn't be able to see!"

"Blurry vision is normal. It should pass within several days." I patted him on the shoulder, looked over at his wife, smiled and said, "I'm going to give your wife some eye drops. Twice a day, once in the morning, and once before bed."

"Thank you, doctor! Thank you a hundred thousand times."

"How about a hundred thousand NT?" I quipped. "I'll see you in one week."

"Okay," he said, and then his wife led him out.

I gave Mr. Lin a clean bill of health at his checkup the following week. He called me three weeks later and asked if I would meet him at a restaurant. He said his eyes were fine and that he had something very important to tell me. I agreed, and met him at an upscale seafood joint about a blow job away from the hospital.

When I came in Mr. Lin was floating at the bar in front of a double martini with three of its slain brothers lined up in a neat little row. I sat on the stool next to him.

"I want to repay you for giving me my complete sight back."

"Oh, there's no need."

"Please, I insist," he said, and drained off half of number four.

"I want you to be my weekend guest at an exclusive club that I belong to—a league of men in my social circle. We are sworn to secrecy, and are only allowed to bring one guest per annum."

I knew his type, a bunch of rich pricks screwing young whores in some VIP karaoke club.

"I'm gay," I said plainly.

"Oh, it's nothing like what you might think," he said. "There are very strict rules, and sex is forbidden." He shot me a grin and chuckled, "Besides, I knew you were homosexual on my first office visit."

"It's that obvious, huh?"

"My last visit you wore pink socks."

"My sister, Meko's," I said. "I forgot to change them from the night before. She used to get so pissed when I'd steal her Barbie Doll's clothes and use them to cross dress my Bruce Lee doll."

"Oh, the staff will love you," he said, and his eyes ran up and down my five foot-two flagpole. I frowned.

"I'm sorry," he said. "You don't seem to be—"

"Self conscious about my height, no-no-no," I lied. "I know I'm a small man, even by Taiwanese standards—even by Pygmy standards."

Mr. Lin laughed, and then his face turned into a granite mask and he said, "Men in my position are constantly under a severe amount of pressure. Thousand of employees and their families depend on me. If I make a mistake, the Taiwan stock market might drop faster than a blind boy's erection after he's just discovered it was the cute neighbor's dog licking his balls, not her."

"Ha!" I laughed. A great ass *and* a sense of humor.

"At our society each man is placed into an environment which requires that he regresses to the emotional and physical level of an eighteen-month-old baby."

"Sounds like medical school."

"Believe me when I say that it's the most relaxing and therapeutic thing I've ever tried, and I've tried them all—drugs, booze, the most beautiful sluts money can buy." And then he cupped one hand over his mouth and whispered, "I've even tried a guru."

"Beards don't do much for me, either. When?"

"Next weekend," he said and smiled. "Can you take Friday off? We really need three days. Please let me repay you for giving me my full sight back. You can't imagine how happy I am that I can see my lovely wife again in vivid color, and my children and grandchildren. Please be my guest! You'll find it to be a truly rewarding and healthy experience. Of course, I'll pay for everything."

"Okay," I said. "I have been stressed from working a lot of OT lately. But, if I don't like it for any reason I want out."

"No problem," he said.

I rode the bullet train to Taipei early Friday afternoon. Mr. Lin met me at the train station at two in a Mercedes limo.

The driver got out, opened the rear door, and a smiling Mr. Lin, who was sitting in the back seat dressed for an inauguration said, "Get in, baby."

I jumped inside. Mr. Lin handed me a double gin and tonic and a blindfold, and said apologetically, "I hope you don't mind putting it on. It's actually to your benefit if you don't know the location."

I set my drink on the small bar in front of me and put the rag around my eyes.

He hesitated, and said ominously, "I should prepare you for your first encounter with the Owl."

"The Owl?"

"The head nurse. There are all kinds of rumors. One is that she used to work in a traveling circus in Romania, where she butchered one of the circus bears and ate its heart after killing it armed only with a knife. Others have claimed she worked in the Ukraine Secret Police and performed special services for the director himself—services that even in Russia were deemed unholy and diabolical."

"I have a patient emergency," I mumbled, and felt my nerves begin to do the jitterbug. "You can let me out at the next corner."

"How could you possibly know that?" he asked. "Your

phone didn't ring."

"I feel these things—like telepathy. I'm clairvoyant. I have a strange gift. You can ask Big Sister Wong, the fortune-teller. I've had fantastic visions while reading Carl Jung's *Archetypes and the Collective Unconscious*, for god's sake!"

"Now, now, don't be frightened."

"Wwait!" I stammered and closed my eyes. "You're not safe either. I can see, I can see you, and there's a woman—a tall, thin Taiwanese woman. She's walking towards you. I've seen nicer legs in the morgue. She's got your Swiss bank account numbers."

"I knew I couldn't trust my secretary," he laughed.

"You want me to spend the weekend at the mercy of the Butcheress of Bulgaria, with her knives, chains, and a stockade? You better pour me a double embalming fluid."

"Now, now, now," he said calmly. "Those are only rumors. Look at me. I've been there a number of times, and I'm fine."

"It might be one of those delayed reaction things. You know, one day you're counting your millions, and then your brain gets the hiccups and they're you know, slapping you in restraints and sending you off to Crazy Acres."

He roared with laughter, paused, slapped me on the shoulder and said, "She can be quite dramatic and quite . . ."

"Quite what?" I asked and nervously slugged down half my drink.

"Some of our members worship her like a goddess—their fascination and obsession borders on; well, they've created a kind of cult."

"What do you mean? They literally worship her?"

"Some have created—idols of her," he said with hesitation, "and other things I'd rather not discuss at this time. You'll find out in due time."

"Come on! What?"

"Well, one member has a tattoo of the Owl's face on his hip."

"You're kidding?"

"It's true."

"Before, you said she can be quite dramatic and what?"

"She can smell fear—like a canine."

Oh, fucking great, I thought. I'm spending the weekend with the daughter of Lon Cheney, Jr. and Morticia Addams. I bet she despised queers.

"And don't worry about anyone finding out about where you were this weekend," he said reassuringly.

"Why's that?"

He smiled proudly and said, "There are several reasons. The staff is paid ridiculously well. And considering that most of them come from poor eastern European countries, well, they're just tickled to have the position." Then his face darkened a bit, and he shrugged and said rather flippantly, "They've also been sworn to secrecy, and been told that if anyone leaks all of their family members will disappear."

That's nice, I thought. Maybe I'll fuck up, and they'll set me up on a blind date with a Ukrainian serial killer.

Thirty minutes later we entered an underground garage and parked.

"Please keep your eyes covered until I tell you it's okay," Mr. Lin said, and led me by the arm to an elevator. I wondered if we were in Taipei 101 as we ascended for a long time.

The lift finally stopped, and he led me down a hallway and halted, and said through an intercom, "Abracadabra."

The doors swung open momentarily. Mr. Lin tightened his grip on my arm and dragged me through. I could hear the doors close behind us as he led me down a long corridor and stopped. The sound of a lock mechanism clicking and moving startled me.

"You have to see this," Mr. Lin said excitedly, and lifted my blindfold.

A round door sprung open for thirty seconds and snapped shut like a Venus flytrap. I couldn't see anything beyond the door except a white background. I looked down. The carpet was red as a butcher's apron.

"Get it?" he asked.

"Uh, not really."

"It's a cervix. They have it timed like contractions during labor."

"Of course!" I said sarcastically. "How could I forget what my mother's 'tunnel of love' looked like when I was born?"

He chortled, rolled his eyes, and said, "Now, put your blindfold down and hold my arm tight. Another contraction will occur in around three to five minutes—and we'll jump through."

I complied, and several minutes later the door's mechanism clicked again, and Mr. Lin shouted, "Hold on!" and we jumped through. A whining, mechanical sound was coming from somewhere in front of us.

"What's that sound?"

"The white screen you saw before is lifting," said Mr. Lin.

I was certain we were backstage at a Miss Universe Contest as a cloud of perfume the size of an elephant fart mixed with ditzy banter engulfed us. Mr. Lin led me thirty feet inside and stopped. It suddenly became silent as applause at an Imelda Marcos tribute. I felt cold as a proctologist's glove. I was being choked by the umbilical cord of this botched delivery. I just knew the Owl was near, and was startled by a hand that jerked off my blindfold—a six-two Caucasian women peered down at me with round, yellow-green eyes. She had a long, flat face and a gummy bear nose. A mouse's tail stuck out of sharp, red lips. Her face was white as her bleached hair. Two black bobby pins in her permed wave looked like a tiny pair of boots sticking out of a snowdrift. Her traditional nurse's uniform fit like a sausage casing—white shoes; hoes wrapped around rutabaga calves disappeared into a smock that hung below her knees. Screech's hefty breasts, encased in a 1950s cone-shaped torpedo bra, were dead level with my face, and I swear, as she pushed those things within inches of my nose I heard the tumblers of a firing mechanism begin to turn. Behind the Owl, a line of eight strapping nurses, all of them over six feet tall and sporting fruit like their boss, stood perfectly still with their arms at their sides—half could've passed for the Owl's sister. There was also an African, a Taiwanese, and a Hispanic. I glanced around the well-lit reception room's empty white walls, and was surprised not to see the stuffed heads of disobedient members staring down upon me. I was trying to figure out exactly where we were, but the windows were completely covered with light-blue placards.

"I'm nurse Zapgun," the Owl said with a soft, high-pitched, voice. She continued to stare me down, and slowly blinked her luminous eyes. "Welcome to Top Boy Society. And welcome back, Mr. Lin."

Her voice sounded so lyrical and pleasant. How could it possibly be coming out of that bird of prey?

Mr. Lin nodded politely, smiled, and said, "Albina."

"Albina?" I blurted out with a giggle.

The Owl snapped her fingers, and one of the blonde nurses ran up and shoved a pacifier into my mouth big enough for a baby hippo.

Screech's face became sour; she leaned into me, her rack of thirty-eights restructuring my nose, and she purred as she eyed me up and down, "There'll be no rigamarole, little man."

Mr. Lin covered his mouth with his hand and let out a muffled laugh.

An evil grin appeared on the Owl's face; she stepped back, glared into my eyes and said playfully, accentuating the last syllable of each word, "No sodomy, no buggery, no paraphilia, no fiddling with yourself, or there'll be retribution only a reptile could endure."

I thought like what, spankings, enemas, and beatings?

The Owl continued, "For the duration of your stay you'll act and be treated as eighteen-month-old boys. As of this moment you may not speak to any of the staff or guests. However, we encourage you to express your emotions either vocally or physically; any anger, fear, pain, joy, regret, or worry that you may have. Bawl, scream, cry, howl, laugh; fucking warble if you'd like. Kick, gouge your eyes out—have a goddamn tantrum until you shit yourself. You may walk, run, climb, crawl, roll, slither, or mope around sucking your thumb with your balls dragging on the floor. Let it all out. These walls are soundproof. Toilets are available. You have the option to defecate and urinate in diapers that will be provided. You cannot change your own diapers. Signal one of the nurses, and she will change you. Whichever method you choose, you must wear a diaper at all times. No cell phones or communication to the outside. The staff and I are at your service to assist you. We're very aware that it is taboo to display emotions of anger or to cry in a social environment in Taiwanese culture. Therefore, we have developed what you may consider unusual techniques to stimulate those who find it difficult to *release*. If you follow these rules and advice, at the end of your tenure you will feel rejuvenated like never before."

The Owl stepped back and waved her arm at the line of nurses, snapped her fingers, and the line bowed in unison, fell apart, and dispersed like a crack military drill team. I know you're wondering if I went "full baby" like some of the others and became a walking Play-Doh Fun Factory. Only once, and it wasn't planned. You'll see.

One of the blondes walked over, picked me up like I were a loaf of rye, gently cradled me in her long white arms, carried me into a dorm room with two rows of man-size cribs flanking either side of the center aisle, and laid me down on a long diaper changing table. Her name-tag read: Nurse Vargo. I liked her immediately. She had round edges and smelled like papaya. She belonged in a TV soap commercial. I looked over and saw Mr. Lin being carried in and set down on an identical table a few cribs away.

"That a boy," Nurse Vargo said and smiled, and with the hands of an oarsman, she quickly stripped me and tossed my clothes into a hamper behind a nearby crib.

She pulled the pacifier out of my mouth, set it down on the edge of the changing table, picked me up again, and as she walked over to a washing area I noticed several guests snoring comfortably in their cribs. She set me down like a priceless jade monkey in one of the several plastic tubs that were being filled with water by one of the other nurses. A naked Mr. Lin was carried over by his nurse several minutes later and set down in the tub next to mine. He cooed and giggled like an infant as his sexy nurse soaped him up. He pawed at her breasts a few times, and each time she slapped his hand hard. Nurse Vargo finished with her abrasive scrubbing, picked me up in a towel, carried me back to the changing table, and set me down.

"Now this may hurt a little," she said softly, and stuck the pacifier in my mouth, grabbed a roll of wide white tape, tore off a two foot section, placed it on my pubic hair and quickly ripped it off.

"Ieeeeeeeeee!" I shrieked. My testicles were on the end of a yo-yo string doing "walk the dog" in the middle of a tap dancing class. I glanced over at the crib next to mine. A crazy-looking man with no teeth and a baby bonnet tied tightly around his fat face stared at me with his chin resting on the top bar of his crib. I knew that face from the TV. One of the wealthiest men in Taiwan! He looked ten years younger; I'd heard he was around sixty.

"Oh, he's been a real mister big britches today," Nurse Vargo said. "He's been a naughty boy. He bit Mr. Washington's arm and ear." The face sunk and disappeared into the crib.

"Oh, I know it hurts dear," she said, and repeated the action with the tape. "It'll be so much easier to clean you up after you pee and poop."

After I pooped and peed! I knew she was going to take my blackberry patch, too. I was right. After she mowed my front lawn, she turned me over and mowed the back—taking out a few hedges and a young palm tree. The last time I cried that much was when Michael Jackson died.

Nurse Vargo sprinkled me with baby powder, wrapped my red baboon ass in an adult diaper, tied a blue and white baby bonnet around my head identical to what sunshine next door wore, picked me up and said, "Let's go have an afternoon snack with some of the other boys, okay."

I glanced over at Mr. Lin, and thoroughly enjoyed hearing him yelp and whimper like a Schnauzer getting its tail cropped as he got his lawn mowed. I thought about his flowery sales pitch: *it's the most relaxing and therapeutic thing I've ever tried.* The fuck it was.

I noticed a naked man wandering around balling at the top of his lungs as the nurse carried me toward a door at the end of the dorm. He carried his diaper in one hand and punched and pawed at the air with the other, which was holding a doll in a nurse's outfit with pointy cannons like the Owl's. I'd no doubt this maniac was one of the founding members of the cult of the Owl Mr. Lin had spoken about.

"Last month his prodigal son ran his flagship into the ground," said Nurse Vargo with an air of satisfaction, and she opened the door at the end of the room and we entered a large kitchen and feeding area.

We walked toward a row of six men donned in diapers and bonnets sitting in high chairs. They were munching on bananas and crackers. As we neared, several of the *boys* stared at me and pointed, and began to laugh and make farting sounds. I immediately recognized several of the high profile big shots—a who's who of Taiwan's elite. They looked absolutely pathetic and hilarious. Taiwan's best and brightest! I realized for the first time just how stupid I must have looked. Several nurses hovered around and gave them more food when signaled. Nurse Vargo set me down in a high chair at the end of the row, fastened on the tray, and slung a bib around my neck. Mr. Lin was carried in and placed in the high chair next to mine. I gave him a dirty look and grunted. He smiled innocently, made the clucking sound of a chicken, and began shoving pieces of banana into his mouth. One of the boys threw a piece of banana that hit the boy next to him in the eye. The others laughed. The boy let out an impressive, angry scream that would have made the hair on my ass stand on end if I had any left.

The black nurse ran over to check if the boy was hurt and said, "Now Mr. Jefferson, you know that's not nice. If you can't be a good boy, no 'milk time' for you today."

Milk time! I was lactose intolerant! They probably had a lactating Fraulein with udders like a heifer stashed away until feeding time gushing with gallons of buttermilk for us all. After dining on bananas and cardboard Nurse Vargo carried me back to my crib and laid me down for a nap.

"I'll come get you later," she said, tucked me in, and left.

"Hey thon," a voice whispered with a lisp. I knew it was toothless next door. I lied still. "Hasth the Owl taken you to *the room* yet?" the voice asked. "It'sth okay for you to talk to me. No one will know if we sthay quiet."

I clamped both hands over my mouth and tried not to laugh. This great and sometimes feared man, this pillar of the community, and an eloquent public speaker who I'd heard several times on TV, was reduced to a lisping idiot. Unable to resist my wily and famous neighbor, I popped my head over the top of my crib, and like a prairie dog wary of possible intruders, quickly surveyed the landscape. All was clear. I looked over and toothless's fat, bonnet-wrapped face smiled at me and he said, "Thom sthay the Owl usthd to work at an asthylum in the Ukraine. Others thay she wath a guesth there. Either way, thomething or thomeone'sth thure kept her talonsth razthor tharp."

"What's *the room*?"

His eyes became wild, darting back and forth, and he whispered, "Everyone goths into the room their first vithit. One guy came out like he'd won the lottery. Another like he'd losth a lung. One never came out."

"How'd you come out?"

He hesitated for a leap year, and then he looked into my eyes, and said somberly, "In a sthraitjacket with a hard-on." Then he let out a long, high-pitched laugh and said, "I'm the guy who won the lottery."

"You're not going to give me the low-down about *the room*? Is that what the Owl meant when she said they have techniques for those who don't act the part of a raving lunatic?"

"Where'sth your senth of fortuity?" he asked with a devilish smile. "Besidesth, the room'sth different for everybody, depending upon the Owl'sth mood. She'sth like a chameleon—and thsarp asth her talonsth. She triesth to give a man what he needsth, be it a sthpanking, a fucking, whatever. Juth hope she'sth not 'riding the red river' when they call your number."

"Did you really bite another guest?"

"Yeah," he chuckled, "and he tathted like thit—much too thalty for my delicate palate. Oh, I'm only kidding. But, he or the nurthseth didn't know that."

He threw the end of a rope from a harness over the side of the crib. A red and white baby rattle fastened to the end shook for a few seconds.

"They've tied you up?"

"It'sth all part of the game."

"So, you don't buy into this?"

"Regrething to the sthate of a child—are you kidding?" he smirked. "I already did that with my firtht wife. She got half the gold mine and my vath deferens in the divorth thettlement." Then he hesitated for a long moment, and his eyes looked past me. He rolled his tongue around on his lips, and said bitterly, "She wath a doll compared to my third ex. I call her my triple X. Lath time I thaw her outhide of a courtroom wath two yearth ago when I found her drunk and nude in a chaisthe lounge by our pool with the thixteen year old neighbor boy hot wiring her ignithon."

I giggled.

He rolled his head around like he was recovering from a sucker punch, and asked, "Firtht timer?"

"Yes."

"I've been coming here for yearths, and I enjoy the hell out of watching thom of theseth foolsth, thom being my competitorths I might add; really thwallow the hook. I've theen more crazy thit happen here than in any whore-wallpapercd VIP room perched over a cathino in Macau. Thay, whath your name?"

"Yellow Boy."

"Where'd you get a name like that?"

"When I was studying in Seattle a couple of rednecks used to say that every time the Neanderthals saw me. So, I reclaimed the slur, and appropriated it just like some African Americans do with 'nigger.'"

"Uh-huh, well have it your way, Yellow. I'm Benjamin

Franklin. Everybody callths me Frankie. Have you run into the Crier yet?"

"I think so. The naked gay wandering around balling?"

"That'sth what I'm talking about. How could any man with a fleet of othean cruitherths and a *Playboy* thcenter fold for a wife that'sth thirty yearths histh junior, pothibly have anything to cry about?"

"Maybe he has personal problems," I said softly, and thought about my homosexuality for the millionth time and how I was sure it would devastate my parents if they ever found out.

Frankie ignored my remark and said, "I think the Thumbthucker'sth here. The General, and the Runner, too. Tho is the Sthleeper. Oh, be glad you mithed the Mathturbator. We voted to revoke his memberthip lastht month. That crazy basthtard liked an audienth, and the rumor wath he had more sthpunk to go around than one of those ponieths in a Brathilian porno video. They tried handcuffths, and his nursth even made him a rig, some kind of chathtity belt. Nothing worked."

I suppressed my laughter and instead let out an appropriate farting sound. "Have you guys tried to vote the Owl out?" I asked.

"Three timesth," he said sadly. "A factthon, who barely hold a majority, well, they're enamored with her and her methodths."

"So I've heard," I said.

"Before her thith place was a retreat for the Roman Thenate. Now we're all part of her experiment."

"How many members are there?" I asked.

"Total? Around theventy-five, I guess. We've agreed that fifteen ith the max number allowed to vithit at any given time."

"Hey listhen," Frankie said, and he cupped his hand around his mouth, leaned out of his crib as far as he could toward me and whispered, "Me and a few of the otherths have been working on a project for months, doing a little bit each vithit. We've managed to cut a peep hole into the wall in *the room,* and althso one in the wall of an adjathent room where all the nursthes hang out and sothialize; you know, thit around and gothip and stare at each others' tiths. Tonight will be our firthst viewing. Do you want in?"

"Oh god, I don't know," I said, and nervously thought about the Owl's menacing gaze.

"Come on, Yellow Boy," Frankie pleaded. "You'll be thafe with me."

"Okay," I said, and wondered if Mr. Lin was part of his crew.

"That a boy. Thoon after lighths out be on the ready. I'll come and get you."

"Okay."

It was quiet at dinnertime. Even the Crier was silent as he munched on his chicken and rice. I looked around at the fifteen men in their high chairs, and wondered how many were in on Frankie's plan. He gave me a few sly winks and nods while he pestered the men on either side of him by barking and sticking food into his ears. Frankie was the first to leave. His nurse, a buxom Taiwanese, led him into one of the playrooms by the five meter rope attached to his harness. I, along with several others, finished eating soon after Frankie. I pointed toward the room Frankie was led into. Nurse Vargo took me by the hand and we walked inside of a big, open room with a wooden floor. Posters of famous Taiwanese singers and actors hung on the walls. Frankie was standing in a small circle with a half dozen other members. He waved me over, and I ran and stood next to him. Soon, the rest joined the circle.

Frankie's nurse walked out into the middle of the circle and clapped her hands, smiled and yelled, "What time is it boys?!"

"Singsong!" all the boys screamed in unison.

Frankie dashed out into the middle of the circle with his harness dragging behind, bent over, yanked his diaper down, turned around slowly, and mooned everybody. Then he pulled his diaper up, crouched down, and did somersaults until he was on the other side of the circle. The others clapped, hooted, and made farting sounds. Frankie repeated his stunt, and when he popped up off the floor in front of me his red, sweaty face was angelic—euphoric. He was absolutely beautiful.

I glanced around and tried to figure out who was who from

what Frankie had told me— the movers and shakers of the Little Dragon. I knew the Crier. He looked ready. His Owl doll was tied around his waist with a string. The Thumbsucker was obvious. I wondered if any of their wives or mistresses knew about this place.

The song "Hokey Pokey" began to blast through loudspeakers in the corners of the room. We all followed the singer's instructions:

"You put your left leg in, you put your left leg out
You put your left leg in, and you shake it all about . . ."

Frankie bolted back into the center of the ring and stood next to his dancing nurse, ripped off his diaper and harness, threw them down, raised his arms into the air and ran out of the circle and around the perimeter of the room. Everyone, including me, screamed with glee, tore off their diapers, and followed after the naked, frolicking seraph—the Pied Piper of Taipei. Frankie's nurse and Nurse Vargo, along with several other nurses who were also supervising, held their hands over their mouths and laughed hysterically as they witnessed the spontaneous spectacle. Frankie led us back into the circle around his nurse after a few riotous laps around the room. We finished doing the "Hokey Pokey" in our birthday suits, and it was one of the most fun and liberating things I've ever experienced. A beaming and triumphant Frankie smiled at me as we were led to our cribs.

An hour later, at ten, the lights in the dorm dimmed and a traditional Taiwanese lullaby began to play over the loudspeaker. Nurses appeared and strolled up and down the aisle whispering, "Nighty-night time boys."

Five minutes later the music stopped and the lights went out. A dozen night lights glowed softly along the dorm wall perimeter. I anxiously waited for Frankie's signal. Ten minutes passed. Fifteen minutes. Twenty minutes—and still no signal from the toothless wonder. I became restless, and popped my head over the top rail of my crib.

"Hey, Frankie boy," I whispered. There was no response. I

looked around, saw that all was quiet, and slowly and carefully climbed out of my crib and crawled to the back end of Frankie's cage. I peered inside. He was gone. A hand grabbed my shoulder from behind and spun me around. It was Mr. Lin.

"The Owl's swooped down and taken him—follow me."

"I didn't hear a thing," I said.

"You never do, kid," he said, and scampered away along the back wall. I stayed right on his tail. He looked over his shoulder and whispered, "If anyone comes, dive under the nearest crib, okay."

I followed Mr. Lin past the bathing area at the end of the dorm. He stopped at the corner of the entrance to the eating area, peered around it, and bolted through the kitchen like his diaper was on fire. I continued to stay on his bumper, and ducked through a doorway and into a dark room behind him. The door closed behind me after I entered. Someone made a chirping sound.

"Is that you, Lin?" a new voice whispered.

"Yeah, and I've brought my friend."

"Who?"

"Yellow Boy," I said, and was greeted with snickers and giggles.

A penlight flicked on ten feet in front of us, illuminating a group of four diaper and bonnet clad billionaires huddled together against the wall.

"Where are we?" I whispered.

"A few feet from heaven," said a tall man with a sallow complexion.

"Or, a few feet from hell," grunted a pudgy man who looked right at home in his baby attire.

"We're in a storage room adjacent to *the room*," said Mr. Lin.

"We're going to see Frankie get the treatment," giggled a small man who had enough hair on his chest and shoulders to knit us all wool sweaters. "That son of a bitch stole my baby that I built from the ground up. He's the master of the hostile takeover."

"Give him a break, would you," barked a tough looking hombre with an unlit cigar in his mouth. "It was all Frankie's idea to cut these peeps. It's goddamn ironic that he's on the other side for the grand opening. Oh hell, he probably planned it this way."

The tall man said, "Listen, we've got to be quiet. Let's quit stalling and start the show."

"Yeah," snarled the cigar man, "keep your damn mouths shut no matter what we see in there."

The faint sound of a violin playing began to seep into our darkened room. Cigar man took the penlight from Hairy, walked over to a poster of Tom Cruise, carefully removed the pushpins, and handed the poster to Mr. Lin. Light streamed through two small holes a meter apart. Cigar man and Hairy pressed their eyes against the holes.

"What do you see?! What?!" the pudgy man asked. The men didn't answer. A minute later their mouths dropped open.

"What? What is it?" asked Mr. Lin.

Cigar man waved his hand like he was shooing away stock brokers. Both men stepped away from the peep holes with guilty looks on their faces. The pudgy man and the tall man immediately took their places at the peeps.

Mr. Lin handed me an empty drinking glass, put the one he held up against the wall, and began to listen. I followed. I heard a violin playing a beautiful, sad tune. And I heard the muffled cries of Frankie below the music. After a few minutes, Hairy and the tall man stepped away from the wall with tears in their eyes. Mr. Lin and I jumped at the chance, handed the drinking glasses to Hairy and the tall man, and pressed our eyes against the peeps. The pair stuck their ears to the wall like they were being pulled by a giant magnet. The room was lit with candles. Vases of tulips and orchids sat on a table in front of a weeping Frankie. The Owl sat across from him in a black gown, playing the violin. She stopped playing, leaned forward, and looked deeply into Frankie's eyes.

I read his lips. "Don't stop," he begged. "Please, don't stop."

He had his teeth! She'd let him have his teeth!

The Owl purred, "I heard about your victory laps tonight."

Frankie straightened up, got a hold of himself like a bottle a cold baby formula had been squirted in his face, and said,

"You should've joined us. It might have helped break your bad habit of pulling out your feathers."

"Your last visit you put gin in all the formula. And, the time before that you molested Nurse Hematoma.

A big smirk appeared on Frankie's face, and he purred, "Yow."

"Now, you've broken my rules again."

"Oh yes, the exalted diaper policy," he muttered sarcastically. "Clearly a matter of national security." Frankie sat silently for a long while, and looked around the room nonchalantly as if he were in a dentist's waiting room. Then he folded his arms across his chest, gritted his teeth, stuck out his chin and hissed, "We could have you removed."

"And, we could have you removed."

"I meant, removed from the planet."

The Owl flinched like Frankie winged her with a 12 gauge. She sat speechless, and began fussing with her whirlybird hair-do.

I quickly glanced at my fellow voyeurs after Frankie unfolded his arms and sat back in his chair, all the while looking cockily at the Owl. Mr. Lin clearly wasn't enjoying watching the Owl's dressing down. Hairy continued to listen with his fat head scrunched up against the drinking glass and wall. He looked disappointed, like his favorite horse threw a shoe down the home stretch. The tall man moved his head away from the wall with a look of disbelief. He clenched his drinking glass with both hands and set it on the floor. Then he put his hands on top of his bonneted melon and shook it back and forth.

Smelling victory, Frankie stared the Owl down and said, "Look queenie, you may well have some of us prancing in your wake tossing rose petals into the air—but you don't have all of us, and you certainly will never have me. Maybe it's time for you to go back to the circus."

"But, I like this one better," she said meekly.

"Then ease up."

She picked up the violin and said, "You're angry about something." She began to play, and the notes rolled over Frankie like an invisible narcotic gas. He shrunk down and softened up like a deflating balloon, and slumped in his chair.

She stopped playing five minutes later and said softly, "Tell me more," and nodded her head.

"My daughter—she hates me," he moaned.

"I didn't know you have a daughter."

"I've seemed to forget that a lot myself. I've been too busy making money to pay any attention to her. Now, she's a beautiful twenty-five year old woman, and I hardly know her."

"It's never too late," the Owl said reassuringly.

"I know how to manipulate a board of directors as well as the stock market. But, I've been terrified to tell my daughter how much I love her."

"What are you afraid of?"

"Oh, it's the curse of all Taiwanese men," he whimpered. "It's engrained in our hides from day one. We can't show affection. We're afraid about the possibility of losing face."

The Owl smiled and said, "You've been a tough nut to crack, big boy. How many times do you think you've been in this room?"

"I don't know."

"Many times, and you've always played the comic. Why today? Why are you telling me this today?"

"My daughter—she's dead," he said softly, bent over, laid his head on the table, and sobbed and pounded his fists causing the candles and flowers to shake.

"Oh, I'm so sorry!" the Owl said, and she stood up, walked over to Frankie, bent down, put her arms around him and began to cry. I wondered if she was acting.

I fell away from the peep, crouched down against the wall, and was overcome with sadness for my new friend. I looked around at the others. Even Hairy, who'd lusted for revenge just a few moments earlier, appeared sullen and shamefaced. Soon, we all slipped back to our cribs without saying a word. I heard Frankie climb into his crib thirty minutes later. He quickly fell asleep and began to snore. As I laid there my thoughts suddenly became so very clear; what the hell was I waiting for? I'd trudged through life encumbered with fear; fear of failure, fear of rejection for being gay, fear of losing someone, so I'd never gotten too close to anyone. Could I find the courage to really love? I'd never told my parents that I love them.

The next morning after breakfast Nurse Vargo carried me through a door at the end of the dorm room and we entered a playroom half the size of a basketball court. Toys and balls of all colors and sizes were strewn around. Eight members were sitting on the floor at the far end of the room playing with toys. Frankie was sitting alone against the wall in the middle of the room sucking on the nipple of a baby bottle. I pointed toward Frankie, and my nurse carefully deposited me on the floor next to him. We sat quietly for what seemed like the length of a film directed by Kevin Costner.

"What you drinking?" I finally asked, feeling awkward and at a loss for words.

"Hemlock, on special request, compliments of Nurse Zapgun," he said, and flashed his teeth at me.

"Feel like sharing?" I said.

Frankie ignored my weak attempt at a joke and said, "You know, I actually feel," then he hesitated and said, "purged, yah, purged. I haven't cried like that since I was kicked off the little league baseball team for doing a 'Pete Rose.'"

"That's funny."

"How much did you peepers hear last night?" he asked like he already knew the answer.

"All of it," I said, and felt the claws of guilt rake up and down my spine. "I'm sorry about your daughter."

"Thank you, Yellow," he said with a faint smile. "That's very kind. How old are you, if you don't mind my asking?"

"Thirty-two."

"I wish I were thirty-two again," he said wistfully and rolled his eyes. "Don't wait, my friend. Whatever you need to do or say to someone in this life, do it now. Don't wait. Don't become a first class loser like yours truly."

"You're no loser."

"I've missed it."

"Missed what?"

"Everything," he said bitterly, and let out a long wheezing breath. "You're looking at an insatiable fool who's spent his entire adult life chasing after money—a man obsessed with obtaining more and more, and wasn't even smart enough to take the time to enjoy it."

"But, now you can," I said consolingly. "You're fairly young. You can change your life."

His voice broke, and he whispered, "My daughter was the only one in my life that didn't want me for my money. Everyone else; ex-wives, boards of directors, stockbrokers—they're barnacles clinging to my hull. I'm alone Yellow, and it's my own damn fault."

"I'm your friend," I said weakly.

"I know Yellow, and I appreciate—"

"Milk time!" yelled the black nurse. "Milk time, boys!"

"That's your cue, chink," he said with a little smile.

"I'm lactose intolerant," I said nervously, and looked around for an exit or something to crawl under.

"Thanks for the warning," he said. "I'll go fetch my umbrella and galoshes. By the way, the word is tonight it's your turn to ride the Owl's boob machine."

Up until my first and only "milk time" session I actually thought I might get out of Nurse Zapgun's funhouse with the same number of neuroses I entered with—I stopped counting at seven. Even now, a year later, merely the mention of the word *lactate* makes me break out with hives, and turns my colon into a writhing python that's just swallowed the Rockettes. As my nurse dragged me into my first milk session, I pictured in my mind a litter of chubby Saint Bernard pups fighting for a seat at the bar as their mother lay calmly on the floor as still as a corpse. Then, instead of pups, I envisioned eight diaper-clad billionaires wrestling for a teat on Four Eyes, a circus freak with four nipples. I wondered what the milk might taste like—a lot like chicken?

Nurse Vargo clutched my hand and led me through two swinging double doors and into a small auditorium with a large movie screen taking up the entire wall on the right hand side. A handful of tycoons were strapped into their seats sucking on baby bottles. I recognized several of them from our peep session the night before. They looked content and glassy-eyed as dopey toddlers. I hoped Frankie would show.

"Today's a special show," Nurse Vargo cooed, guided me into a chair in the middle of the pack, and strapped me in tightly.

One of the blonde nurses appeared with a baby bottle, shook it a few times, stuck it in my mouth and said playfully, "Bottoms up."

I pretended to drink and made loud, sloppy sucking sounds with my lips. Whatever this stuff was, none of it was going down my hatch. My first day, they gave me apple juice and water. This warm concoction smelled mammalian. After a few minutes the lights went down and the screen lit up. I proceeded to squirt half my bottle underneath the seat next to me.

Someone tapped me on the shoulder from behind. I smiled, thinking it was Frankie, put the nipple of the bottle into my mouth, and turned around. The Owl's vacant eyes met mine—she looked like something you could have found perched on a bench in Norman Bates's taxidermy workshop.

"Tonight little man, is fag night," she tauntingly whispered.

I gulped, accidentally pouring a huge slug of milk into my mouth. I held on with bloated cheeks trying desperately not to swallow, and hoped she would leave.

"What's wrong?" she purred. "Do you have air in your tum—"

I blew the mouthful into her face. Several of the fat cats who'd been watching broke into hysterics and began to make farting sounds. Two nurses rushed to the queen's aid and wiped the gook off her face. The shocked and mortified look on the Owl's face still makes me chuckle.

"Enema," the Owl said under her breath to my nurse with gritted teeth, and then she disappeared into the darkness.

My sweet nurse never followed the Owl's instructions. I discreetly expelled the rest of the concoction from my bottle onto the floor under the seats around me. Not a drop of the lactose ran down my throat. I couldn't wait to give Frankie the blow-by-blow of the event. Did I do it on purpose? You bet I did.

For the next hour we were mercilessly forced to watch re-runs of George W. Bush speeches, followed by the cartoon *Sponge Bob.* I thought they went together rather nicely. Half the lucky dopes fell asleep shortly after George began his "dumb ass in the headlights" routine mumbling along with the teleprompter. Actually, George W. was well-liked by many Taiwanese, especially the well-heeled because of his harsh stance against any military invasion by the Chinese communists in Beijing. "Milk time" was a win-lose experience. I lost half my brain cells thanks to rat face and *Sponge Bob,* but managed to get revenge on the Owl for humiliating me my first day in front of Mr. Lin.

I didn't eat much at dinner. The Owl's warning continued to ring in my ears. I knew she had something villainous planned for me. There was no escape. At lights out Nurse Vargo carried me to my crib. There was no word from Frankie. A handful of sleeping pills wouldn't have helped me sleep. I was a mouse, and waited and waited for the flight of the Owl. An hour passed. I thought about finding a place to hide. I wondered how many were waiting at the peep holes in *the room.* That's it, I thought! I could go to the peep room and spend the night. She'd never find me there—it was my last night, too. Ten minutes later I made my move. I looked into Frankie's crib. He wasn't there. I guessed the old rascal was either in the peep room with the others or in the john pushing groceries. Either way, I knew he was a fighter, and I'd see him in the peep room. I couldn't wait to hear more of his funny jokes and play-by-play. I knew he'd be okay. I fucking knew it.

I followed the same path along the wall that Mr. Lin led me the night before. All was clear. I'd made it to the end of the dorm, and crouched down at the corner of the wall outside the kitchen area. I was going to make it! The Owl wasn't going to toy with my fag ass. I peered around the corner and looked into the darkened kitchen—along the floor against the wall. I heard the faint sound of a baby rattle somewhere in front of me.

"Frankie," I whispered. "It's me, Yellow Boy." No one answered. I crept on my haunches along the kitchen wall. Something was hanging in front of me. I scurried to it.

A baby rattle brushed against my face. "Oh, no!" I whimpered in horror.

I grabbed the red and white rattle at the end of the rope, looked up, and gasped. Frankie was hanging by his neck from a high support beam. His body swayed back and forth ever so slightly. I knew he was dead. I unfastened the rattle, shoved it into my diapers, and ran into the peep room to tell the others with my butt feeling gooey as a Hershey bar at a July picnic. Mr. Lin and the same characters from the previous night were ogling through the holes in the wall. After I told them about Frankie I cleaned myself up, changed back into my clothes, found a bottle of Johnnie Walker stashed in the kitchen, sat against Frankie's crib, and got drunk. All the lights were turned on. Nurses and members scurried around like maniacs. Why did I unfastened the rattle and shove it into my diapers? I'm a collector, and I wanted something physical for my memory of Frankie. Do you remember before when I said I crapped in my diapers one time? That was it.

Mr. Lin found me an hour later. He silently sat down on the floor next to me.

"I'm sorry," he said. "I knew you really took a liking to him." I took a gulp of scotch and handed him the bottle.

Mr. Lin took a swig and said, "All members who are present just held an emergency meeting with the Owl. We voted, and the majority has agreed to secretly move Frankie's body to a suite in one of the Taipei hotels he owns."

"How the hell are they going to manage that?"

"These guys own everybody, everything. Key people at the hotel and a few members of the local police will be paid off to keep their mouth's shut." He took another swallow and gave me the bottle.

"So, they're going to stage it like he died there?"

"The coroner's official report will say it was a heart attack.

This place doesn't exist—can't exist. If the press ever found out about this place and that he died here, a suicide; well, the stock market will plunge and the scandal will rock the country for years. There's no sense in getting a lot of people hurt."

"I suppose not," I said, and began to sob again. I handed the bottle back to Mr. Lin and slunk to my crib.

I couldn't sleep. I lay there looking up at the glow-in-the-dark stars on the ceiling with the night's events tumbling through my mind. Was it a suicide, or was it a murder, I wondered? The Owl's creepy face flashed in my mind. It was awful coincidental that Frankie decided to off himself the night after he threatened the Owl's life. And, the night after he spilled his guts to the Owl about how distraught he was about his daughter's death. A perfect opportunity for the Owl to get rid of him by killing him and making it look like a suicide. She certainly could've pulled it off with the assistance of some of her devoted followers. Either way, my new friend was dead. I kind of hoped it was a murder. I'd hate to think how lonely and desperate Frankie might have felt the moments before he took his own life.

The lights turned off an hour later. I was still restless. I laid there for two more hours, long after things got quiet and the sound of snoring echoed through the dorm. I grabbed a penlight that I'd liberated from the kitchen after dinner and did my prairie dog routine before I crept out of my crib. My stomach did a cartwheel as I passed by Frankie's crib. I crabbed three cribs down and stopped to listen for any noise coming from its inhabitant—all quiet. I slowly raised myself up from the back of the crib. A clean diaper was hanging next to me over the side. I peered inside. Mr. Lin was fast asleep. I carefully reached in, lifted up his long T-shirt, flicked on the penlight, and moved it over his naked hip. A life-like tattoo of the face of the Owl stared up at me. Oh my god, my hunch was right! I quickly turned off the light, scurried back to my crib, and climbed in. The ceiling turned into Van Gogh's *Starry Night*. I thought about making a run for it right then and there. But if I ran, and it was a murder, then I could be considered a loose end. I stayed put, and didn't sleep a wink. If the Owl, or anyone else came lurking to my crib I planned to scream even louder than when Jerry the lumberjack played hide-the-weiner. It was the loneliest night of my life.

Nurse Vargo came to my crib at 8:00 a.m.

"The members have decided to close the facility today because of Frankie's suicide," she cooed. "You can put your street clothes on and come for breakfast whenever you're ready. Everybody's supposed to be gone by ten o'clock."

"Thank god," I whispered.

I quickly got dressed, gave everyone I saw a fake smile, and tried to avoid Mr. Lin. He seemed to turn up everywhere I went; in the bathroom, next to me at breakfast. I was paranoid. I belonged in a Woody Allen film.

At 9:45 Mr. Lin approached me and asked, "Can I give you a lift to the train station or to the subway?"

Yeah, sure, I thought. You can drop me at the Jimmy Hoffa station. "Oh, no that's all right," I said. "I've already called for a taxi." I lied.

"Please, I insist," he urged. "I feel just horrible about what happened to Frankie, and what you must be going through after finding him hanging there."

"Thank you for inviting me," I said softly. "I really don't feel like any company."

My "playing dumb" routine went rather well. To these wealthy characters I was just some affable fag doctor from Tainan. In all the commotion and aftershock nobody bothered to blindfold me on my way out. I walked to the elevator bank and discovered that my initial instincts upon my arrival were correct. I was in the Taipei 101 building. If that elevator car had dropped at three hundred miles per hour it still wouldn't have been fast enough. When the doors finally opened at the lobby I scampered for the exit like I was trapped in a right-wing Christian revival meeting. I walked out into the muggy air and took a deep breath. I figured the only appropriate way to go to the train station was to crawl and swim through the sewer.

I took the train back to Tainan. Frankie's words echoed in my mind as it neared my stop, "Don't wait, my friend. Whatever you need to do or say to someone in this life, do it now. Don't wait."

When the hell was I ever going to be a man?

I called Mr. Lin a week later, after I'd calmed down, and thanked him again for inviting me to witness the aftermath of a grisly death. I actually feared for my life, and kissed his tight little ass until it turned black and blue. He came to my office six months later for a routine eye exam. I played the dumb, benign doctor and didn't mention a word about our weekend at the Owl's fun house. I haven't heard from him since. As for the Owl, the high priestess of Top Boy Society; there'll always be predators of her ilk in the world. Sometime, somewhere, she'll cross the wrong person and get her wings clipped.

I miss poor, beautiful Frankie terribly, and still find myself chuckling occasionally at some of the stunts he pulled. I've accepted the fact that I'll never know if his death was a suicide or a murder. Because of him, and the wisdom he passed on to me, I don't regret my weekend at Top Boy Society. However, I do regret not being capable of figuring out just how bad off Frankie was in dealing with the death of his daughter. I wish I could have been there for him, talked to him more, tried to help him. Instead, I was too worried about saving my own skin from more humiliation from the Owl. To honor Frankie's memory, and to help heal the pain of losing him, I've recently drawn a comic of my weekend at Top Boy featuring all of his exploits. I haven't shown it to anyone.

Meko

On a lousy Friday, Meko pedaled down Tainan's SuWei Road as composed as a high wire act in a bombing raid. One trembling hand held an oil paper parasol overhead to shield her from the cruel July sun. In the shadow cast by the mushroom—a customized prize rendered in peacocks and peony, Meko's other hand choked the handlebar of her mother's bicycle; she pretended it was the gills of the previous night's blind date. She couldn't tell whether a hideous grinding noise was coming from the red coaster's dry chain or her teeth. With Napoleon fins and a scorpion's tail, the cold fish embossed his name onto her ass, adding to the bead roll of hopefuls and losers. She knew he'd never see her again. That thought caused her to continue to scowl and restlessly bounce around on her seat as she made her way back to Tainan Hospital for the two o'clock shift, where she had worked for three years as a nurse in the Ophthalmology Department. To secure Meko the plum position, her older brother Yellow Boy, an eye surgeon in the department, called in every marker he had, both real and imagined.

He also lied, begged, and gave the department chief his *A* blow job—three times. As she teetered along, Meko's uniform, a light blue skirt and vest and a white shirt, showcased her titillating figure. Hospital inmates and coworkers constantly took runs at her like aspiring Olympian pole vaulters eager to join the "six meters club."

By Friday, Meko always felt like a creaky, sweat-stained floorboard at a dance marathon because she endured dialysis treatments on Monday, Wednesday, and Friday mornings. On Mondays and Wednesdays she played dead on a cot at her hospital's morgue after the four-hour treatments before resurrecting for her afternoon shift. On this Friday, as usual, she had gone home to eat lunch with her parents at their single-story red brick house on the outskirts of Tainan where she'd lived her entire twenty four years. Meko knew that without the treatments she would've soon taken up residency on the family altar in an alabaster urn picked out by her devoted mother. She'd backed out of several schemes to give herself a piano wire necktie or a Jonestown cocktail, because unlike her suitors, she was never one for quick exits. Dialysis did what Meko's bean filters were supposed to do, as it does for anyone with tanked kidneys: remove waste from her bloodstream. Meko always wore long sleeve shirts, even in the summer, when streets were lined with fire breathers and the wind had emphysema, so people, especially prospective beaus, couldn't detect the permanent catheter in her wrist. The catheter led to a hotline in Diyu, the "Ten Courts of Hell." It rang off the hook. According to many Taoist, Buddhist, and Chinese folk religion beliefs, Diyu is a purgatory where souls are tortured to atone for their mortal sins in preparation for reincarnation.

Meko's mother and grandmother were worried as hens fated for a pot of sesame chicken soup because she wasn't married. On Saturday nights after everyone went to bed, they tried to think of ways to get her hitched while smearing calamine lotion on each others' hives. They knew the truth was glaring as the hole in Meko's wrist; as far as most young men were concerned, she wasn't wife material. They'd thrown money at fortune tellers, prayed to the deity Matsu night and day, and bought enough amulets to hang around the neck of every child at nearby St. Lucy's Orphanage. Meko denied this truth far too often, and it had her stumbling through the sunless, vacant lots of her own private internment camp searching for a husband with a dead flashlight and a box of rubbers. She knew the odds of her seeing her forty-fifth birthday were skinny as a rice stalk. Meko was the goddess of Easy Street before her kidneys went belly up in her mid-teens; she was regal, confident, and vivacious as hell. Since then, she'd wilted like an orchid left on a dashboard in June. In recent months, the Harpies of anxiety, which dwelled in her private internment camp, had multiplied, swatting at her heels as she neared a date she dreaded—her twenty-fifth birthday. She'd be one year closer to the day Taiwanese parents clang alarm bells for their single daughters; their thirtieth birthday.

As Meko continued to ride along, her mind continued to drift to the flying fish she had on the line the previous night. She scrunched up her nose, shook her head, and rode faster, trying to chase the memory away. No luck.

Meko sat up in bed after sex. The merman, a young resident at the hospital, shot his chowder in less than five minutes. He began to doze off.

"Don't you want to talk to me?" Meko asked fretfully.

"Sure." He spit the hook out and began to fall asleep.

"We've been intimate twice and you haven't asked me what I like to do or anything. You haven't even called me by my name."

"Huh?"

"You never want to talk to me!"

"Talk, sure," he mumbled softly.

"I really think we have something special, you know. I can feel it. We have so many things in common it's just amazing, isn't it? Maybe we could try living together? I have some great ideas what we could do to brighten up this place, and I can cook you know. I could make you dinner whenever you want. Hey, I just thought about music. I don't even know what kind of music you like. You know you've never asked me that, either. That's okay, and . . ."

The merman began to snore. Meko quickly put on her clothes and quietly slid under the door.

Meko had this scene down; perfecting the role over the past several years with a string of men long enough to fill a baseball game's scorecard. For the players, the hole in Meko's arm put her in the same league as betel nut girls and hussies; but she wouldn't let herself see that half the time. From the first kiss the prospects knew the relationship would last as long as the lifespan of a housefly. As soon as Meko began buzzing about living together or getting serious, they'd vanish like the bundle of loot former Taiwan President Chen ran off with. For Meko, sex was an escape from the stark reality of her disease. It was an exercise in self-loathing; a magic wand used to fend off demons and charm stray souls lurking in her private internment camp. Screwing doctors and other fatties blew her ego up for about as long as it takes a giant Humpty Dumpty balloon in a holiday parade to float three blocks.

Yellow Boy would often say to their grandmother in private when Meko would sulk around the ophthalmology department after getting tossed by her latest, 'She'd have better luck picking guys out of a police line up—in Detroit.'

The grandmother would reply with something like, 'That girl can read a boy's true intentions about as well as a foreigner reading a Chinese menu.'

This reality grieved everyone in the family except for Meko's father. He had a doctorate in mathematics and a master's in denial. Meko rode into the hospital parking lot teary-eyed, parked her bike, and slogged toward the employee entrance.

She stuck another thorn into her side and whispered, "Am I going to be fucked up for the rest of my life?"

Curtis rode his shiny new black-and-white 125cc Yamaha with a sidecar up Mango Road and parked in front of his grandfather's *san-ho yuan*. A boy of thirteen, in a wide-brimmed bamboo hat, dark pants, and a white T-shirt with the words "drug dealer" scrawled across the front in Chinese characters walked past pushing a wheelbarrow full of cow manure toward the mango orchard. Curtis looked at the boy and chuckled, jumped off the bike, and walked through the courtyard to the house. The old man was sitting in his chair on the front porch smoking a cigarette after lunch.

He glanced at Curtis, then looked out toward the motorcycle, took the cig out of his mouth and grunted, "Well, don't you look some kind of goddamned James Dean."

"Who's James Dean?" Curtis took off his aviator sunglasses and put them in his shirt pocket.

"A young man who could even make a bull dyke's pussy wet. We used to watch his movies when I was in the service. Is that thing running okay?"

"It purrs."

"You keep your ass in college and working to make those loan payments, or I'll fix you up with a job being a skin diver for a septic company." The old man reached into his shirt pocket, pulled out a small plastic bag of betel nuts, popped one into his mouth, took a drag off his cig and said, "The Chin-huang harvest is soon, probably next week. Is auntie going to cut you loose so you can stay out here for a few weeks and help this old man out? I know you have the new job at the candy store."

"It's a 7-Eleven. You know how much I like working with you in the mangos. Auntie won't mind."

"She'd better not. That old carp is dizzier than a tilt-a-whirl."

Curtis laughed, looked toward the mango orchard and asked, "Who's the new boy?"

"The dipshit?" squawked the old man. "That son of a bitch is the softest strawberry I've had yet. He's my strawberry milkshake."

Curtis sat down in the chair opposite his grandfather and said, "I noticed your artwork on his T-shirt."

"The punk got busted dealing drugs at his junior high. His mother came over here three times crying and carrying on something awful before I agreed to take him on. I'm getting too damn old, but his mother is good people, and I won't let her down, even if it takes that sorry knucklehead two summers to get some sense."

"How long have you had him?"

"A week," laughed the old man. "Hell, he turned rabbit the first night and tried to run away. I had to hop on my busted one-lunger and chase him down. I chained him to his bedpost for the next two nights, and then I gave him the *Cool Hand Luke* treatment. That broke him. Now, he's as tame as a neutered gerbil. Go ahead, walk over there and pet him."

"What's the *Cool Hand Luke* treatment?"

"It's from a movie I saw on the idiot box last month."

Curtis shrugged his shoulders and said, "I must have missed it."

"You're always missing it," teased the old man. "I had the dipshit dig his own grave and fill it in three times before he figured out who he was dealing with."

Curtis sat silent for a long time, and said apologetically, "I made an appointment for you to see an eye doctor this afternoon in Tainan City at two thirty."

"You did, did you?" huffed the old man. "An appointment at the whorehouse is what I need. That's where this whole problem started. I gave a pretty young gal there such a good trimming the last time that I saw cross-eyed for two days afterwards. So did she, I'm told."

"You haven't been to a whorehouse since before you met Grandma."

"And they still remember me. They called me Two Gals Lee."

"Why's that?"

"Because I needed two gals before I put my plow up."

The boy smiled and said playfully, "You stubborn old bull."

"Damn right."

"Come on, it's getting worse."

"I hate going to the doctor. They're always jabbing me with needles, or trying to poke something up my ass. Your dear, sweet grandmother—she used to do all my doctoring. She knew all about Chinese medicine. I bet you didn't know that, did you, boy?"

"No, I didn't."

"She could cure about anything with things grown right

out here in these fields—all natural. None of these horse pills from the States doctors now have Taiwanese eating like fucking M&M's."

"You're afraid," taunted Curtis.

"Damn right I'm afraid."

"I'll take you."

"Oh dammit!" said the old man, and he stood up and flicked his cigarette into the bright sunlit courtyard. "Okay, but it's only because I don't have any alternative except to sit here and go blind."

The old man walked out to the boy working in the mango orchard and said, "We're going to town for a few hours, Milkshake. You keep working in the shade here spreading manure until that sun eases off around four." The old man gave the boy a hard look and said, "We know you're good at spreading shit around. You proved that big time back at school."

The boy looked up at the old man and frowned momentarily. Then he quickly got back to work.

"If I'm not back by five go on up to the house. And remember, don't be jacking off in your room and shoot strawberry juice all over hell. You jack off in the bathroom or outside."

The sullen-faced boy nodded and said, "Yes sir."

The old man walked away a few steps, turned back around, looked down toward the main road and said, "Don't even think about it Cool Hand, because I'll find you. And stay out of the damn barn and away from that bull. The randy kid last summer snuck in there with a step-ladder and tried to fuck it in the ass. Damn near got his nuts kicked to Hong Kong."

Curtis was sitting on his motorcycle when his grandfather returned from the orchard. The old man climbed into the sidecar and said, "When my eye gets better you ride 'bitch,' and I'll show you how to move."

Curtis laughed, kicked the motor over, shifted into first and hit the throttle, and headed down the dirt drive past the gleaming mango orchard. The old man smiled.

At 2:20 Curtis and his grandfather walked into the crowded

waiting room of Tainan Hospital's Ophthalmology Department. The old man walked to the counter, presented his Taiwan National Health insurance card to a young nurse, and was given a small ticket with the number 27 printed on it. He and Curtis sat down among the other patients who were watching a Korean soap opera on a flat screen television on the wall.

The old man muttered under his breath, "Fucking Korean this and Korean that everywhere. It's as bad as all those Hollywood B-movies they poison our kids with."

Curtis leaned toward his grandfather and chided in a whisper, "What about James Dean?"

A look of frustration appeared on the old man's face. "James Dean was magnificent," he said, and stuck his nose into the air acting as if he was insulted by the boy's remark.

Ten minutes later the number 27 flashed on the digital screen next to the TV. Meko walked out of one of the three exam rooms and into the waiting room. "Mr. Lee," she called out. "Mr. Lee."

The old man stood up, smiled at Meko, and walked past her into the exam room. Curtis's eyes rolled over Meko's curves like a runaway rollercoaster car as he followed his grandfather. Meko waited for Curtis to enter the room, walked inside, and gently closed the door. Yellow Boy was sitting behind a small desk in a white jacket and tie writing notes concerning the previous patient onto a pad on a clipboard.

The old man sat down in a chair across from Yellow Boy, looked at Curtis and said, "Please wait outside."

Curtis smiled at Meko with a little embarrassment, and went back into the waiting room. Meko winked at her brother and left the room.

Yellow Boy looked up from the clipboard and said, "Good afternoon, Mr. Lee."

The old man looked Yellow Boy up and down and said, "Have you confessed to your folks?"

"Excuse me? Confessed what?"

"That you're a rice queen."

Yellow Boy raised his hands into the air in frustration and

embarrassment and said, "Oh my god, everybody seems to know. How did you?"

"The way your eyes unzipped my grandson's fly and tugged on his onion."

"I apologize. He is quite virile looking."

"Of course," said the old man, and he patted a hand on each of his cheeks. "He takes after this old bull. Hell, when I was his age I was tipping gals over like bowling pins." The old man raised a hand and pinched his thumb and index finger together and said, "I'm about this close to taking that strawberry to a 'barber shop' myself. That kid wouldn't know what to do with a girl if she sat on his face and played 'Moon River' with her pussy."

Yellow Boy laughed and said, "I wouldn't be so sure about that."

The old man saddened, and asked with a hesitant voice, "What's the verdict, Mister Sawbones? Am I going to go blind and have to put on horse blinder sunglasses and go poking around with one of those canes like some feeble old jackass?" He sat silently for a long moment, looked down, and said in a whisper with his voice trailing off, "I don't know if I could take not being able to see my beautiful mango trees."

"I'll do everything I can so you can see your mango trees."

"I'm not cut out to be some damn Cyclops," whined the old man. "What the hell will all my girlfriends think?"

Yellow Boy chuckled. "You'll be fine."

The old man looked up at Yellow Boy, his eyes twinkled, and he smiled and said, "Really?" In an instant a proud, defiant look appeared on his face, and he asked, "Then what in the name of Sun Yat-Sen is wrong with me?"

"Please sit on the exam table and we'll take a look."

The old man followed the instructions.

"Can you tell me your symptoms?"

"My left eye's the lame dog," said the old man. "Sometimes I see bright flashes of light, especially with my peripheral vision. Blurry vision, too."

"When did it start?"

"Two moons ago."

Yellow Boy pulled a penlight out of his shirt pocket, moved close to the old man, cradled the back of his head with one hand, flicked the light on, moved it in front of the old man's left eye and said, "Look straight ahead. Good, now look slowly from side to side."

The old man complied. Yellow Boy turned off the penlight a minute later, stood up straight, took a few steps back and said, "I would like to check your retina."

"What is that, exactly?" the old man asked nervously.

"It's the light-sensitive membrane on the back of your eye. We'll seat you in a dark room, and using an ophthalmoscope, shine a beam of light through your pupil. Then I can see the back of your eyeball. It's painless, and will only take about ten minutes."

"Okay," said the old man.

Meko appeared, led the old man into a small room at the rear of the exam room, and helped him sit in a chair against the back wall.

"What's your name?" asked the old man.

"Meko."

"That's a sweet name. It sounds Japanese."

"It is. It's a nickname I gave myself."

"I'm part Japanese."

"Really?" the girl asked in a surprised high-pitched voice.

"It's a long story." The old man cupped his hand next to his mouth and whispered, "That sporty young man I came in with is no relation to me. I found him wandering on the street and took him in."

Meko laughed.

"You know I'm joking, don't you?"

"Yes."

"He's my grandson," the old man said proudly. "First year in college."

Yellow Boy walked into the room with the flashlight sized ophthalmoscope. Meko smiled at the old man, slid out of the room, shut the door, and turned off the lights.

Ten minutes later Yellow Boy and the old man emerged

from the small room.

Yellow Boy sat down in the chair behind the desk and said solemnly, "Please take a seat."

The old man sat down and studied the doctor's somber face.

"Oh shit. Let's have it."

"Your retina is detached."

"Oh, donkey dip!" bellowed the old man.

"We can attempt to repair it with surgery."

"Attempt! What are my chances?"

"Fifty-fifty."

"Those are hangman's odds." The old man's mouth tightened. "When do you want to cut me open?"

"As soon as possible. How does sometime in the next few weeks sound?"

"I'm a condemned man, you might as well hang me quick."

"I'll check my surgery schedule and we'll set a date, okay?"

"All right."

"Please go back to the waiting room, and my assistant will give you the time and date in a few minutes."

The old man stood up and walked to the door, turned around, and said in a fatherly tone, "I know the torment of living with a big secret. It's heavy as a stone, isn't it?"

A nervous smile crept onto Yellow Boy's face. He felt like he was lashed to a crate of Motion Lotion sinking to the bottom of the Te-ching River. It'd been a whole year since his late pal Frankie from Top Boy Society urged him to out to his parents, and he was just as terrified as before, maybe more.

"Do you want to tell your folks about your gaytitude?"

"Very much."

"Then tell them son, before it's too late." The old man walked out the door.

The old man was silent for a long while as they rode toward home. After twenty minutes he looked over at Curtis and yelled, "He's going to cut me open next week."

"I know. What's the diagnosis?"

"Too much sex."

"Hah! Hah!"

"It's nothing, really. A small problem. Sawbones is going to fix me right up."

"Good."

"While you were out in the waiting room fondling yourself I had a nice conversation with Sawbones's pretty nurse. I talked her up real nice."

Curtis grinned and asked, "Get a date?"

"Could have," bragged the old man. "Hell, the way she was looking at you, why didn't you . . ."

"I've got a date with Meko tomorrow night," Curtis said victoriously. "She's the doctor's sister, by the way."

"She is, is she," the old man said with surprise. "Well, it's about goddamn time you got after it," he quipped. "Where are you going to take her?"

"A KTV."

"Karaoke, huh," the old man grunted with disgust. "Another damn Jap invention. Damn Japs are still crawling all over this island one way or another."

"Come on Grandpa!" Curtis whined with frustration. "We're part Japanese."

"You're right," the old man conceded. He rubbed the top of his head and barked, "But I didn't have any say in that and neither did you."

"I know you don't mean those things," said Curtis. "You're just worried about your surgery."

"Like hell I don't," the old man muttered under his breath. "I'm Taiwanese through and through, and damn proud of it." He looked off into the rice fields, and his mind wandered to the scene at Yellow Boy's office and he thought about his upcoming operation. He was petrified.

That night Meko lay awake in bed, twisted up like a female version of Pepé Le Pew in a *Looney Tunes* rerun. All her previous dates said adieu and blew after a couple of nights in the sack when they discovered her hotline to the "Ten Courts of Hell," she thought. Why would Curtis be any different? At 2:00 a.m.,

Yanluo, the King of Hell himself gave her a crank call. She picked up.

"Hey, kidney bean, still awake?" he whispered followed by the usual heavy panting. "You said before you don't like heights. Good old 7-Eleven has everything you need to off yourself. Why don't you quit fussing and run over and get a bottle of Absolut, a bottle of aspirin, and mix yourself a Stockholm Cemetery? Come on, sugar. We've got a room available in the sixth court where the house special is skinning sinners alive and sawing them in half."

At least the bastard's reliable, Meko thought, and she crept to the family altar in the front room of the house, lit three sticks of incense, and prayed with the shaky hope of a gypsy who had just spent her last dollar on a lottery ticket. Meko started balling and began to hatch a plan to ax her date with Curtis. The smell of the burning incense awoke her grandmother. The old woman with cropped gray hair and a wise face shaped like the moon soon appeared and knelt down in front of the altar next to the girl.

"New boy?"

Meko nodded.

"Let's see your feet."

"My feet?"

"You've been running away from life since you were fourteen. They must be so tired."

Meko cried harder and wrapped her arms tightly around her grandmother.

The old woman leaned back, rested her hands upon Meko's shoulders and said, "I've heard you speak to some of your suitors on the telephone. You can't just throw yourself at a man. It chases them off. On a first date you drop your pants as if they were on fire, don't you?"

"Grandma!" Meko whispered loudly.

"Oh, I know—"

"I'm a slut."

"Nearly bona fide."

"You're right. I'm a runner, too."

"You give it away like free rides at a carnival. You've got boys licking their lips with a sign on your forehead that reads 'human blow up doll' or some nonsense."

Meko's mouth opened to the shape of the letter *O*.

"You're a lion tamer without a whip."

Meko clenched her hands together. "You're right."

"Quit the carnival kid. Let it leave town without you."

"Then I'll be alone."

"You're not your blown kidneys."

Meko began to whimper.

"You're a wonderful, effervescent girl who has a medical problem; and any young man that can't see past the hole in your wrist is too damn dumb to be bothered with. Know what you need to find that's more important than any man?"

"A suitcase full of money?"

The old woman ignored the remark, stuck her chin out and said, "A passion."

"A hobby?"

"God, I detest that word," the old woman moaned. "Hobbies are for old men with hemorrhoids and rice pudding in their arteries."

Meko giggled weakly.

"Like your brother and his comic drawing. You must find something that sets your soul ablaze, something that you do for yourself. It'll fill that hole in your wrist, sweetie."

"And when you were young?"

"Oh, I had no time for any passion when I was a child. At age eight I was helping my mother cook dinner for our family and working in the fields next to my folks six days a week. Girls didn't go to school back then. We weren't important enough for that. Later on, you know, cooking became my passion."

"We love your traditional recipes."

"Hey, how about—"

"Cooking?"

"You've always enjoyed helping your mother and me in the kitchen. Just think how fun it would be to be chef for the President or a saucier at a five-star hotel."

"A chef for the President?"

"Dream big, girl. Why the hell not? Or maybe start your own place. Whatever it is kid, find something you really love."

Meko smiled. "Thanks for the ideas. I'll think about it."

The pair knelt in silence for a long moment.

"Something else is fluttering around in your head."

Meko continued to look away in silence.

"What?"

"Nothing."

"Tell me, child."

"My vagina's too big."

"Too big for what?" The old woman tried not to laugh.

"You know."

"I'll go fetch my sewing kit."

"Grandma!"

"Fashion magazines, again?" The old woman shook her head in disgust.

The sheepish look on Meko's face gave it away.

"Is that where you also got the idea that dousing yourself with enough perfume to gag a water buffalo would attract the right kind of man? Easy on that stuff. I bet you gave your last date a nose bleed."

Meko sniveled and let out a weak laugh.

The old woman gently placed her hand under Meko's chin, lifted it up, looked into her eyes and said, "Your vagina's not too big. Say it."

"My vagina's not too big."

"Again."

"My vagina's not too big."

"Now that we have your plumbing figured out, let's focus on your date. You are courageous. You will be courageous. And I'm so proud of you. What are you kids going to do?"

"We talked about going to a KTV."

"Whatever you do, try to enjoy it. The sunrises are counting down."

"I know."

"Go slow, hot rod girl," the old woman warned with a reassuring smile. "Be strong with this one, and keep your panties on and see what happens."

Meko lied awake after she went to bed and told herself that no matter what happened tomorrow she wasn't going to be afraid anymore. She finally fell asleep at three in the morning.

At nine the next evening Meko changed into a pair of skin-tight designer jeans, flip-flops, and a long-sleeved maroon silk blouse. She walked out of her room, which occupied the right wing of the san-ho yuan, crossed the courtyard, and entered the front door of the house.

"Mom," Meko called out as she walked past the family altar to an open door leading to the kitchen.

"In here, angel," her mother cooed.

Meko stopped and stood inside the kitchen doorway. Her mother, a genteel woman of fifty-eight, was standing near the sink preparing tea. She wore a traditional blue flower print dress. Meko couldn't ever remember not seeing her mother in a dress.

Her mother quickly turned her head toward Meko and asked politely, "Tea before you go?"

Meko's father, who was sitting at the kitchen table behind a bowl of cut papaya, looked up over his newspaper momentarily, and then he quickly descended back down under the sports page.

"Sure," Meko said. She sat down across from the renowned mathematics professor.

Meko's mother carried a handmade ceramic tea pot over to the table, refilled her husband's small cup, and then poured Meko a cup and sat down next to her. Meko's father carefully folded the paper up and put it down on the chair next to him. He placed both hands on the table, held his head high, and slowly inspected his wife and daughter with the discerning eye of a king. He wore a short-sleeve white dress shirt with plenty of starch, a conservative brown tie with dark yellow stripes, and dark brown slacks cut out of plywood.

He cast his supreme gaze down upon his daughter, and said

with the blunt authority of a courthouse judge, "Your mother tells me you have a momentous date tonight. Something epic, that no doubt will prove to be terribly historical; requiring an extra coat of whatever it is you pretty up your face with."

"It's called rouge, dear," Meko's mother meekly lectured.

"Well, young lady?" he said, and picked up the folded newspaper and made a shooing gesture toward his wife.

A nervous smile appeared on the mother's face. She grabbed Meko's hand, smiled at her and said, "Yes, yes she does dear. And Meko thinks he's a very fine—"

"What does Mr. Very Fine do for a living?" he asked, and picked up a toothpick, jabbed a piece of papaya and ate it. "May I be so presumptuous and assume he's an upstanding professional of some sort or other?"

"He's studying at university," said Meko.

Her father took a sip of tea, raised his eyebrows and asked with a slight suspicion, "A younger man? A younger man with no vocation?"

"They're not getting married, dear," her mother said gently.

"He's a few years younger," said Meko.

"How many?"

"Four, or maybe five," Meko said, her voice trailing off into a whisper.

"And his qualities?"

"Qualities?"

"I'm naturally assuming Mr. Very Fine is benevolent, chivalrous, and honorable?"

"Oh, naturally."

"I want you to promise your mother and me that you'll do one thing tonight on this *date*," said her father.

"What's that?"

A little smile crept onto her father's face, and he said, "Have a good time with Mr. Very Fine."

Meko's mother exhaled and smiled, let go of her daughter's hand, and began straightening up the table.

Meko stood up and said, "Thanks, I will," and she said goodbye and walked toward the front door.

Her grandmother was waiting on the front porch. The old woman gave her a big hug, and whispered into her ear, "Pretend tonight's the last night of your life."

"Okay Grandma, I'll try," she said and walked to her bicycle.

A fifty-cent moon the color of a perfectly toasted marshmallow followed Meko as she pedaled boldly down Tainan's Cheng Gong Road toward Curtis's 7-Eleven.

Her grandmother's words echoed and Meko smiled and repeated, "You can do it," over and over.

The kitschy orange and green 7-Eleven sign appeared a kilometer further down. Meko parked her bike next to the front door and walked inside. She noticed that the store was empty of people, which was strange because Taiwan's urban areas swarmed day and night.

"Curtis," she called out. "Curtis!" No one answered.

Meko heard the faint sound of a trumpet playing a slow rendition of "Skylark" as she neared the front counter. The music invited her through an open door behind the cash register. She walked through the storage room and through a door leading outside, and came upon a grandiose banyan tree standing in the center of a small grassy area. Exposed roots at the base of the tree's gnarled and twisted trunk reached out several meters in all directions like the reposing tentacles of a fantastic sea creature. A well-crafted wooden bench sat in front of the tree, and a lone street lamp off to the right cast its warm, muted light upon the scene.

Curtis didn't notice Meko as he sat on the bench playing his sad tune. He wore a Panama hat with a black band, blue jeans, and an orange 7-Eleven vest over a black T-shirt. Meko looked with astonishment at an enormous pink-and-gray-patched pig that stood fifteen feet in front of him. It remained very still as he played, with only its ears wiggling occasionally. Meko moved toward Curtis like a starlet gliding down the red carpet at the Golden Horse Film Awards, and thought he had the same honest face and innocent eyes that dazzled her at the hospital. Curtis stopped playing, delicately set the trumpet down in its case and looked slowly over at Meko.

"They're gonna kill her next week," he said quietly, and he turned his gaze back toward the pig.

"Who is?"

"The owners."

"Oh?"

"A temple ritual for Ghost Month. Choo Choo's tame. See how beautiful and clean she is. They don't mind if I let her out as long as I take her back and lock her up."

"I've never seen a pig in the city," said Meko. "I liked the song, too. You play very well."

Curtis picked up the trumpet, held it tenderly against his cheek, and said proudly, "This was my grandfather's trumpet before he gave it to me."

"I spoke with him at the hospital," she giggled. "He's so sweet and so funny."

Curtis rolled his eyes and said, "He's half son of a bitch and half meteor shower—just kidding."

Meko chuckled and asked, "How long have you been playing to Choo Choo?"

"Since last year when I started working here and going to university."

Meko smiled regally and sat down on the bench several feet away from Curtis. She looked down at her cuff and saw that it was covering her catheter port. She rolled up both sleeves to her elbows, rested her hands palms up on her thighs, and with a poised look asked, "What are you studying?"

Curtis caught himself staring at her catheter, and then he quickly looked up and pressed the trumpet against his cheek again.

"Music major?" asked Meko, and she slid a little closer to Curtis, who continued to gawk at the hole in her wrist.

"I have kidney disease," she said plainly.

"Really?" Curtis said, and looked away with embarrassment.

"I need to have dialysis treatments three times a week at the hospital where I work." She arched her brow and studied the young man's face for a reaction.

"Sounds tough."

"Oh, not really. After treatments I feel the same way as when I made the mistake of watching *Baloney Ranch*."

"How's that?"

"Headaches and nausea, followed by profuse vomiting."

Curtis laughed and said, "That's so cool you can laugh about it." He paused, and said sheepishly, "I'm a diabetic, but I wasn't going to tell you yet."

"Really!" That's uh . . . that's so weird that we both have a special problem." They laughed nervously. Meko couldn't wait to tell her grandmother.

Meko looked at Curtis with compassion and said softly, "It must be difficult having diabetes."

He looked down bashfully and said, "My grandfather always tells me we all have marks, but don't go using it as an excuse to not do anything with your life."

"Sounds like my grandmother."

After a prolonged, awkward silence, the ghost of Marcel Marceau appeared behind them. With a bored expression, Marcel placed one hand under his chin and mimed "a man masturbating" with the other.

"Uh, so what do you like to do?" Curtis finally asked. Marcel wiped his brow in relief, smiled, and mimed the climax. Then he did a few cartwheels and disappeared.

"When I'm not shopping?" giggled Meko.

"Taiwan's national pastime."

"Right. I like to hang out with my friends and go to movies. I love going to hot pot restaurants, and I absolutely love seafood." Meko covered her mouth with her hands and wailed, "Oh god, I sound like some stupid personal ad!"

Curtis cleared his throat, stuck out his chest and expounded, "I'm a straight nineteen-year-old single male co-ed majoring in something that's going to get me a really good job and a big house and I possess a love for stray dogs and farting in elevators and pray for world peace. Please, no fatsos." They both laughed.

Meko curiously studied the trumpet and said, "You're so lucky to have a passion. I need to find something like that, too.

Do you hope to play professionally someday?"

Curtis rubbed the top of Choo Choo's head and said, "Yes, and I think I want to be a mango farmer, too, like my grandfather. My aunt isn't too crazy about either of my career choices. She says I should get a solid career, whatever the hell that means."

"And your parents?"

Curtis turned cold as a hearse driver's delivery list. "They passed away when I was young," he whispered. "I've lived with my aunt ever since."

"I'm sorry."

"Thanks," he said and fondly studied the pig. "I can't let Choo Choo die. She's kept me company on many lonely nights working graveyards. She can dance, too. Watch!"

Curtis began playing an up-tempo version of the famous Cuban folk song "Guantanamera." The pig wiggled its ears, snorted, and began slowly shuffling from side to side, three feet to the right, then three feet to the left and back again.

"Oh, I know this one!" shouted Meko.

"Go dance with her!" urged Curtis. "She won't mind!"

Meko stood up, hurried over and followed the dancing pig's lead.

"Oh my god!" shouted Meko with glee. "I'm dancing with a pig! She really can dance!"

When the song ended Curtis said, "Do you want to learn the words? It's a beautiful tune."

"Okay!"

"You follow me, okay."

Meko followed Curtis line by line as he sang the lyrics:

I am an honest man

From where the palm tree grows

And before dying I want

To share the verses of my soul

Girl from Guantanamera, dance, girl from Guantanamera

"That's Choo Choo's favorite song," Curtis said. "That's the first verse. If you want, I can teach you the rest some other time."

"Okay," said Meko.

Choo Choo ambled over and snuggled up against Curtis's leg. Meko looked up through the tree's majestic canopy of large waxy leaves and grinned.

Noticing her smile, Curtis said, "I like just being near this tree. Sometimes when no one is around, I run my hands along the trunk. I know some people might think that's strange." He looked at her sideways. "Do you?"

Meko shook her head, still smiling. "My grandfather does that sometimes to our papaya trees," she said. "He thinks it gives him strength. Why do you do it?"

"I can't get out of the city as much as I'd like, and it makes me feel connected to nature, to the earth, to touch something so beautiful that has lived so long. I really need that feeling."

"Uh-huh."

"Hey, do you still feel like going to the KTV? My replacement should be here any minute."

"Sure."

"What about Choo Choo?"

"I'll take her back home when Chung gets here."

"I mean, what are you going to do about Choo Choo and the people who plan to sacrifice her?"

"I don't know," said Curtis, and he set the trumpet in its case and closed it. "She just loves sweet potatoes, watch." Curtis picked up a plastic bag beside him, pulled out a baked sweet potato, and held it in front of Choo Choo. The pig quickly gobbled it up.

Curtis rubbed the pig's head and ears and asked, "Want to try?" He pulled another potato out of the bag and handed it to Meko. She giggled excitedly and gently shoved the potato into Choo Choo's open mouth.

Curtis's replacement Chung popped his bushy head out of the back door of the 7-Eleven and said, "Hey, its okay. I'm here."

Curtis stood up and said, "You wait here, okay. It'll only take five minutes to take Choo Choo home and lock her up."

"Okay," said Meko, and she smiled and chuckled as she watched the pig follow Curtis down the street.

Meko felt victorious about the way she spilled to Curtis about her kidney beans as the pair rode through the hectic streets of Tainan City. Curtis turned onto Chengkung Road, pulled over and parked across the street from a monstrous Holiday KTV building with its flashing orange and white sign. Inside, fifty private karaoke party rooms were rocking with drunken, crooning guests. Meko felt capricious as a high school girl on a first date. Curtis gently took her by the hand, and they walked across the boulevard and into the crowded KTV lobby.

Yellow Boy came bouncing up to the couple from across the wide tile reception area, outstretched his arms and wailed with laughter, "Hello, hello." He noticed Meko's rolled up sleeves exposing her catheter port. It inspired him, and he grinned like a cat perched on a barrel of sea bass. "Its 'Queer Night,' we get half off," he laughed, and was shocked he said it.

Curtis gave him a ten cent smile. Meko felt his apprehension, squeezed his hand tighter, and said, "He's just having some fun, aren't you darling?" She winked at her brother.

Yellow Boy looked earnestly into Curtis's eyes and asked, "How's your grandfather doing?"

"Ornery as ever, and scared."

"I'm sure you know his surgery is scheduled for next Tuesday."

"Uh-huh."

"My friends call me Yellow Boy, by the way."

"I'm Curtis."

"Oh, I know. Meko told me. Come on," said Yellow Boy, and he headed toward a wall of elevators. He turned his head and said, "I've booked us a nice room. The others are already there."

They got off on the twelfth floor, walked through a maze of hallways bulging with private karaoke rooms, and entered a plush, dimly lit room with ten young people lounging on black vinyl sofas around the perimeter. They were watching and listening to a sexy, braless young woman in a black T-top and tight white shorts, who was standing alone in the middle of the room singing a Taiwanese pop song into a microphone. In front of her, taking up the entire wall, the bold white lyrics floated across a giant plasma karaoke screen swirling with psychedelic patterns and mountain scenery.

"That's Tiki," Meko said into Curtis's ear. "She's one of the nurses in our department."

Two young women chirped with excitement, sprung off the couch, and bounded over to Meko and Curtis. The women also took notice of Meko's exposed catheter. They knew about Meko's condition, but like her brother, had never seen her show her bare arms in public.

"Curtis, these are my friends Melody and Cherry," said Meko. "I've known them since high school." The women smiled and exchanged hellos with Curtis.

Tiki finished her song and handed the microphone to one of Yellow Boy's colleagues, a heart surgeon from the hospital. He walked to the right side of the room and began to scroll through the immense song selection on a flat screen computer mounted on a stand.

Yellow Boy cupped a hand around his mouth and yelled toward his friend, "In the Philippines six people have been murdered this year for singing Sinatra's 'My Way.'"

"Really?" his colleague purred into the microphone.

"Yeah, they got shot by irate neighbors living next to karaoke clubs—driven insane by all the bad singers constantly singing that song."

The heart doc flashed Yellow Boy a devilish smiled as the opening bars of "My Way" began to blast through the sound system. He sang, "And now, the end is here, and so I face the . . ." Everybody laughed.

Curtis turned to Meko and asked, "Are all of these people from the hospital?"

"Half. The rest are my friends."

"They want to check me out, huh?" said Curtis.

Meko smiled. "Of course. My brother and my friends are very protective, so watch out." She laughed.

"I guess I shouldn't have brought the roofies," Curtis said with a straight face.

Meko smiled and punched him on the arm a few times. Curtis laughed and rubbed his arm pretending he was in pain.

There was a loud knock on the door. It quickly opened, and two staff members, a young woman and a man dressed in white dress shirts, red ties, and black pants, quickly wheeled in a cart full of stir-fry dishes, Taiwan Beer, and soda. They unloaded the spread onto a coffee table that sat in front of one of the sofas. Curtis, Meko, and Yellow Boy sat down together, joining others who were already munching on the dishes.

Yellow Boy opened a can of Taiwan Beer, poured it into a glass of ice, dropped a dried plum into it for sweetness, took a big swallow, and asked Curtis, "Would you like a beer?" He picked up another can and held it out toward Curtis.

"No thanks. I'm a diabetic."

"Oh, really?" said Yellow Boy with surprise.

"On rare occasions I'll drink one beer, but I have to have food first."

"How about a soda, then?" asked Meko.

"Sure, a Coke sounds good."

Meko stood up and walked over to the drink table.

Yellow Boy's colleague began an encore of "My Way," and everybody roared. Curtis walked to the bathroom at the rear of the room to give himself an insulin injection. Meko sat down next to her brother and set the Cokes on the table.

Yellow Boy looked at her bare arms, smiled gleefully and said, "Congratulations!"

Meko grinned and took a sip of Coke.

"What compelled you to be so brave tonight?" he asked excitedly. "Whatever it is, can you rub some of it off on a hopeless pillow biter?"

Meko laughed, looked at her brother with peaceful eyes and said, "Grandma helped. I just got tired of hiding, and of letting my kidney problem ruin my life."

"I'm tired of hiding, too." Yellow Boy looked across the room at his colleagues.

"Pretend today is the last day of your life," Meko said, repeating her grandmother's words. "How do you want to live it?"

A wild and mischievous look appeared on Yellow Boy's face. He looked around at the faces in the room, stood up, walked over and gently grabbed the microphone away from his colleague, faced the small crowd and finished the last few lines of "My Way." Curtis stepped out of the head, stood at the back of the room, and watched the jittering doctor onstage.

When the song ended Yellow Boy smiled meekly and said into the microphone, "I uh, want you to know that I've enjoyed working with you so much. You've truly enriched my life. And Meko's friends, you guys are aces, and I really appreciate the way you've looked after my little sister. I know you probably won't understand why I'm telling you this tonight, up here blabbering like an idiot." Then he hesitated, took a deep breath, and said, "I'm gay."

The room went completely silent. Mouths hung open.

Meko's eyes became teary and she whispered, "Oh my god! Oh my god!" and she looked across the room at her brother's colleague's faces. She stood up and ran to Yellow Boy, put her arms around him, and squeezed until closet door hinge rust and confetti shot out his ears.

Curtis looked on intensely, and was struck by the affection and compassion Meko showed her brother. He was falling for a girl for the first time, and unknown to him, a tsunami brewed in the "Sea of Love" while he innocently frolicked on the beach looking for sand dollars with his trousers rolled up to his knees.

The heart surgeon, who had been singing "My Way" moments earlier, stood up, raised his beer glass and shouted, "A toast to the best eye gouger this side of the Taiwan Strait!"

Everybody stood up shouting "congratulations" and "that a boy," and they gathered around Yellow Boy, tears streaming down his cheeks.

"I'm only half out," Yellow Boy sobbed softly into Meko's ear. "I'm still mortified to tell Mom and Dad."

Meko held her arm around Yellow Boy and said, "I'm so proud of you big brother. Tonight we celebrate you, and how cool and wonderful you are."

As Curtis rushed the stage his eyes cut out Meko's outline and pasted it on his wall next to pictures of his parents and

Derek Jeter. He thought about the tender way Meko had treated his ornery grandfather, and the way she was so confident and forthcoming when talking about her kidney problem. Without warning, the "Sea of Love's" colossal tide crashed onto the beach and broke through the seawall, dragging Curtis far from shore. He didn't have a chance.

Five minutes later someone started playing "My Way," and everyone whooped with laughter and sang along with Yellow Boy. The singing and drinking went on until four in the morning. Meko and Curtis slid out around two.

"Want a coffin sandwich?" Meko asked with a sly smile and hopped on the Yamaha behind Curtis.

"Do you?" asked Curtis, spitting out beach sand with vines of seaweed tangled around his torso.

"Some say it's an aphrodisiac."

"An aphrodisiac?"

"I know another place that serves deer penis topped with whipped cream."

"Really?"

"No silly," she laughed.

"I could go for a coffin."

Ten minutes later they arrived at the Chihkan Coffin Sandwich restaurant on Jhongjeng Road and ordered two coffins to-go. The coffin, a local favorite, is a thick slice of toasted hollow bread with a hinged top filled with seafood chowder. The couple arrived at Curtis's 7-Eleven a short time later.

"Do you want to sit for a little while under the banyan tree?" asked Curtis, and he took a bite out of his casket.

"Sure."

They walked behind the 7-Eleven and sat on the bench under the voluptuous banyan tree. Curtis, still squirming in his seaweed overcoat, trembled in the batter's box. He'd been down to first base a few times, but that was back in the minors. Several terrible minutes passed. Meko grew tired of waiting for him to take the bat off his shoulder; she leaned in and tossed the boy a slow ball. He hit a nubber up the first baseline. For the next few innings Meko gave his tongue a workout and taught him how to steal second. Meko floated home on her bicycle. It was the first time she hadn't dropped her pants on the first date since high school. She went to sleep feeling like she'd won a small victory.

Curtis phoned Meko two days later, and they agreed to meet under the banyan tree at 7:00 p. m. on Saturday. At six the night of, as Meko sat at her vanity, the spray coat of moxie she'd worn on their first date began to flake off like dime store fingernail polish. She grasped for the fleeting voices of spontaneity and confidence, but they'd become faint and distant, like the cries of workers buried in a Chinese coal mine.

"Damn it!" Meko muttered in frustration, glared in the mirror, grabbed her hair, and began giving herself a Friar Tuck. She winced at her small breasts and eyed her padded push-up bra hanging from a drawer. She looked down at her catheter, furiously shook her head and whimpered, "Why am I so fucked up? Why? Why?"

Meko grew increasingly anxious, and decided to call Curtis and feed him a white lie to bail on their date. As she reached for her phone the familiar rumbling sound of a motorcycle made her jump—instantly transporting her to the derelict streets of her private internment camp.

"Curtis?! Oh shit!" she shrieked. "Oh fuck!"

Bogeymen cackled and called to her while they played Big Deuce in the shadows. Meko's nerves were a cat tiptoeing on a nearby electric fence. Someone threw the switch. The cat screamed above the rattle and thunder of a funeral dirge. Meko hastily powdered her nose with a sparring glove, sprung out of her chair, and frantically threw on the loaded bra and a shirt. She made sure her shirt sleeve covered her catheter, cracked the door open, peeked into the courtyard, and let out a panic-stricken gasp as Curtis sat at ease on his motorcycle twenty feet in front of her wearing his newly tailored seaweed overcoat speckled with beach sand. It fit like a ten year old playing dress up with his pop's wardrobe. Choo Choo stood up on the side-car's seat and threw her front legs over the side.

"Hallo!" Curtis said with a big smile.

Meko took a deep breath, flung the door open, ran to Curtis and exclaimed with phony sincerity, "Oh my god! You're here and you've got Choo Choo! My brother gave you my address, didn't he?"

"Yeah. I wanted to surprise you."

"Uh huh," Meko said with a half-assed smile, and then she glanced toward the front door and whispered loudly, "My parents are home! Park your bike around the side of the house next to the papaya trees and wait for me."

"Okay," Curtis said. Once parked, he took a six foot piece of rope that was fastened around Choo Choo's neck, tied it to the sidecar, and waited.

Ten minutes later Meko came stumbling around the side of the house like she was trying to outrun a falling cypress— a Harpy perched on each shoulder; the soles of her shoes caked with pigeon droppings from a thirtieth-story window ledge. Curtis didn't notice. He was too busy fiddling with the starfish boutonnière on his lapel.

"Come on!" whispered Curtis. Meko climbed on the motorcycle feeling light-hearted as a rubber room. "Hold on tight," he said, and Meko wrapped her arms around Curtis's thin waist and leaned her head against his shoulder. He hit the throttle, and the motorcycle roared around the side of the house, past the courtyard, and south on Highway 17 toward the Tainan County countryside.

"Are we kidnappers?!" yelled Meko above the thunder of the motorcycle and the traffic.

"I am!"

"Did you try talking with Choo Choo's owner?!"

"They're not the talking type. You can say I kidnapped you, too."

Meko spewed a fake laugh that trickled down her leg and onto the pavement, taking her grandmother's words of wisdom along with it. She cursed herself for failing to deliver the white lie and asked, "Uh, where are we going?"

"To my favorite place," said Curtis.

"Where?"

Curtis pretended not to hear the question, and laughed boyishly as they drove past betel nut stands and gas stations at the city's outskirts.

"You're not going to tell me?!" asked Meko. The cat on the electric fence bleated.

"Nope!"

Meko thought about feigning ill and asking Curtis to take her home. But she'd frozen up, and had become stiff as a Badouzi skipjack deep-throating a winch cable. Thirty minutes later they entered the plush rice and vegetable fields of Kaohsiung County. Curtis turned off on a narrow farm road and continued south toward Gangshan Township, where hectares of fluorescent green rice fields ready for harvesting spread to the horizon.

"The sunset!" Meko shouted with mock sincerity that Curtis continued not to pick up on. "It's so red! Like a painting."

Meko was no match for the relentless Harpies, and she knew it. The bastards had her balled up about everything—her hair and makeup, her age, the size of her vagina, if she remembered to bring condoms; and a list long enough to fill a shrink's notepad. So Meko did what she'd always done to fend off the Harpies, she summoned her darker self—her old standby the *huli jing*, and told the spicy jade to stay close.

Curtis pulled over and parked on the side of a lonely country road west of Ciatou Township beside a grove of empyrean coconut palms.

"My grandfather brought me here five years ago."

"Oh?" Meko said indifferently, and looked up at the tree's fan-like fronds swaying in the breezy onset of dusk.

"I come here often. I can meditate on this grove for hours. It's profound."

Meko looked at the palms as Choo Choo hopped out. Curtis pulled two sweet potatoes out of a bag under the sidecar's seat and tossed them on the ground. She wiggled her ears and gobbled them up.

"They should be coming soon," said Curtis.

"Who?" asked Meko, and she got off the Yamaha and took

a few steps toward the palms.

"The egrets. They roost here at night. Hundreds of them."

Meko continued to look at the palm grove, and then she clumsily turned around and asked timidly, "Profound. Why is this grove so profound?"

"It's a feeling. My grandfather told me I needed to learn how to *see*. When I'm out here I can see beyond our materialistic world. I think that's what he meant."

"Really?" Meko asked meekly as the cat hung up on the electric fence continued to wail. Meko called to the huli jing, who vaunted over like the Rio Carnival. Her vagina began to tingle. "It makes me feel horny," Meko crooned daringly and waited for the boy's reaction.

"What?" mumbled Curtis. He looked away in embarrassment.

"Oh, nothing," Meko sighed light-heartedly and rolled up her shirt sleeves. The huli jing had taken her over completely, giving her the pluck of a she-wolf. Meko chuckled to herself as she became more aroused by the boy's naiveté, strutted to the motorcycle, reached into the bag and threw Choo Choo a few more sweet potatoes.

Soon several groups of the large white birds appeared, circling above the grove in swooping arcs, and then casually landing in the tops of the palms. More groups came and landed soon thereafter, and a loud racket ensued.

"I wish I could own a grove like this," sighed Curtis, and he leaned back on the seat and folded his arms across his chest.

"Uh-huh, sure," said Meko, and she wondered why Curtis hadn't dragged her out into the middle of the grove, tore her clothes off and fucked her up against one of the palms—every other guy she'd dated would've. "Isn't that why he brought me out here?" she whispered under her breath.

"Let's go," said Curtis, and he kicked the engine over. "I want to get to our destination before dark."

Meko took several lofty strides toward the grove and picked out a tilted palm with a fat trunk. She leaned against it, stuck her shapely ass in the air, and looked over her shoulder at Curtis. He waved her over. Meko crossed her arms in frustration, turned around, and haltingly walked back to the motorcycle. The pair and the pig headed further into the Ciatou countryside. A short while later Curtis pulled off the main road onto the narrow dirt road that ran along the length of his grandfather's mango orchard. Curtis followed the road as it veered left at the end of the orchard. The san-ho yuan soon appeared, glowing in the twilight like a sanguine jewel. He pulled over and parked in front of the house. Choo Choo immediately jumped out and began foraging in the short grass at the edge of the orchard.

"What is this place?" asked Meko, still wet and dizzy from the palm grove.

"My grandfather's."

The words startled Meko. She shooed the huli jing away, who giggled wickedly and strutted around the motorcycle a few times; and then she slowly paraded down the road, stopped thirty feet away, spun around and crossed her arms defiantly.

"Choo Choo?" Meko said feebly, becoming more nervous as the Harpies returned. She didn't want to see the old man, as she was certain he could smell the huli jing a kilometer away. "Does your grandfather know about Choo Choo?" she asked restlessly as she watched the pig move unhurriedly through the orchard.

"Come on," Curtis said gently. He grabbed Meko by the hand and they walked toward the house.

"Did you, uh—"

"Tell him?" said Curtis. "Not yet."

Meko thought again about Curtis's grandfather. Even though they had only met twice, she knew he was tough and no nonsense. "Uh, oh!" she whispered dreadfully under her breath, knowing both her and Curtis were on the firing line.

Curtis turned his head and said, "I'll ease it on him."

Meko wondered why he'd brought a stolen dancing pig on their second date, and thought that he was reckless as hell—wonderfully reckless. But, that's what she liked about him, besides his boyishness. The aroma of baked sweet potatoes overtook the couple.

"Oh, smell those sweet potatoes!" shouted Curtis and he excitedly strode a few steps in front of Meko, who shrugged and pursed her lips into a smile that was radiant as a Shanghai dust storm.

The leathery old man was sitting in a rocking chair on the porch with a white gauze bandage covering his left eye. He was in the middle of grabbing a pack of Long Life cigarettes from his shirt pocket.

"Hello, Grandfather," said Curtis as they walked up to the old man.

"Hello, boy," the old man grunted. He stuck a butt between his dry lips and lit it.

"You know Meko," said Curtis, feeling a little jumpy, as he'd never brought a girl to his grandfather's.

"Of course I do, you damn idiot," the old man brayed, and he turned and winked at Meko. "She's my personal nurse; and the best damn nurse over there. Welcome, little sister. Sit, please."

The couple sat down in creaky wooden chairs next to the old man. He grimaced slightly as he noticed the catheter port in Meko's wrist for the first time, and remembered a friend's wife in town who also had a hole in her wrist—she didn't make it to forty.

Meko had observed the old man's discovery, quickly rolled her sleeves down and asked, "How are you feeling Mr. Lee?" and she cooled down a few centigrade slipping into the role of the dutiful nurse.

"The verdict's still out," said the old man, and he reached up and lightly touched the patch over his eye. "I'm counting on your brother."

"He thinks the surgery went quite well," Meko said tenderly. "Have you been changing your dressing every day?"

"Every night."

"And have you followed the doctor's instructions and kept your eye closed at all times when changing the dressing?"

"Yes, but it isn't easy. I'm anxious for a test run."

"I know but—"

"I have to let the eye heal."

"Yes."

The old man scowled at Curtis, shook his head from side to side, and asked, "Is this bum, this boy behaving himself?"

"Uh, most of the time," Meko laughed awkwardly, trying to conceal her shame. She looked out toward Curtis's motorcycle. The huli jing pointed at Meko and snickered, and then she lifted her skirt and spun around.

The old man fidgeted in his chair.

"Your body language is talking to me," Curtis said. "What happened?"

The old man let out a long wheezing breath. "Oh, some fool from the Kuomintang Party came by today trying to bribe me."

"Again?"

"They'll never buy my vote, not in a million years."

"Why don't you put up a sign?"

"Why don't I buy an attack dog?" growled the old man.

Meko and Curtis laughed.

The old man smiled at Meko and said, "Little sister, I would like to speak with my grandson in private for a few minutes."

"Oh sure," said Meko, and she stood up and walked toward the orchard. "The whip's going to come down on Curtis now," she whispered to herself. Then Meko frowned and looked down the dirt road and nodded to the huli jing, who was puffing on a Hav-A-Tampa and snapping her garters. Meko looked back toward the house at the old man and Curtis, who appeared much younger as he braced for his scolding. Guilt kicked Meko in the rear so hard it knocked a tooth loose. She shook her head and thought she was the biggest chicken and fraud in the world.

The old man gave Curtis a look from the South Pole. "The pig?" he asked.

"How do you know about that?"

"I bought her yesterday. She's mine, snout to ass."

"What?"

"I ought to slit her throat in front of you and have a barbecue."

Curtis's eyed widened with alarm.

"Stealing is stealing, boy, even for a good reason."

Curtis looked down at his feet and muttered, "I'm sorry for disappointing you, Grandfather. I was wrong."

"You bet you were wrong! And never mind how I found out. Didn't you learn anything here, you damn idiot?"

"But I . . . oh, auntie told you?"

"Buts are for assholes," said the old man. He reached into his pants pocket, pulled out a white envelope, and handed it to him.

"What's this?" asked Curtis, and he quickly opened the envelope and thumbed through a modest stack of blue one-thousand-dollar NT notes.

"You owe me two hundred hours in the sun, boy, for the pig, starting next week when you're not working at the candy store. You can work alongside of the dipshit. I'll tie you sons a bitches together like a chain gang." He coughed. "You're going to get the Ching Dynasty treatment this time."

"What's that?"

"Something very bad."

Curtis tightened his lips and looked at the old man sorrowfully.

"Get your thieving ass over to the owner's tomorrow morning and give them all of the money. They're expecting you. You better do it on your knees. You stay in school, boy," the old man said, and he stood up and took several steps out into the courtyard toward the orchard and gazed tenderly and proudly at the strong slender boughs swaying in the cool evening breeze. He spun back around and barked, "Just what the hell was going through your feeble mind when you hijacked that swine and brought her out here?"

"I don't know," Curtis said weakly.

"You're even a crummy thief!" The old man raised his hands into the air in frustration. "You didn't have a plan? Well, you better learn to see farther than your nose if you ever want to make it in life." The old man waved his hand at the boy in disgust and said, "Well, go ahead and call for your sweetheart before she wises up and runs off with one of the neighbor boys. I'm done with you for now."

"Choo Choo!" Curtis called out. "Choo Choo!"

He waved Meko over, and as she walked toward the house

guilt let her have it in the backside one last time. The cat on the electric fence shrieked louder. White smoke rose off its body and across the sky above Meko's internment camp forming into silhouettes of a bottle of Absolut and a bottle of aspirin.

"Choo Choo!" Curtis called out again. "Come on lazy!" The pig ambled out of the orchard, ran through the courtyard past Meko, and sidled up to Curtis.

"Oh my god!" cried the old man. He took a drag off the cigarette. "It'd take me a whole year to eat that."

"Grandfather!"

"I'm only kidding," said the old man with a demure glance at Meko as she approached the porch. "I suppose I'll keep the porker if she doesn't cause too much trouble."

"Oh, yeah!" said Curtis. He patted his grandfather on the back.

"What's so special about the pig, anyway?" asked the old man. He sat back down in his chair and popped a betel nut into his mouth.

"She can dance!" shouted Meko, faking to be excited.

"Oh, I'm barbecuing her for sure tomorrow morning," grunted the old man. "There'll be sweet smoke for miles around."

"She really can," said Curtis. "I'll show you some other time, and I'll have you dancing right along with her."

"I'll dance with the pig if she wants me to," the old man said dryly, and he stood up and asked, "how about right now? I'm in the mood to make a fool out of myself."

"Okay, sure," Curtis said. He stood up, trotted out to the motorcycle, retrieved his trumpet, and quickly returned.

The old man walked out into the courtyard and stood next to the pig. She playfully rubbed her fat head against his leg.

"She's making a pass at me," bawled the old man. Curtis laughed, and Meko pretended to.

Meko stood next to Curtis on the porch, put a hand on his shoulder, forced a smile and looked out toward the old man and the pig. Curtis began to play an old Taiwanese tune that he knew was one of his grandfather's favorites. He'd been practicing it for a few weeks, trying to perfect it to surprise the old man.

The old man looked down at Choo Choo, and she shuffled

several steps to her left then back again. He grinned and yipped with delight, and began shuffling his feet from side to side trying to keep in step with the pig. The old man raised his arms in the air, spun around, did a pirouette, bowed, and outstretched his arms. Meko tittered girlishly as she studied the old man with fascination, surprised by his athleticism and graceful movements. His spontaneity and free-spirited nature had a narcotic effect on Meko. But she knew from experience that the feelings of serenity would last about as long as his three minute jig, and that the Harpies would soon return.

When Curtis finished the tune a few minutes later, the old man marched proudly to the porch, plopped down in his chair, shook his head and said with a chuckle, "She can stay." He was pleased with his grandson's song choice, and the way he played it, but said nothing as he wanted to keep Curtis in the doghouse. The couple sat down next to the old man. Choo Choo lied down on the porch next to the old man and rested her head on his foot.

"She's smart," barked the old man. "She knows who the big dog is." The old man looked at Curtis and said, "Don't miss it, boy."

"Yeah, okay," Curtis replied. The smile they shared seemed to Meko to hold a secret significance.

The old man winked at Meko, stood up, and said to Curtis, "Go into the orchard and fetch Milkshake. He's working the Irwin. Tell him to get his rear end up to the house and get cleaned up for supper, and no funny business." Curtis ran through the courtyard and into the orchard.

The old man grinned and asked Meko, "Are you hungry, little sister?"

"Sure."

"Well, then come on," he said and held out his elbow. He looked at Choo Choo and said, "You too, pig." Meko hooked her arm around the old man's and they walked around the side of the house toward the smell of the baking sweet potatoes. Choo Choo followed behind. The old man's kindness continued to smooth some of Meko's frayed edges; it turned off the electric fence—but it was too late for the cat.

The old man led Meko into a slightly overgrown garden of orchids, flowers, and vegetables. He guided her to one of the wooden chairs, and then he jumped up onto an empty lettuce crate that was up against the back wall of the house and lifted the lid off of a fifty-gallon ceramic pot. He carefully turned the sweet potatoes over with a long pair of tongs so that they could cook on the other side. He stepped nimbly off the crate, placed the lid back on the pot, and quickly walked over to an open space in the center of the garden and began stoking the wood fire underneath a homemade barbecue.

"Do you like seafood?" he asked beaming at Meko.

"Yes."

The old man sat down next to Meko, bowed his head slightly and murmured, "Please forgive this fool of an old man. I apologize for staring at your arm before."

"Oh, that's so sweet," Meko whispered with embarrassment and fidgeted with her sleeve cuff. "Don't worry about it."

The old man smiled lovingly, reached over and gently placed his rugged hand on hers; he was too choked up to utter a word. Meko appreciated the old man's compassion, but she felt that not even the hand of the Goddess of Mercy, Kuan Yin, could've helped her chase away the Harpies.

Curtis soon appeared. Ten minutes later, the shy, sour-faced fourteen year old boy walked out the back door. He had taken off his "drug dealer" T-shirt and replaced it with a clean white one.

The old man turned toward the boy and barked, "Make yourself useful, Milkshake."

The boy hopped to, and began arranging a stack of dishes on a wooden table.

"I see you've got yourself all spiffed up, and changed out of your orange jumpsuit," chided the old man. He stood up and walked over to Milkshake, placed one of his brown, weather-beaten hands upon the boy's slight shoulder, looked at Curtis and Meko and said, "This is my new one, Milkshake. He just might make it out of here alive."

The old man rubbed the top of the boy's head affectionately. An elfish grin appeared on the boy's face.

Meko and Curtis smiled at the shy, red-faced boy, and tried to make him feel at home by lobbing polite questions concerning his family. Thirty minutes later the four of them and Choo Choo were dining on barbecued shrimp, fresh salad greens, sweet potatoes, and ice cold Taiwan Beer. All the while, Meko doted on the boy by putting more food onto his plate, and refilled his soda glass three times. This impressed and fooled Curtis. As on countless dates before, Meko continued to try to act relaxed and genuine; smiling helplessly as the Harpies tripled in number, pinned her in a corner of an empty lot of her internment camp, flicked out switchblades, and carved directions to Ling's Mortuary across her back. Meko looked off at the sky in a daze and thought about the Stockholm Cemetery that Yanlou, the King of Hell, had offered her.

The metallic voice of a carnival barker called to her from the shadows on the far side of the lot, "Tonight's the night! Defying the laws of nature and reason; Meko the 'Human Pincushion!' She's the loneliest woman in the world. She communicates with liar's dice, recites Baudelaire's *The Flowers of Evil* with her pussy and . . ."

Curtis gently touched Meko on her arm bringing her back to reality. The barker's fading voice droned on as the couple said goodbye to the old man and Milkshake soon thereafter.

"What did your grandfather mean by saying 'Don't miss it'?" Meko asked shakily as they approached the Yamaha.

"He always reminds me to slow down and cherish the beauty in life," said Curtis. "Like this orchard and you."

Meko swallowed the compliment like a foul tasting shot of Tong Ren Tang cough medicine. "Thank you," she mumbled.

Other dates had never spoken to her like that. The Harpies stopped the carve job, flitted across the vacant lot, jumped in a Black Mariah and fired it up. Meko's old friend, the huli jing she'd left in front of the san-ho yuan, and in dozens of seedy motels around town, waited nearby eyeing the paddy wagon as she tapped her foot and checked her watch.

After a long silence Meko asked, "Uh, what's your grandfather's sentence?"

"The Ching Dynasty treatment."

"What?" Meko laughed and imagined the old man saying it.

"Two hundred hours working here, but—"

"But, what?"

"He's an expert in the torture arts." Curtis shuddered and thought about the *Cool Hand Luke* treatment the old man had used on Milkshake.

Meko laughed uneasily as the Black Mariah lurched across the lot. The huli jing stamped her foot, tore off her watch and waved it in the air.

"Uh, what's Milkshake's story? Your grandfather said he was his 'new one'?"

"I was Milkshake number one five summers ago. He's taken on a troubled kid like Milkshake every summer since. He called me his Straw Boy."

The Black Mariah gave Meko a Pol Pot pedicure. She had had enough, and again whistled down the huli jing, who came running, flushed as a raw steak. Meko told her to stick around this time and she cooed seductively, "Ooh, a bad boy. I love bad little boys." Her nipples popped out of the toaster and her panties waited for the fire truck.

"He called me a lot of other things too, and when he bawled them out the sky would blacken on a clear day," Curtis said, and flashed a mischievous smile that belonged on a boy monk sneaking a cig behind the monastery; completely unaware that he'd tossed another lit match into Meko's smoldering cotton shed.

"What'd you do Straw Boy to become Milkshake number one?" she giggled, feigning coy.

"I don't want to talk about it."

"Okay, maybe some other time, milky boy." Meko spun sideways, flaunting her s-curve; she jutted her hip and let the cherries roll off the sponge cake.

Curtis's eyes grew big as a hobo's in an ice cream parlor. "Maybe," he said bashfully.

Meko moved in, her face six inches from his, and she said haughtily, "What about this kid?" and stuck her tongue down his windpipe. For the next five minutes Meko did all the driving, roaring down the steep winding turns of Jade Mountain as Curtis held on to the rear bumper.

"Let's go to a love motel," Meko purred with a rascally smile.

"A love motel?!" asked Curtis, clearly shocked.

"Come on. We can order a pizza and anything else you want."

Curtis's face became hot and his cheeks glowed like a Peking duck. "Okay, I guess if that's what you really want to do," he said submissively, feeling overmatched as a sawhorse in the Kentucky Derby.

The couple arrived at the east side of Tainan City fifteen minutes later, and cruised down busy JianKang Road looking for one of the tacky love motel signs.

"I know a place!" Meko yelled into Curtis's ear. "Turn left at the next light."

"I know a place?" mouthed Curtis and felt his guts skip town. He donned Ichabod Crane's riding gloves, impulsively hit the gas and shot helter-skelter through the turn, nearly taking out a scooter mom with four clinging kids. Meko giggled and hung on, mistaking Curtis's fright for excitement.

"There it is!" she giggled and pointed over Curtis's shoulder—the boy strangled the brakes.

The flashing neon sign read in Mandarin and English: You Very Nice Pleasure Love Motel. Curtis pulled into the lane next to the reception office and parked. The couple walked into the small office. A greasy middle-aged man wearing a paternity suit and track spikes was sucking the life out of a Coke Big Gulp behind the counter.

He looked up and said, "Hi Meko," and smiled at Curtis with the sincerity of a used car salesman.

Meko leaned against Curtis, cupped her hand over his ear and whispered, "He came into the hospital."

Curtis didn't buy it. "Sure he did," he said, and smiled wryly like some grizzled Taipei beat cop.

"Would you like your—"

"Could we see a room selection menu, please?" asked Meko,

and raised her eyebrows at the man.

The man winked at Meko, reached under the counter, grabbed a plastic coated menu and set it down in front of the couple. They looked at the color pictures of the rooms, a list of their amenities and prices.

"How about this one?" asked Meko, and she glanced up at Curtis.

He looked at the one she pointed at; a queen bed with a large plasma TV on the opposite wall.

"It has a mirrored ceiling," said the man, winking at Meko.

"Do you have the same room without the mirrored ceiling?" asked Curtis.

"Sure."

"We'll take it," said Meko. She squeezed Curtis's arm. "The one without the mirrors."

"How many hours?" asked the man, and rolled his eyes at Meko. "We have a two hour special tonight that includes an adult film of your choice."

"Four hours," Meko said and looked at Curtis, who nodded.

The man slid a registration form under the couple's noses and said, "Please fill it in and sign it. That's one of our deluxe rooms. You can park in the private garage directly underneath."

"Can we just leave the bike here?" asked Curtis.

"Sure, if you want. Pull it over on the walkway to the right of the office door, okay."

"Why don't you want to park in the garage?" whispered Meko.

"No need," said Curtis. "I'm not hiding from anybody. Are you?"

"No!" Meko said defensively.

The couple quickly signed the form using fake names and information. The man handed Meko the room key. She stepped outside like Cleopatra slumming in the slave quarter. Curtis parked the motorcycle where the man instructed. Meko paraded ahead down the narrow drive past the office, turned left and walked up the stairs next to the private garage. Curtis ran after her with feet cold as a root beer float. Room number 25 came into view as he reached the top of the stairs. Meko boiled into the room like a lava flow. She switched on the lights, set the dimmer low and turned on the TV. A bikini clad Taiwanese girl danced on a sun drenched beach across the screen. Curtis cautiously stepped through the flames licking the door jamb. He sat on the bed and nervously fumbled around looking for a food menu or a pizza delivery flyer. He glanced up and saw Meko stripped down to her red bra and panties. She writhed and danced enticingly in front of the TV screen. Curtis stared at her arousing figure with the awe and fascination of a junior high school boy watching his first sex-ed film. The "Sea of Love" had turned into quicksand. He sunk down to his chest.

"Come on," she purred. "I'll do whatever you want. Fuck me in the ass if you want. I like that."

Curtis felt like bolting out of the room, but his prick broke his legs. With a mouthful of quicksand he pawed the remote and switched to a Yankees baseball game.

Meko unfastened her bra, took it off, threw it on the bed next to Curtis and asked, "How do you feel now?"

His eyes followed her small, jiggling breasts. "Like someone just handed me the keys to a new Maserati and I don't know how to drive."

"I'll do all the driving, Straw Boy." Meko closed her eyes and continued to dance in front of the trembling young man.

"Meko," Curtis said. She didn't reply. "Meko!" he said louder.

She slid over to the bed, jumped on it, and got down on all fours next to him.

"How come you still have your clothes on, Straw Boy?" She rubbed her head and shoulders up against his side like a playful cougar.

"How many times have you been here?" She didn't answer.

"What's wrong?" she whined. "Don't you want me?"

Curtis jumped to his feet. Meko crawled to the edge of the bed, reached for his fly and tried to unzip it. Curtis grabbed her hand and held it tight. He flung her back on the bed. She landed on her back and began to pull off her panties.

"Would you fucking please stop!" screamed Curtis. "Just stop!" Meko began to cry.

Curtis sat back down on the edge of the bed. He said calmly, "If we stay together we'll have plenty of time for this. But, not tonight. Not like this."

Meko whimpered louder, got up, and sat next to Curtis on the bed. She fumbled around for her bra, picked it up, and quickly put it on.

"I just wanted to make you—"

"I'm a virgin," said Curtis.

"Oh, my god!" Meko giggled with embarrassment. She moved back in, slid her hand onto his crotch and squeezed.

Curtis's face suddenly turned pale. He breathed heavily, and fell face down on the floor with a crash.

"Curtis! Curtis!" Meko crouched on the floor, grabbed him by the shoulders and tried to roll him over.

"The motorcycle," he wheezed softly. "Under the seat." He went unconscious.

"Oh shit! Oh shit!" Meko wailed and frantically ripped at the bedding; grabbed a pillow and placed it under his head.

She took the motorcycle key out of his pocket and ran out the door and down the stairs in her bra and panties. Two cleaning ladies pushing a cart at the bottom of the stairs ogled as she scurried past. One of them called the front desk with her cell phone. Meko passed a wispy prostitute standing in an open door, and sprinted to the office. The desk clerk was standing nonchalantly in the doorway talking on his cell phone.

"She's here," he said and hung up. The man's eyes traced Meko's body like he was memorizing it for a police sketch artist.

She quickly unlocked the motorcycle's seat lock and began rummaging around underneath.

"Call the fucking paramedics!" she screamed. "My friend's having a seizure! He's a diabetic!"

The man nodded indifferently, as if Meko had just given him an order for pizza. He dialed the operator with his boney index finger. Two young men walking by on the sidewalk stopped and stared, and began making catcalls.

Meko found Curtis's insulin travel kit, grabbed it, and ran like mad back toward their room. A husky Taiwanese man in blue shorts sprung out of the open door where the prostitute was standing minutes before, grabbed Meko, pulled her inside and slammed the door.

"Help!" Meko screamed. "Help!"

The soundproofing in the motel was state of the art. She could've yodeled like Patty Hearst and no one would have heard her. The man, a midnight character covered with tattoos, slowly rocked from side to side in front of the door. He had a square head and a face that looked like it'd been put together with an acetylene torch and a monkey wrench. He leered at Meko, who shivered two meters in front of him like a snow leopard tethered in a poacher's camp.

His steam shovel jaw swung open, and he crowed to the half-naked prostitute sitting on the bed, "This the stray?"

The devil's sister tugged on her studded dog collar, smiled with a nod and took a sloppy gulp from a bottle of beer. "Looks flexible as a damn baby," she slurred.

Meko tried to charge past the man. The lout stuck out a forearm heavy as a sack of Portland cement and easily pushed her onto the bed.

Meko sprung up, waved the insulin kit at the man and shouted, "My boyfriend needs emergency medical help! His life's in danger!"

"So is yours," he said deadpan. Meko wilted and stepped back toward the bed.

"She's lying anyway," chided the prostitute.

"Oh nice work, detective," he snapped sarcastically.

The man stared Meko down for a long time. Her eyes panned the room. A telephone sat on a nightstand across the Black Sea.

"Triple feature?" blurted the prostitute.

"Clam up Bambi!" hissed the brute.

Bambi convulsed with laughter, accidentally spilled her beer on her lap, and fell over on the bed.

The man winked at Meko, shoved his hands into his pockets, turned them inside out and bellowed with a hideous laugh, "Kiss Bugs Bunny?!"

Meko recoiled in disgust. He dropped his shorts and stood naked before the women.

"Ooh! It's carnival time!" screeched Bambi. She rolled over, sat up on the bed, took off her black bra, cupped her hands under her enhanced breasts, and yelled at Meko with an insane laugh, "Bar's open!"

Meko turned and caught herself staring at Bambi's perfectly round breasts.

"Show off," said the man. He looked at Meko and asked, "Like her rack? Tits right out of a manga comic book by some Thai body and fender man."

"No one could pound all her dings out."

"Hah! Hear that?" laughed the man.

"Ooh! Jealous?" Bambi snickered.

"Handcuffs!" the man barked at Bambi. "The furry ones."

Bambi grabbed her hand bag that was laying on the bed and rifled thought it. She pulled out the handcuffs, held them up like a dead rabbit and squealed, "A Greek phonics lesson?"

"Shut up, or I'll use you for a drop cloth," squawked the man.

Meko tightened her grip on Curtis's insulin kit until the veins in her lean arm popped out like a junkie ready to drop the hammer. Her other hand was clenched into a fist at her side. The slob took a step toward her. He reeked of diesel and a bad childhood.

"Back on the bed next to Bambi," he sneered.

Meko slowly backed up toward the bed. She turned in a flash, leaped across the bed past Bambi, knocked the telephone receiver onto the floor and pressed the emergency call button. The man dove across the bed and pounced on Meko, pulled her bra down with the finesse of a polar bear, and began slobbering on her breasts. Bambi grabbed Meko's wrist and handcuffed it to the bed post—she kicked and screamed. The door flew open. Bambi yelped as the lazy-eyed office clerk sprung into the room. The bear looked over his shoulder. The clerk rushed over and gave him a face full of pepper spray as casually as if he were washing windows. The naked punk fell on the floor moaning and rubbing his eyes.

"Where's the key asshole?!" shouted the clerk. He turned

and pointed the pepper spray at Bambi's face.

"Okay, okay. I have it here somewhere," she slurred with a giggle and began looking through her purse.

"Hurry!" yelled Meko.

"Hurting poor Mr. Wet Noodle wasn't really necessary, was it?" chided Bambi. "Look at him."

Bambi handed the key to the clerk. He unlocked Meko's handcuffs. She snatched the pepper spray out of his hand and let Bambi have it in the eyes. The prostitute screeched in agony and fell back on the bed.

"Are the paramedics here?!" wailed Meko. "Are they?!"

"No," the clerk said softly.

A terrified look appeared on Meko's face. "Why the fuck not?!" she pleaded. "Is he uh—"

"Dead?" cackled Bambi. She sat up on the bed rubbing her eyes. "He's dead sweetie."

"Shut up!" screamed the clerk.

Meko hastily pulled up her bra, and raced out of the room and up the stairs. The nosy cleaning ladies were pretending to be working outside the open door of her and Curtis's room. After she ran into the room they quietly moved to the side of the door and peered inside.

Curtis was sitting on the bed watching the Yankees game. He turned to Meko and smiled.

"What's this?!" Meko blurted and huffed. "What the hell is this?! Are you all right?"

"One good con deserves another," he said calmly.

"Oh you! Oh my god! Oh my god!" she screamed, her face turning red. She thought about telling him about her abduction.

"I'm all right," Curtis said sheepishly.

"Well, I'm sure not all right! No, I'm not all right by a long fucking shot." Meko flung the insulin kit at him and hurriedly began to get dressed.

"I didn't know how else to wake you up," said Curtis. "Come on," he pleaded, realizing his stunt went too far.

"Wake me up?! You could've awoken the bleeping dead with a stunt like that! By the way mister, the paramedics are coming." Meko finished getting dressed.

"No they're not. I already called your pal from the *hospital*."

"I'm taking a cab," Meko said and blew out of the room.

Curtis jumped up, ran to the door, and watched her until she disappeared down the stairs and around the corner. The cleaning ladies stepped back away from the door, looked at each other, shook their heads and grinned. Ten minutes later, two police officers stepped out of the room Meko was pulled into and escorted a handcuffed Mr. Wet Noodle and Bambi to their patrol car.

Meko called Curtis's cell phone two chewed fingernails into a taxi ride. He didn't answer. Memories of the several men she'd let grip her like a bowling ball and toss into the gutter at that particular love motel flashed in her mind. She looked at her catheter. The hotline from the "Ten Courts of Hell" began to ring again.

"You're hopeless," she whispered to herself. "That's why you ran out of there."

Meko leaned her head over the front seat and asked the driver, "Could you drop me at the 7-Eleven on Cheng Gong Road near Chikan Street instead?"

"No problem."

A fingernail later, the driver dropped Meko off in front of the 7-Eleven where Curtis worked. She rolled inside like a blood bank hoofer, and bought a bottle of Absolut and a bulk bottle of aspirin. The clerk, a peach-faced boy of seventeen, didn't connect the dots. He was too busy trying to keep his hard-on leashed. He smiled at Meko as she walked around back and sat on the bench underneath the banyan tree where she'd first met Curtis and Choo Choo. She twisted the cap off the vodka, put the bottle under her nose, and took a big whiff.

"Yuck!" she cried out. She'd never tried booze before.

She set the bottle down, popped the cap off the aspirin bottle, and dumped half of the pills into her hand. She looked around at the banyan and the empty space, began to weep uncontrollably, lied down on the bench, and bawled until she fell asleep half an hour later. Two hours later she was awoken by the hotline from the "Ten Courts of Hell."

A recorded message sneered repeatedly, "Rooms available. Roly-poly, mama's little fatty, gonna die today."

Meko buzzed a taxi and arrived home at three bells. No one heard her come in.

Yellow Boy drove his new Nissan to his parents' home two weeks later, on a balmy, clear Sunday evening. He'd been going there for dinner once a week for years out of respect, knowing it pleased his mother and father. He parked in front of the san-ho yuan. Meko was waiting for him in the moonlit courtyard as he walked toward the front door.

She ran to her brother and giggled with excitement, "Hello big brother! Mom and Grandma went all out tonight."

"Really?" Yellow Boy stopped halfway through the courtyard and faced his sister.

"She's prepared Three Cups Chicken with a little extra sesame oil and rice wine the way you like it."

"Sounds like a wonderful last meal for a man going before a firing squad."

"What?" Meko laughed, and shot him a quizzical look.

"Never mind," Yellow Boy said with a sneaky smile. "What else?"

"*Dan zai* noodles, shrimp, and rice with sweet potatoes. And Grandma made her scrumptious suncake. Don't say anything about the suncake. She wants to surprise you."

"Okay."

"Come on, then." Meko took a few steps toward the front door.

"Hey, have you talked to Curtis since the fight you were so vague about?"

Meko stopped and turned, wrinkled her nose and said, "No. He's called a few times." She didn't tell her brother that she tried calling Curtis three times, and each time he didn't answer.

"What the hell happened on your date?"

"A potential headline."

"Which would have read?"

"Bimbo abducted."

"Abducted?! You're kidding!" Yellow Boy clamped his hands on top of his head.

"Nope."

"You mean blindfolded and and handcuffed and and ransom notes and fed those radioactive sandwiches from 7-Eleven?!"

"Just about."

"You could've been famous or— "

"Dead." Meko laughed nervously.

"Oh, god!" Yellow Boy blurted, clearly frightened. He clammed up and walked around in small circles.

"But, I'm ok."

"You've got to be careful," he scolded with tears in his eyes. "Mom and Dad know?"

"Are you kidding?!"

"Want to talk about it?"

"No."

"Come on."

"Emphatically, no."

"Did you learn anything?"

Meko looked her brother in the eye and said, "Yeah, I did. You could say I got 'scared straight.'"

"Oh, I'm so glad!" Yellow Boy said, and exhaled loudly. He looked at his sister with a sly grin and said, "Nice choice of words by the way. If I was going to ever get 'scared straight,' it would've been when I got my first ass pounding by Jerry the lumberjack from Tacoma—AKA The Human Redwood."

"Ouch," giggled Meko.

"More ball slapping and dribbling went on in the back of his camper than at a basketball summer camp."

"Hah!"

"Don't play too hard to get with Curtis, or the bee might find another flower."

Meko shrugged and said, "Maybe I'm too old for him?"

"You don't fool me, sister. You're smitten. Sure you're okay?"

Meko stuck her nose in the air playfully and said, "Yeah, let's go inside."

As they walked into the house they were overcome by the

delicious aromas coming from the kitchen.

Meko called out, "Mom, Dad, he's here."

Meko and Yellow Boy walked into the kitchen. Their mother, dressed in a handsome blue and pink dress, was stirring the big pot of Three Cups Chicken on the stove.

She looked up quickly and said, "Sit, please."

The pair sat down at the table and gazed at the platters of food.

"Are you expecting anyone else, like the Tainan Lions?" quipped Yellow Boy.

"All for you, honey," she said, and picked up the pot of chicken and set it on the table.

The grandmother soon appeared and sat down at the table.

"Hello Doc," she said, and gave Meko a wink and a smile.

"Hi beautiful. Where's Grandpa?"

"Coming right along. Your father's helping him."

Several minutes later the father and grandfather appeared. The ancient old man could barely walk, even with a cane. The math professor held him steady with one hand on his shoulder, and the other under his arm.

When the ancient one saw his grandson Yellow Boy, he wrestled out of his son's arms and wheezed with pride, "I can do it myself you damn fool," and he hobbled to a chair with his cane and slid into it. Everybody laughed, even the stoic and grandiose professor.

The family enjoyed lighthearted conversation and bantered playfully throughout the dinner.

Yellow Boy looked around as everyone was finishing their suncake and tea, and said in a low voice, "Last year I met a man named Frankie who has had a profound effect on me even though he died a few days after I met him."

Everyone stopped talking and stared at Yellow Boy. His face became tense. His eyes met Meko's. She smiled and stood up, walked over to her brother, knelt down next to his chair, put her arm around his shoulder and squeezed.

"What is it dear?" asked his mother with a small nervous smile.

Yellow Boy turned and looked at his father, and ran his eyes over his wide shoulders. He was wearing a white short-sleeve shirt, a thin black tie, and glasses. A girlish smile appeared on the grandmother's face.

"I need to tell you something," said Yellow Boy in a trembling voice.

The father clenched his fist that rested on his thigh.

"You have given me so much with medical school and everything, and I haven't given you anything." He paused again. His eyes filled with tears and fretfully darted around the faces at the table.

"You can do it," Meko whispered into his ear and squeezed his shoulder.

"I'm gay."

Everyone's eyes turned to Yellow Boy's father. He sat expressionless, turned slightly and glanced at his wife. He looked across the table at his son and said, "Is that all that's bothering you, young man?"

"What?!" Yellow Boy asked, completely shocked.

Tears welled up in his mother's tender eyes. She shot her husband a quick, worried smile.

"We've all known that for years, you dummy," barked the grandfather.

"Why didn't someone tell me?" brayed Yellow Boy. "Everybody always knows! Even you guys?!" His shoulders slumped.

His mother said gently, "We thought that if you ever needed to talk about it dear, well, then it would be best if no one pushed you. You'd come to us."

Yellow Boy anxiously looked at his father. The exalted one seemed to have doubled in size. His father straightened up, rested his long arms on the chair's armrests, and clenched them tightly.

He peered down at his son and said plainly, "I have but one concern."

"What?" Yellow Boy glanced at Meko for support.

"Are you okay with your true identity?"

"You mean with being a hopeless queer?" said Yellow Boy with a weak, mischievous smile. His eyes danced around the table.

The room became silent as a cemetery during Ghost Month. Everyone looked at his father for a response. The stoic king sat stone-faced for a very long moment.

His lips tightened, and he said, "Yes, son. Are you okay with being a hopeless, cocksucking queer?" His face cracked into a huge smile.

Everyone roared. The grandfather laughed so hard that his dentures fell out onto his plate.

Several minutes later, when everyone had calmed down, Yellow Boy said to his father, "Yeah, I'm okay with being a fag now."

"That's all that matters," his father replied. "You have been a most honorable and dutiful son."

"And grandson," said his grandmother.

Meko wept with happiness and threw both of her arms around her brother's narrow shoulders. Yellow Boy felt absolved—light as an ultra-thin condom. His heart was floating with the spirit of the wild man who called himself Frankie.

Yellow Boy looked at Meko affectionately and said, Thanks little sister for being there for me."

The mother stood up and asked, "More cake anyone?"

For the next thirty minutes the family talked and poked fun at one another while enjoying cake and wine. The piercing sound of a trumpet coming from the courtyard silenced everyone.

"He's here!" squealed Meko. She jumped up and ran toward the front door. Her mother and grandmother tore after her.

"Another horn blower!" wailed the grandfather.

Yellow Boy pointed at his grandfather and howled with laughter, "Outrageous!"

The old man chuckled and rubbed his belly.

The father winked at Yellow Boy and asked playfully, "The cougar's boy?"

Yellow Boy nodded. "He's still wears his maternity ward bracelet." The father and grandfather laughed.

The mother caught Meko by the arm as she neared the front door. The grandmother rushed over and said calmly, "Make him wait, honey."

"She's right," said her mother. "Don't go running crazy legs out there like the house is burning down."

The three women went into a nearby room, crouched down

in front of the window, and peered out into the courtyard. Curtis straddled his motorcycle and continued to play the tune "Skylark."

"That's our song," Meko moaned, and remembered when he played it under the banyan tree.

"He's got flowers," giggled the mother.

"I don't see them," said Meko.

The grandmother reached into her housecoat, pulled out her glasses and put them on.

"Sticking out the sidecar's far side," said the mother.

The grandmother saw the flowers, too. Meko stood up and walked toward the door.

"Get back over here girl," snapped the grandmother.

Meko obeyed, and asked, "What if he leaves?"

The mother stood up, moved to the side of the window, looked out smiling and said, "He's not going anywhere."

The grandmother said, "Your mother's right. Wait until he finishes the song. Then we'll see what his next move is."

The young man finished playing five minutes later, put the trumpet in its case, jumped on the kick starter, hit the throttle, drove slowly and stopped ten meters in front of the front door. He primped his hair in the motorcycle's mirror, hopped off the Yamaha, and walked to the door with the fresh bouquet of lilies and knocked.

The grandmother answered the door. "You must be the prankster," she said with a youthful smile, and disappeared back into the house.

Curtis wandered around in the wide courtyard. Ten minutes passed—fifteen minutes.

Meko appeared in the doorway. The hotline from the "Ten Courts of Hell" began to ring. Meko smirked proudly and cut the line. Curtis meandered toward her with the confidence of a door-to-door salesman with a dead chicken for a necktie.

"On parole?" she asked and crossed her arms.

"I escaped."

"Oh, really?" Meko chuckled.

"What's so funny?"

She looked at the flowers. "Going to a funeral?"

"I'll let you know in about five minutes."

Meko couldn't keep a straight face. She eyed the orange lilies and asked, "How's the Ching Dynasty treatment going?"

"I drew up my will yesterday."

"Hah!"

"I'm donating my internal organs to a dog food factory."

"Your heart, too?"

"What's left of it," he said and looked down. Then he popped his head up and blurted, "It was wrong what I did at the motel."

Meko shook her head and thought about the brute that pulled her into his room. "You don't know the half of it, flower boy."

"You're starting to sound like my old bull of a grandfather."

"Good."

"Maybe you can tell me about it sometime."

"My grandmother said I deserved it."

"Did you?"

"We all deserve it."

"Uh-huh."

"I guess the sleazy way I acted at the motel was about as dumb as bringing a stolen pig on a date."

"I thought you liked that."

"I did Straw Boy." Meko walked up to him.

"You know if I didn't care about you, about us, I wouldn't have said those things at the motel," he said shyly.

"I know."

"Then what?"

"You scared the shit out of me. And had me running around almost naked in front of a bunch of strangers and— "

"I bet they get a lot of that at that place."

"They probably do." Meko paused and asked, "Think we can start over?"

Curtis pondered her question, groping for the right words. "My grandfather says there's no 'do overs' in life—only forgiveness."

"Can you forgive me for acting like such a slut?"

Curtis looked down with embarrassment. "I already have." He paused and said, "Maybe, we need to uh, you know. Maybe we need to spend more time together before we— "

"Go for a spin in the Maserati?"

"I think so."

Curtis turned, looked back toward his motorcycle and said, "I've got to go. I just wanted to tell you in person."

"Sure."

Curtis handed her the lilies, turned around, and walked toward the Yamaha. Meko's heart fell into a butcher's scrap bucket. She unconsciously took several steps toward him.

He stopped next to the motorcycle, turned around, and asked, "Would you like to go out to a movie with me next Saturday night? I know you're tired on Fridays because of your treatments."

Meko swooned and ran to him. They knotted up and kissed.

She whispered into his ear, "No more love motels until *you* decide we should go there."

Curtis grinned.

"Can you play me a song?"

"Now?"

"Uh-huh." Meko smiled jubilantly and said, "Know what else?"

"Huh?"

"I've found my passion!"

"What?"

"This week I started taking classes to become a pastry chef."

"Really?! Congratulations!"

"My grandmother encouraged me, and she and my parents have been so supportive. In a few years I hope to open my very own bakery."

"That's so cool," Curtis said and smiled, reached into the sidecar, took the trumpet out of its case, and began playing a traditional Taiwanese love song. Meko's mother and grandmother were still watching from the window. They turned, gave each other high fives, and pranced toward the kitchen to deliver the news.

Yellow Boy and Meko drove out to Mango Road two days later at dusk. The waning sun washed the clear sky a gorgeous pinkish blue. The car rumbled up the long dirt drive bordering the mango orchard and parked in front of the san-ho yuan's court-yard. The old man twitched in his chair on the porch nervous as a boy before his first day of school. His ears pricked up at the sound of the approaching car. He lifted his sinewy left hand off his lap and gently patted the bandage covering his eye. Choo Choo lay at his feet like a trusted hound.

"Easy now," the old man shakily whispered to himself and popped a betel nut into his mouth.

From the orchard, Curtis and Milkshake looked up and saw the roiling cloud of dust rise from the road. They stopped working and walked toward the house. Meko and Yellow Boy turned and watched them approach.

"Nice shirt!" Meko called out.

Curtis looked down at his T-shirt. It had the word "thief" scrawled in Chinese characters with a magic marker across the front.

"Welcome to Mango Road Prison," he bantered.

Milkshake squirmed around shy as a newly weaned puppy a few paces behind Curtis. The old man had added a scrawl to the back of his T-shirt. It read "ninety percent strawberry."

"How is he?" asked Yellow Boy, and looked toward the old man on the porch.

"He said today there's going to be a hanging," said Curtis.

"Hopefully, not mine," said Yellow Boy. Everyone laughed uncomfortably, and they walked across the courtyard and up to the porch.

"A house call?" barked the old man, his good eye running over the foursome.

"You're the first," said Yellow Boy, and he sat down in the chair across from the old man.

"Came out here to help bury me, didn't you?"

"Returning a favor."

The old man gave him a puzzled look and said, "If you want to do me a favor you could take these two clowns off my hands," and he glared at Curtis and Milkshake.

"I saw a traveling circus setting up their tents back down the road," said Meko.

"Pack your bags, boys," yawped the old man. Everyone giggled.

Yellow Boy looked down at Choo Choo and said, "The famous dancing pig. We meet at last." Choo Choo wiggled her ears and snorted.

"She likes you," said Curtis.

"I taught her the jitterbug the other day," the old man said proudly. "She told me she wants a boyfriend." Everyone laughed.

"I might know someone," joked Yellow Boy.

"One of your queer friends with an animal fetish?"

"Uh-huh." Yellow Boy opened his black medical bag, pulled out a penlight, and put it into his shirt pocket.

"I'd like to alone with the doctor for the unveiling," said the old man, and he looked at Curtis and jerked his head to one side. He turned his gaze toward Meko and said tenderly, "Little sister, would you please escort these good-for-nothing cons to the nearest cliff."

Meko, Curtis, and Milkshake walked through the courtyard and stopped in front of Yellow Boy's car. They kept their eyes fixed on the two men on the porch.

"Let's get rid of Bluebeard's eye patch," said the old man.

"And how have you been feeling?" asked Yellow Boy, and he began to carefully remove the tape from the right side of the bandage.

"I need some pussy," the old man squawked, and squeezed the armrests of his chair.

"Hah! Hah! Hah!"

"I've never been any damn good at waiting," whispered the old man.

"Uh-huh. Unfortunately, I have."

"What?"

"I finally told my parents last night."

"Oh? Oh! Good for you, son. Their reaction?"

"They've known for years, like everybody else."

"That's the trouble with all you closet homos. You think you're carrying around some big goddamn state secret. Hell, I spotted you for a fairy right off, remember?"

"I remember."

"Most folks don't give a shit one way or the other if a fella likes it up the tailpipe. They're too busy worrying about bills and how they're going to save money to send their kids to college."

"You're right. And thanks for the advice the first time we met."

"Call it even if my blinker's okay."

"If it's not?"

"Run like hell. I keep a shotgun inside the front door."

Yellow Boy chuckled, "Please keep your eye closed until I tell you to open it." The old man wiggled around restlessly as the doctor carefully continued removing the layers of tape.

"How do you feel now that you're out of the rice queen closet?"

"Absolutely sublime."

"If you keep using fancy pants words out here I'll charge you. I told you you'd feel redeemed."

"You did, and I do," said Yellow Boy, and he finished removing the tape from the right side of the bandage and swung it slowly across the old man's eye. The old man tightened his grip on the armrests until the chair began to creak. Meko, Curtis, and Milkshake couldn't control themselves. They quietly walked back through the courtyard, stopped several meters in front of the porch, and continued to watch intensely.

Yellow Boy removed the bandage, flicked on his penlight, held it in front of the old man's eye and said, "Okay."

The old man took a deep breath, as if he were about to swim the length of an Olympic swimming pool underwater, and slowly opened his eye.

Yellow Boy asked, "Can you—"

The old man sat very still and opened and closed his eye several times as if his eyelid weighed a ton. He jumped up out of his chair and cried out, "I can see! I can see!"

Yellow Boy grinned and stood up. The old man gave him a bear hug and wouldn't let go.

"Oh, thank you doctor!" he sobbed. "Thank you Kuanyin!"

Curtis, Meko, and Milkshake rushed over to the embracing pair. The old man turned and hugged each one of them, tears streaming down his face.

"My mangos!" he shouted merrily. "My mangos!" He scrambled through the courtyard like a teenager, stopped in front of the grove, outstretched his arms, and beheld the swaying trees.

The others and Choo Choo followed behind. They stood with the old man and watched the sunset. Shortly thereafter, Yellow Boy and Meko said good bye and left, followed by Curtis on his motorcycle.

That same evening around ten, Curtis's grandfather strode off his porch, kicked off his sandals, stripped off his shirt, walked through the courtyard, crossed the dirt drive and stopped in front of his mango orchard in the bright moonlight. He looked up at the stars that twinkled above the dazzling landscape. His gaze slowly turned to the majestic mango orchard. He smiled and began practicing the elegant movements of tai chi. The boy he called Milkshake, and Choo Choo, the liberated pig followed close behind. The boy peeled off his shirt, stood next to the old man, and began following his flowing movements. Choo Choo stood on the other side of the old man, wiggled her ears, and shuffled from side to side.

"That's it Tiger Boy, breathe," said the old man.

Moon Hill

Five a.m. sat on my motorbike in a grove of coconut palms waiting for the light atop Moon Hill, and far below, Thai migrants' dreams poured out the ivory smokestacks of Formosa Plastics like an eternal drift of swallows heading out to sea never to return, rolling languorously across the most beautiful red-pink sunrise I've ever seen—time to go to work.

The Pilgrimage

Taiwan's Taoist temples dwell on sun-swept plains somewhere between life and death. During my first year in Taiwan I'd visited many temples in Taipei and had become obsessed with their beauty and the mystery of Taoism. On a stormy April afternoon during that first year—with lightning strikes pointing the way, I rode a rented motorbike toward a rural Taipei temple, where a revered Taoist holy man was waiting for me. A friend's father had arranged the meeting. I'd hoped the master would share some of his wisdom concerning Taoism. My camera bag contained an old friend, a half pint of Jack Daniel's, and my dog-eared translation of the ancient Tao text, the *Tao Te Ching*. I'd read it twice that week, and numerous times previously.

I arrived at the temple an hour later, walked up its steep staircase, and as I passed through the arched doorway, the bearded and menacing looking Yu-Chih, one of the ten-foot tall door guards, swatted away an evil spirit and slipped a Mickey into my carton of red tea. He smiled down upon me in approval when he spotted the copy of the *Tao Te Ching* I held in my hand, placed one of his large boots on my rear, and sent me flying into the hall. Taoist gods began to pop up everywhere—like creatures in an arcade funhouse, glowing bright red, green, and yellow. I looked around. My eyes couldn't swallow the scene. Everything was red, and every square inch from floor to the golden, Baroque ceiling was covered with beautiful artwork. My legs turned into Cream of Wheat and my heart began doing the samba on my breastbone. The last time my senses were this overloaded was when I thumbed through a *Playboy* magazine for the first time when I was ten. My eyes were blinded by incense smoke that poured out from a large dragon urn outside the main door. Worshippers from all walks of life held sticks of burning incense as they poured in and out of the several round portals on either side of the main entrance. Then, through the smoke, a beautiful mural of the goddess Kuan Yin (goddess of mercy) protecting three rural farmers from creatures from the underworld came into view through a forest of two dozen towering red columns. Other murals depicting heroic acts performed by gods adorned the walls. I walked to the main altar, which was covered with hand-painted vases of lilies and orchids, and many small idols. The Three Pure Ones (the highest Tao deities) sat upon their gilded thrones at the center of the temple's rear wall—flanked by idols of the gods Kuan Kung (god of war and prosperity) and Tu Di Gong (the earth god). To my left, a group of ten kneeling sutra-chanters dressed in brown robes droned.

"Michael!" boomed a voice behind me.

I turned around and a tall, smiling, robust man of sixty, in a hand-woven red robe bounded toward me out of the smoke like a fullback chugging toward the goal line.

"Master Lee?" I said, and lowered my shoulder and braced myself for the Laughing Buddha's impact. He bounced up, sweat dripping from his red face, and stopped so close to me it felt like we were wearing the same pair of shoes.

"Ivan the Terrible, at your service," he said with a laugh. Then he stepped back, bowed and whispered, "Some of my eccentric American colleagues used to call me that."

"Your English—it's excellent. Why did they call you Ivan the Terrible?"

He ignored my inquiry, smacked his lips and said, "USC, class of 1974. Oh, Los Angeles—that glorious reptile pit, that grand celebration of individualism." (He told me later that he graduated *cum laude* from USC with a master's degree in religious studies.)

I couldn't take my eyes off of his intricate silk robe—decorated with flying birds, flowers, geometrical designs, and five white circles containing scenes of white cranes against lush green backgrounds.

He held out his hand. I placed my hand in his and he squeezed it tightly, and then he looked through me with the penetrating eyes of a prophet, and he laughed and shouted, "California! You too, eh?" and reared his head back exposing enough gold in his teeth to feed a family of six for a year.

"Right, how did you . . ."

"The golden mountain," he bellowed with sarcasm. "The land of —"

"The dead," I said, and thought his loud, fast-talking manner and charisma reminded me of Burt Lancaster playing the lovable con artist in *Elmer Gantry*.

"Yes, yes, that too!" he chortled. "My assistant informed me of your background."

"Come," he said, and led me to a room off to the right. We sat down in hand-carved wooden chairs at a royal table and he began preparing tea.

After a long silence he leered up at me—Elmer Gantry's maniacal face had completely disappeared. The Master's eyes darkened, drilling holes through mine, and he said deadpan as a Folsom Prison lifer, "My assistant told me why you've come." Then he waited another long moment, ran one of his hands over his sweaty, shaved scalp and recited slowly, gravely, the first line from the *Tao Te Ching*, "The Tao that can be spoken is not the true Tao."

I cursed myself for not bringing the joint of Phnom Penh Thunderfuck I'd left on my dresser. Perhaps that could've assisted me in my clumsy attempts to grasp this elusive sparrow.

"The Tao is indescribable," he continued—his face changed again, and it began glowing with intensity and excitement. "It existed long before man created religion, government, money, and the other follies."

The other follies I smiled and thought; countries, war, banks . . . what a beauty! This holy renegade's so illuminated that he sells power to the grid.

He poured us tea, grinned and asked, "Do you find this temple spectacular?"

"Quite."

"Taoist temples represent the *religion* of Tao. The Tao is a philosophy, a simple way of life, not a religion. People come here to pray, but the Tao cannot answer their prayers or accept their offerings."

"And, the temples? Aren't there thousands of them in Taiwan?"

"Around seven thousand. People need," and then he hesitated and said, "in the old days the temple was the social center of the township."

"People need hope?" I asked.

He brushed away my question like an annoying insect and said, "Ancient Chinese had strong beliefs in spirits, magic, fortune telling, and ancestor worship. They relied on shaman to send and interpret messages to and from the unseen world. Buddhism arrived from India with its wide array of gods, and with Confucianism many rituals were added to the pot. Thus, the religion of Taoism was born out of all of these ideologies."

I nodded, hoping he would continue, and set my copy of the *Tao Te Ching* on the table.

He reached over, picked it up, opened it to the introduction and said with approval, "An adequate translation. Can you read Chinese?"

"Uh, no."

"The ancient text in its mother tongue is pure, like cherry blossoms lining a dirt road in the countryside. But, this will be fine for you." The Master set my book on the table, and quickly ran his fingers back and forth over the cover like a blind man reading Braille and said, "Go on a pilgrimage. The experience may resonate, and like a calm wind lead you to other paths. Take photographs, if that pleases you. But, if you want to try to understand the *philosophy* of Tao, you must take something else."

"What's that?"

"The eyes of a child," he said, and he reached over and took my hand and held it, kneading it tightly in his. Then the seer looked into my eyes and smiled—sweat streamed into the thick folds of his face and he said, "Please don't be offended when I say, your heart is hard as a clay burial pot."

My hand quickly pulled away, acknowledging that he had spoken the truth.

"Learn to forgive," he said and smiled.

"Who?"

He looked at me in silence for a long while. I felt naked—overmatched. Then he said, "Everyone, beginning with you."

My eyes filled with tears, and images of my deceased father and scenes from our tumultuous relationship during my youth came to mind.

The Master placed a giant paw on my shoulder and said compassionately, "Many times, our most trying experiences prove to be the most beneficial," and he pulled off his robe, exposing scars the size of silver dollars—one on his shoulder, and the other on his abdomen.

"These are my South Central stars," he said plainly.

"You got shot!?"

He nodded and said, "This is why they called me Ivan the Terrible."

"In L.A.?"

"Watts in 1969 was no place for a dumb, nineteen-year-old gook like me."

"What happened?"

He paused, slipped his robe back on, and said, "It was very hot in L.A. in August 1969—the fourth anniversary of the first day of the 1965 riots was taking place at Will Rogers Park—a festival for the black community. I'd just completed my freshman year at USC and was feeling cocky as a young dragon.

With my head filled with moon dust, and my lungs filled with butane, I told my friends I wanted a cultural experience, and drove alone down to Watts around one o'clock in the afternoon. There was no parking near the park, so I drove around and parked a few blocks away—across the street from a neighborhood convenience store. While walking across the street toward the store to buy a soda I noticed three black men hanging around on the nearby corner. They boiled and strutted around in tight T-shirts—clearly agitated, with big Afros, and long sideburns. The vibrations they gave off painted a swath the color of coal that ran along the street, up my back, back down onto the street, up every telephone pole and tree, and billowed into the sky creating an immense cloud that stole my shadow. Filled with fright, I quickly looked back toward my car—it was floating upside down in the Yangtze River. I had ventured too far, and found myself alone, stranded out in the middle of the flood plain. My fear transformed the tall, gangly leader—in an orange muscle shirt and platform heels, into a Congolese warrior wearing a bone through his nose and a leopard skin headdress. He gave me the *evil eye* as I hurried into the store. It wasn't much better inside. Other fierce looking characters who smelled like bottles of gin brushed past me and gave me the once over. My eyes darted around looking for a back door, a trap door, any door. The door to hell would have been fine— no luck."

"When I came out the unhappy trio were waiting on the curb sharpening their lances."

"The leader swaggered toward me all elbows and knees, and he cried out in an eerie, high-pitched voice, 'You lost slope? Hey, look at this Buddha head we got here.'

'You shouldn't have come down here today, yellow cake,' crowed one of the other men.

"I walked as fast as I could toward my car, but the leader, he cut me off —and then he pulled a pistol and shot me."

"Jesus!" I said. "Did they rob you?"

"No," he said. "I don't remember much as I went unconscious after a few minutes due to blood loss. A young black couple witnessed the shooting. They called the police from the payphone next to the store—that's what the police told me later. I would have bled to death right there if those two young people hadn't assisted me." Master Lee sat in silence for a moment, smiled and said, "While recovering in hospital I rediscovered the *Tao Te Ching*. I'd read it before in high school, but at that time I wanted to become an engineer—my initial major at USC. I've tried to follow the ways of the Tao ever since."

"What happened to the man who shot you?"

"He went to jail for attempted murder. But, he had been in his own prison long before that. I found out from the police that his father was killed during the riots in 1965. I hold no ill feelings toward this man."

"My friends at USC began calling me Ivan the Terrible after the shooting incident. My English name was Ivan, and they said I was some sort of *bad ass* as you Americans say, for going down there alone—getting shot."

"Thanks for sharing your story," I said.

"You're most welcome." Ivan the Terrible hesitated for a long while; took a sip of tea, smiled and gently said, "Don't expect to find any answers on your pilgrimage."

I thought of another quote from the *Tao Te Ching: The more you go in search of an answer, the less you will understand.*

"Live simply, humbly," he said. "Follow the way of nature."

I thanked him, walked out to my motorbike, took a long pull off the bottle of Jack, and rode back toward Taipei.

I adhered to Master Lee's advice, and a month later, on a misty, humid May morning I ventured south from Taipei to Tainan County on my first pilgrimage to a traditional religious festival. It was the birthday of Taiwan's most popular Taoist folk goddess, Matsu. She has been revered since early Han immigrants looked to her for safe passage as they made the often perilous journey across the Taiwan Strait. Initially venerated by local fisherman, Matsu's glorification increased dramatically in the twentieth century, and she came to be considered Taiwan's patron saint. I woke at five the day of my departure, took twenty rolls of film out of the fridge, stuffed them into a bag with my two cameras and my copy of the *Tao Te Ching*, and lit out onto the dusky street promising myself I wasn't coming back until at least fifteen rolls were cooked. I wouldn't be flashing the camera like a dime-store cop badge only pretending to take pictures like I'd done on several occasions. I'd waited for this day, anxious as a thoroughbred kicking in its starting gate—visions of blood-splattered spirit mediums and crowds of frothing pilgrims rocking on their heels that I'd only heard about had kept me awake half the previous night.

At six I met my friend Nadine and her mother, who was a member of a small neighborhood Taoist temple in Taipei, and we went to meet a group of around twenty-five others at the temple in the Wan-hua district. A rented bus idled out front. I took notice of a group of musicians were also part of the pilgrimage. They were passing around bottles of rice wine near a small blue truck that carried big drums, cymbals, horns, and a small idol of Matsu. Some of the men had nasty scars on their foreheads and between their shoulder blades.

I thought of Master Lee's gunshot story, and about one of the last things he said to me, "Don't expect to find any answers on your pilgrimage."

It had finally occurred to me what he meant. He was talking about my life—don't expect to find any answers on your pilgrimage through this life.

"What's with the tread marks?" I asked Nadine as I continued to stare at the men.

"Oh, the scars?" she said with a sly grin, and stuck a cigarette in her lips and lit it. "You'll see. Wait until you see the weaponry they use."

"Weaponry?" I said, unable to control my fascination.

"Some of them are spirit mediums. We call them *jitong,* it means divine boy servant."

"Shaman?"

"Not quite. Taoist shaman have power to gain control of forces in the spirit world. A jitong is a boy or man who's been chosen by a god as the earthly vehicle for divine expression—

and the jitong is completely under the god's control."

"How do gods express themselves through jitong?"

"By speech or by spirit writing. Sometimes they'll write messages in sand or in incense ashes on a special plate at the temple."

One of the mediums dropped a small yellow bundle of paper on the ground, bent down, and lit it with his lighter. Instantly, several of the men's faces contorted and became dour, ugly, inhuman, and then they began to walk around the bundle with their eyes closed, waving their arms around.

"That's ghost money," said Nadine. "It can be bought at temples. It's believed that the money, once burned, can be used by ancestors or gods in the afterworld."

The men stopped dancing, killed off the bottles, and climbed into the back of the truck with the musicians. I grinned in anticipation of photographing these men in action over the next two days.

We headed south toward Taichung. Someone passed around a big plastic bag of mystery food. I kept an eye on it as it neared us. A girl of seven sitting in front of us with her mother took the bag, pulled out two barbecued chicken feet, and began gnawing away.

"Jesus," I said. "Look at the claws on that rooster."

Nadine laughed, and said with embarrassment, "You think that's gross, huh?"

"Where's the meat?"

"It's supposed to be good for girls," she said as the girl passed her the bag. "We eat everything here because we used to be such a poor country," she said, and passed the bag to the seat behind us.

Unknowingly to Nadine, her humble remark caught me off guard and rained embarrassment upon my head. I knew of Taiwan's colonial past, but she was the first person that I'd met here to put it so bluntly. I would come to love Taiwanese cuisine, but I never could warm up to those claws or fish head soup because in my upbringing they were always discarded. One of the pilgrims appeared in the front of the bus with a microphone—a petite, harmless looking middle-aged woman wearing a Marie Osmond wig and enough make-up to wax a fleet of buses.

The driver switched on a TV monitor above his head. I gazed up and noticed speakers from an AC/DC show that ran above our heads the entire length of the bus. Nadine looked at me apologetically and gave me a weak smile. I was trapped in karaoke hell with the Osmonds and we had hundreds of miles to go. Karaoke music began blaring through the speakers. The pilgrim began to wail with a voice delicate as a chainsaw.

"What's she singing?" I shouted above the noise.

"A traditional Taiwanese folk song."

A commotion came from the back of the bus. I spun around and saw the spirit mediums huddled together cackling like a brood of Satan's helpers, shirtless, their eyes glowing like red coals. I thought of Michelangelo's *Last Judgment*. One of them raised a bottle of rice wine with his long, forked tail and motioned for me to join them. I did. They all roared after I poured down a slug of the Sherwin-Williams—boysenberry, my favorite color. The racket went on until we stopped at the first temple in Taichung County an hour and a half later.

With one camera slung around my neck and the other in hand, I jumped out ahead of Nadine poised to get my fix, pushed through the mass of bodies, looked to my left and saw hundreds of pilgrims from other temples pouring out from several buses.

Master Lee's words echoed in my mind, "Take the eyes of a child." I told myself to try to really feel this—not just see it.

"I'll find you later!" I shouted at Nadine, and ran through a tall, ancient arched gate where two Buddhist monks in long yellow robes begged for money.

People lit thousands of firecrackers to ward off evil spirits in a large open area in front of the temple. I ran through the crowd toward a group of spirit mediums, four of them in all, dancing around in slow deliberate gestures in the white smoke, stripped to the waist, waving medieval-looking spiked clubs and swords in the air. Their assistants stood by vigilantly with small two-wheeled carts full of other weapons . . . clubs and straight blades and curved swords. An immense circle of on-lookers surrounded the mediums. I ran inside the circle, crouched down next to one of the assistants, and began taking pictures. He looked down and smiled—his teeth were stained reddish black from years of chewing betel nut. The closest spirit medium was twenty-feet away with his back toward me. Small spots of blood dotted the area between his shoulder blades. He stood rigid, as if in a trance. Big drums pounded. High-pitched horns screamed. Cymbals clanged. Incense fumed from a giant bronze urn at the foot of the temple steps. Several four-inch-square bundles of ghost money smoldered on the ground. One of the spirit mediums began to walk around the bundles in chicken steps—his face contorted and his eyes stared blankly. He pointed to a spot on the ground with his sword. His assistant immediately dropped three more bundles of ghost money in front of him and lit them on fire. A nearby pilgrim ignited a dozen beer-case-size boxes of firecrackers with a propane torch. The deafening explosions and smoke began to disorientate me. The spirit medium closest to me moved closer and quickly spun around. I got a good look at his monstrous face—it looked like a Frankenstein mask that had been gouged, torn, and pulverized with a hammer. A large pile of ghost money blazed in front of him, throwing his grim shadow onto the crowd. His eyes rolled back into his head completely, as if someone had stuffed a soft-boiled egg into each socket. Sweat covered his naked torso, and blood streamed from his forehead down his nose onto his chest. The assistant ran out and wiped some of the blood off his face with a rag. The assistant reached into his cart, grabbed a club spiked with nails, and handed it to the spirit medium, who bent over slowly until his torso was almost parallel to the ground, and then began beating himself furiously on the back with the club.

Past the circle of onlookers, near the buses, a long line of women dressed in white representing the goddess Kuanyin carried fish baskets of white flowers through the smoke. They weaved through the many piles of burning ghost money. Several pilgrims entered the circle with ten-foot replicas of popular gods worn over their heads; Shou Xing (god of longevity), Fu Shen (god of happiness), and Qiye and Baye (low level generals). They strutted around waving long phony arms paying homage to these deities. A procession of a dozen people from a different temple in matching tracksuits moved unsteadily through the crowd. They carried a large elaborate wooden box (palanquin) on two long poles. They seemed to be wrestling with this thing as if it were alive. It pulled them around as they fought to get inside the temple. They believed that the goddess Matsu was inside the box causing all the commotion. The horns and drums heaved and lurched in a chaotic frenzy. I was overcome by the noise and the intensity of the scene before me. I weighed a thousand pounds—my ears rang and my eyes burned and my heart pounded. I trudged through the smoke after the pilgrims carrying the palanquin like a young kid trying to keep up with his older brothers. The spirit mediums and procession swayed and lunged toward the temple's big wooden doors until they were all suddenly sucked inside as if by some invisible tempest. The immense cloud of white smoke began to lift after several minutes. I remembered Nadine and her mother. I couldn't find them. I stumbled to the busy temple staircase and found a place to rest.

The excitement and humidity had completely drained me—but I felt ecstatic as I'd already shot three rolls and couldn't wait for the bell to ring for the next fourteen rounds, which it did over the next two days as we raced south to several temples in Tainan County and in Beigang.

Soon after I arrived back at my ramshackle place in Taipei, I phoned Nadine and thanked her and her mother again for inviting me to accompany them on the pilgrimage. Then I dived onto my bed, put on The Doors' first record, smiled, and thought about how the experience was more than I'd hoped for—and the sixteen cooked rolls of film in my bag. Nobody, including the mediums, seemed to care that I was taking photos right up in their faces as they performed their sacred rituals. It was very different in Prague, where locals, especially older folks who had endured decades of Soviet communist oppression, were at times frightened by the sight of my camera. I swear, some sneered as they could somehow detect my imperialistic hide. I thought the same thing might occur in Taiwan, considering the way the KMT marched over the island with iron boots for nearly fifty years. The tolerant Taiwanese had continued to prove me wrong since the day of my arrival.

In the ensuing years, I've often visited these "other worlds" of Taoist temples to escape the delirious pace of Taiwan urban life. I'm not a Taoist, nor do I belong to any religion. But, I do consider myself to be a spiritual person, and the temples give me a wonderful sense of peace and tranquility. I'll never grow tired of visiting these pearls of Taiwanese culture.

I often think about my interview with Master Lee and his words of wisdom concerning the Tao, "Live simply. Live humbly. Follow the way of nature."

I try to do that, and fail half the time. But, I keep trying. I'm so very grateful that he took the time to speak with me, to get to know me, and because of him I'm able to *see* a little more of the road I'm traveling.

Happy Go Drive Thru

Mr. Leonard Thing and his Taiwanese girlfriend, Linda, were driving along Taipei's RenAi Road on a drizzly overcast afternoon in her new turquoise Volkswagen Beetle. Linda was taking Leonard somewhere; she said it was a surprise for his birthday. Leonard was a junior corporate lawyer at a large international export company, while Linda continued with her graduate studies in engineering at the renowned National Taiwan University.

"Your mom called," Linda said as she changed lanes. "She said she'll be connecting in L.A. instead of San Francisco on her flight from LaGuardia next month."

"Dear mumblety peg," Leonard said sarcastically, and he tucked in the front of his "I Survived Driving in Kaohsiung" T-shirt.

"Come on! It's been two years since the incident."

"Yeah. I've been in her doghouse for so long that I have to visit a veterinarian for my annual physical. Jesus, it's a big problem! My insurance won't cover it! I hope she remembers the Reese's Peanut Butter Cups and the knockwurst this time."

"She forgave you," cooed Linda.

"How could any mother, especially my JAP mother from Yonkers, forgive her son after he yanked off her fiancé's toupee at his son's bar mitzvah?"

"It was hilarious. And you and I and everyone else were pretty drunk by that time."

"Well, old Yedidiah didn't take it so well. He's sharpening the knives and planning revenge, Old Testament style, I know it."

"Your mom thinks Taipei's so exotic," chirped Linda, trying to change the subject.

"About as exotic as a ham sandwich," said Leonard. "She was humoring you. Brooklyn's more exotic than Taipei."

"Really?" Linda said with a frown.

"Come on, you know you have to go to southern Taiwan to get underneath."

"Anyway, happy birthday!" Linda screamed enthusiastically, throwing her head back. "Look in the glove box." She giggled.

Leonard opened the glove box and pulled out an envelope.

"Come on sleeve, open it."

Leonard opened the envelope and pulled out a white card. The front read:

Happy Go Drive Thru Circumcision

Leonard winced and opened the card. Inside it read:

Congratulations!

This certificate good for one super deluxe circumcision. Limited offer only. Good at any of the six Happy Go stores in Taiwan. Offer expires December 31.

Thank you for choosing Happy Go!

Leonard closed the card and placed it back in the envelope as if it contained something infectious.

"Jesus!" he said finally. "I know we've talked about it. But a drive-thru! Are you wacko?!"

"It's a new thing," Linda pleaded. "You know how Taiwanese demand and expect fast service. There are thousands of 7-Elevens on this little island."

"And at 7-Eleven they're not trimming foreskins off penises while they heat up some pathetic and carcinogenic 'food product' in the microwave," whined Leonard.

"Well, that's where we're going! It's your surprise!"

"Now?!" shouted Leonard. He opened the glove box and pulled out a plastic bag that contained his *soo zee* ball. He squeezed the golf-ball-size hunk of soft, pliable black rubber a few times until he calmed down. "I am tired of going around with this dork," he said softly.

"That's my line," laughed Linda.

Leonard laughed nervously.

"Don't worry, it's all done automatically with a machine," she said reassuringly.

"Oh great, a machine!" moaned Leonard. "What kind of machine? A hot dog steamer crossbred with a bread slicer?"

"Close."

"Christ, I think I'm going to have an historic episode, like the finale of some pathetic TV show!" Leonard blurted. "What if there's some kind of malfunction? I'm not a gecko or an earthworm, you know; I can't regenerate."

"Come on, Leonard," pleaded Linda in a soft voice. "Trust me."

"That's what Custer told his boys," said Leonard. "God, I'm too healthy," he continued fretfully. "I think I'm taking too much ginseng. I've developed this tic lately. When I'm sleeping on my side my leg twitches like a dog having a dream. I'm like a Ferrari with the idle set too high. I can't calm down."

"What about your mantra?"

"Soo zee, soo zee," repeated Leonard slowly over and over. He continued to gently squeeze the ball as he repeated his mantra.

"What happened to *chuck roast*?" Linda asked, surprised.

"At my appointment this week, Dr. Bender said it was associated too much with death and Baltic religions. You know, thick characters with names like Otto or Boris with bloody aprons and cleavers."

Linda glanced at the ball of rubber. "What is that stuff, anyway?"

"It's the goop they put between the joints of concrete for sidewalks," said Leonard as he continued kneading the rubber. "We used to pull it up when we were kids, and it just felt like it should be called *soo zee.* "

"Feeling better?" asked Linda.

"Soo zee," Leonard said, nodding his head.

"Now, remember what we talked about?" asked Linda. "I would really love to be able to give you more oral sex, and this way it'll be more hygienic and won't, uh . . ."

"I know," admitted Leonard. "Won't smell so bad."

"The heat and humidity are a big factor," she said consolingly.

"Maybe they should have a sign at the airport," said Leonard. "Beside the sign that says *Welcome to Taiwan, the Penalty for Drug Dealing is Death*, there should be a sign that reads: All Dorks Beware, Enough Smegma Will Grow On Your Uncircumcised Penis Here To Fill A Million Bottles of Smelling Salts."

"Honey, you know you're also extremely self conscious about the way your penis looks," Linda said gently.

"Now, that is true."

"This could help your low self-esteem. Don't you think so?"

Leonard groaned.

"Oh look! There's the sign," said Linda. "That's it."

"My god!" squealed Leonard. "It looks like a Wendy's Hamburger without the crazy little girl on the sign."

"It actually used to be a Wendy's," said Linda. "Wendy's might be the only American fast food chain that's been unsuccessful in Taiwan."

The couple pulled in and stopped at the drive-thru menu. A young Taiwanese woman poked her head out of the drive-thru window twenty yards ahead, took a quick look at the pair, and then ducked back inside.

The large flimsy plastic menu read:

Welcome to Happy Go Drive Thru Circumcision

Please choose the ring type you would like:

High and Tight

Eraser

Wing Nut

Old Kentucky

Mr. Lucky

Leonard leaned across Linda's lap and yelled into the speaker, "I'll have a cheeseburger, hold the mayo, small fries, and a large Frosty! Oh, and one circumcision!"

"May I please take your order?" said a small female voice through the speaker.

"And two lobotomies with everything!" yelled Leonard into the speaker. "Oh, make those extra crispy. It's my birthday."

"Sorry, they don't sell hamburgers here anymore," said the small voice.

"Hi, we have a gift certificate for one super deluxe circumcision," Linda said slowly and politely into the speaker.

"And the ring type you desire?" asked the small voice.

"What's Mr. Lucky?" asked Leonard.

"Oh, it's our most popular," said the small voice. "I guess you could say its normal, like the kind you would get at the hospital as a baby."

"One Wing Nut to go," said Leonard.

"Are you sure?" asked Linda.

"Can you do an Abe Lincoln?" Leonard asked the girl. "Something in a stovepipe?"

"Sorry," said the girl.

"How about something in a mushroom cloud?" asked Leonard.

"I'm afraid we can't," said the girl.

"Can you do some kind of buff and shine or hot wax at the end?" asked Leonard.

"Sorry," said the small voice. "Oh, I forgot!" shouted the girl. "We have a new one!"

"What's it called?" Leonard asked excitedly.

"It's for the truly adventurous," she said.

"Yes?" asked Leonard.

"The Arrowhead."

"The Arrowhead?" said Leonard with astonishment. "I'm trying to picture it in my mind, and all I keep seeing is two retrievers stuck together after humping, and some old neighbor lady trying to separate them with a garden hose."

The voice from the speaker giggled.

"Okay, Mr. Lucky, then," said Leonard.

"Sure this time?" asked Linda.

Leonard nodded.

"We better switch places," said Linda.

The pair got out of the car and changed seats. Leonard slowly drove up to the drive thru window, stopped, and shifted the Beetle into park. A young, sexy Taiwanese girl was standing at the window holding a clipboard and a caliper. She was wearing a yellow bikini top and a red miniskirt. The nametag on her miniskirt read "Ginger."

"Hello, I need some personal information before we proceed," said Ginger with a smile.

"Are you a doctor?" Leonard asked nervously. "Ginger, how does this work?"

"What's your full name, please?"

"Leonard Thing."

"No middle name, Mr. Thing?"

"No, they cut it off at birth instead of my foreskin."

"Now Mr. Thing, we need to measure," she said, still smiling.

"Please, tell me there's a physician here."

"Dr. Drill committed suicide a few weeks ago. We're waiting for a replacement."

"Really?! How did Dr. Black and Decker off himself?"

"Swimming pool."

"He drowned himself?"

"He ate his rubber pool."

"One of those little plastic blow-up pools for kids?"

"Exactly."

"Jesus! At least he was original."

"Let's get you measured," she said. "We usually get kids and babies most of the time."

"It looks a lot younger than it actually is," said Leonard. "And it has extremely low mileage. Does that qualify for some kind of discount?"

"Please slide your pants off, sir," said the young girl.

Leonard pulled his shorts down.

"Jesus, I have freckles!" he shouted. "I guess I've never really examined it outside before. Well, there was the catastrophic incident when I was caught red-handed in a circle jerk at summer camp when I was in junior high."

The girl quickly and deftly placed the calipers around Leonard's penis and took measurements of both length and girth. She jotted the measurements down on the clipboard.

"You're not going to post my manly man details on the Internet or sell them to some other penal cottage industry like penis lengthening or straightening or bending or what have you, are you?" asked Leonard.

"Come on Leonard," pleaded Linda. "Relax."

"All strictly confidential," the young girl said with certainty.

"That's what blank said to blank," said Leonard.

Linda handed Ginger the gift certificate.

"Wait one minute," the girl said, and she turned around and disappeared from the window.

She returned shortly carrying a shiny silver aluminum box the size of a shoebox. In one end there was a four-inch hole.

"Jesus, it looks like a giant pencil sharpener or a coffin for a chinchilla!" Leonard shrieked.

"Please, uh—" said the girl with a giggle.

Leonard cut her off and said, "I know what you want to say."

"Can I?"

"I've heard them all. In school they called me *The Thing* after the movie."

"Okay," Ginger said with a playful smile. "Mr. Thing, could you please put your thing in the—"

"Thing," Leonard said finishing her sentence.

The girl became suddenly calm. "Please set this on your lap, and whenever you're ready, place your penis into the hole," she said professionally as she handed the box to Leonard. "Relax, and the machine will do the rest. It will all be over in approximately seven to ten minutes."

"Will this hurt?" asked Leonard.

"Tomorrow," the girl replied with an apologetic smile.

Suddenly, a pudgy, frantic middle-aged European man with a mustache appeared and ran up to Linda's window.

He stuck his sweaty head into the car window and stammered in broken English at the top of his lungs, "I, I has the, the mold! In my, my refrigerator! I has the mold in my refrigerator! It's like a p-p-poison!"

"Congratulations," sneered Leonard. "But we don't need any mold. We have plenty at home. Check back with us next month."

"I need a cleaning agent!" the man said desperately, and he put both hands on top of his head.

"Wipe the mold out with a damp cloth and then wipe the inside of the fridge down with fresh lime juice," said Linda.

"Lime? Juice?" asked the man. "Oh, thank you. You are charitable so much."

"If that doesn't work," Leonard said, looking the man up and down, "try hanging some of your soiled under shorts in there for a week or so. That should kill anything. It works better than baking soda. Hey, have you been circumcised?"

"You crazy damn Americans!" the man said, shaking his head as he scrambled away.

"Are you ready?" asked the sexy girl in the drive-thru window.

A Taiwanese man smoking a cigarette pulled up on a motor scooter behind Linda's VW. He tried to drive up to the window in the narrow space between the VW and the building.

"He's trying to get in front of us!" Leonard said in amazement. "Just like some of these pushy bastards butting in front of me in line at the 7-Eleven. Can you believe it?!"

There wasn't enough space for the man's scooter to make it to the drive-thru window. He hopped off the scooter and ran up to the window, stood between Leonard and the young girl in the window, and tried to hand the girl money. She politely told him he had to wait his turn. He hopped back on his scooter and drove off.

"Go ahead, honey," said Linda.

Leonard took hold of his penis with one hand and slowly placed it into the hole at the end of the silver box. He reached over and took Linda's hand and squeezed it tightly.

The machine began to make a humming sound.

"I can't feel my dick," Leonard said in a quiet, nervous voice.

"Don't worry," assured the girl. "It's just the local anesthetic taking effect."

The machine stopped humming eight minutes later.

"Very slowly and gently take your penis out of the machine," instructed the girl.

Leonard followed the girl's directions by gingerly taking his penis out of the machine. The entire shaft was wrapped in heavy gauze.

"See!" said Linda.

The girl handed Linda a medium-sized brown paper bag.

"It's enough gauze and saline solution to last for ten days," she said. "Change the dressing twice a day. And, no sexual activity for at least two weeks."

While driving home, Linda asked, "Leonard, what's a circle jerk?"

"It's not a subject for nice girls."

"I'm not so nice sometimes."

"Okay. But you've been counseled."

"Go ahead, counselor."

"As with all conspiracies, this particular circle jerk was thought out with ruthless cold precision that only truly psychotic and unhinged individuals are capable of," Leonard said sternly. "I was at summer camp, Camp Silver Spoon, somewhere upstate when I was fourteen. There were the typical cliques of jocks and pretty boys and guys like me they called nerds or freaks because we excelled in academics not sports."

"Oh yeah, I saw that funny movie *Revenge of the Nerds*."

"Well, the good guys didn't win at Camp Happy Shit. About the fifth night a bunch of us guys were at a campfire sing-a-long. It was a coed camp, so there were girls there, too. The leaders made us do these kinds of stupid activities. I mean, sing-a-longs are cool when you're seven or eight. When it ended, the girls went to their side of the campground where they had their tents. Around midnight our leaders went to bed, so it was just about ten of us guys sitting around all full of energy."

"One of the jocks said, 'Anybody want to make some money? It'll cost you five bucks to play.'

"The rest of us kids huddled around the picnic table where this kid was sitting. A dozen new aluminum pie tins sat on the table in a neat stack."

'It's real simple,' he said with an evil grin. 'We sit in a big circle and put out the fire until it's so dark we can't see nothing.'

'Then what?' asked some other kid.

'We all jerk off, and the first kid that comes in his pie tin wins all this loot. Fifty bucks!'

'That's fucking bullshit!' said another kid.

'Chicken?' snickered the boy. 'No one can say nothing to anybody cause we all are jerking off together, stupid.'

"One boy we all liked said he was game, and the rest of us followed. We each took a pie tin and sat in a big circle with about ten feet between each boy. A few kids put out the fire, and it was pitch-black with nothing but a million stars twinkling so poetically."

'Don't any of you assholes start until I say go!' the boy called out.

'Fuck you!' another kid said.

'Okay, now, when I say *go*, start jerking off, and when you shoot into the tin call out. First one wins the cash, okay?'

'Okay,' a bunch of kids muttered nervously.

'Go!' yelled the boy.

"I tore my briefs off and started masturbating as fast as I could. I was determined to win all that moola. I was fantasizing about this pretty girl in math class and was really working my pecker, and after four or five minutes I came into the pie tin and yelled out, 'I'm done! I win!'

"I was immediately flooded with cold beams of burning light from the other kids' flashlights. I couldn't see anything, but I could feel in my bones that I had made a mammoth error in judgment. A life-threatening, suicidal mistake. The other kids ran to me, laughing hysterically, and circled me with their flashlights still shining on me. They all had their clothes on, and each one dropped his dry pie tin in front of me."

'Jesus Christ!' yelled one kid. 'Look at that little load!!'

"The other boys continued to laugh and squeal and call me names, like jerk-off and circle-jerk king and flash in the pan. I can't describe to you how humiliated I felt. About an hour later, after everyone was asleep, I gathered my stuff and snuck out of camp. I hitchhiked to a Greyhound station and took the long, sad bus ride back to Brooklyn."

"I'm so sorry, Leonard!" said Linda. "Oh my god! It is a funny story, though."

"It is. I was just a dumb fourteen-year-old."

"Did you ever get revenge like in the movie?"

"I don't believe in revenge. Besides, none of those kids went to my school. They were from all over the state, so no one back home ever found out about it."

Leonard and Linda were at home late one evening two and a half weeks later.

"Want to ring the bell?" asked Leonard.

"Really think you're ready?" asked Linda.

"Yeah."

"Oh, I can't wait to, uh . . ."

"Unveil it?" said Leonard. "Are you still mad at me for not letting you see it?"

"Well, at least you could have let me help change the bandages."

"I wanted it to be a surprise. You know, our first time since the, you-know . . ."

"Let's take it real slow," said Linda. "We don't want to give you a . . ."

"Rupture," said Leonard.

"Yeah."

They went into the bedroom and quickly took off their clothes. Linda dimmed the lights very low. Leonard sat on the edge of the bed. Linda knelt down and slowly began to unwrap the gauze from his penis. When she finished, they looked at each other in shock.

"It glows in the dark!" squealed Linda. Leonard's penis emitted a soft blue light that lit up her face.

"I'm a comic book hero!" cried Leonard.

"Leonard, it's beautiful! Your penis!"

Linda took the blue glowing member in her hands, placed it gently in her mouth and began to suck on it.

"I'm a blue light special," Leonard said proudly. "What about when I go camping with the guys in Kenting? I guess I could use a sock."

"Uh-huh," Linda moaned as she continued sucking.

"Do you really like the way it looks?" asked Leonard. "It feels straighter now that it's hard. Maybe they threw in an alignment?"

"It's absolutely wonderful," Linda said, and she took the glowing penis out of her mouth and slowly stroked it. "Does this hurt?"

"I'm okay. Hey, do you need sunglasses? Was this part of the surprise?"

"No! I didn't know anything about this! Look at it! It's getting brighter as your dick gets harder."

"I know! Like a glowworm! Ever heard of the Green Lantern comic-book hero? Call me the Blue Lantern."

"They did a wonderful job with the circumcision, Mr. Lucky," Linda cooed before putting the glowing penis back into her mouth.

"Yeah, it looks great," cackled Leonard. "Maybe we should buy it a tux."

"It's so sexy, and it makes me so hot! Fuck me! Fuck me with your big blue cock light!" pleaded Linda as she lay down in the middle of the bed.

"I'm glad she likes blue," Leonard quipped and he lifted her legs over his shoulders and entered her. "I almost forgot how sexy you are without any clothes," he said.

An hour later the exhausted naked couple was relaxing in bed.

"You know, we can't go back to Happy Go," Leonard said, and he took a huge bite from a dreamy melted-cheddar-and-tuna sandwich.

"Oh, I know," said Linda as she sipped red tea. "If the Taiwan media ever found out, they'd strip our bones like piranhas. Remember how pissed off Elton John was the last time he came here when they smothered the poor man at the airport?"

"Fucking hyenas," said Leonard.

"I lost my virginity listening to the *Yellow Brick Road* album," said Linda.

"With your father doesn't count," laughed Leonard.

"Funny, lantern boy," chortled Linda. "Leonard, I have a confession to make," she said bashfully.

"About what?"

"I've been fantasizing all night about you having sex with Ginger, you know, the young girl from Happy Go."

"Really?"

"Yeah, all three of us are in our bed with the lights down low, and I'm watching your magnificent glowing blue cock slide in and out of her."

"Oh Jesus, you're making me horny with talk like that."

"Yeah?"

"You know, I've been fantasizing about the same thing, and I give both of you a good working over. I really take you to town."

"You're kidding, right?" asked Linda.

"What, it's okay for you to fantasize about me schtupping Ginger, but I can't?"

"Leonard!"

"I'm kidding."

"I don't believe you."

"But of course, if there was a gun to my head I just may be able to have sexual intercourse with the girl."

"Want to do it again?" asked Linda, and she sat up in bed and pulled her T-shirt off.

"Sure."

"Let's dim the lights again, okay, so I can see your wonderful blue boner."

Linda sat on top of Leonard, straddling his thighs, and leaned forward so that he could reach her breasts with his mouth. She knew this always got him off. A few minutes later she gently placed his glowing blue erect penis inside of her.

"Jesus Christ! Look at your tits!" shouted Leonard. "They're blue like me!"

Linda looked down at her glowing blue breasts, smiled and asked, "Does it hurt?"

"I'm okay."

"My ass feels warm," she said and looked over her shoulder and down at her buttocks. "Oh, shit! It's blue, too!"

The sight of Linda's glowing blue breasts excited Leonard. He blew up the bag faster than microwave popcorn.

It went on like this for the next month. Leonard's penis and Linda's breasts and buttocks continued to glow with a bright blue light each time they had sex.

One evening in bed six weeks after their visit to Happy Go, Linda said, "I told somebody."

"Oh, Jesus! Who! I thought we promised each other to keep this secret."

"Professor Turner."

"The Brit from school?"

"Yeah."

"Why?"

"He swims with some very aristocratic fish."

"Tell me the old boy doesn't know where we live or our phone number?"

"He doesn't know where we live or our phone number."

"I feel a tiny bit better," whined Leonard. "As if a doctor just told me I have cancer but not to worry because it's only spread to half of my internal organs."

"Extremely privileged people like him and his crowd are easily bored. It's nothing for them to travel halfway around the world to a secret dinner of animals on the endangered species list. They do that like we go to a movie."

"What's this got to do with my blue dick and your blue tits and ass?"

"He knows people who will pay a fortune to see it."

"My dick?"

"Uh, huh."

"What kind of fortune?"

"Fifty thousand US dollars."

"Holy Moses! To see it once?"

"Yup."

"What about the media and getting eaten alive like Elton John? They'll find our blue skeletons floating in the Danshui River, and your sister will get the fifty grand and your VW."

"They have no motive to go to the media," said Linda. "They're filthy rich. Beyond filthy rich."

"Keep talking."

"And they want to keep this very discreet and have the presentation at one of their private homes. The place will have more security than a military base."

"What exactly do they want?"

"A little live sex show with the lights down low so they can get a good look at your gorgeous surprise."

"Live sex show with who?"

"Oh no, not me. I've been guaranteed that she will be a clean, sexy professional who will also get paid extremely well."

"She could go to the news."

"Who would believe her story? She'll have no proof, and you'll be wearing some type of mask so she won't be able to identify you."

"Will you be there?"

"Of course. Come on Leonard! One show for fifty grand cash. We can pay off my college loan and put a down payment on a house and take a long vacation to Europe like we've always dreamed about."

"When do they want the show?"

"Next weekend, if possible."

"How many people will be there?"

"Eleven total. Five couples and Professor Turner."

"No cameras or cell phones?"

"Nope."

"Do they know you glow, too?"

"No. That's our secret, sweetie."

"Fuck! Why me!"

"Cause you're special, Mr. Blue Lantern."

"Okay, I'll do it. But I'm only doing it for us. I wouldn't do it for myself alone."

"That's why I love you, sweetie."

On Saturday evening Linda and Leonard drove to a secluded home on a tree-lined street in Taipei's wealthy Neihu district.

Professor Turner was standing between two black Mercedes limos, which were parked in front of the house. He held a martini in one hand and a black briefcase in the other.

As Linda stopped the car, the professor walked over to her window, opened the case so that she could see inside and said, "As promised dear, fifty thousand US dollars in cash."

"Do you want a receipt?" Leonard quipped.

The professor frowned, handed the briefcase through the window and said, "They're waiting."

The couple followed the professor into the lavish home. Their audience was standing around a bar in tuxedos and evening gowns chatting and dipping their paws into a fine spread of crab, lobster, Beluga, exotic cheeses, and champagne. They all stopped talking and stared at Leonard.

"We forgot to put on your mask," Linda muttered, and she began to dig around in her purse.

"He looks like Alfred E. Neuman without the missing tooth," chuckled a pudgy American to his cake-battered wife.

"Alfred who?"

"*Mad* magazine's cover boy."

"Oh, yeah, he does, doesn't he?" she giggled while gawking at Leonard with detestation.

"This is like a pathetic Benetton commercial," whispered Leonard, and he put his mask on and glanced around at the racially diverse couples.

"Yes, indeed, we have patrons from Japan, the US, New Zealand, Singapore—and Taiwan, of course," the professor said proudly.

"Patrons?" said Leonard sarcastically under his breath. "How about freaks?"

"Leonard, shhh," Linda said.

The professor led the couple through a wide set of double doors and into a plush fifty-seat home-movie theater that looked like a miniature version of the state-of-the-art commercial venues found around the world. A double platform bed sat on the stage in front of a red satin curtain. The stiff mattress was covered with a single white slipcover.

"Where's the girl?" asked Linda.

"Getting ready."

"Where's she from?"

"Russia."

"Really?!"

"There's a huge market for Russian exotic dancers and prostitutes in places such as Macau. That's where we found her. You won't be disappointed."

"Does she know anything about Leonard's gift?"

"We thought the element of surprise on her part would add more drama. Would you like a drink or anything?"

"When do we start?" asked Leonard.

"Thirty minutes."

"White Russian," said Leonard.

"She's white."

"My drink."

"Oh, righto."

"Me, too," said Linda.

"Make mine a double," said Leonard.

"While I get the drinks, why don't you two go to your dressing room and relax. It's behind the stage. I'll come get you when we're ready to start," said the professor, and he walked out of the theater.

The couple found the dressing room.

"Want to be my fluffer?" asked Leonard as he began to undress.

"How much will you pay me?"

"Twenty-five grand."

"Okay."

"Don't take me over the falls, okay? We don't want to melt the ice cream."

The professor brought their drinks a short while later and left. He returned forty minutes later, knocked, and said, "Showtime. Stand behind the curtain and wait for your cue, please."

"Are you going to watch?" asked Leonard. He hugged Linda.

"Of course," she said, and adjusted the flamboyant gold colored mask that covered Leonard's eyes.

Leonard walked out of the dressing room naked with half a tuna and stood behind the curtain. He glanced at the bottom of the curtain and could see the stage lights dim way down.

"And now, what you've all been waiting for, ladies and gentlemen, I present to you the Blue Lantern," announced the professor, and as the curtain slowly rose and Leonard's glowing blue penis came into full view, the audience gasped with excitement.

With a confident smile, Leonard looked at the well-dressed patrons seated in the first two rows and the beautiful Russian woman kneeling on the bed. She was a striking brunette with a devil-may-care look in her eyes. She wore sheer thigh-high nylons and a sheer white bra that was pulled down underneath her large breasts. Leonard walked over to the edge of the bed. The composed girl gently took hold of his penis and began to slowly stroke it. Leonard's penis began to glow brighter as she continued stroking, and it became fully erect a few minutes later. The woman got down on all fours and Leonard entered her from behind. Leonard fucked her slowly. After ten minutes, the girl's breasts and ass began to glow with the same blue light, just as Linda's had. The audience clapped and hooted. Fifteen minutes later the blue light had spread to the girl's back, abdomen, and thighs.

"I feel really hot!" she cried out.

The audience clapped louder.

"Jesus! I feel really fucking hot!" screamed the girl, and her entire body began to glow.

Leonard fucked her harder. The girl glowed brighter and brighter until the patrons had to shield their eyes from the intense light.

"I'm going to come now!" moaned Leonard as he took his foot off the brake.

The Russian's body stopped glowing moments after Leonard pulled out.

The audience stood up, clapped, and yelled, "Bravo! Bravo!"

A few of the aristocrats muttered amongst themselves that they weren't entirely convinced. They thought it was an act, some kind of magician's illusion like the fantastic shows in Las Vegas they had witnessed. Leonard hurried backstage, dressed quickly, rushed with Linda out to the car, and drove down the hill toward Taipei.

"Her entire body was glowing!" Linda said.

"Christ! I know! I know! Did that really happen?"

"Did it?"

"How come I didn't turn totally blue, too?" Leonard asked.

"Let's try to calm down, okay?" urged Linda as her cell phone began to ring. "It's the professor!" she cried. "How did he get this number?" She stared at the phone.

"Talk to him," said Leonard, and he leaned over so that he could hear the conversation.

"Professor," said Linda.

"She's dead."

"What?"

"The girl died five minutes ago."

Leonard grabbed the phone from Linda and said, "What the hell do you mean she's dead?!"

"I know a private doctor. I can take the both of you to see him tonight. We must hurry! It's your only chance. But I'll require half of the fifty thousand back tonight or I go to the police."

"How did you even get this number? She's not dead, asshole. Go ahead, call the cops."

"Be reasonable," purred the professor. "If we don't get you to the doctor, it's only a matter of time before the two of you end up like that poor Russian girl."

"We know it's all a con."

"What?"

"You and the Russian set up these dominoes," Leonard said. "You were going to get the cash and spend the next month monkey-fucking her in some Macau high-rent slum."

"Meet me with the money at the Sun Yet San Memorial in an hour, and I'll take you immediately to my doctor," demanded the professor, and then he hung up.

Leonard and Linda didn't know what to do. Linda suggested that they drive back to the professor's house and investigate. Leonard disagreed, and said that they should stash the fifty thousand, sit tight and do nothing. When they got back to their apartment, Leonard hid the money. Ten minutes later they decided to drive to one of their favorite Japanese restaurants, where they dined on fresh sushi and sashimi and Sapporo beer.

"Maybe we should cruise over to Happy Go and try to find Ginger," suggested Linda as they drove home from the restaurant.

"Oh, I don't know about that," said Leonard. "I know how they did it!" he laughed.

"How?"

"The professor rubbed some kind of invisible cream or liquid on her body in her dressing room before the show."

"And then they activated it somehow while you two were having sex?"

"Yeah, and the light got brighter and brighter, and it wasn't the same color blue as me—only at first her breasts and ass glowed like me and like you."

"We don't have to worry about that fool professor," Linda giggled confidently. "We're rich!"

"Hey, I did the job I was paid to do, and I'm not going to worry about some greedy lame noodle of a prof."

"What, me worry?" said Linda.

"Let's get some ice cream, richy."

"Okay," said Linda as she stopped at a traffic signal. "Then can we go to try to find Ginger?"

"I'm going to count how many people run this red light," Leonard said ignoring her question. "There's one, two—"

"Leonard! Right now I don't want to hear one of your diatribes about how people drive here. After all, you come from the land of road rage."

"Okay! Okay!"

Linda's phone began to ring again.

"It's him," said Linda.

"Don't answer it."

"Right."

The traffic was as heavy and chaotic as usual, clogged with cars, bicycles, and motor scooters. A young Taiwanese man around twenty pulled up and stopped his scooter next to Leonard's window.

"Look at his bleached hair and those piercings," marveled Linda.

"You know who are the real rebels of Taiwan society?" said Leonard. "I mean the really defiant ones?"

"Who?"

"Kids his age who turn their back on society and become monks, and live the rest of their lives in a monastery in the mountains. That takes a lot of chutzpa."

"But the monastery is just another institution with its politics and control."

"At least they can escape this endless hell of the pursuit of material possessions. Taiwan's getting so much like the US that way. It's sad."

"Ever had sex in a car wash?" asked Linda.

"With another person, never," Leonard said with a straight face.

"I got gang-banged by three neighbor boys in a car wash when I was seventeen."

"Really?" asked Leonard with a shaky whimper.

"Got you! You should've seen your face. You looked completely mortified."

"Christ! I'll get you back, you sly little trickster."

"I can't wait."

"If there were more caves in Taiwan, monks could live there beyond any institutional power or control," said Leonard.

"I know where one is."

"A cave?"

"A car wash, dummy."

"Could you live in a cave to be free from all of this?"

"If I could have my weekly stinky tofu fixes."

Fifteen minutes later Linda pulled into the parking lot of an ice cream store on Chungshan Road. She leaned over and gave Leonard a sloppy wet kiss.

"Look Leonard!" she cried with horror, and she looked at her glowing blue face in the rearview mirror.

"The light!" screamed Leonard, and he pulled up his shirt and examined his glowing torso.

"It's spreading!" yelled Linda. "Your neck is glowing, too!"

"You're glowing more, too!" shouted Leonard, and he pulled up her shirt. "Look at your stomach. Oh my god! You're a goddamned comic book hero, too!"

"Oh, my fucking god!" Linda screeched as she examined her glowing abdomen.

"Better cover your face!" Leonard said. He opened the glove box and pulled out a surgical mask similar to the ones they wear whenever they ride his scooter.

Linda quickly put it on. The horde of traffic and people on Chungshan Road fizzed in front of them.

"Is anybody looking?" she asked.

"Only a group from a tour bus," said Leonard as a throng of twenty Chinese tourists crept toward them.

"Oh god!"

"Floor it! Some of them have cameras!"

A few minutes later the couple was safely lost in the maze of traffic.

"Keep your head down," commanded Linda. "We're glowing like an electrocution."

"What the hell are we going to do?" cried Leonard.

"Let's go over to Happy Go right now! We can't be the only ones this has happened to! Somebody there must know what to do about it!"

"No, honey! What if this is just a fluke? What if we go to Happy Go and they turn the media on us? We've got to go home and calm down and think of the best thing to do."

"Oh, the Russian girl!" Linda said with barely concealed terror. "Maybe we should go to the hospital."

"Okay, okay," Leonard conceded as his hospital phobia began to bite him on the ass. "Let's go to Happy Go."

I love you," Linda said smiling, and she stepped on the gas.

They arrived at Happy Go fifteen minutes later.

"Park across the street," said Leonard. "Let's see if we can spot Ginger."

Linda parked on the other side of Chungshan, but they couldn't see the drive-thru window well enough to notice if Ginger was there.

"Let's wait for them to close," she said. "Then I'll drive up, and you get out and try to grab her."

"Sounds good, flame girl."

Happy Go's lights turned off thirty minutes later.

"Floor it flame!" shouted Leonard.

Linda hit the gas and the Beetle zoomed across the street and into Happy Go's parking lot.

"Christ! There she is!" screeched Linda, and she jammed on the brakes in front of the girl.

Leonard jumped out, ran up to Ginger, grabbed the frightened girl by her arm, and dragged her into the backseat of the car and slammed the door.

"Remember us?" asked Leonard, and he pulled up his shirt while Linda sped away.

Linda pulled her mask down and quickly turned her head to give the trembling girl a good look.

"Oh, no!" Ginger whimpered. "Not you, too!"

"How many other blue freaks are running around Taiwan?" asked Leonard.

"Is your, your penis you know—"

"Blue as Superman's tights," said Leonard.

"Five maybe," said Ginger. "I don't know. It was Dr. Drill. He controlled everything."

"Five!" shouted Leonard. "That's just grand. We could all meet for therapy sessions on Tuesday evenings at the Holiday Inn right after Betel Nut Chewers Anonymous."

"What do you mean Drill controlled everything?" barked Linda.

"There were all kinds of strange rumors about the doctor. One was that he loathed himself so much because he had a small uncircumcised penis; a micro-penis, and that he used to masturbate with an old welder's glove. You know, the kind with the little rubber teats all over the palm for a better grip.

"Jesus," Leonard moaned with laughter.

"Another was that he used to work on the secret military base in Area 51 in Nevada. And he experimented on dead aliens, and that's where he got the technology to make human skin glow blue. There's red and green, too."

"Oh, like pretty Christmas lights," chided Leonard.

"And the nut case used this technology on the Happy Go

machines?" asked Linda.

"Yeah, but nobody knew and no one directed him. I'm so sorry. They told us after his suicide that all of the machines that he had tampered with to make skin glow were found and destroyed. I would have never put you at risk if I knew that there were any left."

"So, I've got E.T.'s dick?"

"Kind of," whispered Ginger.

"And all I wanted was a stovepipe with some chin whiskers like Honest Abe."

"Has anybody died?" asked Linda.

"Died?" said the girl with surprise. "I don't think so."

"Why make penises glow blue?" asked Linda.

Ginger shrugged and said, "Who knows? He was crazy, I guess."

"Any cure?" asked Leonard.

"I'm sorry," she said. "The mad genius is the only one who knew the secret."

"Maybe if I rub it long enough it will wear off like one of those temporary tattoos," said Leonard.

Ginger laughed nervously as Linda pulled over and parked along the side of Chungshan. Linda turned around and said, "Promise that you won't go running to the press or tell anybody."

"I promise," said the girl.

Leonard opened the door and let her out. The tired couple drove toward home without stopping for any ice cream.

The professor phoned Linda twice more, but she didn't answer either of the calls. The couple arrived at home at one thirty, too tired to think about it anymore. They went to bed, agreeing that Leonard would call in sick the next morning and they'd spend the whole next day thinking about possible solutions.

At 4:00 a.m. Leonard awoke having to urinate and discovered that his entire body was glowing with the same blue light that had been emitting earlier from his penis, thighs, and buttocks. He looked over at Linda, whose face was glowing. He pulled back the sheets. Her entire body was glowing with the blue light.

"Linda! Linda! Wake up!"

She rolled over and said, "Huh? Leonard?"

"We're all blue!" he cried. "Look!"

"Oh, my god Leonard! We're not having sex, either."

"I know! I know! Like the Russian! What the hell are we going to do?"

"Leonard, my body feels really hot."

"Me, too."

"Hold me, Leonard!"

Leonard got into bed and tenderly embraced Linda.

"I love you, honey" said Leonard.

"I love you, too, sugar pie," whispered Linda, and she held onto Leonard tightly.

Their bodies erupted in flames. The bedroom was badly burned, in spite of the sprinkler system and the fire department's quick response.

The police and fire department spent the next two days going through the couple's apartment trying to determine the cause of the fire. Their results were inconclusive. A week later Linda's relatives removed the couple's furniture and personal belongings that weren't too smoke damaged.

Once Leonard and Linda's apartment was rehabbed, Miss Amparo Pagaspas, a humble, hard-working, overweight twenty-year-old Filipino maid, was assigned to clean up the mess and make sure everything was ready for prospective tenants to view. She came across something unusual as she was cleaning the bathroom closet. Behind the top shelf, she found a false wall. She pushed open the one-foot-square panel with the end of a broom. There she found two large plastic freezer bags stuffed with stacks of US one-hundred-dollar bills. She carefully removed the money, placed it in her purse, and slung the purse over her shoulder. Then she replaced the false wall, locked the front door behind her, and walked to the nearby subway station.

Atom Gun

The pineapple-field workers toil while a Pingtung County sunset splatters the zigzag clouds with their ancestors' blood. The workers' joints creak and snap like the lever action of a Winchester 30-30. Machetes . . . heavy leather gloves . . . wide-brimmed straw hats . . . Long Life cigarettes. Head to toe, the women's bodies are covered with lightweight cotton clothing, slits for eyes and mouths. Bend, grab hold, slash, then alley-oop the pineapples into the back of a flatbed—all day until the rust-barrel sunset falls, until night snuffs out the flame. Bend, grab hold, slash, with their babies playing around by the line of parked motorbikes on the hill above the field. In the distance, a cluster of brick houses that have seen a hundred summers buzzing with beautiful kids shine hot red-orange in the crosshairs of the sun's atom gun. Their parched courtyards are flanked by east and west wings that reach out to the cane like loving mothers. The surrounding fields dusky, glorious, filled with the bones of good men and women, bulls, monks, teachers, and musicians—a fine place to die. The voice of an old-time Taiwanese singer coming from a scratchy transistor radio slays the birds and knocks down the cypress trees. The air smells like Um's marmalade and thousand-dollar bills . . . the high-pitched whelp of a far-off motorbike with a fat dinner duck strapped across butterfly handlebars. The field crunches under plodding rubber boots. Bend, grab hold, slash, then alley-oop into the back of the flatbed.

Voodoo High

Taichung's main vein was a boilerplate special on a Friday
night hot and a little dangerous like a drunk with wild eyes
and a smile like a flatfish Sunset Union wheels oozed out of
karaoke clubs on alligator paws with powdered teen fairies in
the breast pockets of sharkskin suits sandwiched between a cell
and an American Express and a bankroll fat as a duck sandwich neon went to the stars lighting up the promenade of slick
company men with black briefcases short-sleeve white dress
shirts and ties a nun would approve of and office girls string-
ing out a chum line dressed better than the sexy mannequins
in the big windows teens with glazed eyes on voodoo highs
watched straight-backed good girls float by on blue seahorses
the intoxicating noises of the street the sky began to spit someone was madly turning the key to the city cranking the handle
on top of Tuxedo Tower to get this cotton candy machine
jump-started I was on an all-nighter full of forty weight and
taxi cab exhaust chomping on a Cuban chasing the seahorses
like a madman on a Taiwan raid with no thoughts of the past
or future right there in Buddha's lap seeing every inch of this
noodle dish all the beautiful sweet people who let me sneak
into their muggy dream.

Want To Drive To the Sea?

Gregorio Gregarious was shaving naked in the tiny bathroom of his cramped Keelung apartment. He was smiling and gently humming the Beach Boys song "Wouldn't It Be Nice" and thinking about how relieved he'd feel once they had enough money saved to move back home to Manila and buy a house—back to Sunday services with the whole family at St. Phillip's Catholic Church and the traditional get-together at his parents' house afterwards with much wine and traditional delicacies such as *lechon* (whole roasted pig), a hearty chicken stew called *tinola*, and his favorite, *kare-kare*—ox tail with vegetables in peanut sauce.

Gregorio sniffed the air deeply with a nose as flat and dark as a halibut and thought, "Camia flowers, yeah, that's what she smells like after we make love."

His slim and sultry wife, Carmen, was lying on the bed in the other room flipping through a comic called *Me, Me, Me*, which spoofed the fashion industry.

"What are you doing in there?" she asked in a seductive voice.

"Are you going to put on the things I bought you?" Gregorio said as he gazed vainly at his trim muscular physique with his slightly bulging eyes.

He could hear her moving around on the bed, putting on the lingerie. That was the best part, he mused, the thought of her lying there waiting for him. She made his low-paying, sixty-hour workweek cleaning hotel rooms worth it. Carmen worked in a laundry Tuesday through Saturday. They had been working that way in Taiwan for three grueling years. He really loved her, even though she could be eccentric. She insisted, for instance, that they listen to the theme song from the game show *Jeopardy!* while they made love. She even had recordings of the original show dating back to the 1960s.

"What the hell is it with Art Fleming?" he wondered, not for the first time.

Gregorio took his time, finished shaving, tugged on his half erect penis a few times, and walked out of the bathroom.

Carmen smiled girlishly, slowly unfastened her bra, looked down at her breasts, and asked, "Hey, handsome, want to drive to the sea?"

A week later Gregorio came home from work early. He wanted to surprise Carmen. As he entered the apartment he could hear her laughing hysterically over the theme song from *Jeopardy!* from behind the closed bedroom door.

"What the fuck?" he muttered, and his mind raced to the scene of three years earlier when he caught Carmen humping their Manila employment recruiter. She begged for forgiveness and promised it would never happen again. He wanted to believe her. Gregorio looked around the apartment to see if anything was out of place. "Should I grab the Tongue Dinger or the baseball bat before I go in there?" he asked himself as he rummaged clumsily through a kitchen drawer filled with an array of sex toys, hunting knives, and marijuana paraphernalia.

Then, with a lime Tongue Dinger in one hand and the bat in the other, he gently pushed the bedroom door open. Carmen was sitting on the bed wearing red shorts, a black bra, and a cheap plastic Yogi Bear Halloween mask. A half dozen other masks were strewn on the bed, including Deputy Dog, Bugs Bunny, and Porky Pig.

Carmen turned and looked at her husband and then burst into wild laughter.

"What the hell is going on?" pleaded Gregorio.

Carmen continued laughing.

"That's our sex music!" he said, and walked over and sat on the bed next to his wife. He lifted up her mask and observed her pupils. They were as big as poker chips.

"I took some LSD, big boy!" she giggled.

"Jesus and Maria! With who?"

"Tony at work gave it to me. I'm so fucked up!"

"Tony the baloney?"

"Tony the salamander face!" Carmen said, and burst out laughing.

"Oh, that Tony," said Gregorio with a frown.

"Do it with me! Okay?"

"What is it?" asked Gregorio.

"Orange Sunshine or Sunshine Up or something," she laughed and handed Gregorio a small Ziploc baggie containing six tiny squares of paper blotter acid.

"Remember the last time? How many did you take?"

"One, or maybe one hundred," she laughed.

Gregorio took one of the small pieces of paper out of the baggie; held it up to his face and studied it closely.

"Put it on your tongue, and it'll dissolve like a goddamn Pez!"

"I know, I know," Gregorio said, rolling his eyes.

He ate the acid and picked up a couple of the Halloween masks. Carmen picked up the Porky Pig mask.

"That's the right one for you today," she giggled.

Gregorio put the mask on.

"Your entrance with that bat and the Dinger!" Carmen blurted out and began laughing so hard she fell off the bed and rolled around on the floor. "You looked so pathetic and dumb!"

"I suppose I did."

"You sure did, Mr. Cheerios. Mr. Dildo."

"What about you with that mask and Art Fleming?"

"I got horny after I ate the acid. But that wore off when you came in because you're so funny."

"Did Tony eat any?"

"No, he had to work today."

"Have you ever fucked Tony?"

"Remember the rules," she snickered playfully. "That's not an acid question, big boy."

"I'm sorry," he said sheepishly.

"Jealous?"

"Yeah, a little," Gregorio said and set the dildo on the nightstand. "I've seen him give you the look."

"He's a horny little guy; gives all the girls at work the look."

After ten minutes the LSD turned Gregorio into cheese dip. He stripped down to his boxers and switched masks to Dudley Do-Right. He found a bottle of Jack Daniel's, and they began taking shots; after each shot they stuffed a wedge from a freshly cut orange into their mouths.

"Let's go outside!" yelled Carmen.

"Where?"

"Let's eat some elephant penis!" she screamed with laughter. "I have some!"

"I want chocolate gumbo!" squealed Gregorio.

"Come and see," Carmen said as she walked into the kitchen, got down on her knees and opened the refrigerator door.

Gregorio took another shot of JD, stuffed a slice of orange into his mouth and walked into the kitchen.

"Here it is!" Carmen yelled out as if she'd found a hidden treasure.

She held up a two-foot-long piece of ox tail.

"That's quite a hot dog!" yelled Gregorio. "Did you get any buns?"

"I've got buns," she winked.

There was a loud knock on the door. The couple looked at one another and burst out laughing.

"Ask if they have any buns," said Carmen.

Gregorio went to the door and looked through the peephole. "Jesus! It's those two freaky Mormon kids again," he whispered loudly. "Get a shirt on, peaches."

Several weeks before, two Mormons had approached Carmen on the sidewalk as she walked up to the apartment after work. This was their third visit. On the first visit Gregorio had told them politely that he and Carmen weren't interested in hearing about what the Mormon religion had to offer.

On the second visit the Mormons weren't so lucky. That time Gregorio had opened the door and found the same two smiling young men standing there very straight and resolute.

"They all look the fucking same," Gregorio had thought. "It's always two young white guys with nice hair, around twenty-two, short-sleeved white dress shirts with name-tags, ties, and dark dress pants. And the bicycles. Those fucking bicycles."

The tall Mormon said, "Hello again. We just wanted to say that if you ever need any help—"

"Need any help!" Gregorio interrupted. "Need any help! You psychos! You poor little lost psychos!"

"I'm sorry, sir, did I say something wrong?" said the tall Mormon apologetically.

"Okay! Okay!" Gregorio said. He leaned against the doorjamb, trying to calm himself down. "Doesn't it seem outrageously arrogant and pitiful to you," he said slowly, "that a small group of people are actually naive enough to believe that their religious worldview is the only correct one, and that all the rest of us poor helpless heathens need them to save us from eternal damnation?"

"Well, sir, uh," the blond Mormon said ruefully.

"Well, what?" Gregorio said sternly and looked both Mormons in the eye. "The Taiwanese don't need you. You probably need them. You're fortunate that most Taiwanese are open-minded and tolerant of people like yourselves and that they allow you to invade people's privacy the way you do. Your wiring's fucked up, Brigham. But you've been programmed all too well not to see what you're doing, what you are. You boys are young, and it's really not your fault you are the way you are. But now you are men, and it's time to wake up."

"We're just trying to help," the tall Mormon said softly.

"I know you are," said Gregorio. "Did you notice the Taoist

temple across the street?"

"Uh, not really," said the blond Mormon.

"Ever visited a Taoist temple? There must be thousands of them on the island."

"No."

"Think for a minute what would happen if hundreds of pairs of young, devout Taiwanese Taoists went to Salt Lake City and started banging on doors with the intent of rolling Mormons in flour and throwing them into the Taoism frying pan."

The boys chuckled nervously.

"Tell me what would happen," Gregorio said firmly.

"They'd probably get arrested or be asked to vacate the city limits," said the blond Mormon.

"Or lynched," Gregorio said. "I have a cousin in the States that married a gal stationed in the Air Force somewhere in Utah. Ogden, maybe. He told me that the Mormon block leader in his neighborhood used to regularly come knocking on their door asking for money—not a donation but a kind of tax or extortion for living among the Mormons. My cousin told the guy many times that they weren't Mormons. They guy said that it didn't matter. Obviously, my cousin and his wife didn't make many friends in Utah. He said it was the most miserable and alienating two years of his life, and he was elated when his wife got transferred to Colorado. That's the problem with your cult and so many other religions. You think that anybody with different beliefs is fucked up. That's so childish. Know what really pisses me off?"

"I don't—" replied the tall Mormon.

"The way the Mormons ripped off Christianity and twisted it all up to make fools out of us all. You took my Jesus and made him a sham."

"Um," said the tall Mormon.

"Go home tonight and think about what you just said and what I said," said Gregorio. "Maybe there's hope for you yet."

"Hope for what?" the blond Mormon asked innocently.

"Wisdom," Gregorio said sympathetically, looked both young men up and down and gently shut the door.

"You got a shirt on?" Gregorio whispered loudly to Carmen. "I'm going to let them in."

"Yeah, okay," said Carmen.

"Can you hear me?" Gregorio whispered even louder as he scampered into the kitchen. "Put some of the acid in some food, okay?" he said, and pinched his wife's ass and scooted back toward the front door.

"Okay," laughed Carmen.

"Tar and feathers, tar and fucking feathers!" sang Gregorio in a low, mischievous voice behind his Dudley Do-Right mask. He pushed the mask up until it rested on top of his head, set the bottle of Jack Daniel's down on an end table, and slowly opened the door. The two Mormons stood erect and proud with the same confident looks on their faces they had had on their previous two visits.

"Looking for more disciples?" asked Gregorio with a sly grin.

"Hello, sir," said the tall Mormon. "We're actually on a mission from the Church of Jesus Christ of Latter-day Saints. Remember our previous conversations?"

"LDS, huh?" chuckled Gregorio. "Come on in, preachers!"

The tall Mormon smiled triumphantly at the blond Mormon.

"I'm sorry, it's against church rules to enter someone's home while on mission," the blond Mormon said.

"This is a special case," whispered the tall Mormon to the blond Mormon. Then he marched into the apartment with the ghost of wild-eyed Joseph Smith riding on his shoulders.

The blond Mormon hesitated for a few long moments and then followed his partner inside.

"Please, sit down," Gregorio said, and waved his hand toward the living room sofa.

Carmen came capering in from the kitchen with a plate of four chewy M&M cookies. She was still wearing the Yogi Bear mask. She tried unsuccessfully not to laugh as she set the plate down on the coffee table in front of the Mormons and sat down on the sofa with them.

"Try one," she said. "They're homemade."

Gregorio sat down on the sofa between Carmen and the Mormons. The Mormons quickly ate two cookies each. Gregorio wondered if they were starving them back at the Mormon base camp.

"We brought some of our literature for you to look at," said the tall Mormon, and he handed Gregorio two small pamphlets whose covers contained color paintings of Biblical scenes.

"Uh, how many orange M&M's did you put in the cookies, peaches?" asked Gregorio casually, sliding his wife a mischievous look.

"Two."

"Oh, okay."

"Each," she giggled.

"Praise Jesus!" roared Gregorio.

Gregorio and Carmen waited for the LSD to take effect on the Mormons. For the first time they listened without interrupting to the young men's rehearsed speech about how Joseph Smith founded the religion in Utah, and how they too could be saved from the wrath of the devil. After ten minutes, the blond Mormon went to use the bathroom.

"God! Jesus looks so strange right now!" said the tall Mormon as he paused from flipping through one of the pamphlets explaining the works of Jesus.

Carmen burst out laughing.

"What do you mean?" Gregorio asked with a smile.

"He looks, he looks crazy!" said the tall Mormon, and he began to laugh uncontrollably pounding his fists on his thighs.

"Well, Halle-fucking-lujah!" screamed Gregorio at the top of his lungs and raised his arms over his head.

"Huh?" laughed the tall Mormon.

Gregorio slid over closer to the tall Mormon and looked deeply into his eyes. The tall Mormon leaned back.

"Church of LDS, welcome to the church of LSD," said Carmen.

"What church do you go to?" The tall Mormon screamed with laughter as his cheeks turned red.

"What church do you go to?" Carmen mimicked. She and Gregorio laughed crazily.

Gregorio took a swig from the Jack Daniel's and handed the bottle to the tall Mormon.

"I'm not supposed to," said the Mormon.

"You're not supposed to be bugging the shit out of people, either," chided Carmen.

"I'm feeling over-stimulated! I'm feeling over-stimulated! I feel so funny!" the tall Mormon yelped in a childish voice.

"We put LSD in the cookies," said Gregorio.

"LSD?"

"You know, acid?" said Carmen.

"Oh yeah, they taught us about that in missionary training, but I can't remember now what that means."

"Lysergic Acid Diethylamide," Gregorio stated plainly. "It's a powerful hallucinogenic."

"How much did we take?" asked the tall Mormon.

"Enough to light up the entire Mormon Tabernacle Choir 'til the Second Coming!" howled Gregorio and handed the young man the bottle of whiskey.

"Enough to make you guys see in Panavision or X-Ray vision or any kind of vision you want!" said Carmen, laughing uproariously.

The tall Mormon took a small sip of the Jack. Carmen quickly picked up a slice of orange and stuffed it into his mouth. He sucked on the orange and began to laugh in a crazy squealing manner.

"How long will this stuff last?" he asked.

Gregorio and Carmen looked at one another.

"Longer than you could possibly imagine," said Gregorio.

"Maybe two days," said Carmen.

"And you may have flashbacks after that," said Gregorio.

"Flashbacks?" asked the tall Mormon.

"They're like bad dreams, but you're awake."

The tall Mormon got on his knees on the floor in front of the sofa, folded his hands, and pressed them against his chest and recited loudly, "Oh Jesus! Please help us through this!" and he fell over and began rolling around on the tile floor, laughing wildly.

"Ever been to a rodeo?" asked Carmen.

"No! We can't do anything!" bawled the tall Mormon. He sat

up and loosened his tie. "But I watch TV sometimes in secret."

"What do they call the cowboys that ride the bulls?" she asked.

"Bull riders I think," giggled the young man. "Those guys are really nuts!"

"And those bulls have names like Ol' Leather Nuts and Sinbad, right?" laughed Gregorio.

"And how long do they usually ride the bull?" asked Carmen.

"Ten seconds, I think."

"Imagine a bull ride that will last for two days," she said. "That's what you and blondie are in for. So, you have got to hang on tight."

"Will you be our rodeo clowns?" asked the tall Mormon innocently.

Carmen and Gregorio smiled at one another.

"Sure," Carmen said as she tried to compose herself.

"Don't go outside alone before you come down," warned Gregorio. "The cops will put you in the funny house."

"Could I have some extra black coffee, please?" asked the tall Mormon.

"Even a coffee enema won't help you now!" cackled Gregorio.

Carmen jumped up and stood over the tall Mormon with her hands on her hips.

"He's right," she said. "Don't fight it. Go with it."

"Coffee enemas!" the tall Mormon shrieked with laughter. "With Danish?"

"Sure," said Gregorio. "Two coffee enemas and two Danish, you know one for blondie, too."

"It's Halloween!" Carmen said enthusiastically. "We have plenty of food and other stuff."

"Hey, get the masks," said Gregorio, and pulled the Dudley Do-Right mask back over his face.

"Oh, that's right!" she said and hurried into the bedroom and returned quickly with several of the Halloween masks. She set them on the coffee table in front of the tall Mormon.

"Go ahead, try one on," she said.

The tall Mormon picked up the Deputy Dog mask, put it on, and when he looked up, Carmen and Gregorio were standing in front of him spinning Hula-hoops around their waists. The tall Mormon giggled with glee as he watched Carmen's lithe, sexy body move. His lustful gaze didn't get past Gregorio—who became anxious as thoughts of the Manila recruiter and Tony and others he suspected of screwing Carmen filled his mind.

"Come on and try!" she urged.

The tall Mormon adjusted his Deputy Dog mask, stood up, and hopped over to Carmen, pretending to be a rabbit. Carmen slid the Hula-hoop over her head and placed it around the young man's waist.

"Now move your hips around like Cheerio over there!" she screamed and laughed.

As the tall Mormon was Hula-hooping, a small white booklet fell out of his shirt pocket onto the floor. He scrambled for it, but Carmen picked it up first and looked at the cover. In black print across the top it read "Mormon Missionary Handbook."

"I really need that," he pleaded as Carmen began to page through it. "My White Bible!"

"Number 75; Never be alone with anyone of the opposite sex," she read aloud. "Number 3; Read only books, magazines, and other material authorized by the church."

Gregorio snatched the booklet away from Carmen.

"Number 38; Do not watch TV," he said. "Number 60; never jack off. Okay, I just made that one up. Hey, wait a minute. Oh my God! Your partner!" Gregorio ran to the bathroom.

Carmen and the tall Mormon followed Gregorio down the short hallway. They found the blond Mormon lying curled up on the bathroom floor. His hands were clenched tightly together underneath his chin.

"Let's get him up," said Gregorio, and he and the tall Mormon lifted the sweaty and frightened young man to his feet.

"He's having a bad trip," sighed Gregorio.

"It's going to be okay," said Carmen reassuringly.

The young man broke free, bolted out of the apartment, ran down the three flights of stairs, and scampered frantically across busy Keelung Street and into the Taoist temple. Gregorio, Carmen, and the tall Mormon caught up with him soon after he disappeared through one of the wide openings in the temple's gorgeous and elaborate facade. Several of the temple worshippers gawked at the scene as the three masked foreigners dragged the blond Mormon outside and back across the street. He broke loose again, jumped on his bicycle, and began to peddle like mad down the street blurting out, "He's at the river! He's at the river!" Then he lost control and crashed into a palm tree.

"Try to save some souls now, asshole!" cackled Gregorio. He and the others ran, gathered up the blond Mormon and his bicycle, and managed to get him back inside the apartment and plop him down on the sofa.

"Elder William, we're all messed up," said the tall Mormon. He sat down next to his companion and placed his hand on the young man's shoulder.

Gregorio and Carmen sat next to the tall Mormon and looked coolly at the blond Mormon.

"Drink, please," said Elder William softly and tried to wipe the sweat from his face.

Carmen hurried into the kitchen and brought back a cold can of Pepsi.

"They were drugs in the cookies," said the tall Mormon.

"LSD," said Carmen. She handed the soda to Elder William.

"I feel like I might get sick," said Elder William.

"I hope you puke all the way back to Salt Lake," said Gregorio, and gave the blond the evil eye. "You boys pulled the tiger's tail too many times. Hey, what's your name," he asked, took a pull off Jack and turned his gaze to the tall Mormon.

"Elder Perry," he said.

"Well Perry, I'm Gregorio and this is my wife Carmen. Tell me the *real* reason why you two fanatics have come to our house three fucking times? Why are we so special?"

"We just wanted—"

"Just wanted to help, my ass. You want to fuck my wife, don't you *katoto*?"

"Gregorio!" Carmen laughed, grabbed the bottle of Jack and took a swig.

"No, I swear! That's not it at all."

"Then why?"

"Joseph Smith told us to," said the blond Mormon. "He's at the river. He called to me from the river outside just now."

"You bring Joseph Smith here and I'll let you fuck my wife and me in the ass until the Rapture."

"Joseph Smith," giggled Carmen. "Now, there's an acid head if there ever was one."

"Hell, yeah!" Gregorio said and stuffed an orange slice into his mouth. "I'll tell you what, boys. How much cash do have on your person?"

"What?" asked Elder Perry.

"Ten-thousand NT dollars for one hour with Carmen."

"That's strictly forbidden," blurted Elder William.

"We'll even throw in the theme song from *Jeopardy!*"

After a long moment of silence Gregorio stood up, chuckled and said, "Just joking. Now come on! Let's ride the waves!" he said, and picked up one of the Hula-hoops and began swinging it around his waist.

The others immediately joined Gregorio and the four fried in the apartment for the next two hours, laughing hysterically at normally mundane things. At the stroke of each hour a cuckoo clock on the wall burst open and a small cuckoo sprang out and made an insane racket along with bells and chimes. Each time the cuckoo clock went berserk the four of them got up and ran around the house mimicking the cuckoo bird. After some time the blond Mormon, Elder William, became quiet and sat alone on the sofa. He then began to babble unintelligibly as he slowly rolled his head around. Carmen and Gregorio sat on the sofa and stared at him.

"What the hell's wrong with him?" Gregorio asked Elder Perry.

"He's speaking in tongues," said Elder Perry.

"Can you interpret?" asked Carmen.

"Yeah," said Gregorio. "What did he say?"

"He say, oopy doopy! We have fun!" laughed Elder Perry.

Elder William sprang up from the sofa and stood next to his

companion. The two Mormons began to sing:

"What he say?

He say oopy doopy! We have fun!

Go go gophers, watch them go go go.

Go go gophers, watch them go go go.

Ooboo blah glug oo oo ba ba—"

Elder William abruptly stopped singing and shouted wildly with glee, "I can see! I can see!" as if God himself had dumped a shovel full of angel dust onto his head.

"See what, you goddamned knucklehead?" laughed Gregorio.

"Do you see it, Elder Perry?" asked the blond Mormon. "The world of spirit matter."

"What do you see?" asked Carmen.

"God the Father and Jesus. They're sitting on the most gorgeous thrones on Kolob."

"You're becoming exalted," Elder Perry said in awe. He got on his knees and folded his hands in prayer. "Place your hands upon me."

Elder William placed his hands upon the tall Mormon's head and sang, "We wish you a Merry Christmas! We wish you a Merry Christmas!" Then the blond began to laugh hysterically.

"The spirit of the Lord is upon him," said Elder Perry. "He's transcended the mortal plain. Praise God! Praise Jesus! Don't you understand?"

"What?" asked Gregorio. He pointed the remote at Elder Perry and pretended to change channels.

"This is a holy house now! We must erect a church here!"

"The only thing I'm going to erect is a gallows for you two blathering idiots."

Elder Perry pleaded, "Try to understand! We all can become god-like. But you have to possess the purest mortal eyes to see the world of spirit matter."

"Stand up, both of you," Carmen commanded. The Mormons stood up.

"Now bend down so I can see your heads." The Mormons reluctantly complied.

"I knew I'd find it," said Carmen as she felt along the blonde

Mormon's scalp.

"Find what?" asked the tall Mormon. He began feeling around on his own scalp.

"A zipper."

Gregorio laughed until he turned blue. The Mormons tumbled off of their peak and sat back down on the sofa.

"So, you sons of a gun have watched some TV," laughed Carmen.

"You know *Underdog*?" asked Elder William.

"The cartoon?" asked Carmen.

"Polly Purebred," Gregorio reminisced fondly. "Poor Underdog never did put his thing into her."

"We got a lot of TV shows from the US when we were kids," said Carmen.

"*Go Go Gophers* usually played after *Underdog*," said Elder Perry.

"What did he always say about Polly?" asked Gregorio.

"When Polly's in trouble, I am not slow, its hip, hip, hip, and away I go!" chimed the two Mormons.

"That's right!" laughed Carmen.

"I would have screwed her if I were a cartoon dog on that show," said Gregorio.

"Get off Polly Purebred, for Christ's sake!" said Carmen.

An hour later, Elder Perry walked out of the bathroom naked holding a copy of *Playboy* magazine across his chest. His erect penis bobbed around like a divining rod. It began to deflate as he silently approached the other three, who were sitting on the couch watching TV, transfixed as Charlton Heston parted the Red Sea in *The Ten Commandments*.

The tall Mormon walked in front of the TV, stopped, turned to face the couch and said in a solemn manner, "These are the original golden plates given to Joseph Smith by the angel Moroni."

Carmen stared at his long, twitching penis.

"That's *Playboy's* May issue, preacher," cackled Gregorio. "And I see you've checked it out, Mr. Slinky. Now get the hell out of the way. Chuck's about to set his people free."

"Chuck?" asked the tall Mormon.

"Moses, you six-toed hillbilly," scolded Gregorio. "Any jackass can figure out old Joe Smith stole the story of the Ten Commandments after he ate peyote and had a root beer enema and concocted his fairy tale about the golden plates."

Elder William stood up, gently took the magazine away from his companion and began to flip through the photo spreads. "We need a seer stone," he said.

He looked around the room, walked to the front door, opened it, and stepped outside. Elder Perry followed him. Gregorio and Carmen ran to the door and watched dumbfounded as the two Mormons got on their bicycles and slowly rode away.

Gregorio ran out into the street and shouted, "Your clothes preacher! Your clothes!"

The Mormons stopped along the side of the darkened street, looked back toward Gregorio, and got off their bicycles. The blond Mormon stripped down to his boxer shorts and gave his pants to his partner. The tall Mormon put the pants on and the two continued their journey into the night. Gregorio returned to his front door where Carmen was waiting for him. They looked at each other for a long moment, and then they burst out laughing as they walked back into the house, shut the door, and locked it.

During the ensuing months Elder Perry and Elder William stopped by the apartment several times to say hello and visit with Gregorio and Carmen. Gregorio was cool and distant toward them each time that they visited.

After the Mormons left the house on their latest visit Gregorio cracked a beer, looked at Carmen and said, "I feel sorry for them in a way, and hoped that their LSD experience might open their minds and free them from their spiritual bondage."

"Me, too," Carmen said with a weak smile.

Six months after frying with the Mormons, Gregorio came home from work early one afternoon with the stomach flu and heard the theme song from *Jeopardy!* coming from behind the bedroom door. He chuckled to himself and slowly opened the door, but when he'd opened it about six inches, he heard voices below the loud music. His jaw tightened as his bulging eyes took in the scene. The two Mormons were tied up and hand-cuffed to kitchen chairs. Their naked bodies were covered with baby powder. Carmen strolled before them in a black vinyl dominatrix nurse outfit—a miniskirt with a T-top, black nylons and garters, a choker, and a pointy hat.

"Say it!" she said, and twisted the tall Mormon's nipple and ruffled his powdered hair.

"Watch me!" bleated the blond Mormon.

"Watch me what?"

"Watch me shoot the goo."

"That's my holy boy," she purred and delicately ran the tip of a riding crop across his chest.

Gregorio closed the door very slowly. The others hadn't noticed him.

"Did I do this?" he moaned. He walked outside, got back into his car and drove to the Cement Factory, a run-down bar frequented by local and migrant Filipinos.

Gregorio mulled over the entire experience with the Mormons while he soaked his head in a glass of San Miguel.

"Did I go too far?" he mumbled to himself, and sucked the rest of the blood out of the saint. "It was my idea to invite them in and give them the acid. Maybe she would have had sex with them, anyway—even if we didn't do any acid. Yeah, all three of them are fucked."

The bartender quickly poured another beer and slid it under the blue Filipino's nose. Gregorio gulped half of it down, and glanced around the round, semi-crowded barroom. His eyes found a sophisticated-looking bargirl who was sitting alone over a champagne cocktail at a table in the center of the room. She was svelte as a panther and no older than a blackjack, wearing a little yellow linen dress that fit like wet cheesecloth. The girl looked out of place as a birthday candle on a cow pie. Gregorio picked up his beer, walked over to her, and sat down.

He studied her drink and asked, "They serve champagne?"

"The bastards will if they want me to keep this dump on my trap line."

Gregorio nodded, clearly impressed. "A wild filly. No stable for you, eh?"

"Strictly freelance."

"Can you give a discount for a 'hate fuck'?"

"Wife or girlfriend?"

"Wife."

"Sure, why not."

"How much?"

The bargirl's eyes weighed Gregorio for diseases and neuroses. She smiled and said, "You don't smell too bad. Some guys smell like a bait shop. You can ride the pony for two-thousand NT an hour. If you want to wear spurs it's another thousand."

"Oh, I don't want to slam dance. Does it look like I do?"

"Your eyes are so—"

"Fanatical. I know."

"I was going to say, impassioned."

"You're a good saleslady. Are you from China?"

"Vietnam."

"How'd you end up in Taiwan?"

"Three years ago I was a 'mail-order bride.'"

"Not anymore?"

"Instead of special delivery, my Taiwanese husband had me shipped fourth class."

"Nice. He knock you around?"

"Oh no, nothing like that. All the oversexed moron wanted to do was fuck me three times a day. He was a 'minute man,' too. I know what you're going to say and—"

"How many times do you have sex every day now?"

"As much or as little as I want. I decide, and the money's great."

"Uh-huh."

"I couldn't take it, so I lit out of Chiayi and came up here about a year ago."

"Jesus and Maria!"

"Still want a 'hate fuck'?"

"Okay."

The bargirl jumped up and pranced toward a flight of stairs in back like she was heading down a fashion show runway.

Gregorio followed her upstairs with Carmen's riding crop sticking out of his ass; his eyes saddened with each step, carving an SOS into the hustler's Brie. The girl disappeared down a beat-up hallway that was murky as a urine sample at a VD clinic. She jerked a door open; a beam of sunlight flooded past her. The room swallowed her like a bum wolfing down an egg tart. Gregorio walked into the light in front of the open door—the shadow of a rat snake appeared on the wall behind him. He entered the room unglued as a firefighter cadet on his first marshmallow roast. The bargirl was sitting on the bed beneath a crucifix. Gregorio crossed himself and sat down next to her, remembering the lies he told at his last confession.

"And the cash?" she asked softly, and began to slip off her cheesecloth.

Gregorio pulled out his wallet and handed her two crisp one-thousand-dollar NT notes. He didn't give a shit if his hard earned money vanished faster than an eight ball at a stag party. Gregorio watched as the girl finished stripping down to her white bra and panties. He glanced up at the crucifix. Jesus mooned him.

The girl stood up and said, "Want me to dance for a little while? That gets a lot of guys revved up."

"Sure."

She began to dance as if she were born sliding down a firehouse pole. Several minutes later she took off her bra and tossed it onto the bed. Gregorio continued to sit and watch.

"Go ahead," she urged. "Strip."

"I'm okay."

The bargirl sat down next to him and said, "She really whittled you down, huh?"

Gregorio paused, put his hands over his face and whispered, "From a railroad tie into a fucking tongue depressor."

"Jesus! I'm sorry."

Gregorio didn't utter a word for a long moment. Then he said softly, "I've never cheated on my wife, until today."

"We haven't fried the *longganisa* yet, *ginoo*."

"I cheated in my mind—in my heart."

The bargirl placed her delicate hands on his shoulder and said, "You're a real sweet guy. You know that, don't you?"

"What's your name?"

"Misty."

"Misty, you're a nice girl, too. I think I'd just like to sit here and talk until my time is up. But, I'd like to see you again next week when I'm not so, uh, you know."

"Okay."

Three days later, Gregorio took an extra hour for lunch and rode his scooter to the Mormon Field Office in Keelung. He flung the glass door open and strode inside. The long, narrow room was cheery as a leper colony. A wrinkled man a few miles past fifty was sitting behind a wooden coffin reading the Book of Mormon. His soul had been skewered and charred over an open fire at a Joseph Smith sing-along when Nixon was President. He had a mug that looked like he spent his spare time bobbing for apples in a barrel of weed killer. He was wearing "the uniform;" a clean, white short-sleeved shirt, and dark slacks.

Gregorio stomped up to the coffin, looked up at a framed painting of Jesus hanging on the wall behind the Mormon and said, "Get yourself a new front man. He's taken."

"Uh, may I help you, friend?" asked the man without looking up from his bible. He slicked back his well-groomed salt and pepper hair.

"I said get yourself a new fucking front man!" Gregorio said raising his voice. "You Mormons stole our boy."

The man looked up and said, "Please refrain from using profanity, son. I'm here to offer you enlightenment."

"Nice desk—some kind of gimmick?" sneered Gregorio, ignoring the man's remark as he eyed the coffin. "Hey, where's your bike, preacher?"

"Come again?" the man asked. Gregorio heard voices coming from the back room.

"Two of your sheep have been fucking my ewe."

The man's eyes inflamed and found Gregorio's. "Excuse me?" he asked, and tried to regain his composure. He nervously put the book down on the coffin and tapped the cover with his finger-tips.

"You better hold on to that Bible, mister. You're gonna need it more than ever by the time I'm through here." He slammed his hands down on the coffin and hissed, "This goddamned Salt Lake overcoat, too."

"Son, what exactly do you want?" he asked gently.

Gregorio noticed the man's hand begin to grope and squeeze the Book of Mormon.

"Looking for a rip cord, preacher?"

"Huh?"

"Are they here?"

"Who?"

"Your fornicating missionaries. The dildo brothers. Perry and William."

"The Elders are in back, having lunch."

"You best summon your sheep."

"Elder Perry! William!" the man shouted, and turned his head toward the rear of the office.

After a few moments the two Mormons casually walked out of a rear room that was fifty-feet behind the man at the coffin. They stopped when they saw Gregorio, and gave each other frightened, wide-eyed looks.

The man stood up, turned to face the young men, and commanded, "Front and center."

The two Mormons walked slowly to the man and stopped.

"Ask them where they were and what they were doing three days ago at around three in the afternoon," Gregorio growled in a low voice, barely holding in his anger.

"Well?" asked the man. He put his hands on his hips and looked piously at the young men.

"We were at this man's home," whispered the tall Mormon.

"And did you violate our laws of chastity with this man's wife?" asked the man.

The two Mormons stood in silence.

"You goddamned posers! You motherfucking hypocrites!" screamed Gregorio.

The man turned toward Gregorio and asked, "Sir, can you please tell me what took place at your home?"

"I caught these two having sex with my wife. My *wife!*"

"Is that true?" the man asked. His eyes hardened and bounced between the Elders' faces.

The young men nodded.

"Both of you are immediately relieved of your mission for violating your mission code of conduct. Return to your living quarters and pack your belongings."

"Yes sir," the Elders said, and they walked past Gregorio and out the front door.

Gregorio did all he could to control himself from lunging at the young men.

"Please sit down," the man said, and he sat back down behind the coffin. "I'm terribly sorry, and you have my deepest apologizes on behalf of the Church of Jesus Christ of Latter-day Saints."

"Oh, thanks a fucking lot," Gregorio said, and rolled his eyes. "That means a lot, especially coming from a lunatic who thinks that after his death he'll be banging women for eternity in a garden on his own fucking planet."

The man gave himself the sign of the cross and said, "The Lord forgives you for your profane outbursts. So do I, son."

"Fuck forgiveness. I want revenge. I want my wife!"

"You can be assured that the two elders—"

"What's going to happen to your lost sheep?" Gregorio asked and sat down across from the man. "A shearing? A butchering?"

"You can be assured that the two elders will be flown back to Salt Lake tomorrow morning and undergo an inquest. I would like you to write a detailed description of the events you witnessed concerning these missionaries," the man said. He slid a form and a pen across the coffin. "And I can assure you those two will never be able to bother you again."

For the next thirty minutes Gregorio wrote in graphic detail what he had witnessed two days earlier when he caught the Mormons diddling Carmen.

When Gregorio finished, he stood up, looked the man in

the eye and said, "Close down your gag store and go back to Utah. The world doesn't want you or need you."

The man gave Gregorio a fretful smile and opened his Book of Mormon.

"What's with the coffin, anyway?" Gregorio asked, shaking his head in disgust, and ran his hands over the wood.

"Oh, yes," the man chirped quite pleased with himself. "I use it to remind our Elders how fleeting life is, and not to tarry with their mission work."

"Real fucking cute—the coffin, it suits you. And it's a perfect example how out of touch and culturally insensitive you fanatics really are."

The man frowned and asked, "How's that?"

"Putting a symbol of death in a Taiwanese business is as taboo as you can get. It's like staking your wife spread-eagle on the lawn and inviting the devil and his cadres over for a game of Twister. I bet the neighbors around here love you. You've probably got them burning incense and praying day and night that you'll leave. But, you weren't aware of that, were you preacher?"

Gregorio didn't wait for a reply. He spun around and walked out with his head held high, jumped on his scooter, and rode back to work.

He never told Carmen what he'd seen through their bedroom door two days earlier, about his encounter with Misty, or about his visit to the Mormon Field Office.

Penghu

On a bright, sweltering July morning I flew from Taipei to Magung on the small archipelago of Penghu, which sits west of Taiwan in the 110-mile-wide strait that separates Taiwan from mainland China. Magung is Penghu's main city. There are stone walls built by hand to protect the fields from the fierce winds ... weathered coral houses huddle together in ancient villages ... the people smell like the sea. I stayed at a cheap motel and felt like a big shot in the lumpy potato-sack bed ... locals got a kick out of seeing me sputtering around on a motorbike ... the salty air coated my face ... wore a long-sleeved white cotton shirt to fend off the brutal sun ... the heat melted the bike's tires and we sank together into the gooey tar ... passed many scenes that stick in my memory—hundreds of fish drying in the sun on big screens, their black eyes staring at the blue yonder ... a proud old gal hoeing dirt behind a rock wall ... sea ladies puffing cob pipes and jabbering on benches in the shade; they stared as I rode past with my glowing white skin ... women digging clams in the low tide and farmers leading chocolate cows to bright green pastures . . . came upon many houses whose ornate doors pulled me in . . . an abandoned village in the salty sun at five o'clock . . . an old man told me ghosts kept the place clean. Tu Di Gong, the earth god, has been protecting these noble farmers for centuries . . . to honor him the local people have erected many small, enclosed shrines in the fields around the island—crept into one of them on all fours and found a small icon of the earth god perched on a tiny wooden table. The colors were saturated all over Penghu . . . the bright blue sky, the fluorescent grass, and the white coral houses—ran my hands along the old walls. . . . Came upon an abandoned house with a big buzz saw set up next to the front door . . . fresh sawdust was scattered all around . . . the door was very old and magnificent with Chinese characters carved into stone around the doorframe . . . the characters told stories from old times . . . the wind whipped through the slats and sang in a fierce pitch. . . . Further down the narrow alley, all the houses were gutted, with only coral walls standing . . . slowly wandered through the ruins. . . . Fell in love with Penghu and wished Julia and I had our own little coral house overlooking the broad stretches of white-sand beach . . . parked the bike on a tall bluff overlooking the ocean . . . could see out for miles to the thin line of the horizon . . . the sky a mesmerizing deep reddish orange—the phone poles and house silhouettes like some old Monument Valley in a John Ford film. . . . Each night returned to the flop happy with a bag full of spent film. The woman who ran my small hotel let me keep beer and food in her refrigerator, like I was staying at a friend's house. On my last day, used my jackknife to pop off a small piece of coral from one of my favorite abandoned houses, and filled my pockets with beach sand. That night I sat by the window smoking a cigarillo, reminiscing about the week's adventures . . . closed my eyes smiling, and in my mind I could see my darling Julia back in Kaohsiung making soft cooing sounds while she slept. Below me, on the oily street, a pack of kids on motorbikes zoomed past like a swarm of honey bees.

Lester Moore

Smoker's Paradise in downtown Kaohsiung is a tobacco shop that sells Cuban cigars, imported European pipe tobacco, and single malt scotch that is also often consumed on the cozy and tranquil premises. At one time the shop was immensely popular with local fishermen; however, for the past few years, only a small and select group of patrons have met there regularly. Late one airless and hot June evening two white men, one a gifted German scientist and the other an esteemed Australian professor of English literature who had witnessed sixty summer solstices, lazed in luxurious maroon-leather chairs in the rear sitting room in a haze of cigar smoke and soft amber light.

They conversed in low voices as a comely American woman of twenty-seven, wearing a white cotton camisole with spaghetti straps and a lavishly embroidered front, faded Wrangler cutoffs, and cowboy boots, half-dozed in a nearby chair. A straw cowboy hat with a wide black-leather band and a silver conch in the center was tilted over her face. She was employed as a psychologist in the cargo-shipping industry. Her vessel, an enormous container ship from Singapore christened the *Edmund John* was safely anchored in nearby Kaohsiung harbor with deck and hull laden with software and electronics.

A wooden ceiling fan whirled hypnotically over their heads. Handsome framed cigar and tobacco advertising posters hung on the dark wooden walls, along with a lithograph of a single piece of toast burnt to a black smoldering crisp against a cream-colored background. One line of type spanned the bottom of the poster: Peaceful Rising Bread Company.

Mr. Tsai, the amiable shop proprietor, sat behind the front counter enjoying every puff of a Royal Jamaican torpedo. It was so stifling and humid outside that the shop's front windows were almost completely fogged over. Mr. Tsai could barely make out the seven stately and magnificent palm trees that grew in front of the store. Like guardians of some eternal secret, they stood stoically and motionless in the sweltering, heavy darkness. Outside, the fences moaned.

"Tell us one of your tales, Miss Vivian Lin," the Australian pleaded in a deep, soft voice.

Vivo rustled in her chair, sat up, took a short pull from her glass of Balvenie, picked up her cigar from the ashtray and said, "Hmmm."

"I hope I'm not being too forward, but is it true what Samuel told me concerning your captain?" asked the German scientist as he eyed the striking tattoo on Vivo's shoulder of the state of Texas and a yellow rose.

"He's doing a stretch for forgery," Vivo said plainly, and slid the cowboy hat back, exposing her cropped hair. "Caught him in Singapore with a suitcase full of Benjies."

"And the company?" asked the professor. "Insured?"

"Oh yeah, wasn't even a scratch on the rattlers," replied Vivo.

"You were quite fond of him, hey?" said the professor. "I remember you speaking of him in a rather Homeric and romantic manner in previous yarns."

"So much for heroes," said Vivo a little despondently.

"Brilliant!" exclaimed the German. "Your southern US accent is absolutely fantastic." Then he hesitated for a long moment, took a drink, and whispered loudly as if he were sharing a secret, "The professor has informed me of your unorthodox *methods.*"

"He has," Vivo replied with mock surprise, and she turned her head and playfully snarled at the professor. "I suppose that my methods do fly in the face of western medicine's ritual of stuffing patients so full of pills that they can't take a crap."

"Oh, lord!" the German exclaimed. "What exactly do you do aboard ship?"

"I wake the dead."

"I bet you could," proclaimed the German. His eyes darted over Vivo's sensuous figure.

"I'm a shrink. Cargo ship crews are a rough, hearty bunch—prolonged time at sea away from their loved ones. Often heavy alcohol and drug use. This can induce abnormal levels of depression and anxiety related disorders."

"How do you wake the dead?"

"It's case by case. I've used sky diving, cream pie throwing, and in a few rare cases, various sexual stimulation therapies."

The two men raised their eyebrows and looked at one another.

"Oh no, not by me," she lied. "We hire professionals."

"And what does the company say about these methods?" asked the Australian.

"A thirty-thousand-dollar bonus last year," Vivo said proudly.

"Excellent," said the German, and he thought she came off a little arrogant.

"To the company the crew is part of the ship, no more important than any of its moving mechanical parts," she said. "They don't care what I oil them with, as long as they meet their performance standards. I guess that's why they hired me. I've got the right kind of oil."

"So, you enjoy your work," said the German.

"I love the challenge of working with eccentric individuals," she said boldly, looked down and began to dig around in her purse for her lighter.

The professor quickly leaned over toward the German, cupped

his hand over his ear and whispered, "She's a real little Miss smarty-pants, isn't she. Thinks she's got everyone's number."

"Samuel tells me you're originally from Taiwan," said the German.

Vivo relit her Cuban, took a big drag, and blew a hell's rainbow that floated between the two men and dissolved. "My parents are Taiwanese," she said. "I was born in Taichung and lived in Taiwan until I was thirteen, when my father, the Colonel, landed a plum job on the Texas coast."

"School in the States?" asked the German.

"At knifepoint," she said dryly.

"Ha!" laughed the professor. "She's being modest. PhD in psychology and an IQ that's higher than a crocodile's weight," he said proudly.

Vivo shrugged her shoulders as if to apologize for the professor's remark, kicked off her three-hundred-dollar Tony Lama cowboy boots and threw her long, skinny legs over the side of the chair.

"A tale, Mädchen?" said the German with a large grin.

She took another drink and paused. After a long moment her eyes lit up, and an impish smile exposed teeth that were too white from frequent bleaching.

"This ain't no fib nor tall tale nor Huckleberry stretcher, or may Stonewall Jackson and the seven horsemen come hunting me up," she said in her Texas twang.

"Brilliant!" exclaimed the German.

The Australian grunted happily.

"About two years ago we were anchored here with a catch from Japan. The usual consignment. I came ashore alone that time cause my regular go-ashore partner drank a whole bottle of Tabasco sauce on a bet, and you can imagine where he spent the next few days."

The two men laughed.

"Son of a bitch won five hundred US dollars on that deal," said Vivo. "About the third day in port I woke up on a welder's workbench under the hot blue arc of a cutting torch. My mouth was full of horsehair and puke. A nearly empty pint of Tondeña rum chided me from across the room."

"Drambuie on pancakes," said the professor.

Vivo cocked her head at him.

"What you said reminded me of the time I had Drambuie on pancakes. I'd heard it was a cure for a hangover."

"I thought chocolate-chip pancakes with whipped cream were bad enough," Vivo said, "but Drambuie on a stack; that's one thing you couldn't find even at IHOP."

"International House of Pancakes," said the German under his breath. "Another American monstrosity."

"Here's something I've meant to ask you," the professor said. "Why in hell do they put carrots and peas and gobs of sugar in the potato salad here?"

"The same reason most Chinese food in the States sucks," said Vivo. She took a gulp of the scotch. "You play to your audience."

"Well done," quipped the German.

"Now about my hangover," she said. "Two shots of bear bile from Mr. Lee's traditional Chinese medicine shop and a roast pork sandwich straightened my needle. Gassed up a rented motorbike to go to the night market. I'd seen a guy there the night before, and I kept thinking about him. No, it wasn't like that, y'all. Every night he stood at the entrance to the market with an old Rollei around his neck and a chimpanzee on a leash. Foreigners called him the cameraman; locals called him the monkeyman. I heard he was from the South, too, and I wanted to know his story."

"The rental bike was a 250. Compared to these little 125s I'm used to, it felt like two tons of Virginia coal barreling toward Fongshan City. I could see the night market half a mile away. It was lit up like a goddamn prison yard, puffing and spurting like an enormous roman candle. Out front on the wrangling street a thousand whining motorbikes squirmed and wiggled around like yellowfin trapped in a gigantic net. Hundreds of other motorbikes were parked out front and filled a club sandwich next door."

"It was typical as far as Taiwan night markets go. A bloated church bazaar. A roiling, smoking honeycomb of food and rag vendors. Music blared. The narrow stalls were filled with fake

Converse All Stars, clothes, jewelry, CDs and DVDs, exotic birds, and the like. I took a look around first, caught a wave to the wide glass doorway of gracious tattoo master Yang Jin-Hsiang, who was carving into the shoulder of a grimacing, bespectacled, dark-looking older Taiwanese—the kind of guy that can handle himself in a scrape. I splashed around with middle-aged locals arm wrestling slot machines and spilling beer out of plastic cups. A few cripples and Buddhist monks wandered around begging with signs in a heavy fog from stinky tofu, frying steaks, and seafood. A divorcee named Miss Lucy sat in a stall removing two small moles from a young gal's chin with a tweezers (Taiwan tradition says some moles bring good luck and some bring angry spirits). Old men threw horseshoes behind a tent. Fake fur coats on white mannequins with big round tits. Bored teenagers bopped along."

"Then I circled around and walked up to the cameraman. He was still doing a Jerry Lewis near the entrance. He was a white confederate in his mid-fifties, thin as an ice pick, and mysterious as a Hitchcock flick. The camera strap pinched the skin around his withered neck. When I got close, I could see that he was nervously fidgeting and shuffling around, like a downed power line flopping and hissing on wet pavement— a five-foot-nine dildo with fresh batteries. Christ, I thought he might explode! There it was—that urge—I wanted to help him. But what the hell could I do? How about a twelve-gauge? His pet chimp did summersaults and cute tricks for the kids, wearing a cowboy outfit and six-guns that were actually cap guns. He'd twirl the guns around and shoot them off. He even had a little lasso that he fumbled around with. The tourists and locals alike couldn't get enough of his act. Folks plunked ten-NT-dollar coins into a tin cup Billy waved under their noses. The monkeyman told me the chimp's name was Billy."

Vivo paused. The German scientist poured her another Balvenie. She relit her cigar and took a few long leisurely puffs.

"And," the Australian professor said anxiously.

"I found out it was true that there wasn't any film in his camera. There never was. The story goes that each night for the past seventeen years he pretended to take pictures of every bus that snarled by. Some said his Taiwanese wife was canceled by a bus on that very spot. The other line was that he was ex-paparazzi who got tapped on the head with a frozen lungfish by a famous local actress. And some said he was a lottery winner who gave it all to the Holy Sistine Sisters of the Beloved Virgin Bowling Team and Convent in Manila. I did know that he and Billy lived over at the Neptune, on the seventh floor."

"I asked, 'How come crazy people always hang out in city parks?'

'When I was young I could move like a house afire,' he said, looking past me into the distance as if he were addressing a vast gathering.

'Zippy looks tired,' I said.

'Must be the new dog food. I like it okay, but it makes him phosphorescent.'

'Come on. I'll buy you a neutron soda,' I said.

'I just live over there at the Neptune,' he said.

'I know.'

"He raised his eyebrows."

'Billy says it's all right to have company tonight,' he mumbled after a prolonged pause.

"The Neptune teetered in a jungle of neon and food vendors a few blocks away. It was seven stories of red brick and Super Glue that belonged in an earthquake safety film or a Ralph Nader telethon."

'What was this before?' I asked as we entered the drab lobby.

'Nutto house,' he said proudly.

'For?' I asked.

'The KMT,' he said.

"A service elevator took us up to the seventh floor. As I followed the pair down the hall, I could hear Gene Autry singing 'Don't Fence Me In.'"

'That's my fat rodeo boy,' the monkeyman said with a smile.

'The singing cowboy,' I said.

'That fat fuck recorded a lot of his songs live from his radio show. Golly jeepers, he had a hell of a smokestack.'

"His voice had changed since we'd come inside, and he wasn't so jittery. I started to wonder if maybe I'd been had. He opened the door to his room, and a dozen rodeo bulls snorted past. The place was decorated in authentic American Old West."

'Where you from?' I asked.

'Abilene, mostly,' he drawled, threw the Rollei down and stripped his shirt off.

'I heard about you. I knew it was all an act,' I said.

'We're all harlots, ain't we?' he said, matter-of-fact.

'Not my mama,' I said.

'I make people feel needed. They throw a few bucks to a loser and feel like they helped somebody.'

'What's your name?' I asked.

'Lester Moore,' he said.

"The chimp dug in his shirt pocket, pulled out a business card, and handed it to me. On one side of the card it read:

'Here lies Lester Moore

Shot dead with a forty-four

No less, no more.'

"On the other side, the card read:

'Justin Case

Undertaker.'

'I want that to be my epitaph,' he said.

'Which one?' I asked.

'What do you think?'

'Where'd you get Lester Moore, off a filling station wall?' I asked. 'I've heard that before.'

'I'm the one who wrote that on every gas station wall between El Paso and Houston,' he said proudly. 'I'm the original.'

'And I'm Annie Oakley.'

"He sat down in a wooden chair and set a bottle of brown liquor on a scratched-up oak coffee table that looked as old as the early Tom Mix and John Wayne movie posters and Native American rugs on the walls. I sat on the opposite couch. The bottle's label contained a painted image of an Indian chief's head and the words *Cut Throat Bourbon.*"

"As he poured two glasses, Lester smiled and said, 'Did you

know that in the Old West some saloons cut their whiskey with gunpowder and turpentine? Don't worry. This stuff is okay.'

'We're all cutting our stuff with something, aren't we?' I said. 'Where'd you get all this?' "I looked around at the walls."

'I've got an arsenal, too,' Leonard said calmly.

'Guns?'

'I know it's not legal in Taiwan for a regular fella to own a gun, but they're already here. Just like the aliens.'

'Who's here? Chinese communist spies?'

'Oh, hell and tarnation,' he drawled in a whisper. 'Everyone knows that.'

'Uh-huh.'

'It ain't the commies we need to worry about. They lack the imagination to pull off something really exceptional.'

'Then who?'

'Never mind,' he said smugly. 'Let's shoot some birds.' "He stood up and walked down the hallway with his drink in hand and went into a small room."

"Billy and I followed. I brought my own glass and the bottle. One of them big screens you see in video arcades took up one whole wall. A plastic shotgun sat on a wooden bench against the opposite wall. Lester was standing near the bench holding a second plastic shotgun. Billy squealed with excitement when he saw Lester holding the shotgun, and then he strapped on his six guns, scurried over to a boom box, and put in a CD. The melody from 'Pop Goes the Weasel' began playing. It sounded like a wheezing old circus organ."

'What's that?' I asked.

'Buck Naked and the Bare Bottom Boys, or I don't know. Billy loves it. Look at him.'

"The chimp began to run around in small circles shooting his cap guns off into the air."

"A gravelly voice began slowly singing:
'Round and round the mulberry bush
the monkey chased the weasel
Farmer John brought his four-ten around
Pop goes the Weasel

Na na na na na nanana na ee ee ee Oh!
Farmer John brought his four-ten around
Pop goes the Weasel . . ?
'What you want?' Lester asked. 'I got skeet, people, and animals.'
'What people?' I asked.
'Oh, there's modern-day politicians, famous folks like movie stars, pretty girls, and uh . . .'
'Purty girls? Any naked guys?' I asked.
'Oh, it's too much. The girls are completely naked, and they have assault rifles and when they, uh . . ?'
'Skeet to start,' I said.
"Old Les was a good shot. I kept up with him pretty good from all the trap and target shooting I used to do with my dad back in Brownsville as a kid."
'Who you like better for an outlaw, Jesse James or Doc Holiday?' he asked.
'Was Doc Holiday an outlaw, really, or just an ornery and dangerous man?' I asked after I knocked down my third bird in a row.
'That all depends on what the definition of an outlaw is. Doc did kill more folks than Jesse, something like seventeen, but he didn't rob no banks and trains. He made all his money playing an honest game of poker, whereas Jesse was a bona fide outlaw glorified and vilified in the Missouri newspapers.'
'If I had to choose, I guess I'd choose Doc cause he had a reason to be ornery with his TB and all,' I said. 'But I still don't think he was an outlaw.'
'I suppose you heard all the stories about my wife,' Lester said softly, and he sat down on the bench.
'Some. But mostly stories about you,' I said, and I sat down next to him.
'I did it William Burroughs style about twenty years ago. You know the tale about the skinny old fag, don't you? Hey, you want to shoot at some of them naked gals?'
'No thanks,' I said. 'Mexico City, wasn't it? Burroughs?' "I took a swig of the chief."
'Some friends goaded him into exhibiting his marksmanship with his newly bought pistol, so he placed a glass on top

of his wife's head and missed. Shot her in the melon. He only served thirteen days in jail. He fled to the US and was convicted of homicide in absentia and sentenced two years that was later suspended. Do you think he meant to kill her?'

"He didn't wait for me to answer."

'I used to like seeing whores all around Asia after I done it,' he said. 'Until I met this one sweet gal in I can't remember where, and when I asked her, what's it like being a prostitute? She said it was like being a cold slab in a busy city morgue. I've never had the desire to buy sex since.'

'Have you talked to a shrink about it?'

'Only Billy,' he replied with a straight face and looked fondly at the chimp. 'Isn't that right, Billy boy?'

"Billy grabbed his crotch with one hand and flipped Lester off with the other."

'What did he say?' I laughed.

'He said piss on shrinks.'

"Then his eyes slowly crawled over me like a Gila monster, and he asked with suspicion, 'What in the hell do you do anyway, cowgirl?'

"Oh shit, he's got me treed, I thought." 'I'm a life experience counselor,' I said.

'Well, that's some real nice PC shit, lady. And I'm a damn hominoid exhibitor. Talk Texan now, darling.'

'Okay, I'm a shrink.'

'That's why you're here?' he said with disappointment. 'And I thought it was on account of my boyish figure.'

'I wanted to mostly meet you because we're fellow Texans.'

She's telling one of her Huckleberry stretchers, thought the professor, and he looked at the German and raised his eyebrows.

'You're here to shrink my head like one of those troll dolls?'

'Maybe just a little,' I said.

'Why don't you shrink Billy? That damned chimp's been jerking off to that yellow-haired gal on *Three's Company* something awful for two months now.'

'I have cigars that would go good with this hooch,' I laughed, and pulled out two Macanudo fatties. 'Want one?' I asked.

'Sure,' he said.

"We lit them up. Lester blew perfect smoke rings over Billy's head. The chimp squealed, rubbed his face, and did several back flips on the floor."

Lester drawled, 'Carla was from Taitung. She farted a lot for a girl, I thought, and she grew these beautiful tomatoes.'

"He paused and took a big gulp of the whiskey."

'I live the life of an ass because I should for what I done. For what I did to my sweet gal and her folks. All this Old West is my way, you know, to forget. I've got damn near every western film made, from *Stagecoach* to everything Clint Eastwood ever did. My way to try to occupy my mind, but the guilt keeps me down. Way down. I'm drifting along on the bottom of the sea covered with horse apples.'

'How'd you get off?' I asked. 'Make it look like a suicide?'

'And a few payoffs. I guess it wouldn't take a Sherlock Holmes to put the finger on this sad story,' he said.

'I'm real sorry, Lester,' I said and drained my glass.

'Some shit we never . . . you know,' he said.

'Maybe you need to try something different to get yourself pointed down a new road,' I said. 'Something to shake you loose. Shake you up.'

'Like what?' he asked.

'How about anal sex?'

"Outrageous!" howled the professor. The German's eyes bugged out.

'With me being the receiver?' Lester barked in a low voice.

'Yeah, and with a gal throwing strikes.'

'Shit fire!'

'Think of it as erotic electroshock therapy.'

'I'd rather get shocked by fucked-up jumper cables.'

'You know, without the electrodes strapped to your head or the rubber thing they put in your mouth so you won't swallow your tongue.'

"It's called a—" said the German scientist.

"I know what the damn technical term is," she said, making a shooing gesture with her hand.

'The jolt just might clear your slate,' I said to Lester.

'Jesus Christ! That's some gummed-up crazy shit!' he exclaimed. 'Is that the medicine you give to all your patients? My bad heart can't take that kind of action, anyway. I've already had one heart attack.'

'Only a select few, and this won't hurt your ticker. You need to relax. Tell me you've never had a gal slide her finger up your anus and do a drumroll on your prostate during sex. Tell me you didn't like it. What's the difference if it's her finger or a dildo up there?'

'A big fucking difference,' he said. 'That's half queer.'

'It ain't queer when a heterosexual couple engages in anal sex. It's just being adventurous.'

'A fella lets gals fuck him in the ass with all kinds of dildos, then pretty soon he'll want some summer sausage.'

'You find yourself an adventurous girlfriend,' I said. 'One that has a special talent in this area, but not no sadistic butch chick in leather with whips and stuff. Just a real sweet, sexy gal that is gifted with a strap-on. Let her give you a real thorough machining, and then you get her doggie-style and return the favor, and man you'll step on the gas like you're driving a souped-up stock car from San Anton to Tucson, and the orgasm you'll have will take you to I-don't-know-where.'

The German rolled his eyes and gave the professor a quick smile. This is one kinky shrink, the professor thought, and became entranced by the wild, insane look on Vivo's face.

'Paint me a picture, cowgirl,' he drawled. 'Tell me about the last ass you jacked up on a hoist and reamed.'

'One guy who lost his wife in a car accident asked me to do it. He said it was like jumping out of an airplane. And he didn't go queer, as you put it. It could expand your awareness,' I said.

'Expand my cornhole to a size nine hat. And jumping out of an airplane is just about as crazy,' he said, shaking his head.

'You are living with a chimpanzee, Lester,' I said.

'Well, he's more human than some folks.'

'I'll agree with that.'

'And did you like it?' asked Lester.

'The back door? I liked it all right,' I said. 'And, I definitely use only my own tools. No borrowed wrenches.'

'The pistol Burroughs used to kill his wife was the same model that Robert Ford used to gun down Jesse James in Missouri in 1882,' he lied, straightened up and pushed his shoulders back. 'A Smith and Wesson nickel-finished forty-four.'

'Like hell!'

'You know the story?' he asked.

'Everybody's had a friend like Robert Ford,' I said, 'the friend who shoots you in the back.'

"Lester opened a drawer and produced a small latched cedar box and set it on the bench next to our whiskey glasses."

'Be my William Tell tonight. Go ahead and open it. You know what it is. We can make it look like I done it to myself,' he said.

"I felt heat surge through my chest and head." 'No way in hell, Lester!' I said.

'Billy!' Lester called out.

"It all happened real fast. The chimp hopped onto the bench and flipped the box open. Inside was an old black-handled pistol. Lester put his empty whiskey glass on the top of his head. Billy grasped the pistol with both of his small hands and shot the whiskey bottle I had set down on the end table. Whiskey and glass sprayed everywhere. Then that damn monkey just sat there real still with the gun pointed at Lester. Then a policeman came barreling in through the front door. I guess he heard the shot. Before the cop could get down the hall to our room and draw his pistol, Billy fired two more, knocking old Les off that bench like one of those dummies at a carnival shooting gallery. The first bullet went into his mouth, and the second blew part of his right ear off. The cop finally drew and shot the chimp. There was blood and smoke, and then I remembered the card the chimp gave me. Jesus and Mary!"

"Here lies Lester Moore, shot dead with a forty-four. No less, no more," said the professor.

Vivo paused and relit her cigar. After a few puffs she said, "The cop took me down to the station. I had to make a sworn statement and sign it. Christ, it took half the damn night." She didn't tell them the rest.

"Americans and their guns," the professor said, softly shaking his head.

"A terrible and fascinating culture," said the German. "Although any country that can produce the likes of Sam Cooke, Elvis Presley, and doo-wop is ultimately all right with me," he sighed.

"And, how about you?" asked the professor. "How did you fair after what you witnessed that evening?"

"Indeed," exclaimed the German. "It must have *shaken you up*."

"Hell, I've seen worse shit happen at a rodeo," she said unconvincingly, and thought about the month leave of absence that she took immediately following the incident, and all the humiliating hours that she'd spent on her colleague's couch the following ten months.

There was a sustained silence. Then Vivo shrugged, pulled on her cowboy boots, rose, and walked toward the front door of the shop.

"You will stop in and have a drink next time you're in port?" asked the professor.

"Sure."

"Adios, senorita," said the German.

"Ciao, y'all," she drawled, and walked out the door and into the oppressive darkness.

The seven stately palm trees lining the front of the shop rustled momentarily as a cool onshore breeze swept over the muted harbor.

"See, we needed a witness with a straight back. Not some flimflam dodgy foreigner who comes through Taiwan as often as a minnow looking for the biggest piece of cheese," Lester Moore said as he finger banged a bottle of Buffalo Trace bourbon in the Sunset Room of Kuala Lumpur's Sheraton Imperial Hotel. "We needed someone that the Taiwan police and the insurance company wouldn't mind if they woke up next to in bed. We waited months for her. She was perfect. And she dropped right into my lap like a ripe Georgia peach. The cop got half. Do you know how it feels to be dead?"

"My first marriage."

"That's fucking funny. Let me tell you, those Christians, they don't know shit about how it feels to be reborn. It's absolute freedom." Lester Moore had waited two years to tell his tale, but he figured enough time had passed, and this ninety-year-old tycoon was so stinking rich that he wouldn't want any of Lester's money.

"And the shooting?"

"I worked with that ape for weeks practicing the same scene over and over. It was always three shots. The first one at the bottle, and the next two at me. I must have spent a thousand dollars on Snickers bars."

"Blanks?"

"That little feller just loved them damned Snickers. Poor Billy. He was a good friend."

"Why'd the cop shoot him if the bullets were blanks? They were blanks?"

"Not quite. That first round was real. It had to be if we were going to sell the girl a shit-pile '74 Pinto with bald tires and a busted speedometer."

"How did you know the chimp wouldn't shoot you with that first real bullet?"

"That was the exciting part. I didn't."

"You're one theatrical son bitch."

"The beauty is the girl still doesn't know anything."

"She thinks you're dead?"

"Yup. She's completely and peacefully innocent."

"Why the girl? You didn't really need her."

"Her statement shined the cop's badge up real nice so he came out looking like the Lone Ranger. I also just wanted to see if I could pull it off. And it was something, I have to say, to fool a sharp gal like that. A psychologist, to boot."

"The insurance company?"

"They're still sniffing around a little, I heard."

"Worried?"

"The dead don't worry. Besides, I planned this five years out. That's when I bought the policy."

"The beneficiary?"

"My sister."

"She didn't have a problem with it?"

"There's not a straight piece of lumber in the whole family."

"And the girl, this psychologist wasn't in on it?"

"Scout's honor."

"Uh-huh."

"Really."

"The cop showed up right on cue, didn't he?"

"I signaled him when the girl and I went into the building. He was always on the ready on weekend nights. That's when the foreigner traffic is highest at the night markets."

"How did you find the mark?"

"Dumb luck, mostly. A pretty gal like that strutting around Taiwan in a cowboy hat and boots sticks out like tits on a bull. A friend of a friend told me what she did for a living—and that she was cocky as hell thinking that she's got it over on everybody. That's when I really started playing it up as a local wacko."

"I take it the whole tale about you killing your wife William Burroughs–style never happened?"

"Course not. I've never been married."

"And did you ever try it out, the girl's suggestion for shaking things loose?"

"That's none of your damn business," Lester said, grinning.

"Any guilt about bilking the insurance company out of a cool US million?"

Lester looked at his friend. They both began to laugh.

After treating his friend to a steak and crab dinner, Lester Moore bought a Cuban cigar at the bar and retired to his penthouse suite. He plopped down in a plush leather chair, turned on the big screen TV, and began to watch the western *Johnny Guitar*. An hour later there was a knock on his door.

Lester stood up, walked to the door and said, "Yes?"

"Room Service," said a female voice. "Compliments of your dinner companion."

"That old son of a gun," Lester said with a big grin.

He opened the door and a thin blonde rolled in a cart carrying a bottle of champagne chilling in an ice bucket.

"Over there by the TV," said Lester, and he shut the door.

He eyed the blonde's appealing figure as he strolled into the bedroom to get cash for a tip. When he returned he looked up and saw Vivo standing in the middle of the room with her legs spread apart. She held a blonde wig in her left hand and a 9mm Beretta wearing a potato in her right.

"Annie Oakley," Lester drawled with amazement.

"William Burroughs. Or, should I say Mrs. Burroughs—resurrected."

"What you been doing cowgirl, besides filing your teeth?"

"Target practicing."

"Hah, you were purty good already," winced Lester.

"I also picked up how to castrate a bull."

Lester eyeballed the Beretta and its long silencer. "Where'd you get the glue gun?"

"7-Eleven."

"Looks like I'm stuck in the crap shack without any TP."

"Where you been these last two years?"

"Happy hour."

Vivo ran her eyes over Lester's expensive linen shirt, rust colored slacks, and ostrich skin cowboy boots. "I liked you better in the chalk outline."

"That was a rental."

Vivo paused and said, "The dead ain't supposed to be scared. You look scared, Lester."

"I wish you would've come later."

"Why?"

"Joan Crawford's about to draw her guns on that purty brunette gal," he said. He nodded his head toward the TV. "How did you—"

"Saw you by chance three days ago. You should have left Asia, asshole."

Lester asked playfully, "Still mad because I wouldn't let you fuck me in the ass?"

"The way you fucked Billy, and me? Billy is dead, isn't he?"

"That's funny coming from the poster girl for cyberdildonics. The ape, yeah, he's a gonner."

A disgusted look appeared on Vivo's face. She twirled the pistol and said, "Wondering if it's loaded?"

"How about a drink?" Lester asked, trying to conceal his anxiety.

"Whisky neat. Pour yourself a cyanide."

"Funny!"

"So, you threw a lasso over the insurance company."

"You're a sharp one," he drawled. "Yup, they filled my pond with catfish."

"And soon they'll all be floating belly up, along with their Texas caretaker."

Lester stood up, walked over to the mini-bar and poured two whiskies. "I've got one hundred thousand of them whisker fish here in the safe. You can have it all."

"Let's go get it, Mister Burroughs," she said. Vivo followed Lester into the bedroom. He opened a small safe that was on the floor of the closet and pulled out a bulging white envelope.

"Set it on the bed." Lester complied. Vivo raised the pistol and pointed it at Lester's chest. She bent down and picked up the envelope. "Now, go get your drink and sit your ass down, showboat."

Lester walked out of the bedroom. Vivo followed behind with the pistol pointed at his back. He picked up one of the drinks off the bar and sat back down in the chair in front of the TV. Vivo stood ten feet in front of him.

"You haven't even looked at the money," he said, trying to look around Vivo to watch the TV.

"I can smell it."

"What the hell do you want?"

Vivo shot him a wicked smile.

"For—"

"For using me just like you used that poor chimp. I'd never seen anyone get killed before. I was so stressed out and depressed that I almost lost my job. I was on the couch for damn near a year. I really wanted to help you."

"Bullshit. You were slumming—getting your kicks off the local nutcase. You did it all for you, wanted to see how good you were. You were such an easy mark."

Vivo thought about her therapy sessions and knew he was half right, but she pretended not to hear him.

"Set your drink on top of your head," she commanded, raised the pistol, and pointed it at Lester's melon. Lester held the drink on top of his head with one hand.

"Please! Please darling!" Lester shouted. "I can get you more money! Anything!" We, we can work together on another job. Fifty-fifty."

"Let go of the damn drink, Lester."

He let go of the drink and rested his trembling hands on his thighs. The glass began to wobble, but it didn't fall off.

Vivo walked closer and stopped ten feet in front of the frightened Texan. She held the pistol pointed at his head for a very long moment. After two minutes Lester began to sweat profusely. His two-hundred-dollar linen shirt and slacks felt as if they were on fire. Two more minutes passed.

Then Vivo slowly lowered the pistol, pointed it at his chest, and yelled, "Billy!" and fired twice.

Lester Moore heaved loudly and jumped up a foot out of his chair. His drink crashed onto the floor. He slumped over and didn't move. Vivo checked for a pulse on Lester's neck. He was dead.

"Shit fire and jumping jackrabbits," Vivo drawled in a low voice. "A damned heart attack. Your poor, bad heart. How did you like them blanks, fucker?"

She wondered if she would've used any of the remaining

live ammunition in the clip if her plan with the blanks had failed. Vivo quickly unscrewed the silencer and put it in her hip pocket, stuffed the pistol into the rear of her pants, and made sure the long hotel uniform shirt that she'd pilfered from a laundry hamper was covering it. She picked up the envelope of cash and tucked into the front of her pants, put the blonde wig back on, wiped her prints off everything that she'd touched, pushed the cart out of the room, and quietly shut the door.

"No less, no more," she chuckled, and thought about the card Billy had given her as she strolled completely unnoticed to the nearest elevator.

Absinthe with Joseph Beuys

Holed up above a Taitung firecracker shop with a bottle of absinthe watching Joseph Beuys on the screen in a squalid downtown Hamburg hotel room ... a fox crouched all miserable in the corner with small paws up like a shadow boxer and fangs at the ready cause old Joe has a sheet over his head and is acting like some German gunder ghost from East Berlin. . . . Learned the art of drinking with the Green Fairy in Prague in the bowels of a five-hundred-year-old cellar grog shop ... kids were rolling joints on a big round table and me and Anthony the baker's son from Long Island who copied my *The Good The Bad and The Ugly* soundtrack were up at the bar a shoulder in with the sugar and the Zippos we poured slugs of green heaven into glasses then dumped the sugar in lit it up and after a few hours of that with pints of luscious Czech black pivo and joints had to close one eye and it took me five hours to make the twenty-minute tram ride home to U Trati Street in Strasnicka cause I was walking Memphis miles spinning faster than a forty-five rpm and had to get off a lot to nap and sing into the nearest alley man we really went to town and Prague is a great drinking town cause the cops won't do anything if they find you in a pile somewhere they'll walk on by like you were a dog or a soda can.

In Taitung I was with the Green Muse and Joe Beuys after days of taking pictures of Taoist temples, and I heard a loud, strange humming outside my door. I stayed with Joe a while longer, but curiosity kept nudging my shoulder, so I went and opened it and a young man in a purple robe walked past me into the room as if I weren't there. He appeared to be some kind of holy man. He was slender, calm, and about twenty-five, with a shaved head. As I turned around, the robe dropped off his body, and he stood naked facing me. A huge pair of transparent dragonfly wings unfolded from behind his shoulders. They started beating as fast as a hummingbird's, blowing photos and maps off the bed. The noise sounded like a busy airplane hangar. He started flying around the room. He crashed into the walls and bounced off the ceiling like an injured fly trying to get out. His long legs were spread wide apart. His entire body turned transparent, and pictures of me flashed like a movie across his torso. I grabbed the bottle of absinthe and held it up like a club and felt myself backing into the nearest corner, excited and terrified. Ten minutes later three young men in the same purple robes rushed into the room. They wrestled the winged man down onto the bed; his face was red, sweaty—ecstatic. He laughed hysterically. One of the men lunged at him waving a machete. The other two got the machete away from him and tied up their friend's wings with yellow nylon rope. I went over to one of them and felt around on his upper back and shoulders—normal. They bundled up their friend and carried him out.

One of them turned toward me with pleading eyes and said, "Please no talk! No talk!"

I sat on the bed and smoked a joint, poured a double of the Green Fairy, set her hair ablaze, and continued my journey into the "long dream." The fairy slit time's throat with the panache of a matador … we crammed its bloated carcass under the mattress.

A tin Palomino stuck its head through my window and flapped its gums, "The plain amigo. Let's go."

The fairy clutched to my shoulders, and I stumbled into the bright sun with the bottle of absinthe and my camera. The Palomino kicked up dirt with his front hoofs . . . the words "Yamaha Rental" painted in white across the length of its body. I mounted and we loped across a sunbaked Mexican plain . . . the sun was a zebra's poon fart—a spinning black and white target with a bull's-eye. It pulsed bright to dim every ten seconds. A horde of blackbirds were perched in a grove of fluorescent yellow mesquite heaving in the wind like a gaggle of drunk prostitutes swaying to Mariachi on an Ensenada stage.

One of them squawked, "Emerald City is the other way, round eye." They all laughed.

"Albino!" another cawed.

Tarantulas the size of rototillers tore around sandy red hillsides . . . flowering blue agave cactus big as houses were everywhere. . . . The sun suddenly turned into a red and yellow target with a pink bull's-eye . . . I instinctively reached behind, grabbed a Henry rifle out of its scabbard, and took a wild shot that missed the orb.

"Ding! Ding! Ding dickhead!" cackled one of the blackbirds.

"Hit the bull's-eye when it's bright, and day will turn into night, and you'll be king of Chacota for a day," another one cried.

"Any mescaline there?" I yelled, aiming with one hand.

Another barked, "You'll need penicillin, not peyote wine, flour face."

"Chacota's a den of wolves and losers," screeched one with a cig in his beak. "You'll be right at home."

Another squawked, "Follow the white crosses—five miles ahead."

I turned, aimed the Henry at Cig Beak and said, "And if I plug one of you?"

"We'll bake you a pie," sung a group of baby birds that buzzed past us.

"Watch out for the one called El Coyote," warned Cig Beak as he flew by my side keeping pace with my horse.

"Who?"

"An Indian shaman. A trickster. He's a being who slips back and forth through the horizon line looking—"

"Looking for what?"

"Assholes like you who stray too far past the periphery."

"And, if El Coyote finds me?"

"He'll try to keep you here, gringo."

"I like it here."

"Tell me that after you've spent a night in Chacota," he smirked.

"I'm not scared," I lied. "I spent a night in a San Felipe jail on crooked charges waiting for the meanest Federale in Baja to get his fat drunken ass across the desert."

"What happened when fatty arrived?"

"After they stripped my friend's car?"

"Si."

"The greasy son of a bitch and his deputies swatted at us like we were piñatas until the customary bribe money jingled out."

"Well, El Coyote's no stinking Federale, hombre. He doesn't want your money."

"What does he want?"

"To give your soul a paint job."

"The Catholic Church already tried that."

"And?"

"It peeled off when I hit puberty." I became more scared, but didn't let on and kept riding and firing and missing. I hollered, "Can't someone slow that blinker down?"

"Come on crack shot!" another blackbird chortled. "Keep missing and we might get bored and decide to peck your bleeping eyes out!"

The Henry turned into a Dachshund . . . jelly bullets streamed out of its muzzle.

"Ding!" cried Cig Beak as I'd finally hit the bull's-eye when it was bright, and the sun fell with a bang and a thud behind the chocolate Mexican hills.

Day instantly became night. My rifle, the Dachshund, disappeared. The blackbirds turned into a cloud of bats, and zoomed past us toward the dark horizon . . . could hear faint yelling and whooping coming from up ahead . . . the sun clanging around behind the hills like a giant tin plate. A quarter mile further we came upon the arched wooden gate of Chacota. A crowd holding torches boiled in the dusty main street, which consisted of a saloon, a bank, a handful of shotgun shacks, and a Catholic church. A white stucco auditorium with a golden dome sat at the end of the wide main roll. I scanned the crowd searching for the man called El Coyote.

"That's him!" someone yelped as we rode up.

"The Wonder Bread Kid!" shouted another. They all pointed mockingly and yipped with laughter.

"Hey gringo boy!" yelled a handsome, barrel-chested man wearing a gaudy red sombrero. "You've caused quite a hubbub!" You're king for a day! What you want?"

"*Huevos rancheros* and a cold Pacifico," I replied, and wiped the dust from face.

"That's all, after knocking the used up blonde out of her penthouse?" heckled Barrel Chest. He looked around in disbelief. "What a dumbfuck!" Everyone laughed. "We've been known to make a man swing from the bank clock tower for less. How about some action?" he asked smiling, turned, and held his arm out toward the auditorium.

Everyone turned and gazed at the lions and tigers and panthers lounging in front of the main doors.

"I'm not interested in stirring the soup with any sporting ladies," I said. Everybody laughed and whooped louder.

A bearded old man with yellow eyes and a red macaw perched on each shoulder muscled through the crowd.

"El Coyote!" someone yelled with reverence.

The medicine man strode up to me and resounded mockingly, "Lonely Miguel! Some big shot! You and this horse! Hah! Riding in here like Don Quixote. Your important work. Your noble photographic endeavors. Your hoity-toity 'cross-cultural dialogue' mumbo jumbo!"

"So what," I blurted defensively.

He flashed his eyes and twirled his mustache. "What are you *really* looking for, Miguel? Tell me it's not pussy."

The crowd hushed.

"Rainbows," I said sarcastically, and jumped off the horse.

"Bullshit!" he growled. One of his macaws screeched. El Coyote's fiery eyes cut out my silhouette. Then his eyes found mine. "No, Miguel. You're looking for redemption—for a life pockmarked with transgressions and disappointment."

I paused, and replied, "Maybe that's part of it."

He smiled and said, "You don't need redemption, amigo."

"Then, what?" I asked.

"Let go of them—the dark memories," he whispered. "You're much more than that. I can take you to a place. Somewhere beyond time where strange beings roam the desert. They can teach you."

"Teach me what?"

"To dance, even when all appears to be lost."

Cig Beak, the loud-mouthed blackbird, appeared and landed on my shoulder. "Don't go!" he screamed. "It's a trick!"

El Coyote turned into a red-tailed hawk and we all watched him fly away with his macaws.

Barrel Chest took off his hat, waved it around and proclaimed, "Weeeeeell! Ooh! So Don Quixote, you like hanging on to the Devil's tail, eh? To the bad memories?"

"Sucker!" someone squealed.

"So big shot, how about that action?" asked Barrel Chest, and he looked back over his shoulder at the auditorium. "Maybe it'll help you forget about your past."

"I told you slim, I'm not—"

"Jesus and Joseph!" he resounded in frustration. "It's not a whorehouse. It's *Lucha libre*! The wrestlers! The holiest of the holy! The holy moly wrestlers!"

"El Gordo! Chupa the Magnificent! Julio the Wolf Boy and many many more!" shouted a star struck young woman.

"The greatest show in all Jalisco!" yelled Barrel Chest. "The greatest show in all of Mexico! Before the match, when the *luchardos* come parading out in capes and *mascaras*, it's better than seeing the Holy Father himself!"

Everyone whooped and began dancing around with their

hands raised above their heads.

"I don't believe you," I said. "Beer first, then maybe," I wheezed with cotton mouth, and handed the reins to a giggling retarded stable boy with ears the size of a jackass's.

As I walked into the saloon I looked over my shoulder down the street . . . the auditorium and the big cats lying in front of it were gone. I dragged my ass up to the bar with the foaming crowd following behind. . . . The place was filled with laughing, frolicking Mexican cowboys, who were hooting and flinging wisecracks at a line of buxom dancing girls onstage. The red-tailed hawk came out of nowhere and appeared on the bar in front of me flapping its wings, sending glasses of beer and tequila flying. I jumped back and felt my heart thump like the bass pedal on a Wurlitzer. With a roll of quarters in her fist, the Green Fairy reared back and socked me in the ribs, knocking a battery cable loose. . . . Suddenly, I found myself back in Taitung careening around in the darkness on my beat-up Yamaha rental near a traditional puppet show in front of a Taoist temple . . . parked the bike and sneaked behind the stage . . . loaded my camera, grabbed an old sheet, draped it over my head, and blundered out front oblivious to the audience of old men watching the show . . . clumsily tried to snare the fox I thought I saw jumping around on the small stage—like a kid trying to catch a butterfly with his bare hands. The Green Fairy sat on the edge of the stage giggling at me and slapping her thighs. The old boys, who were sitting on wooden chairs drinking beer and smoking, eyed me and chuckled to one another . . . their chuckles soon turned into screeches and peals of laughter that came spinning toward me like throwing knives . . . the spry fairy took off running without looking back . . . I did a Boris Karloff into a nearby alley . . . crept through the shadows back to my hotel . . . flopped onto the bed. I was a Mars Bar one of the crew had left on the cylinder head of a top fuel dragster, and the Christmas tree lights ahead turned from amber to green . . . with a grin on my face, I went to the stars with all my clothes on.

Special thanks to my wife Julia Wu, my mother Joan Hickey, Uncle Dave and Aunt Kathy Walsh, Patrick Huang, Dr. Gerald Liu, Simon Shih, the late Ken Rignall, Attorney Jerome Garchik - San Francisco, Dr. Mark and Helen Griffin, Mina Chou, Mrs. Chou, Ivan Lee, Kevin Hu, Susan Ciriclio, Kaohsiung tattoo master Yang Jin-hsiang, Zone 5 Professional Photo Lab - Taipei, the Fulbright U.S. Student Program; and Dr. Wu Jing-Jyi, Julie Hu, and staff (1998-99) of the Fulbright Foundation for Scholarly Exchange in Taipei.